AFTER THE EXHIBITION

A church art exhibition turns deadly...

Jack Haldean expected Lythewell and Askerns' exhibition of church art in Lyon House, London, to be a sedate affair, the last firm to be associated with mystery, violence and sudden death. Or so it seemed – until after the exhibition...

Further Titles by Dolores Gordon-Smith

The Jack Haldean Mysteries

A FETE WORSE THAN DEATH
MAD ABOUT THE BOY?
AS IF BY MAGIC
A HUNDRED THOUSAND DRAGONS *
OFF THE RECORD *
TROUBLE BREWING *
BLOOD FROM A STONE *
AFTER THE EXHIBTION *

The Anthony Brooke Spy Series

FRANKIE'S LETTER *

* available from Severn House

BlackpoolCouncil

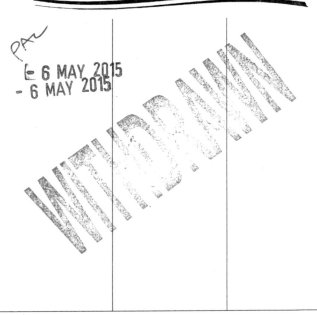

PAL

E 6 MAY 2015
- 6 MAY 2015

Please return/renew this item
by the last date shown.
Books may also be renewed by
phone or the Internet.

Tel: 01253 478070
www.blackpool.gov.uk

AFTER THE EXHIBITION

A Jack Haldean Mystery

Dolores Gordon-Smith

Severn House Large Print
London & New York

This first large print edition published 2014
in Great Britain and the USA by
SEVERN HOUSE PUBLISHERS LTD of
19 Cedar Road, Sutton, Surrey, England, SM2 5DA.
First world regular print edition published 2014 by
Severn House Publishers Ltd., London and New York.

British Library Cataloguing in Publication Data

Gordon-Smith, Dolores author.
  After the exhibition. -- (The Jack Haldean mysteries)
  1. Haldean, Jack (Fictitious character)--Fiction.
  2. Christian art and symbolism--Exhibitions--Fiction.
  3. Murder--Investigation--Fiction. 4. Novelists,
  English--Fiction. 5. World War, 1914-1918--Veterans--
  Fiction. 6. Detective and mystery stories. 7. Large type
  books.
  I. Title II. Series
  823.9'2-dc23

ISBN-13: 9780727897626

Severn House Publishers support the Forest Stewardship Council™
[FSC™], the leading international forest certification organisation. All
our titles that are printed on FSC certified paper carry the FSC logo.

MIX
Paper from
responsible sources
FSC
www.fsc.org   FSC® C013056

Printed and bound in Great Britain by
T J International, Padstow, Cornwall.

Dedicated to fellow mystery lover,
J.K. Rowling,
with admiration and gratitude.

One

At the breakfast table of Whimbrell House, Whimbrell Heath, Surrey, silence reigned. Daniel Lythewell, partner of the firm of Lythewell and Askern, Church Artists, Furnishers and Monumental Masons, the cause of the heavy and, he hoped, meaningful silence, had progressed from dissatisfaction to irritation and was now on the verge of downright annoyance.

He sighed, buttered a piece of toast, sighed again, poured himself a cup of coffee and rustled the *Daily Telegraph* in a significant way. Despite all this, Maud, his wife, remained oblivious. It was frankly appalling the way she ignored him.

Lythewell stolidly ploughed through the headlines, the political comment, glanced over the leader column, disagreed with it – silently – and turned to the classified adverts. Dammit, Maud *knew* he always commented on the morning paper.

He rustled the newspaper once more. Maud drank her tea, flicking through the pages of some fashion magazine or other. It was as if, Lythewell thought with a sense of outrage, as if she hadn't noticed. Hadn't noticed! Despite his determination to be silent, he was goaded – absolutely goaded – into speech.

He tossed the paper to one side.

'I really think you should reconsider your decision, Maud.'

'What decision, Daniel?' said Maud Lythewell absently.

'About the exhibition,' he said testily. 'What the dickens do you think I'm talking about?'

Maud smothered a yawn. 'I've really no idea.' She glanced down at the pages of *Modern Woman* and read at least three paragraphs. 'Is that why you're so grumpy this morning?' she said in a bored voice. 'You're like a bear with a sore head.'

'I don't think you realise how important the exhibition is, Maud. Naturally, I expected you to cancel any other appointments—'

'Cancel my appointments?' She gazed at him in wide-eyed bewilderment. 'Don't be silly, darling. I told you a week ago I had a dress fitting. I can't possibly cancel it.'

'I expect your support,' Lythewell continued, as if she hadn't spoken. 'I think there's every chance that the Winterbourne woman will place a commission.'

'Don't be silly, darling,' repeated Maud, picking up a piece of toast. Her gaze went back to *Modern Woman*. 'If Miss Winterbourne wants you to decorate her school chapel, she'll ask you whether I'm there or not.'

He breathed in heavily. 'If you don't want to come, then I suppose there's nothing more to be said. However, I must insist that Betty attends the exhibition with me.'

Maud put down *Modern Woman*. 'But I *need* Betty,' she wailed plaintively.

8

Betty Wingate was Daniel Lythewell's niece. Left unexpectedly stony-broke following the death of her father, Charles Wingate, she had come to live with the Lythewells three months ago.

Maud Lythewell had quickly realised that Betty had a great capacity for hard work. She liked, as Maud expressed it to herself, to be kept busy. Maud was indulgence itself in encouraging her to fulfil this particular liking.

'Betty's so useful when I'm in Town,' Maud protested.

Daniel Lythewell's forehead furrowed in a frown. 'Betty was a pupil at Rotherdean.'

'Rotherdean?' questioned Maud.

'Miss Winterbourne's school,' said Lythewell. 'We've been through this, Maud. As a former pupil, Betty knows Miss Winterbourne well. She might very well sway Miss Winterbourne's decision to award us the commission.'

Maud's gaze flicked back to the magazine. 'Decorating a chapel isn't like buying a new hat. Miss Winterbourne won't be swayed by Betty. She must be fearfully strong-minded. Headmistresses of girls' schools usually are, I imagine.'

'Nevertheless, I must insist.'

'You really are being completely unreasonable, Daniel.' She noticed his frown and decided to compromise. 'Oh, very well, have it your own way if you're going to make such a beastly fuss, but Betty's so useful when I'm in Town,' she said once more.

'Don't you think you sometimes treat Betty a little too much like an unpaid servant?' said

9

Lythewell. 'She is my niece, after all.' He was still annoyed with Maud.

'A *servant*?' Maud was shrill with indignation. 'Are you mad? We've given her a home, made her welcome, been unfailingly generous. Of course she wants to help. Think of the poor girl's feelings. Of course she wants to show some gratitude. It's a matter of self-respect.'

'All right, Maud.' Lythewell shrugged. 'I sometimes feel sorry for her.'

'There's no reason whatsoever to feel sorry for her,' snapped Maud. 'If she wasn't so young and pretty, I doubt you'd feel quite so sympathetic, niece or no niece.'

Daniel Lythewell suddenly laughed. 'Don't tell me you're jealous.' He found the idea flattering.

'Don't be ridiculous.'

She was jealous, thought Lythewell. He cleared his throat to indicate a change of subject. 'It doesn't matter, anyway. I think there's every chance Betty won't be with us for much longer. From what I saw the other day I thought she seemed very taken with young Colin Askern.'

Maud didn't like Colin Askern, as he well knew. He derived real satisfaction from her snort of indignation.

'Colin Askern! Don't speak to *me* about Colin Askern.'

'Why not?' demanded Lythewell, determined to argue. 'He's a perfectly decent young feller. John Askern's son. There's nothing wrong with him. *He's* coming to the exhibition.'

Maud's shoulders went back. 'As Colin Askern is a member of the firm, of course he is attending

10

the exhibition, but Betty has seen far too much of him in the last couple of weeks. His manner towards her is far too familiar. Perhaps she does not appreciate that informality may be construed in the wrong way. I will grant that he is a remarkably good-looking young man, but his looks are all he has to recommend him. Not only is he completely unsuitable but there have been unsavoury rumours about him.' She paused significantly. 'Need I say more?'

Daniel Lythewell's eyebrows shot up in enquiry.

Footsteps in the hall urged Maud Lythewell to be cautious. *'Signora Bianchi,'* she hissed. 'And you know what they say about her!'

In her bedroom, Betty Wingate, the hem of her dress in one hand and a needle in the other, yelped as the needle slipped and jabbed into her thumb. Damn! She quickly grabbed her handkerchief and dabbed her thumb, anxious not to get any spots of blood on her old blue dress.

It might be old and the hem might need catching up, but it was one of the nicest dresses she had. She really hoped Uncle Daniel would persuade Aunt Maud to let her attend the exhibition.

Admittedly, an exhibition of church art didn't promise to be exactly rollicking, but at least it was better than fetching and carrying for Aunt Maud while she debated which hat and gloves she simply couldn't live without. It was hard – very hard – not to feel envious of the way Aunt Maud casually acquired some really lovely clothes, while she had to make the tiny income Dad had left stretch to almost impossible lengths. Every so often Uncle Daniel would slip her some spending money, which was nice of him, but it wasn't much.

Uncle Daniel's and Aunt Maud's invitation had come when she was nearly at the absolute end of her money and just about at the end of her tether. To act as Aunt Maud's unpaid companion was no sort of life, but at least she had a roof over her head and could eat.

If only she'd been *trained* for something! Then she could earn her own living, but training cost money. Rotherdean had provided an excellent education, but no training. The expectation was that the exceptionally gifted girls would go on to university and, eschewing husbands and the prospect of a family, embrace a teaching career, while the rest would marry. There really weren't many other options open, but Betty felt she'd tried them all.

Marriage ... It was almost inevitable that Colin came immediately to mind. She liked Colin, liked him a lot, and he liked her. She knew that well enough, even if he did treat her like a kid sister. Money was the key to that, too, she thought savagely as she sucked the blood from her thumb. Colin was a very practically minded man. If she'd been well-off, she knew Colin's manner would be different. Less matey and more respectful. It wasn't that he was mean or grasping, but he was ... Well, practical.

All of which made his liking for Signora Bianchi even more mysterious. At the thought of

Signora Bianchi, the needle nearly slipped again. What the *hell* did he see in her?

The rumours had flown thick and fast, but Colin seemed oblivious to gossip. Eventually, unable to stand the barely concealed innuendo, Betty had taken the bull by the horns and asked Colin outright what was going on.

The conversation, if you could call it that, predictably ended in a row, with Colin declaring it was none of Betty's business and if she wanted to listen to village gossip rather than trusting him, that was her affair.

But it was her business – or she'd like it to be, anyway. Betty had no doubt that Signora Bianchi was a man-eater, pure and simple. Colin had aquiline cheekbones, butter-coloured hair and vivid green eyes. He was a very good-looking man; exactly the sort to attract Signora Bianchi as a sort of ... of *hobby*, she supposed.

She really had her hooks into him, Betty thought savagely, her sewing suffering as a result. She *couldn't* have any real feelings for him and, if she did, that would be just pathetic. She was years older than Colin. She was like a cat, dark, sleek and sophisticated. Colin thought Signora Bianchi was glamorous. He referred to Betty as a *nice kid*.

It wasn't, thought Betty, reaching for her scissors, as if Colin was the only one. She hadn't mentioned this to Colin, as it really wasn't any of her business, but Colin's father, John Askern, had been seen leaving Signora Bianchi's cottage more than once. Mr Askern was still a very good-looking man. Daphne, his wife, was indulgent and pleasant and worth two of Signora Bianchi.

Men were fools, she decided, putting her dress on to a hanger. The hem would have to do. Signora Bianchi really was rotten to the core. Mrs Askern was a nice woman. She might not be sophisticated or glamorous, but she was generous and kindly and didn't deserve to be treated like that.

With a feeling of grim determination, Mrs Daphne Askern went into her husband's dressing-room.

John Askern paused in the act of adjusting his braces and looked at her enquiringly. At the sight of her expression his heart sank. She couldn't have found out, could she? He looked at her with a consciously enquiring smile. 'What is it, my dear?'

'Never mind the *my dear.* I want a word with you, John. I thought there was something wrong.'

Askern's stomach twisted. She couldn't know. She just couldn't know. 'Something wrong? You're mistaken, Daphne. I realise I may have seemed abstracted recently...' *Abstracted! That was an understatement!* '...but you must realise how busy I've been with the exhibition coming up. I've had a tremendous amount to do.'

'Never mind the exhibition,' said Daphne Askern. She swept a coat off the dressing-room chair onto the bed and sat down, glaring at her husband. He fell silent under her accusing stare. 'It's not the exhibition I want to talk to you

14

about, it's *this.*'

To Askern's horrified gaze she produced an envelope addressed to him. The envelope was written in a flowing hand in violet ink. He knew exactly what it was and who had written it. Carlotta Bianchi. How the devil had Daphne got hold of it?

'I found this,' said Daphne, 'in your coat pocket.' There was a steely glint in her eyes. 'I'll read it, shall I?'

Askern's mouth was suddenly dry. He made a noise in his throat as she took the letter from the envelope. 'I haven't got time to discuss the matter now, Daphne,' he blustered.

Daphne Askern's eyes were like gimlets. 'Oh yes you have. You never have faced up to unpleasant facts, John, but you are going to face up to this.' She unfolded the letter.

'Mio caro John,' she read, glaring over the top of her spectacles. 'That, I presume, is some sort of foreign greeting. *I can see you this afternoon at three. We shall be alone. Carlotta.* Well?'

Askern pinched his forehead between his thumb and his fingers. How could he have been such a fool as to leave that letter in his pocket? Anger, futile and ineffective, flared. 'What were you doing, poking round in my things?'

If Daphne Askern had been angry before, she was furious now. 'Poking round in your things! How dare you? I looked in your coat pockets because you had left your coat on a chair. I was hanging it up. I was looking after it for you. That, John, is the sort of thing a wife does. A *wife*, John.'

15

'It's ... it's not what you think,' he began weakly. 'No, it really isn't.' Sudden inspiration struck and, raising his head, he met her blistering stare. 'It's Colin.'

'I beg your pardon?'

'Colin,' he repeated, with growing confidence. 'I heard rumours he's been seeing the woman. I didn't want them to come to your attention. I ... I thought you'd be upset.'

He saw her expression change. 'As a matter of fact,' she said grudgingly, 'I know there's been some talk.'

Daphne Askern, a comfortably off widow, had married John Askern, a widower with a growing son, some years after her first husband had died. She'd thought John rather a romantic figure. He was an artist, a gifted artist, but a respectable one, a partner in Lythewell and Askern. Her more worldly friends, dwelling on both his lived-in good looks and his profession, warned her that there might be incidents, as they phrased it. Daphne had dismissed their warnings. She enjoyed having a husband, a stepson and a house to look after and, so far, she'd been very happy.

She was enough of a realist to know that John wouldn't have married her if she'd been badly off, but she had never troubled herself overmuch with ifs and buts and how things would be if the circumstances were different. Such speculations were, she thought, a complete waste of time.

She sighed deeply, considering the matter. She wasn't entirely reassured. Finding that note had been an awful shock and, although the note was short, it seemed very familiar in tone. For one

16

thing, the woman had addressed him as John and signed it with her Christian name, but...

Daphne Askern had a comfortable life and didn't want it disturbed. She had asked John to account for the letter and he had accounted for it. She knew her husband cared very deeply for Colin. That *was* believable.

'So you went to see Signora Bianchi to find out the truth of these rumours about her and Colin?'

'Exactly,' said Askern in relief. 'I wanted to know what was going on.'

'I see,' said Daphne guardedly.

'So I ... er ... made an appointment with Signora Bianchi.'

There was a pause while Daphne Askern took this in. 'And what is the truth behind the rumours about her and Colin?'

'Signora Bianchi assured me that there was nothing more than friendship between her and Colin.'

'Friendship?' Daphne Askern was incredulous. 'How on earth can they be friends? They can't have anything in common.'

Askern swallowed. 'Art, you know? And films. You know what a keen film fan Colin is. He talks to her about films and art and culture and photography and so on.'

Daphne considered this. It sounded credible. Colin, although he hadn't inherited his father's talent, was enthusiastic about modern art. He was certainly an avid film fan and was a keen amateur photographer.

John Askern saw her expression change. 'She takes a great interest in his photography,' he continued, pressing home the advantage. 'She's very cultured and she's travelled widely.'

'I see,' repeated Daphne. 'Is this the truth?' she asked sharply.

'Of course it's the truth, my dear. Do you honestly think a woman like that would hold any attraction for me?' He gave a laugh which, even to his own ears, sounded unconvincing.

Daphne hesitated for a long while, then folded up the letter. 'It's a great pity, John, you didn't see fit to confide in me.' She sniffed. 'I consider it to be a most unsuitable friendship for Colin, but he's a grown man and that's his own affair.'

'Unfortunately, I have to agree, but you can see why I was worried about the boy.'

Daphne sighed deeply and stood up. 'Your breakfast is on the table, John.' It was the white flag, if not of surrender, but certainly of a truce.

After she had left the room, John Askern leaned against the dressing table and took a deep breath. After a few moments he shook himself, then lit a cigarette with trembling hands. That had been *close.*

Colin Askern adjusted the camera on its tripod, ducked under the black cloth, checked the focus and re-emerged. 'Don't move,' he pleaded. 'The sunlight's catching your face at just the right angle.'

Carlotta Bianchi sighed and readjusted her posture. 'Like this?'

'That's the ticket! Bingo,' he muttered.

Signora Bianchi frowned. 'Bingo? What does that mean?'

'It means,' said Colin, 'that I've very nearly finished.' He glanced up once more. 'Stay exactly as you are...' He pressed the bulb on the camera and counted the seconds for the exposure. 'That's it!' He smiled. 'You can relax now.'

Signora Bianchi stretched her arms in an extravagant gesture. 'When can I see the picture?'

'When I've developed it.'

'You take too much trouble for a photograph.' She snapped her fingers together. 'Photographs, they should happen like that.'

'I wanted a proper portrait, not a snapshot,' said Colin.

'A portrait?' She laughed, then stopped as she saw his hurt expression. 'I shall have it with a – what do you call it? A surround, yes?' She indicated a square in the air.

'A frame?'

'Yes, I shall have it beside...' She looked round the room. 'Beside the clock.'

The grandfather clock was one of the few pieces of furniture in the sitting room of Signora Bianchi's cottage that Colin didn't think of as cheap rubbish. Even so, the clock was far too large and, Colin thought, far too noisy for the room.

Signora Bianchi had taken Beech View Cottage, complete with furniture, for three months. It didn't suit her and neither, thought Colin, did Whimbrell Heath. She belonged somewhere modern, with large windows, full of sun and air, not in this small, dark, cramped space. Signora

Bianchi was elegant, modern and gracious and her setting should reflect her personality.

Although well into her forties – perhaps older – she looked, with her healthy complexion, perfect make-up and dark chestnut hair, far younger. It was still early and she looked delightful in a cerise negligee, her feet enclosed in elegant kid leather slippers and her hair tied loosely back with a ribbon.

A large tabby cat jumped up on the chair beside her. She reached out and idly scratched it behind the ear.

'Where on earth did that cat come from?' asked Colin.

'He came all by himself. I like him. Mrs Hatton – you know Mrs Hatton?' Colin knew Mrs Hatton, the daily. 'She tells me he catches the mouses.' She shuddered. 'I don't like them, the mouses.'

'Mice,' corrected Colin with an affectionate grin. 'He doesn't go with your style. If you must have a cat, it ought to be something sleek and glamorous.' He grinned. 'Witches always have black cats.'

'A witch?' demanded Signora Bianchi, affronted. 'You think I have a hooked nose and the green skin?'

'You're not that sort of witch,' said Colin.

Signora Bianchi scratched the top of the tabby's head to a fusillade of purring. 'A witch,' she said thoughtfully. 'You think so?'

'An enchantress, I'd say. Have you any idea,' he asked abruptly, 'how glamorous you are? I don't know what it is, but there's something about you that knocks most other women into a cocked hat. You could be the star of any film.'

Signora Bianchi smiled in genuine pleasure. 'That is nice, yes?'

'Yes, and it's true.' He hesitated. 'I ... I don't know if it's altogether a good thing. People are bound to ask questions.'

She gave a gurgle of laughter. 'Ask the questions? They ask so many questions, Colin. The women who live here!' She waved her hand dismissively. 'They are small, I tell you, small!'

'What have you told them?'

She laughed again. 'Nothing much. They are of no account. I tell them I am Italian and my husband, he is dead.'

'Dead?' questioned Colin.

She shrugged. 'What should I say? Marco is dead. I was so sad. Even though he was not my husband by the church, I was so sad when he died.'

She was obviously in earnest, but the mention of the affair still made Colin Askern uncomfortable.

'You do not like me to say Marco and I were not married, do you?' she said acutely. 'You are very strict in many ways, I think.'

Colin Askern looked even more uncomfortable. 'Appearances matter,' he said awkwardly. 'Especially for you. I know people have rotten, low minds and I don't want them saying rotten, low things about you.'

She laughed once more. 'You are sweet, *tesoro mio*.' She suddenly became serious. 'You are sweet and so very 'andsome, too.' Colin looked

21

rebellious. 'No, no, no, no, no! I like it, the good looks on a man. They will be useful to you, the good looks. It is nice, also, that you worry about my reputation, that you want me to be respectable. I do not think you would worry about such things. You like the art, yes? Artists, they are not respectable.' Her smile faded. 'They are easily frightened, the respectable.'

'My father's an artist and he's respectable,' said Colin thoughtfully. 'I'd say he's worried.'

A calculating look came into her eyes. *Buono. That is very good.*

Two

'Thanks for coming to the exhibition, Jack,' said Chief Inspector William Rackham as he and Jack Haldean negotiated their way through the crowds on Oxford Street.

The two men, although both dressed in formal morning wear, in black coats and grey trousers, provided a real contrast in appearance.

Bill Rackham, solid and ginger-haired, with an easy-going manner and good-natured face, somehow always managed to look slightly rumpled and unmistakably British, whereas Jack, taller and slimmer, with olive skin and intelligent dark eyes, looked as if he'd be at home in Barcelona or Madrid. Although his mother had been Spanish, Jack had been born and brought up in England and it sometimes came as a shock to those meeting him for the first time, to hear his completely English voice.

'Yes, it's good of you to come,' continued Bill. 'Colin Askern asked me to bring a pal to the opening. I couldn't think of anyone who'd be interested, apart from you.'

'That's all right,' said Jack Haldean. 'I can see that the amount of blokes who'd leap at an opportunity to attend an exhibition of church art would be pretty limited. I've never heard you mention Askern before. Have you known him long?'

'Absolutely ages, but we haven't seen each other for years.' Bill gave a sudden grin. 'I first met him when he was flung at my feet.'

'I beg your pardon?'

'He was flung at my feet. Literally, I mean. It was during the war. I was in a fire trench outside Arras, minding my own business, when Askern sailed over the top of the trench and buried himself in the mud beside me.'

'The German artillery gave their involuntary assistance to this athletic performance, I take it?' said Jack with a grin.

'Got it in one. There wasn't much wrong with him. He was a bit taken aback, of course. So was I, come to that. Anyway, we shared a couple of cold sausages and a Woodbine, then he set off in search of his platoon. I bumped into him a couple of times afterwards but I haven't seen him since the war. I ran into him the other day on the Strand. We did the usual catching up, and he told me he'd joined the family firm.'

'The family firm being...?'

'Somebody and Askern, church artists. The Askern in question is his father.'

'Is Colin Askern an artist?' asked Jack with interest. He enjoyed painting, which was presumably why Bill had thought of asking him along in the first place.

'No. His father's an artist but Colin never did anything in that line. He's nuts about films and very keen on modern art. You should get on with him. He wants to bring the firm up-to-date, but I think he's finding it pretty uphill work.'

'Yes, I can see that. Church art tends to be a bit conservative.'

They turned into the quiet, tree-lined fastness of Gospel Commons, the noise of Oxford Street dying down behind them. A crowd of top-hatted, morning-suited men and elegantly dressed ladies halfway down the street marked out the entrance to Lyon House, where the exhibition was to be held.

They took their place by the steps, Bill scanning the crowd for Askern. He groaned as he saw a plump, middle-aged woman with a determined expression and bearing a tray of flags and a collecting tin, see the crowd, scent business and changing direction, approach them hopefully.

'Honestly, these flag-sellers are an absolute menace,' Bill grumbled. 'It's just licensed begging.'

'Don't be such a skinflint,' said Jack easily. 'It'll be for a good cause. She's marked you out, Bill.'

Bill stepped smartly behind Jack. 'After you.'

'Hoy! If I'm getting nobbled for a flag, so are you.'

'Of course,' said Bill smoothly. 'As you say, it's all for a good cause. She's heading straight for you,' he added. 'You must have an obliging sort of face.'

'Or, to put it another way, I look like a mug,' Jack muttered. He broke off and smiled with as good a grace as he could muster as the flag-seller singled him out with expert efficiency.

'Would you like to buy a flag, sir?' asked the flag-seller, holding out the collecting tin invit-

25

ingly. 'It's for the Waifs and Strays Society,' and added, as if she'd been listening to Bill and Jack's comments, 'it's for a very good cause.'

Jack looked at the picture of the pathetically ragged and wide-eyed child on the tin, and, as the flag-seller was obviously doing, mentally contrasted it with his own immaculate top hat and morning clothes. He sighed and dropped a shilling in the box.

'Thank you very much, sir,' she said, stepping back. 'It's all for a good cause.'

Jack looked at her curiously as she pinned a flag into the silk of his lapel. He couldn't place her accent and that intrigued him. She sounded English enough, but her inflections were, somehow or other, in the wrong place. He mentally shrugged. He could hardly quiz the woman about her origins.

'My pal said it was for a good cause. He'll buy a flag—' Jack broke off and looked round.

The doors had opened, the crowd was dispersing and Bill had slipped away to the top of the steps. He gave Jack a thumbs-up, winked, and vanished into Lyon House.

Jack gave an indignant laugh and turned to the flag-seller. 'Can you come back in a couple of hours? The gentleman I was with would just *love* to buy a flag from you. What's more, I'll make sure he coughs up a decent donation. Ten bob if you're here at one o'clock. That's a promise.'

'All right, sir,' said the flag-seller, obligingly. 'I'll do my best.' She moved on to the rest of the rapidly thinning crowd, leaving Jack to go in search of Bill.

Lyon House dated back to the seventeenth century, and the exhibition room, with its wood panelling, painted oak screen, ornate plasterwork and long sash windows would usually have caught Jack's attention. At the moment, however, he was only interested in Bill.

'So there you are!'

'Hello,' said Bill. His face was straight but his eyes sparkled. 'I see you've got a flag.'

'This flag,' said Jack, tapping it meaningfully, 'has just cost you ten bob. And,' he added, as Bill spluttered a protest, 'you're not wriggling out of it. I promised the flag-seller you'd be outside at one o'clock sharp and, come hell or high water, that's where you'll be.'

'Ten bob! You must be mad.' Bill broke off as a fair-haired young man tapped him on the shoulder. It was Colin Askern.

'Hello, Rackham. I'm glad you could make it.' He looked inquisitively at Jack as Bill introduced them.

Askern, thought Jack, was a remarkably good-looking bloke, with the sort of face that was usually referred to as chiselled. He'd make a killing in the movies, with leading-man looks like those. His next remark certainly endeared him to Jack.

'Jack Haldean...?' Colin snapped his fingers together. 'Got it! You write detective stories, don't you? I think they're awfully good.'

'Thanks very much.'

'Not at all. I loved that last story of yours. You know, *The Twisted Shroud*, where the barmaid discovered what the landlord was doing with the

27

chemistry set in the cellar. I always buy *On The Town* when your name's on the cover and I've got about four of your books at home. They'd make corking films. I don't suppose you've ever considered that, have you?'

'I'd like to consider it,' said Jack, 'but it's not as simple as all that.'

'You should look into it. It's a real pleasure to meet you. Are you interested in church art?'

'Art, yes, but I can't say I know much about church art specifically.'

Colin laughed. 'That's reassuring. It means I don't have to apologise for the work we've got on display.'

He gestured across the room to where three large, gilt-framed Victorian-looking panels displayed the Last Supper, the Crucifixion and the Ascension. 'Take a squint at those,' he said in disgust. 'That stuff is our bread and butter. Those paintings were completed last month, would you believe.'

'Are you sure?' said Jack. 'They're well done, but the style's very dated.'

'Exactly,' said Colin in satisfaction. 'And yet, would you credit it, those paintings have been sold to a church in Highgate. I sold them,' he said morosely. 'It's decent business but it drives me nuts. It's as if the past thirty years or so had never happened. Impressionism, Vorticism, Cubism, all the work of artists such as Picasso, Nash and Chagall is completely ignored. I know artists who could take exactly the same themes – classic themes – and really make something of them. The world has changed. There's things happen-

28

ing in cinema photography, with lighting and contrast, that are really stretching the boundaries of how we think about visual images. You know what's happening with art – *real* art – at the moment?'

He looked round, checked no one was listening, and lowered his voice. 'Ever since the Pre-Raphaelites discovered medievalism, church art has more or less been stuck in a rut. It needn't be like that.' He turned to Bill. 'Think,' he demanded, 'of those wonderful African bronzes from Benin. Just think of them!'

Bill's eyes widened and he drew back. 'African bronzes?' he repeated doubtfully, looking to Jack for help. 'Er ... what about them?'

Jack came to the rescue. Poor old Bill obviously didn't have a clue what he should think about the Benin bronzes. 'They're full of energy,' he said, throwing Bill a lifeline.

'Energy,' repeated Bill.

'Distilled energy,' said Jack, feeding him another adjective.

'Distilled!' said Colin Askern triumphantly. 'That's the exact word. They're *full* of latent energy, the sort of energy you get from a motion picture, distilled into bronze. I'd love to bring that sort of force into our work.' He ran a distracted hand through his hair. 'What I want to do is to challenge our clients to see traditional subjects in a fresh way. I know artists who could really let things rip, but neither my father nor old Lythewell will hear of showing them to prospective clients.'

A girl, a brown-haired, attractive girl with

freckles, approached and slipped a hand through Colin's arm. 'Colin, what on earth's the matter?' she said. 'You look really put out. You're not complaining about modern art again?'

'It's more the lack of modern art,' said Jack.

Her eyes glinted in appreciation. 'I've heard that conversation before.'

Jack suddenly thought how nice she seemed. In fact, she seemed very nice indeed, the sort of girl who took an interest in the person they were talking to. A comforting sort of girl, he thought, a girl who you'd look forward to meeting again.

'I don't think we've met.'

'Sorry, Betty,' said Colin, 'I should've introduced you. This is Miss Betty Wingate. Miss Wingate, this is Bill Rackham and his friend, Major Haldean. You've got to be desperately respectful to Rackham, Betty, because he's a chief inspector at Scotland Yard, and he saved my life outside Arras. No, absolutely you did,' he said, holding up his hand to cut off Bill's protests. 'That cold sausage and cigarette you gave me was just what the doctor ordered. I've never forgotten it.' He turned to Betty. 'Have you spoken to Miss Winterbourne?'

'I was nabbed as soon as I came in. She was my old headmistress,' she explained to Bill and Jack. 'She's thinking of redecorating the school chapel and Uncle Daniel – that's Mr Lythewell – wanted me to do my bit. Uncle Daniel's got her in tow now.'

'Good kid,' said Colin approvingly. He broke off as a middle-aged man – from his looks an older edition of Colin – bore down on them with an enquiring expression. 'Hold on a mo,' Colin muttered. 'Here's my Pa. Dad, come and meet a couple of pals.'

'So you're interested in art, gentlemen?' asked Mr Askern, once the introductions had been made.

'Major Haldean is,' said Bill quickly. 'He's a great devotee.'

'Bill...' muttered Jack warningly.

'We were discussing the Crucifixion you've got on display,' added Bill wickedly. 'Major Haldean made some very perceptive comments about it.'

Mr Askern brightened. 'The Crucifixion is a very fine piece of work. A little old fashioned, perhaps, but there's still a taste for the more traditional forms of art. Let me introduce you to the artist, our Henry Cadwallader. I'm sure you'll have lots to talk about.'

There was nothing for it but to bow to the inevitable. 'Thanks, Bill,' Jack muttered.

'You'll love it,' said Bill softly. 'You can ask him what he thinks of African bronzes.'

As Mr Askern led him away, he heard Bill say, 'Excuse me, Miss Wingate, do you live in London?'

Jack sighed inwardly. Bill's conversation with Miss Wingate promised to be far more interesting than a discussion of antiquated painting.

Henry Cadwallader, the artist, was a short, elderly, whiskery man, who stood by his paintings with a morose and rather defensive expression.

'Ah, there you are, Cadwallader,' Mr Askern

said. 'Let me introduce you to Major Haldean. He's a great devotee of art and admires your work.' He smiled at Cadwallader with gracious condescension. 'I'll leave you to it. No doubt the Major is interested in your techniques, eh, Major?'

'My techniques?' repeated Henry Cadwallader. He regarded Jack dubiously and chewed the notion over for a while.

A conversation with Mr Cadwallader, thought Jack, wasn't going to be one of your lightning quick, razor sharp exchanges of ideas.

'Technique,' said Henry Cadwallader ponderously, 'is something I pride myself on. Technique is something that a lot of youngsters can't be bothered to learn.'

Jack cast around for something to say in reply. This was going to be uphill work. If Bill got away with putting anything less than a quid in the flag-seller's tin, after making him swap getting together with Miss Wingate for a chat with Henry Cadwallader, it wouldn't be for want of trying. 'Your technique is excellent.'

He winced in agonised self-awareness. He sounded like some patronising art critic about to judge a school prize.

Henry Cadwallader eyed Jack suspiciously. He'd evidently caught the whiff of art criticism. 'It's not enough to be an artist, I often say, you've got to learn to be a craftsman, too. Craftsmanship, sir!' Cadwallader's eyes gleamed. 'That's what lasts. Never mind telling me you've got a vision. What use is a vision?'

This could have been an interesting topic of

conversation, but Jack saw no remark was called for, even if he'd been able to chip in. Out of the corner of his eye, he could see Betty Wingate talking and laughing with Bill and Colin Askern, but Mr Cadwallader was in full, relentless flow.

'*Anyone* can have a vision, but it takes a real craftsman to put it onto canvas. There's far more to art than most people realise, including many a one who calls himself an artist.'

Mr Cadwallader reached up and ran a loving hand over the painted surface. 'Look at this glazing. Go on, take a good look. You've got to get the glazing right. It changes the hue, the value and the intensity of the colouring. If you get it wrong, you might as well not bother painting the piece at all. Get it right, and the whole painting comes to life. It's a real craftsman's skill. Glazing,' he repeated with satisfaction.

As Henry Cadwallader went through the merits of his craftsmanship, Jack started to feel slightly glazed himself. He had nothing against saints and angels and crucifixions as such – he was a Roman Catholic, after all – but he was conscious of the heretical thought that once you'd seen one saint in startled raptures, you'd seen them all. And there did seem to be an awful lot of gold leaf.

Technically speaking, the Last Supper, the Crucifixion and the Ascension *were* excellent, but the blank-eyed faces, languid figures and the lavish use of gold seemed to Jack to be about fifty years out of date. They were just like the illustrations in a book he'd had as a child of King Arthur and the Knights of the Round Table. He

33

was irresistibly reminded of Burne-Jones and the Pre-Raphaelites.

Jack mentioned Burne-Jones.

Mr Cadwallader swelled with visible pride. 'Burne-Jones? I take that as a real compliment, sir. My word, yes. He was a real artist, not like the rubbish that's called art nowadays. I'd be ashamed to put my name to some of the things I've seen that pass for art. Take young Mr Askern, for instance,' he rumbled. 'Some of the things he wants to put in a church are downright scandalous. He talks about using ideas from films. Films! Young Mr Askern has modern views. No one wants that in a church.'

Jack passed over this interesting theological assumption without comment.

'As I said to Mr Askern – that's Mr Askern senior, of course – you need proper figurative drawing, painting and composition in a church. Mr Askern,' he said ponderously, 'can paint. He understands craftsmanship. Perspective, golden triangles, dead colouring – aspects of art that a mere art lover knows nothing about – *and* anatomy. Some of these so-called artists must've learned their anatomy in the zoo! Mr Lythewell – he started the firm when I was just a boy – now he *was* an artist. He never touched paint, mind,' Henry Cadwallader asserted pugnaciously, as if Jack was about to dispute the point.

'No?' said Jack politely.

'No. He was a metal-worker and wood-carver. You should see the work he did in the chantry in Whimbrell Heath.' He sighed deeply. 'The chantry was Mr Lythewell's labour of love, his life's work. Not the Mr Lythewell who's here, you understand, but his father. He's been dead a long time and sorely missed, if you ask me. Young Mr Lythewell,' he added, 'never had the gift. He just runs the firm.' He sighed heavily. 'This is him, now. What does he want, I wonder?'

'Ah, Cadwallader, there you are,' said Mr Lythewell. 'I'd like you to come and have a word with Miss Winterbourne.' He nodded briefly to Jack. 'Can you excuse us?' He lowered his voice. 'This could be an important commission, Cadwallader. Miss Winterbourne's the headmistress of Rotherdean and she's planning a refurbishment of the school chapel.'

'All right,' said Cadwallader grudgingly. 'I suppose I must if you want me to.' He turned to Jack. 'I'll see you later, young sir. It's been a pleasure talking to someone who appreciates proper art.'

Betty Wingate was gratifyingly pleased to learn that Bill was a chief inspector at Scotland Yard. 'Are you really a policeman? You don't look like one.'

Bill, who out of sheer force of habit, had run through a mental description of Betty Wingate (light brown hair, blue eyes, freckles, height about five foot two inches, age early twenties) felt relieved that his inward reflections hadn't betrayed him as hopelessly official.

'What does a policeman look like?'

Betty Wingate hesitated. 'More formal?' she hazarded. 'Sort of intimidating, I suppose.' She

35

paused. 'Who's that man you were with? I thought he looked like a foreigner, but he's English, isn't he?'

Bill laughed. 'Major Haldean? He's English, right enough, despite looking like the gypsy king.'

'You wouldn't be talking about me, would you?' asked Jack, arriving beside them. He looked round and shook his head. 'Whew! I thought I was never going to get away. That Cadwallader bloke has to be one of the most adhesive characters I've ever come across. He's threatened to nab me later on.'

'Henry Cadwallader?' said Colin Askern. 'Bad luck. He's a permanent fixture at Whimbrell Heath. I've known him all my life.'

'He didn't mention old Mr Lythewell, did he?' asked Betty, with seeming innocence.

'He did touch on him, yes,' said Jack. 'Why?'

Betty giggled and glanced at Colin. 'You explain.'

'Henry Cadwallader worshipped old Mr Lythewell,' said Colin wearily. 'He's a complete bore on the subject. According to him, every aspect of the firm and every painting we commission should be something that old Josiah Lythewell would approve of. He worshipped the ground old Lythewell trod on and he'll never let anyone forget it.'

'Why?' asked Jack.

'It's like something out of Dickens,' said Betty. 'He'll tell you all about it, unless you're very lucky. I was very sorry for him until I found out he testifies to it at chapel and what-have-you.'

'Sorry for him?' repeated Colin. 'He wallows in it.' He lowered his voice. 'Apparently Cadwallader used to be a proper little street urchin, a real Artful Dodger type, and old Lythewell caught him picking his pocket one day. Well, instead of handing him over to the police, Lythewell took him under his wing instead.'

'That was good of him,' said Betty. 'You've got to admit it, Colin.'

'I suppose it was, but I've heard the story so often, and always in the context of how wonderful Mr Lythewell was and how appalled he'd be at the changes I want to make, that it's worn a bit thin. What on earth did you say to him to make him so friendly, Haldean? He usually disapproves of the young.'

'I compared his painting to Burne-Jones and, as a result, he looks on me as some sort of soulmate.'

Colin laughed. 'No wonder he was all over you. Hello! I think your admirer's turned up again.'

With a sinking feeling, Jack turned to see Mr Lythewell bustling towards them, with Henry Cadwallader bringing up the rear.

'Major Haldean?' asked Mr Lythewell. 'Could I ask you to spare us a few moments, sir? I wonder if you'd be kind enough to speak to Miss Winterbourne. She's interested in Mr Cadwallader's work.' He laughed self-consciously and added, in a murmur, 'Excellent chap, Cadwallader, excellent, but he's a little bit of a rough diamond, perhaps. As someone who truly appreciates Mr Cadwallader's paintings, Mr Cadwallader thinks you are the ideal person to point out the merits of his work to her.'

'Be a sport, Haldean,' murmured Colin Askern. 'Talk him up. We need the commission.'

There was nothing else for it. 'Of course, Mr Lythewell,' said Jack, lying manfully. 'I'd be delighted.'

It was about ten to one when Bill found Jack in the hall, smoking a cigarette. 'So there you are. D'you fancy a spot of lunch?' He glanced at the rapidly thinning crowd. 'It's about time we pushed off.'

Jack held up his hand for silence. 'Peace, friend. All I need is this cigarette and a complete absence of Henry Cadwallader.'

Bill laughed. 'C'mon. It couldn't have been as bad as all that.'

Jack's eyes gleamed dangerously. 'Not as bad? It was far, far worse than bad. If you think my idea of a dream morning is one spent praising the merits of a short, whiskery, outdated artist – against all my better judgements, let me tell you – to the headmistress of a girls' school, think again.'

'Relax. What else were you going to do this morning?'

'I could've spent it talking to that corking girl, for a start.'

'Miss Wingate? That short, freckly girl, you mean? She was a bit of a pipsqueak, but she seemed nice enough.'

'She seemed exactly the right sort of height to me. A morning spent talking to her would've been a very pleasant use of my time. Let me tell you, the only thing – the *only* thing, mark you – that's kept me going is the thought that I promised the flag-seller you'd be here at one o'clock.'

Bill raised his eyebrows in surprise. 'You're not going to hold me to that, are you?'

'Just watch me,' said Jack with feeling.

'Oh, all right,' agreed Bill. 'I'll brass up, if you're going to make such a song and dance about it. How much did you say I'd give this wretched woman?'

'I promised her ten bob, but call it a straight quid and I'll consider us quits.'

'God strewth! You must think I've got money to burn.' He saw Jack's expression and held up a placatory hand. 'Okay, I'll do it. I'd never hear the end of it if I didn't.'

They got their coats and hats from the cloakroom and made their way outside.

At the bottom of the steps Mr Askern and Mr Lythewell, together with Henry Cadwallader as a silent third, were holding an impromptu inquest on the exhibition whilst waiting for a taxi. Betty Wingate was chatting to Colin.

'I have great hopes of Miss Winterbourne, Askern,' said Mr Lythewell in a satisfied way. 'She showed great appreciation of Cadwallader's work,' he added, as if Henry Cadwallader were miles away and not standing right beside him. 'Cadwallader definitely appeals to more traditional tastes.'

'We could certainly do with another commission,' agreed Mr Askern. 'Yet despite the interest Miss Winterbourne showed, I'm beginning to wonder if Colin has a point in advocating spreading our net wider and perhaps introducing a more modern element into our work. Some of the work on display today incorporated modern ideas.'

'I'm open to any idea that can be shown to be commercially sound, Askern, but...'

Mr Lythewell and Mr Askern plunged into a discussion of art and business.

Bill drew Colin Askern to one side. 'Thanks for inviting us, old man,' he said breezily. 'We both thoroughly enjoyed it, didn't we, Jack?'

'Absolutely,' said Jack. There didn't seem to be anything else he could say.

'Colin!' called Mr Askern. He nodded an apology to Jack and Bill. 'Excuse me interrupting, gentlemen. Colin, can you recommend an artist or artists whose work reflects modern ideas? We're looking for someone who would be both commercially sound and suitable for our purposes.'

'I think so, Dad. I ran into a chap the other day who was very excited about new ways of dealing with old forms. Betty!' he called. 'What's the name of that Polish bloke we met at the Carmondys'? You know, in Bloomsbury. The one who talked about rhythmic structures?'

'It sounds like complete tosh,' said his father reprovingly. 'We want someone who can paint.'

'But this chap can. He's produced some marvellous work.'

Unnoticed by Mr Lythewell or the Askerns, the flag-seller approached and mounted the steps to where Bill and Jack were standing.

40

'Buy a flag, sir?' She smiled at the sight of the flag in Jack's lapel. 'I remember you, sir. Didn't you say your friend wanted to buy a flag?'

'Bartkowiak, that's the name,' said Colin Askern. 'And don't be too dismissive about rhythmic structures or any other language of that sort. Art's moved on. We need a new language to describe new concepts.'

'Nonsense is nonsense, even if it is about art,' said Lythewell.

'Will you buy a flag, sir?' the flag-seller repeated.

'Yes, of course,' said Bill in a slightly harried way.

'A generous donation, remember,' muttered Jack.

Bill took a ten-shilling note from his wallet and, with Jack's eye upon him, reluctantly added another.

The flag-seller's eyes brightened. 'Thank you very much, sir.'

'Bartkowiak produces some damn good – some jolly good, I should say – art,' affirmed Colin with some vehemence.

'Tradition's what's needed,' put in Henry Cadwallader, 'not this so-called abstract nonsense.'

'Will you buy a flag, sir?' asked the flag-seller. Henry Cadwallader looked scandalised at the idea.

'Even if it was produced last week and not fifty years ago, art's still art,' insisted Colin.

The flag-seller recognised defeat in Henry Cadwallader and moved on to Mr Askern. 'Will you buy a flag, sir?'

41

'Art, my dear boy,' said Mr Askern, absently reaching into his pocket for money, 'especially sacred art, needs tradition. Cadwallader is perfectly correct on that score.' He tutted in irritation. 'Excuse me, Lythewell, have you any loose change? I gave mine to the cloakroom attendant. Tradition is the bedrock of our art...'

He broke off, staring at the flag-seller. She was gazing at them in a fixed, unnatural manner. 'Art,' she said, her voice scarcely more than a whisper. 'Art! Oh my God, art!'

Her face seemed to lose all definition and become flabby. As they watched in horrified amazement, her skin turned an unnatural shade of putty-coloured grey, shocking against her dark hair. 'Art!' she repeated. Her eyeballs rolled up into their sockets, showing only the whites. She made a funny gasping noise, swayed danger-ously and staggered forward.

For a frozen fraction of a second no one moved, then both Bill and Jack leapt forward, catching her as she fell. Supporting her weight, the two men guided her to the steps where she collapsed in an ungainly heap.

'What the devil happened to her?' said Colin Askern in shocked bewilderment. 'What on earth came over the woman?'

'You know as much as we do,' said Bill. 'She's out cold. Jack, can you get that tray from round her neck?'

Jack was already trying to remove the tray of flags. The ribbon was entangled round her neck, caught up between the loose skin of her neck and her coat collar. He tried to loosen the ribbon, then wrenched it away from the box, gently unwrapping it from round her neck.

Bill undid her coat, struggling with the large buttons, and put a hand on her chest. 'She's alive,' he said after a few tense moments. 'Askern, go back into the hall. You can telephone from there.' He turned to Jack. 'Where's the nearest hospital?'

'Charing Cross, I'd say.'

'Me too. Askern, phone Charing Cross and tell them we need an ambulance now!'

Colin Askern, galvanised into shocked movement, raced up the steps.

Betty Wingate, who had watched with wide, disbelieving eyes, came forward. 'Who is she?'

Jack could answer that. He had seen her name written on a label sewn onto the inside pocket of her coat when Bill had unbuttoned it. It was a decent coat, he had noted automatically. A new, good-quality, grey-wool wrap-over coat with three large black buttons matching the trim on the collar. 'She's a Mrs J. McAllister,' he said, pointing to the exposed label.

Betty shook her head. 'Mrs McAllister?' she repeated, staring at the woman slumped on the steps. 'She must have had a heart attack, poor woman.'

Jack knelt beside her. 'Mrs McAllister?' he said gently. 'Mrs McAllister!'

There was no response.

'What do you make of it, Jack?' asked Bill quietly.

'I'm damned if I know what to make of it,' said Jack. 'I suppose Miss Wingate's right. She must have had a heart attack to keel over like that.'

'What a dreadful thing,' muttered Mr Askern. His face was very pale.

'We've all had a shock,' said Mr Lythewell. He, too, was pale. 'I think all of us are in need of a restorative.'

'Why don't you get a taxi to your club, sir?' suggested Bill. 'You do have a club, don't you?'

'Yes, of course, but...' He looked indecisively at Mrs McAllister, slumped on the steps with her eyes closed.

'I really think you'd better leave this to us, sir,' said Bill firmly. He waved his hand at a cruising taxi on the opposite side of the road. The taxi driver turned the cab and drew into the kerb beside them.

'What's all this?' demanded the driver, his elbow over the side of the window, looking at Mrs McAllister. 'D'you need a hand?'

'No, there's an ambulance on its way,' said Bill. 'But you can take these gentlemen to the...' He broke off and turned to Mr Lythewell. 'Which club, sir?'

'Reynolds,' said Mr Lythewell in a distracted way. 'Reynolds in St James, but I really think we should stay.'

Colin opened the door of the taxi and helped his father into the cab. 'There's nothing you can do, Mr Lythewell,' he said, turning back to him.

'Oh, very well,' agreed Mr Lythewell. He turned to Colin. 'Askern, it might be as well if you escorted my niece home.'

'I'll be fine, Uncle Daniel,' said Betty. 'Don't worry about me.'

The clang of a distant bell sounded. Mr Lythe-well got into the taxi beside Mr Askern and, with a concerned backwards look, they drove away as the ambulance turned the corner.

Three

The clanging of the ambulance bell stirred Mrs McAllister into semi-wakefulness. She opened her eyes and struggled to sit up.

The bell stopped as the ambulance came to a halt. The driver and his assistant got out and came up the steps. 'Is this the lady who collapsed?' asked the driver, looking at Bill and Jack. 'Are you relatives?'

'No,' said Bill. 'We're just passers-by. I'm a police officer. Neither this gentleman nor myself have ever met the lady before, but she's got her name sewn into her coat. She's a Mrs J. McAllister.'

The ambulance driver stooped over the woman. 'Mrs McAllister? Can you stand up for us?'

She nodded and he put a hand under her arm. 'That's the ticket,' said the driver. 'We won't need the stretcher, Alf,' he called over his shoulder to his assistant. 'Not if these gents can give us a hand to get her into the ambulance. Come along, Mother,' he said in a loud, cheerful voice to Mrs McAllister. 'You've had a nasty turn, but we'll soon have you right.'

She stared at him in bewildered incomprehension. 'Art,' she muttered.

'What's that?'

'She said *art*,' said Jack.

The two ambulance men exchanged puzzled looks.

'I can't understand it,' put in Betty Wingate. 'We'd just come out of the art exhibition' – she gestured to the building behind her – 'and this poor woman came up to us with her tray of flags, heard us talking about the paintings and so on, yelled "Art!" and keeled over.'

Out of sight of Mrs McAllister, Alf tapped the side of his head in a significant gesture. 'Maybe she had a touch of the sun,' suggested the driver tactfully.

This suggestion seemed to Jack, in view of the fairly chilly April day, to be monumentally unlikely, but he let it go.

'Never you mind about art, Mother,' said the driver with brusque kindness. 'You come along with us and we'll have you there in two shakes of a duck's tail. You'll be as right as a trivet in no time. A nice cup of tea and a sit-down is all you need, I shouldn't wonder.'

'Art,' muttered Mrs McAllister once more, but she allowed herself to be helped into the ambulance.

'Poor woman. She must be off her head,' said Betty as the ambulance drove away.

And that, thought Jack, was probably the top and bottom of it.

The following Thursday Jack spent six productive hours tidying up next month's issue of *On The Town*. Duly liberated and with Archie Keyne, his editor, placated – for the time being, at any rate – he walked along Fleet Street to the

47

Strand. Coming towards him, by Lowther's Arcade, he saw a middle-aged, dark-haired woman he vaguely recognised.

Instinctively he raised his hat, but instead of passing on with the expected nod and smile of greeting, the woman stopped and drew herself up haughtily.

'Are we acquainted, young man?'

As soon as he heard her voice, with its odd swoops and inflexions, he remembered who she was. It was the flag-seller from the exhibition.

Jack's heart sank. The last thing he wanted was to be involved with a woman who, however rational she might seem at the moment, was, on the evidence of their last meeting, definitely odd.

'It's Mrs McAllister, isn't it?' he asked guardedly.

Her air of haughtiness increased. 'That is my name, yes. You'll excuse me if I say I cannot recollect you.'

'I was there the other day when you had your little ... er ... mishap.' That was as good a way as any of describing someone who'd keeled over, stretched out on the pavement and raved about art. 'Outside Lyon House. I helped you into the ambulance,' he added hastily as her eyebrows shot up to alarming heights.

Mrs McAllister froze for a moment, then suddenly relaxed, smiled and tittered in a manner that could only be described as girlish. 'My word, *what* you must have thought of me, Mr ... er...'

'Haldean.'

'I'm sure it was so kind of you to take the

48

trouble to come to the aid of – well...' she tittered once more, 'a *damsel in distress*, if I can describe myself as such. I really don't know what came over me. I can only think how lucky I was to have such a gallant gentleman close at hand. I was completely overcome. The doctor at the hospital – so kind, everyone was so kind – agreed that it must have been the heat and spending so much time on my feet. I am glad to sell the flags. It really is *such* an important cause, but, as the doctor said, it really was just too much for me.'

She tittered once again but Jack was suddenly struck by her acute gaze.

She's lying, he thought. She's seeing how I'm taking it. Why?

'The doctor was probably right,' he said reassuringly, noticing how she relaxed. 'I hope you're taking things easy.'

She smirked as if he'd shared a private joke. 'Take things easy? I certainly intend to,' she said warmly. 'Very easy indeed in the very near future.'

That was difficult to find an adequate – or, indeed, any – answer to, so he changed tack. 'I'm glad to see you suffered no permanent ill-effects.'

'No, none whatsoever, I'm glad to say,' said Mrs McAllister brightly. 'I was up and about again in no time.'

'I'm very glad to hear it. Excuse me, Mrs McAllister, but I couldn't help wondering why you said *art* before you collapsed.' She gave him a quick, guarded look. 'I just wondered what you meant, that's all,' said Jack with a laugh. 'It seemed such a strange thing to say.'

She laughed unconvincingly. 'I suppose it might seem strange, but I've always been very sensitive. As a girl, I was noted for the intensity of my feelings. "Joan," my dear Mama used to say, "you shouldn't *feel* things so deeply." Like everything my dear Mama said, it was good advice, but one cannot change one's essential nature. In fact, it would be wrong to try. To be true to one's essential nature is paramount, I believe. To be able to feel, to experience true sympathy with another's plight, is a real gift, wouldn't you say?'

'I suppose I would,' said Jack, as she looked at him expectantly.

'And really, Mr ... er...'

'Haldean.'

'When I saw you all outside the exhibition, so well-dressed, so affluent, so disdainful of money, well, the *contrast* overwhelmed me.'

'The contrast?' asked Jack, perplexed.

Mrs McAllister's eyes gleamed. 'With my cause. The cause of the poor waifs and strays for whom I was collecting those few spare coppers. A mere trifle to you, no doubt, but life and death to those poor mites. I was asking for pennies, that was all, while in that building the rich were prepared to spend hundreds – thousands even – on *art*. Why is it that painted representations of human beings are so much more valuable than actual people?' She sighed deeply. 'I tell you, Mr ... er...'

'Haldean.'

'The bitter irony of it struck me to the heart. Art, indeed! Art, when children are homeless and starving. What is the good of art?'

'Your feelings do you credit, Mrs McAllister,' said Jack gravely. Inwardly he was dying to laugh but, more than that, he was puzzled. He was certain she was attempting to pull some very sanctimonious wool over his eyes.

She grasped his arm. 'I am very glad to have met you, Mr ... er ... Haldean, was it? Very glad indeed. I am grateful for the opportunity to offer you my thanks in person. Indeed, I have been comforted by the thought that, even among the idle rich, there exist good Samaritans who do not hesitate to come to the aid of one in dire need.'

'Don't mention it,' said Jack with a smile. He could hardly call the woman a liar to her face, and if she didn't want to tell him the whole truth, that was, strictly speaking, none of his business.

She released his arm. 'Good day, sir, and thank you again for your help.'

'Not at all.'

She inclined her head and walked away.

And what, thought Jack, was that rigmarole all about?

'Did you ever hear anything more of that woman who collapsed outside Lyon House?' he asked Bill Rackham that evening, over a game of snooker in the Young Services club. 'Mrs Joan McAllister?'

'No, I can't say I have,' said Bill, leaning over the table and sighting the cue ball. He chinked the red into the pocket. 'Why?'

'I ran into her outside Lowther's Arcade this afternoon,' said Jack, leaning on his cue. 'The thing is, I asked her what she meant when she said *art*, and she came out with what I'm convinced was a load of old rubbish, about the contrast between us, who she categorised as the idle rich, and the waifs and strays she was collecting for.'

'Good grief,' said Bill, lining up on the yellow. 'Idle rich? I wish. If there were any plutocrats amongst us, I didn't meet them, and as for that girl, whatsername...'

Jack frowned. 'Miss Wingate?' he guessed.

'That's the one. She's as poor as a church mouse, despite having been to a fancy school. She's a bit of a waif and stray herself, by the sound of things. Askern told me about it. Apparently her father was a solicitor who tried to get clever with investments. When he died, there was only a pittance left.'

'Poor kid,' said Jack. 'That's really tough. What did Miss Wingate do?'

'There was damn all she could do. She's had odd jobs, but there aren't many opportunities for a girl in her position.'

'Yes, I can see that,' said Jack thoughtfully. 'A well-educated girl scares off a lot of people. I've noticed that before.'

'Well, they don't fit in, do they? They're too posh to be a junior and they don't know enough to be useful. She'd never met the Lythewells, but when her father died she dropped them a line to tell them the news. Then, a few months ago, just when she was at the end of her tether, Mr

Lythewell and his wife invited her to stay. According to Askern, it's a dog's life. Mrs Lythewell treats her as an unpaid companion, there to do her bidding and calling.'

'Poor kid,' said Jack once more.

'Yes, that's more or less what Askern said,' said Bill, potting the yellow. 'Reading between the lines, I think he rather likes her.'

Jack took the yellow ball from the pocket and tossed it from hand to hand. 'So there might be a happy ending after all?'

'I'm not so sure,' said Bill, sighting the red. 'Askern's a practical sort of beggar. If Miss Wingate had some money of her own, that'd make a difference, but as it is...' He shrugged. 'I just don't know.'

Jack felt oddly indignant on Betty Wingate's behalf. 'That shouldn't matter, not if he really likes the girl.'

Bill laughed cynically. 'I agree it shouldn't, but it does though, doesn't it? It's not really our concern. I don't suppose either of us will ever see her again.'

Jack felt oddly put out by the thought. 'No, I don't suppose we will.'

But as it happened, both of them were wrong.

It was the first Thursday in May, a glorious spring day with the promise of real warmth in the air.

Far too good a day, thought Jack, as he finished a late breakfast, to stay indoors. Feeling pleasantly full of bacon, eggs and toast, he stuffed some tobacco from the jar into his pipe and,

53

going to the window, creaked open the sash and, striking a match, leant out.

The sun caught the soot-streaked red brick of the buildings across Chandos Row and turned the grimy windows into sheets of gold against an impossibly blue sky. From Oxford Street came the subdued hum of traffic, the sound hollowed out as it funnelled between the brick canyons of the city.

He was thinking, in an idle sort of way, of Betty Wingate, the Lythewells and Colin Askern. Funnily enough, he thought he'd come across the name Lythewell before. Presumably he'd seen an advert for the firm somewhere or other, but that didn't seem quite right. He hoped Colin Askern didn't let Betty Wingate down. She seemed a nice girl, a good kid, someone who deserved better than to be a fetcher and carrier for her aunt. Her eyes were bright and kind and he liked the way her hair waved—

'Oi!' came a call from below.

He looked down and there, three stories below, was Bill Rackham and, unlikely as it seemed, Betty Wingate.

'Excuse us dropping in,' said Bill, minutes later as Jack ushered them into the room. 'Miss Wingate turned up at the Yard wanting to see me. It's actually my day off, but Miss Wingate was very insistent that she saw me, so they gave me a call, and here we are.'

'I was sorry to disturb you, Mr Rackham, but I couldn't think of who else to turn to,' put in Betty.

'I knew you wouldn't mind us coming along,'

54

said Bill. 'It's an odd story, Jack, and I thought it best that you heard it at first hand. It's a rum sort of business.'

'Better and better,' said Jack cheerily. 'I love odd stories.' It was unexpectedly good to see Betty again. 'Please sit down, won't you?'

Betty looked at the heap of papers on the sofa and hesitated.

'I'm sorry,' said Jack apologetically, coming forward to clear a space. 'I was working last night and my wretched papers get everywhere.'

'Don't worry about it being untidy,' said Betty. 'I just want someone who'll listen to me. No one in Whimbrell Heath believes me. I've been arguing about it all week. Uncle Daniel, Aunt Maud and Colin all say I must have had a bad dream. It's very strange, I know.' She shrugged. 'I wanted to come up to Scotland Yard. Aunt Maud was horrified by the very idea. She said no one would listen to me, but then I thought of Mr Rackham,' she added, turning to Bill with a smile.

'It never hurts to listen,' said Bill, looking rather awkward.

'Anyway, things came to a head last night. Colin tried to lay the law down and forbid me to come, but he just can't *do* that.' Her blue eyes narrowed in determination. 'He's convinced nothing happened, but he's just being pig-headed. He hates the idea of me making a fuss. He threatened to bring Aunt Maud into it, to get her to actually forbid me to come to London, but that's ridiculous. And mean.'

'You're not going to have a row, are you?' asked Jack. 'With your aunt, I mean?'

She tossed her head rebelliously. 'I don't care if I do. Well, I suppose I do, really, but I left before they were up this morning.' She rubbed her nose, frowning. 'I don't suppose they'll be very pleased, but there's nothing they can do. Yes, I know I should be grateful to Aunt Maud and Uncle Daniel, and consider their wishes, as Aunt Maud says, but they don't own me. Why shouldn't I come to London if I want to? Colin will be furious, but I couldn't rest until I'd told someone my story.'

'I'm very glad to hear it, Miss Wingate,' said Jack, in the act of clearing a heap of newspapers off the sofa.

He felt sorry for her. It was perfectly true that neither her aunt nor uncle nor Colin Askern could physically stop her, but he could guess at the recriminations and accusations of ingratitude that would follow her act of defiance. She shouldn't have to argue the toss to be allowed to come and go as she pleased. However, looking at her determined expression, she didn't want sympathy, she wanted someone to listen to her.

He took a cigarette from the box, put it on the table beside the sofa and indicated the vacant space. 'Here you are.'

He lit her cigarette and, lighting one himself, stood back with an encouraging smile.

Betty Wingate sat down, crossed her legs, drew deeply on her cigarette and braced herself, her eyes defiant. 'The thing is, Mr Haldean, although everyone says I let my imagination run away with me, I know what I saw in Signora Bianchi's cottage.'

Jack drew up a chair. 'Miss Wingate,' he said, his eyes bright, 'you have my complete attention. Tell me what you saw.'

'Well,' she said. 'It happened last Saturday...'

It was getting dark as Betty Wingate alighted from the Portsmouth train at Whimbrell Heath that Saturday evening. She'd spent the afternoon in Hindhead, visiting Doris Beckett, a fellow ex-Rotherdean girl.

Doris had been married for six months and, once she learned Betty was living in Whimbrell Heath, had begged her to come for the day to see her, her new house and her new husband. Doris couldn't understand why Betty hadn't been before, but it wasn't as easy as Doris thought to abandon Aunt Maud. There always seemed to be some reason why she was needed at Whimbrell House. However, Aunt Maud had reluctantly spared her, and it had been a golden afternoon.

She picked her way down the cobbled walkway by the side of the station and crossed the noisy little River Whimm by the wooden footbridge to Bridge Street, where a straggle of cottages marked the outskirts of the village.

It was a chilly spring evening. In the distance, she could see the lights of the Brown Cow. Outside the pub, a group of five or six men, Luke Padbury and his friends, were laughing and talking loudly. Her heart sank. Padbury's crowd shouted and wolf-whistled at any passing girl and Betty hated it.

She certainly didn't want to walk past them, so she turned down Greymare Lane, which ran round, rather than through, Whimbrell Heath. It was a longer way home, but at least there were no pubs on Greymare Lane. In fact there wasn't much of anything on Greymare Lane. The occasional cottage was interspersed with fenced-in stretches of scrub and trees; the sun was close to the horizon now and the fast-darkening spring sky made the trees into clumps of rustling inky blackness.

As the keen wind whipped round her, Betty shivered and half-wished she'd kept to Bridge Street, rather than choosing to walk along this dirt-track road on a muddy grass verge with a deep ditch beside her. This would be pretty enough in daylight, she supposed, with the branches meeting over the road, but it was dark under the trees and, she admitted to herself, just a little bit scary.

'Like one that on a lonely road doth walk in fear and dread,' she quoted to herself. Why on earth had that come to mind? Doris, of course. They'd laughed at the memory of Miss Fitzwilliam, their old English teacher, an intense woman with hair that was always escaping from a bun in an untidy straggle.

Miss Fitzwilliam had taught them 'The Ancient Mariner'. Betty had had to recite those lines in class. Almost despite herself, she couldn't resist completing the verse drummed into her years ago. *'And having once turned round, walks on, and turns no more his head. Because he knows a frightful fiend doth close behind him tread...'*

It was, under the encroaching trees, an unsettlingly appropriate piece of verse. She stepped off the soft grass of the verge and walked across a side road that ran onto Greymare Lane, almost expecting to hear footsteps behind her.

For Pete's sake, this was crazy! She'd be giving herself nightmares soon. There were no fiends, fearful or otherwise, and she was being silly.

Prove it. *Look behind you!* The childish pantomime chant seemed like a dare. She got to the verge on the other side of the turning, took a deep breath, stopped and looked round.

Nothing. Nothing at all, but the lonely road and the trees and, a little way off the road, among the trees, the darker bulk of a cottage. With a surge of relief she suddenly knew exactly where she was. This side road was Pollard Wynd.

Pollard Wynd ran from Greymare Lane into the village proper, where there were shops, houses and people, and that cottage she could see through the trees was Signora Bianchi's.

She turned up Pollard Wynd. Partly to take her mind off how dark and lonely it was in the twilight and partly because she was genuinely intrigued, she thought about Signora Bianchi.

There was no doubt about it, the woman was a puzzle. Colin aside (it was a big aside!), she had to admit that Signora Bianchi was glamorous, charming, beautifully dressed and, apparently, had something that was referred to as 'A Past'. 'She calls herself a widow,' Aunt Maud said icily, 'and exactly why she's come here is a complete mystery.'

It *was* a mystery. Whimbrell Heath, a sprawling village on the verge of becoming a town, was being vigorously developed. It was less than an hour to London by train, and new houses, with all modern conveniences, such as bathrooms, electricity, gardens and tennis courts, were springing up like mushrooms. At the far end of the village what the builders called amenities, such as new shops and a golf course were planned. The Electric Theatre, which had catered to Whimbrell Heath's cinema-going public since 1913, had changed its name to The Palace, with a new façade to match. There was even talk of a lido.

There would be no mystery if Signora Bianchi lived amongst the newly arrived, but instead she lived in old Whimbrell Heath, in a pokey cottage amongst the fields at the end of Pollard Wynd.

'There's those who live on the wages of sin, Miss,' said Mrs Cosby, the cook, who was of an Evangelical turn of mind. 'I couldn't rest easy in my bed, even if I did have fur coats and jewels, knowing how they'd been come by.'

As a solicitor's daughter, Betty had heard enough tales from the law courts to give her a reasonable grounding in some of the wages of sin. How Signora Bianchi paid for her mouth-watering sable coat was her own affair, but her relationship with Colin was a different matter. He seemed to be enthralled by the woman.

He'd been seen going in and out of her cottage at all sorts of odd times and yet refused point blank to speak about her. All he would say was that Signora Bianchi was misunderstood, the classic excuse of the besotted.

With characteristic directness, Betty had asked

60

Colin outright why Signora Bianchi had come to live in Whimbrell Heath. Was it, she asked, to be near him?

Colin came as near to losing his temper as she'd ever known. It had come to something if a man couldn't have a few friends without being subject to constant gossip. Just because a woman was good looking and didn't see fit to tell everybody her business, everyone thought the worst and Betty was as bad as any of them. Signora Bianchi could live anywhere she chose without having to account for herself and that was that. Oh, and by the way, the gossip mongers could have some time off because Signora Bianchi was going away for a few days. They'd have to find someone else to pick on.

Betty stopped by the front gate of Signora Bianchi's cottage. It was lighter here, out of the shadow of the trees. It was a modest Victorian cottage with lead-paned windows and a tiny front garden, filled with the yellows and blues of spring. She could just about make out the colours in the last remnants of daylight. It would be dark inside the house. No wonder there was a light in the window...

Light? Hold on a minute, *what* light? Colin had said Signora Bianchi was away, but there was a light, a moving light, an oil lamp at a guess, behind the red-curtained window. Betty felt a grim suspicion growing. Colin had said – made a point of saying, perhaps? – that Signora Bianchi was away. So who was in the cottage? Could it be Signora Bianchi? And could she be with Colin?

61

Betty put her hand on the latch of the gate, then hesitated. Even if Colin and Signora Bianchi were in there, it really wasn't any of her business.

The light was steady now. Someone had put the lamp down.

Something brushed against her leg and she gasped in fright. A plaintive meow sounded and Betty slumped in relief. A large tabby cat ran past her up the garden path to the front door. It sat on the step, turned its head to Betty, meowed again, then scratched at the door with another meow.

That settled it. It was only neighbourly – wasn't it? – for a passer-by to knock on the door and tell the householder that the cat wanted to come in. No one could object to that.

Betty's arguments didn't actually convince her, but she was inquisitive enough to act, all the same. Without further ado, she unlatched the gate, walked up the path and knocked on the door.

To cover her nervousness, she bent down and scratched the tabby's head. The tabby purred loudly, then, in a move obviously born of long practice, rose up on its back legs, rattled the latch and pushed at the door with its front paws. The door creaked open a couple of inches and the cat vanished into the dark hallway.

She really did have to say something now. If Signora Bianchi came into the hall and found she'd apparently opened the door without invitation, she would have every right to be annoyed. She had to explain about the cat.

'Signora Bianchi!' Betty called, opening the creaking door. She could see a wedge of light spilling round the parlour door. 'Signora Bianchi!'

There was silence.

'Signora Bianchi?' Betty called again.

The wedge of light abruptly disappeared.

It was so unexpected, Betty felt a little jolt of fear. Why didn't Signora Bianchi answer her? 'Signora Bianchi,' she called once more.

Again there was silence.

Betty swallowed. It couldn't be burglars, could it? It seemed so unlikely at this end of Whimbrell Heath. What could there be worth stealing in a cottage? On the other hand, Signora Bianchi was such an unlikely person to have rented the cottage, someone might have decided to see what they could pick up.

With the dim light from the open front door behind her, she walked to the parlour, knocked on the door, pushed it open and called, 'Hello!'

The door swung open and Betty stepped into the room.

The room was pitch dark. There was an odd smell in the parlour, a smell that reminded her of hospitals. She stopped, and from somewhere in the darkness came a soft breath.

She was suddenly very, very frightened.

'Who's there?' she called, her voice quavering.

Again, she heard that soft breath.

Betty gulped. It wouldn't be so bad if she could *see*. She backed towards the door, fumbling in her bag for a box of matches. Her nerves made her clumsy. The matches spilled on the floor and

63

she stooped down, groping on the floor to find one.

She heard the creak of a floorboard and, nearly on the point of panic, found a match and managed to strike it on the floorboard.

She held up the light. In its brief glare, she saw someone sitting on the sofa.

The match went out.

Betty fumbled for another match. 'Who's there?' she called again as she ran her hands across the floor.

Maybe it was Signora Bianchi on the sofa. Maybe Signora Bianchi had come home and been taken ill. Maybe she couldn't speak, poor woman, and was waiting for someone to come to her aid. Maybe...

Betty found another match, struck it, held it aloft and screamed.

There *was* a woman on the sofa. In the brief flare of the match, Betty saw a face from a nightmare.

The woman's eyes were bulging, her face was mottled blue, her wide-open mouth was flecked with blood and her tongue protruded at a ghastly angle.

Betty dropped the match and, in that same instant, knew there was someone behind her. A strong arm came round her shoulders and a sickly smelling cloth was clamped to her mouth.

Betty struggled and tried to scream once more, frantically trying to break free of the clutching hands. The hands were strong, very strong. She wanted to fight, but her limbs felt as helpless as a rag doll's and she couldn't breathe...

She awoke with panic coursing through her. She tried to move but her arms and legs felt leaden. There was a horrible taste in her mouth and her stomach heaved as if she were going to be sick.

Fighting down the sensation, she scrunched her eyes shut and consciously lay still, her breath coming in little shallow gasps. She was lying on her side on the floor.

Cautiously she opened her eyes again. The room was dark, but there was a faint patch of light from the curtained window. She reached out a hand and felt the knotted fringe of a rug.

Something soft pushed against her hand. She gave an involuntary yelp of fear and started away. The soft something pushed against her again.

She suddenly realised it was the cat and nearly laughed in relief. The sound came as a harsh croak. Her mouth was horribly dry and tasted foul.

The cat rubbed itself along her, purring loudly. Betty rested her hand on the sofa for a moment before pushing herself unsteadily to her knees. With one hand on the wall, she managed to stand upright.

She took a couple of faltering steps across the floor to where she knew the door was, and, with the cat wrapping itself around her legs, managed to get across the room, into the hall and into the kitchen.

The kitchen curtains were drawn back and the scudding moonlight showed her the sink. Moments later she had reached the tap and was gulping water from her cupped hand.

With the water came strength. She bowed her head, resting it on the cold stone of the sink, letting the splash of the water from the tap soothe her forehead. She gripped the sink, trying to think what to do.

It was cold in the kitchen, colder even than in the parlour. She bit back a cry as something flapped on the floor. The cat pounced and she realised the flapping thing was nothing more than the kitchen rug, stirring in the draught that swept across the floor.

Giddy with relief, she raised her head and realised, with a little shock, that the kitchen door was open. Then she heard a sound that made her senses flare into terrified life.

Someone was crunching up the path outside the kitchen door.

With a whimper of terror, Betty flung herself out of the kitchen and into the hall, sheer panic swamping all thought and all sensation in blind terror. She scrambled to the front door, sobbing in relief as it opened.

Minutes before she could hardly walk, yet now she ran, fear fuelling her muscles, hurtling herself down the path, along Pollard Wynd and back to the village, not seeing anything but the path in the moonlight.

She must've been two hundred yards away from the cottage before her legs gave out. She managed to stagger a few more feet to a lamp-post and leaned against it, fighting for breath.

It seemed to take ages for her mind to stop whirling. She knew she should get help. She

66

should tell the police, but that meant Constable Shaw, and his cottage was up the hill at the far end of Whimbrell High Street. She simply could not face the walk.

A moving light briefly lit up the sky and, from somewhere out of sight, came the distant sound of a car engine, growing louder against the silence of the sleeping village streets.

The headlights illuminated the stone of the houses at the top of the road. Summoning up her strength, Betty staggered into the road, waving for the car to stop.

The car, an open tourer, pulled up to the kerb.

'Betty?' the driver called in astonishment. 'Betty? What on earth are you doing here?'

It was Colin Askern. He climbed out of the car and came towards her. 'Betty, are you all right? What are you doing out alone at this time? It's way past midnight. You ought to be at home.'

Betty tried to speak, couldn't, and, much to her distress, burst into floods of tears.

Colin drew back in alarm. 'What the devil's happened?'

Betty reached out her hand to him. 'Colin! It was dreadful!' Tears overwhelmed her again.

Colin took her hand, then, after a moment of indecision, put his arm around her shoulders and took a handkerchief from his pocket. 'Here, use this. Tell me what's happened.' He gazed at her sharply. 'Has someone attacked you?'

Betty nodded and Colin, with startled apprehension, drew back again. 'Look, perhaps you'd better tell them all about it at home. Get in the car. I'll run you home.'

'It's murder!' Betty gasped desperately. 'Signora Bianchi.'

'What?' She saw his face, ghastly in the moonlight. He seized her shoulders. His thumbs pressed hard through her coat and she knew he was within an ace of shaking her. 'Betty! What d'you mean? What are you talking about?'

'It's Signora Bianchi,' Betty said miserably. 'I've just come from her cottage. She's been murdered. She's on the sofa in the parlour.'

'No,' said Colin, in a dazed voice. 'No, she can't have been. Get in the car, Betty,' he said abruptly. 'You wait here. I've got to see about this.'

Exhausted, she gratefully allowed herself to be escorted to the car, where she sat slumped in the passenger seat.

'Stay there,' said Colin, taking a rubber torch from the driver's door. 'I'll be back soon.'

Betty put her head back against the cool leather of the seat. She didn't exactly fall asleep, but drifted into semi-wakefulness.

She came to with a start when Colin climbed into the seat beside her. 'Well?'

'Nothing,' he said curtly, throwing the torch into the pocket on the door. 'The cottage is locked up, tight as a drum, but I shone the torch through the windows. I could see the sofa in the parlour as plain as day and there's nothing out of place. That damn cat gave me a dickens of a turn. It came clawing at my ankles when I was looking through the window, little beast.'

'So you don't know if there's anything there or not?'

'There's nothing there,' said Colin shortly, starting the car. 'You've had a bad dream, Betty. That's the only explanation. It beats me what you were doing in Signora Bianchi's cottage in the first place.'

'I saw a light,' Betty said wearily. 'I saw a light and then the cat opened the door.'

Colin paused with his hand on the gear lever. 'The cat opened the door? Betty, are you feeling all right? You're not ill, are you?'

'Don't be stupid, Colin.' She was irritated by his lack of understanding. 'The cat ran down the path and clicked the latch with its front paws. The door swung open and I ... I went in.'

'Why?'

'Never mind why!' she snapped, her irritation growing. 'I just did.'

Colin's hand still rested on the gear lever. 'As a matter of fact, I've seen the cat do that before,' he admitted. 'Tell me exactly what you thought you saw.'

'I *did* see it,' she muttered. As briefly as she could, she told him what had happened.

Colin looked at her in disbelief. 'Honestly, Betty, it sounds like a nightmare. You must've been dreaming.'

'I wasn't,' she protested. 'It wasn't a dream, I tell you.' A sudden memory came to her. 'Colin! The cat!'

'What about the wretched cat?'

'The cat was *inside* the cottage, not outside. Someone must've shut it out. I told you I heard footsteps. Someone went into the cottage and moved the body. There's the curtains, too. They

69

were pulled together in the parlour but you looked through them. Someone must've drawn them open.' She sat back in the seat. 'We have to report this, Colin. We have to tell the police.'

She could see his face, indecisive in the gas light from the lamp-post.

'Give me a cigarette,' she said. 'I dropped my handbag in the cottage.'

He absently pulled out his case and, lighting a cigarette for her, took one himself, then sat, chin in hand, thinking.

'You dropped your bag in the cottage?' he repeated.

Betty nodded.

'That's something that can be proved, at any rate,' he muttered. 'All right, Betty, we'll tell the police.'

Four

'And did you tell the police?' asked Jack.

'We did, Mr Haldean.' She raised her hands and dropped them helplessly into her lap. 'They found what Colin found, which was nothing.'

'And this was last Saturday, you say?'

'That's right. Colin drove me to the local police station and Constable Shaw went with him in the car to investigate. They didn't go in, but looked through the window. As there was nothing out of place, Constable Shaw said he'd go back the next day.'

'And did he?'

'Yes. He came up to the house and returned my bag. He'd spoken to Signora Bianchi's daily woman, Mrs Hatton. She'd found my bag in the parlour. She'd thought it must belong to her mistress, but couldn't explain how it got there.'

'What about Signora Bianchi herself?'

'That's just it. Apparently Signora Bianchi left Whimbrell Heath two days previously. She told Mrs Hatton she'd be away for a few days. She didn't know when she'd be back.' She looked at him with wide, puzzled eyes. 'I didn't know what to do. Everyone in Whimbrell Heath says I had a nightmare. That's the polite version, but all I can say is, if I did have a nightmare, it was the most realistic nightmare I've ever had. In the

71

meantime, Signora Bianchi is missing. I'm convinced she's been murdered, but no one's doing anything because they all think I'm nuts or something.'

Jack glanced at Bill. 'It would be a good time to commit a murder, wouldn't it, Bill? Wait until the intended victim has announced she's going away for an indefinite period, bump her off, hide the body, and it could be weeks before anyone raises the alarm.'

'M'yes,' said Bill. 'Signora Bianchi would have to come back to the cottage, of course.'

'There might be any number of reasons why she'd do that. She could've received a message saying there was some crisis or other, or someone could've arranged to meet her there. The person who sent the message would have to know where she was, of course, but if he – I say he for convenience – was planning a murder, that's not too far-fetched. There is another explanation, of course. Rather than being the victim, Signora Bianchi could be the murderer. She could've asked an unsuspecting victim into her cottage easily enough'

'Blimey, Jack, isn't this complicated enough for you as it is? The trouble, as I see it, is that Askern didn't believe anything untoward had happened, and neither, by the sound of things, did this Constable Shaw. The result is that he wouldn't have made a proper investigation and so what we're left with is Miss Wingate's story.'

'You believe me, Mr Rackham, don't you?' asked Betty urgently.

'Oh yes,' said Bill heartily. Just a shade too

72

heartily to be absolutely convincing to someone who knew him well, thought Jack. 'Absolutely, I do.' However it reassured Betty Wingate, who looked relieved.

'And can you do something about it? The local police won't lift a finger, but you're Scotland Yard, aren't you? I mean, you're in a different league. I've told you what happened and if you investigate it properly, then I'm sure you'll find something, something to prove this poor woman has been murdered.'

Bill rubbed the side of his nose with his finger. 'Well, I'm sorry, Miss Wingate, I don't know if I can. It doesn't work like that, I'm afraid.'

Betty Wingate's brows drew together. There was a flash of anger in her blue eyes. 'You don't believe me! You said you did and I thought you would, but it's just like talking to Colin and Aunt Maud and everyone else.'

'It's not a question of belief,' said Jack, hastily throwing some metaphorical oil on these troubled waters. 'As you said, Bill is part of Scotland Yard. But Scotland Yard can't just roll up off their own bat. What happens is the local police force have to be faced with a crime that the chief constable decides they need specialist help with. That usually means something big, like murder, which the local chaps have probably never dealt with before and where the solution isn't obvious. So they call in the experts, who are the Scotland Yard detectives, to conduct the investigation. A lot of chief constables don't like calling in the Yard as they see it as an admission of failure.' He grinned disarmingly. 'They have to be convinced that a crime has occurred, of course, and it isn't just, if you'll excuse the phrase, a mare's nest.'

Betty was visibly mollified. 'I didn't know that's how it worked. In the films, Scotland Yard just come and catch the crook.'

'That's films for you,' commented Jack wryly. 'Real life with the awkward bits left out.'

'I can't believe this red tape!' said Betty passionately. 'Signora Bianchi has been murdered! I didn't know her well and I didn't like her much, but *she's been murdered*! I've told everyone who I can think of telling, but no one wants to do a thing to help.'

'We didn't say that, exactly,' murmured Jack. 'Bill brought you to see me, Miss Wingate.' He put his head on one side and lifted an eyebrow at his friend. 'I rather think there was a reason for that.'

Bill grinned in embarrassment. 'It's an awful cheek. It's just that...' He broke off, glanced at Betty, then looked away. 'I can't do anything, Jack, but you're a free agent. Sorry. You've probably got quite enough to do as it is without looking for work. Forget it.'

Jack linked his hands together behind his head and stretched out in his chair with a smile. 'Forget it? That's even harder than doing something about it.' Besides that, he added to himself, it'd be nice to see a bit more of Betty Wingate.

'Then you'll do it?' asked Bill. 'Thanks, Jack. You're a pal.'

Betty looked at them both blankly. 'I'm sorry, but did I miss something? I haven't a clue what you're talking about. What is it Mr Haldean's going to do?'

'Investigate your mysterious vanishing lady,' said Jack, reaching out for a cigarette. He lit it and blew out a long mouthful of smoke. 'Run round, ask questions and generally make an absolute nuisance of myself to all concerned.'

'But why?' demanded Betty. 'I mean, I could do that. I have done that.'

'Ah, yes, but I'm a pocket genius,' said Jack with a smile. 'If only I was wearing a false beard and whiskers, I could tear it off and you would see the celebrated features of the modern Sherlock Holmes. Conundrums confounded, secrets solved, deceptions detected – that's a blinking good bit of alliteration off the top of my head, even though I say so myself – crooks caught and murders ... Damn! I can't think of a word that starts with M and means solved, but you get the drift. All this done while-you-wait. Distance no object. No job too small and families waited upon daily.'

Bill smothered a laugh but Betty looked at Jack blankly. 'Excuse me? I don't think I understood any of that.'

Bill intervened. 'What Haldean is trying to tell you, Miss Wingate, is that, despite all the evidence to the contrary, he's not certifiably loopy but is actually very good at solving mysteries.'

Betty looked at Jack in disbelief. 'You're a private detective?' She paused uncertainly. 'I can't...' She swallowed, then met his gaze squarely. 'I can't afford to pay anyone to investigate.'

'Don't worry about that,' he said. 'I don't do

this as a business.' He looked at her and grinned. 'I hope you don't mind me asking, but tell me, Miss Wingate, after your adventure, did you suffer from spots?'

'Spots?' She looked understandably affronted. 'What d'you mean, spots? Are you serious?'

'I'm very serious. Spots as in little pimples, you know? I'm sorry if it's a rather personal question.'

'It's certainly that.' Betty shrugged. 'That's the weirdest thing I've ever been asked. Does seeing a murder usually bring on spots?'

'So did you? Have spots, I mean?'

Betty bridled with irritation. 'Yes, I did, if you must know, although I—'

'Were they round your mouth?'

'Yes, as a matter of fact they were.'

Jack turned to Bill. 'Chloroform, Bill. You must've thought the same when you heard Miss Wingate's story and she talked about the hospital smell.'

'I still don't see what you're getting at—' began Betty, when Jack interrupted.

'You were chloroformed. That's what knocked you unconscious. One of the after-effects of chloroform applied to the skin is a rash of tiny blisters.'

'Gosh,' said Betty, impressed despite herself. 'So that's what it was!' She looked at Jack with growing respect. 'It sounds as if you might be good at this, after all.'

Bill laughed. 'He's not bad. I told you as much.'

'So you're going to look into what I saw,

then?' demanded Betty.

'Absolutely I am. Were you going back to Whimbrell Heath today?'

Betty nodded. 'I don't want to be away longer than I can help.'

'Then why don't we run down together? My car's garaged round the corner and it should be a pleasant trip.' He caught the expression on Bill's face and added, 'Can you come too, Bill? Not officially, you understand, but just for the ride.'

Bill smiled and put his hands wide. 'As I said before, it's my day off, and a trip to the country with friends sounds just the ticket. Thanks, Jack. I thought I could rely on you.'

Jack parked the Spyker beside the Brown Cow in the middle of the village. It was a pleasant spot, with a bench in the shelter of a shady oak tree. The post office and a parade of shops stood across the square and, behind them, a wide grassy bank led down to where a stream, nearly wide enough to be a river, gurgled against the piles of a stone bridge.

'The car should be safe enough here,' said Jack, climbing out and offering his hand to Betty. 'Is it far to Signora Bianchi's cottage?'

'About half a mile or so, but there's nowhere closer to park.'

Beech View Cottage was much as Jack had imagined it from Betty Wingate's description. It was a small, brick-built Victorian building with a slate roof, a black-painted wooden porch and a small, flower-edged lawn in front. It was attractive enough in a homely sort of way, but certainly not a likely place to find the sophisticated sort of woman Betty had described Signora Bianchi as, living or dead.

The cottage stood by itself, its nearest neighbours two or three hundred yards up the road on the corner of Bridge Street. The name of the cottage faithfully represented the surrounding countryside. There were plenty of beech trees and, for that matter, lots of other types of trees to view. There were trees behind the house, trees across the narrow road and a line of trees running along the edge of the fields which bordered Greymare Lane.

It was a delightful place on this sun-filled afternoon, but Jack could imagine it having a very different atmosphere by the light of a scudding moon, with the wind soughing through the branches.

Bill looked up and down the road and frowned in disapproval. 'This was a pretty isolated place for you to find yourself in, Miss Wingate.'

'I know,' she said with a shudder. 'I don't mind admitting, I got thoroughly rattled.'

'Let's take a closer look,' said Jack, opening the gate and walking down the path. 'I don't suppose there's anyone in, but you never know your luck.'

Rather to his surprise, his knock was answered. A grey-haired woman wearing a wrap-around apron and holding a duster came to the door. She must be Mrs Hatton, the daily.

'Good afternoon,' said Jack, raising his hat. 'We were hoping to see Signora Bianchi.'

'She's away for a few days, sir. I'm not sure

78

when she'll be back, I'm sure.' Mrs Hatton looked up and nodded in recognition at Betty. 'Hello, Miss. Did you get your bag back? Bert Shaw told me as how it was yours. I couldn't think how it came to be in the parlour, but Bert told me some tale about how you'd been in the house. How the door came to be unlocked I don't know, because I'm always careful to make sure everything's fast before I go.'

Jack glanced to the side of the porch where there was a large flowerpot holding a straggly yellow azalea. There was a rim of earth where it had been moved. 'You don't leave the key under the mat, by any chance? Or under the flowerpot?'

Mrs Hatton drew back. 'Now how did you know about that flowerpot? It's true, as sure as I'm stood here.' Her eyes narrowed. 'You haven't been watching me, have you?'

'No, of course not,' Jack reassured her. 'It's just that I've got an aunt who lives in the country and she always leaves a key under a flowerpot.' That wasn't strictly true but it placated Mrs Hatton. 'And if I could guess where the key's kept, maybe someone else could guess as well.'

'I suppose so,' said Mrs Hatton doubtfully, 'although who would be wanting to break in, I don't know, without it being one of those nasty tramps we get. It's been dreadful since the war, with tramps looking for what they can scrounge, but I'm sure no one like that's been in this cottage. I'd have noticed if anything was missing. Bert Shaw asked me if there was anything missing and I told him no, there wasn't.'

'Did you hear what happened the evening Miss Wingate left her bag here?' asked Jack. 'About what Miss Wingate saw, perhaps?'

Mrs Hatton glanced at Betty, cleared her throat in embarrassment, and looked away. 'Well, I did hear something. It's not that I listen to gossip, Miss,' she added defensively to Betty, 'but it's been the talk of the village. You must've been dreaming, I daresay. You most probably had something that disagreed with you for supper. My mother, she could never tolerate trotters. Used to carry on awful after she had trotters, she did, and I expect you had something similar.'

Betty turned to Bill and Jack. 'You see? Everyone thinks I'm making it up, but I'm not.'

'I didn't say you did it *deliberate*, Miss,' said Mrs Hatton in a wounded sort of way.

'That's just it, though,' said Jack. 'Some people are saying Miss Wingate's making up a story deliberately, and so she's asked me and Mr Rackham here to see if we can get to the bottom of it. So, although I don't want to put you out, I was wondering if we could come and have a look inside and see if there's anything we can discover.'

Mrs Hatton looked very doubtful. 'I'm not sure. It's not really my place to be letting folks in to the house, what with the mistress being away.'

'It's all right, Mrs Hatton,' broke in Betty. 'You know who I am, and these gentlemen are my friends and friends of Mr Askern's, too. You served with Mr Askern during the war, didn't you, Mr Rackham?' she added, turning to Bill.

'Yes, that's right.'

80

Mrs Hatton wavered. 'Well, I'm sure as it'll be all right, being as how it's you, Miss. You'd better step inside. You'll excuse me getting on with my work, though, won't you? I've got the upstairs windows to do yet.'

'That'll be fine, Mrs Hatton,' Jack said with a smile. 'The last thing we want to do is hold you up.'

Mrs Hatton ushered them into the minute hall, hesitated by the stairs for a few moments then, as if reassured they weren't about to immediately start looting the place, went back upstairs.

'It's lucky she was in,' murmured Bill as her footsteps sounded overhead.

'It is,' said Jack. 'Although there's usually a key around somewhere.'

'As a guardian of the law, I'll pretend I didn't hear that remark. What are you hoping to find, Jack? After all, if anything happened...' He broke off as he saw Betty's expression. '*Whatever* happened, I mean to say, it all happened days ago now.'

'Yes, it did,' agreed Jack. 'I wish we could have been here sooner, but we have to take our crimes as we find them. I must say, I don't really know what we're looking for, but let's start in the parlour. That's where Miss Wingate saw the body.'

Betty shivered as they went into the room. 'I wish it had been a dream,' she said. 'I'll never forget striking a match and seeing that woman's face. It was horrible.'

The parlour was a small, low-ceilinged room with dark sham oak panelling and well-used

81

furniture. An attempt had been made to brighten the place up with some bright cushions, but the only items of real note were a grandfather clock and an unframed portrait photograph, propped up on the sideboard.

'This is very good,' said Jack, picking up the photograph. It showed a striking dark-haired woman, her head tilted to one side so the sunlight caught the angles of her face. She was relaxed and happy and obviously felt at ease with the photographer. 'Is this Signora Bianchi?'

'Yes,' said Betty, grimly. 'That's Signora Bianchi all right.' She picked up the photograph. 'Colin must've taken it. He's keen on photography.' Her voice wavered. 'He's never taken my picture.'

'I'm glad he took this one though,' said Jack. 'It'll be useful if we have to find out what happened to her.'

Betty looked suddenly horror-struck. 'Of course! You'll need a picture of her. I'm sorry. When I think what happened to her, it seems so petty to feel anything but sympathy.' She broke off and tossed her head impatiently. 'Colin saw a lot of Signora Bianchi.' She wriggled unhappily. 'There were no end of rumours.'

Bill and Jack exchanged glances. 'What sort of rumours?' asked Bill.

She wrinkled her nose as if she'd smelt something rank. 'Unpleasant ones. People said...' She drew a short, exasperated breath. 'I suppose I'd better tell you. The gossip was that Colin was having an affair with her. I flatly refused to believe it. I couldn't see what the attraction was.'

She bit her lip. 'She's *old*, isn't she? *Old*.'

Jack looked at the photograph. There was no denying Signora Bianchi had an indefinable air of glamour. He could see very clearly where the attraction lay.

'You might as well know,' continued Betty. 'I asked Colin to stop seeing her but he said it was none of my business.'

Jack scratched his nose thoughtfully. It was nothing to do with the case, but he really wanted to know how Betty felt about Colin Askern. 'Why should it be your business?' he asked with seeming guilelessness.

'Because Colin and I have become good friends,' she said flatly. She looked at him with earnest appeal in her blue eyes. 'Can we leave it there? I'd rather not say any more. Colin said he enjoyed her company because she'd travelled widely and knew about art and films and culture and so on. I never thought that was the whole truth.'

'Have you any reason to think it isn't the whole truth?' Jack asked gently. It was obviously a very delicate topic and the last thing he wanted to do was upset her further.

'Not real reasons, no.' She ran her hand through her hair. 'I don't suppose it matters now what Colin thought of her.'

Jack and Bill swapped glances. They knew each other well enough to know what the other was thinking. If Signora Bianchi had indeed been murdered, then Colin Askern's relations with her could be very important indeed. Rather to Jack's relief, Bill didn't find it necessary to point that out to Betty Wingate.

Jack went to replace the photo on the sideboard, then, changing his mind, put it in his jacket pocket.

He looked round the room thoughtfully. There was a tiny black mark on the rug beside the sofa. He stooped down and rubbed his finger over it. 'Is this where you dropped the match? There's a burn on the carpet.'

'I was standing about there, yes.'

'And the woman was on the sofa? Was she lying down or sitting up?'

Betty frowned in remembrance. 'Sitting up, I think. Yes, that's right. She was sitting up but with her head slumped back.'

Jack knelt down by the sofa and examined it carefully. The sofa was a cheap wooden frame, deal varnished to look like oak, with red upholstery cushions tied to it.

The cushions had evidently been plumped up, presumably by Mrs Hatton. Jack moved them to one side and examined the frame with minute care.

'There's a hair trapped in the angle of the frame,' he said. 'It wouldn't be a natural place to put your head if you were merely sitting down.' He gave the wooden arm of the sofa an experimental shake. 'This seems firm enough for normal use.'

'I don't think much of a sofa that catches your hair,' said Bill. 'It sounds damn painful.'

'Yes, it does, doesn't it?'

Jack sat on the sofa, shifting his weight experimentally. 'Under normal circumstances, I think the arm would remain fairly solid. Let me try something, Bill. I'll sit here and, if you don't mind, would you strangle me?'

'Strangle you?' said Bill with a grin. 'That's a turn up for the books. It's usually me that gets cast as the corpse in these little re-enactments.'

'Just do it,' said Jack, hutching himself into the corner of the sofa. 'Now I'm presuming, because Miss Wingate was attacked with chloroform, that Signora Bianchi was also chloroformed and therefore helpless. So I'll look invitingly help-less, yes?'

He slumped forward. 'Come on, Bill,' he muttered into his chest.

Bill stepped forward, tentatively wriggling his fingers. 'And you want to be strangled?'

'Stop short of the *coup de grace*.' Bill grasped Jack's throat. 'Ouch! Not quite so firmly, old bean. Thumbs on my windpipe – there's no need to press! – and now force me back.'

Under the pressure of Bill's hands, Jack's head went back into the corner of the sofa. 'Now take your hands off my throat, as I don't fancy being a second victim, but press my head back hard.' He gave a little yelp of pain.

'I'm sorry,' said Bill, standing back. 'You said to press hard.'

'It's not you,' said Jack between gritted teeth. 'It's this damn sofa. As I went back into the angle, the wood gaped apart and trapped my hair.'

He sat up, rubbing the back of his head, then knelt down beside the sofa once more. 'Let's see what we've got. A couple of short hairs – mine –

and this longer dark one to add to our previous hair. And, judging by what we've just seen, I think the only way hair can be trapped in the frame is if someone is exerting force from above.' He glanced up at Betty. 'One up to you, Miss Wingate. Does Signora Bianchi have long dark hair?'

'She has dark hair, certainly,' said Betty. 'I don't really know how long it is. She always wears it up.'

Bill put the long hairs in an envelope and made a note on the outside. 'I'll keep these. It's some sort of evidence, at any rate.'

'What did you do after you saw the body?' asked Jack.

'That's when I was attacked. I remember the ghastly smell of the cloth over my mouth. When I came round I was incredibly thirsty and it was pitch dark. I found my way into the kitchen. The curtains were open and the moon was shining. I was able to find the sink in the moonlight and I had a drink and splashed my face with water. Then I realised that the kitchen door was open and I heard footsteps outside. I was really scared.'

'You poor kid,' said Jack sympathetically.

'I panicked. I ran for the front door and got myself out of the house and up the street as fast as I could. Then I met Colin and the rest you know.' She looked at them ruefully. 'He couldn't find a thing and nor could anyone else.'

'Let's see if we can do better,' said Jack. 'Have you any idea how long you were unconscious for?'

Betty shrugged. 'I've thought about it, obviously. I can't say for certain, but it must have been a few hours. The train arrived at quarter to nine and it was after midnight when Colin came along. I suppose it must've taken me twenty minutes or so to walk here from the station, so say I was knocked out at half past nine or so. That's about as close as I can get.'

'That means you were out cold for about two and a bit hours,' said Jack thoughtfully. 'Now in that time, our murderer was doing ... what?'

'Moving the body, obviously,' said Bill. 'It wasn't here when Askern looked through the windows, so he has to have moved it in that time.'

'Exactly. Shall we have a look in the kitchen? That might give us a clue where he moved it to.'

The kitchen, with steps down to the adjacent scullery, was, like the other rooms in the cottage, small. A stone sink stood under the window and an unlit cooking range against the opposite wall.

Jack looked out of the window. The cottage had a long back garden with a line of trees at the bottom, separating the garden from the fields beyond. An old wooden fence ran across the back of the garden, with a gate leading to the fields beyond. Between the trees the land fell away, but rising in the distance, about a field's width away, was an imposing stone building that looked like a church with a dome.

'What's that building between the trees?'

'That's the chantry,' said Betty. 'It belongs to Colin's firm, Lythewell and Askern. It looks like a chapel but there's never been a service said in it, as far as I know. Mr Lythewell's father built it years ago.' She grinned. 'Colin hates the chantry. He reckons it's a mausoleum with some of the worst art he's ever seen.'

Jack turned to Bill. 'What d'you think, Bill? It's quite a landmark, isn't it? A good place to hide a body, perhaps?'

Bill gave a dismissive laugh. 'It *could* be. So could plenty of other places. Why don't we look outside? As Miss Wingate heard steps approaching the back door. it's not too great a stretch to say the murderer took the body out that way. We might,' he added hopefully, 'find it in the coal bunker or something.'

'And I thought I was the optimistic one,' muttered Jack. He led the way down the steps and through the scullery, with its copper for the wash and collection of mops and zinc buckets, to the back door.

Immediately outside the cottage was a small paved yard with a dustbin and a coal bunker. The flagstones of the yard were green with algae. Beyond the yard ran the garden path, covered with cinders. It divided the garden in two, running through the patchy grass of the lawn and vegetable plot, leading to a low brick-built building that, Jack guessed, had once been a pigsty.

In deference to Bill's suggestion, he looked in the coal bunker, which, predictably, contained nothing but coal, then crunched down the garden path towards the sty.

Betty gave a little cry and the colour left her cheeks. 'That's it! That's the noise I heard that night!'

Jack paused and pressed his foot experimentally into the cinders. 'What, my footsteps you mean? It'd certainly be a very sinister sound after the experience you'd been through.'

'It was,' said Betty with feeling. 'I've never been as scared in all my life.'

The pigsty, a small, uncovered yard and roofed shelter, obviously hadn't been used for years. The gate which led into the yard stood open, hanging from one hinge, firmly wedged in the mud.

'Hullo,' said Jack, stooping and pointing to the rutted mud. 'Look at this, Bill. The mud's pretty churned up, but do those look like footprints to you?'

Bill examined the marks with a frown. 'They're not very clear. There's been a fair old bit of rain in the last week, so we'd have no hope of matching them to a particular shoe, but yes, I'd say they were footprints.' He stood up and looked over the wall of the sty. 'There's some gardener's tools in the covered part of the shed. Maybe the prints belong to the gardener.'

'That one doesn't,' said Jack, pointing to a print which was protected by the shelter of the wall. It was the print of half a heel, sharply incised into the mud. 'That's an ordinary shoe, not a gardener's boot.'

Bill nodded. 'You're right. Don't go in through the gate. I want to keep those footprints as they are.' He sat on the low wall and swung himself over into the sty. Jack followed him.

The inside of the shed was evidently used by Signora Bianchi's gardener. A spade, a hoe, a fork and a rake stood against the wall, with more tools and a collection of plant-pots on a roughly-made shelf. A wooden wheelbarrow occupied one corner, and two packing cases, clearly used as a chair and table, took up the rest of the room. A pile of sacks, an old newspaper and the stub of a candle stuck onto an old plant-pot holder stood on the packing-case table.

Jack stood with his head to one side for a moment, then, taking the handles of the wheel-barrow, pushed it out into the light. He crouched down beside it and examined it carefully. 'This wood's fairly rough, Bill,' he said, running his hand over the grain. 'Granted that our murderer came down the path and, judging from the foot-print, came into the sty, I'm hoping that there might be something here for us.'

'There is!' cried Betty, craning over the wall of the sty. 'I saw something flutter in the breeze. By the handle. Can you see it?'

It was a snag of brown silk, nearly impossible to see against the wood of the wheelbarrow.

Bill gave a whistle and, detaching the threads, held them on the palm of his hand. 'This,' he said seriously, 'is shaping up to look like real evi-dence. Well spotted, Miss Wingate.'

'I only saw it because it moved.' She swallow-ed. 'Mr Rackham, does this mean you believe me?'

'I believe *something*'s happened here,' said Bill. 'I can't think of any legitimate reason why a gardener should carry silk around in a wheel-barrow.' He put the silk threads into an envelope.

'Do we assume the murderer put the body in

the wheelbarrow and took it through the gate?' asked Jack.

'Why not?' said Bill. 'It's as good an idea as any.'

The garden gate led onto a tussocky field. A couple of hundred yards away, a flock of brown-faced sheep looked at them enquiringly with their mild eyes, then returned to their placid grazing. A rough path led round the edge of the field.

'You take that way, Bill,' said Jack, pointing left, 'and I'll take right.'

'What are you looking for?' asked Betty.

'Traces of the wheelbarrow,' said Jack. 'It'd be a pig to push over the field, so I'm assuming it was taken along the path.'

They set off, carefully scanning the ground. It was only a few minutes before Jack gave a call.

'Bill! Miss Wingate! I've found something.'

The path had narrowed and the paling fence enclosing the cottage gardens had been replaced by wooden posts and strands of barbed wire. On the other side of the fence the ground fell away into a scrub of trees and hummocky ground.

'Here, Bill,' said Jack as the others joined him. He pointed to the path. 'That's a wheelbarrow track.' His eyes were bright with discovery. 'You can see how the tracks are confused. The ground's pretty bumpy and I think the wheel-barrow slipped and went into the fence.' He pointed to the barbed wire. 'What's more, look at this.' On the barbed wire were caught a few more threads of fine brown silk.

'Got him,' breathed Bill in satisfaction. He

added the brown threads to his envelope and made a note. Then he stepped back and looked at the rough ground beyond the fence. 'I wonder if the body's been dumped in the woods?'

Jack scrambled under the barbed wire and, bent double, examined the ground carefully. 'I can't see any sign of the leaves being disturbed,' he said eventually. 'That's not to say they have not been, of course, but let's follow the path to the end.' He ducked back under the wire. 'Do you know where the path comes out, Miss Wingate?' he asked, turning to her.

She thought for a moment. 'I can't say I've ever been along here before, but I suppose if it comes out anywhere, it'll run down to the road leading to Lythewell and Askern and the chantry.'

'I said it was a good landmark,' said Jack with a smile. 'Come on.'

They found traces of the wheelbarrow at intervals along the path, before the ground opened out and ran down to where a field gate barred the entrance to the road. The mud, churned with the feet of sheep and cattle, was clearly useless for spotting any more prints.

Jack latched the gate shut behind them as they walked out onto the road.

The road was wide, bending away from the outskirts of the village. The buildings of Lythewell and Askern were a few hundred yards away, but dominating the surroundings, surrounded by a low stone wall, stood the chantry. They crossed the road and looked over the wall.

The chantry was a brick-built, domed building

and looked exactly like a small Victorian Italianate chapel. It even had a noticeboard, red with gold lettering, which looked as if it should carry the name of the chapel and times of services. What it actually said was: *Property of Lythewell and Askern. Church Artists, Furnishers and Monumental Masons. Private.*

Although the grass on the slope running up to the chantry was mown, the building had a cut-off, neglected look. Beyond the chantry the road bent round to a yard housing a series of single-storey brick buildings from which they could hear sounds of intermittent hammering and shouted instructions.

'Those are the workshops and offices,' said Betty. 'Colin should be here at this time of day. Shall we go and find him? I'd like to tell him that you've proved I'm not making it all up.'

Bill hesitated. 'Just for the moment, Miss Wingate, I must ask you to not mention anything to anyone about what we've discovered.'

Betty looked muleish. 'Why not? That's why I asked you to come here in the first place, to prove I wasn't dreaming things.'

'Not to discover what happened to Signora Bianchi?' Jack asked mildly.

Betty had the grace to look ashamed. 'Well, that too, of course.'

'That's certainly why we came,' said Bill. 'You were convinced you'd seen a murder and, on the strength of what we've found, I certainly agree there's something which merits investigation. However, a murder means there's a murderer.'

'That's right. I heard him, remember?' said

Betty with a shudder.

'Well, the last thing we want to do is to give him any sort of warning.'

'I was only going to tell Colin!'

Jack lit a cigarette. What Betty Wingate didn't seem to realise – what had obviously never crossed her mind – was that Colin Askern could easily be the man they were looking for.

Judging from both the portrait photograph and the village gossip, Colin Askern had a warm relationship with Signora Bianchi; he was on the spot when Betty had made her escape, and he was the one who had first visited the scene of the crime. He could've easily carried the body down the garden path to the pigsty either while Betty was unconscious or, with Betty safely in the car, when he was supposed to be looking through the windows. With Betty on the spot as an eye witness to the fact that there'd been a body, it wouldn't take much thought to realise that the police were going to be called in sooner rather than later.

It was Colin Askern, albeit with Betty's prompting, who'd taken Constable Shaw to Signora Bianchi's cottage. Jack was prepared to eat his hat if Colin Askern hadn't been radiating disbelief to the constable. That sort of mood was very catching. Constable Shaw wouldn't be human if he didn't find the idea of a hysterical, over-imaginative woman far easier to comprehend than a mysterious death involving the still more mysterious disappearance of a body.

He glanced enquiringly at Bill. Bill gave a very slight shake of his head. They were clearly thinking more or less the same thing.

'Please don't tell him, Miss Wingate,' urged Jack, softening the words with a smile. 'I can understand why you want to, but from what you've said, it sounds as if Askern was fairly attached to Signora Bianchi. If you convince him she really has been murdered, he's not going to keep it to himself, is he? He's going to kick up a dickens of a fuss and demand a proper investigation.'

'You don't realise what it's been like,' said Betty reluctantly. 'I *hate* everyone thinking I've been seeing things.'

'Just for the time being, that could be one of our greatest assets,' said Jack. 'A murderer suffering from a false sense of security is a man who won't take obvious precautions.'

Betty's muleish expression intensified. 'Precautions? What precautions?'

Jack took her hand and looked her straight in the eyes. 'Murder. Murdering *you.*'

Betty's eyes widened. 'He wouldn't,' she said helplessly.

'Why not? You're convinced we're dealing with a man who's murdered once. You're a witness. The penalty for murder is hanging. He could kill again but he can only be hanged once. Think about that for a moment. At the moment no one, as far as he knows, believes you. Good. That makes you safe. Let him have the slightest suspicion that there's any evidence that Signora Bianchi really was murdered and you're in danger.'

Betty swallowed hard. She was silent for a few

moments then looked up at him wonderingly. 'But that means you'll never be able to investigate the murder.' She was obviously rattled. 'Not without him coming after me, that is.'

'That's not true, Miss Wingate,' said Bill reassuringly. 'I need permission to conduct a formal investigation. Once that's granted and the investigation is underway, the murderer will know that anything you saw is now known to us and is being acted upon.'

'There'd be no point him trying to bump you off then,' said Jack, rather more cheerily than he felt. Betty was in real danger and he wanted to make her realise it, without scaring her witless. 'In fact, it'd be worse for him if he did try anything, because that gives us more evidence to go on, you see?'

'More evidence?' She managed a wobbly smile. 'My dead body, you mean?'

'You've got it.'

She stared at him. As she saw the sincerity in his face, she swallowed once more. 'You really mean it, don't you?' Jack nodded. 'In that case, I'd better keep things to myself.'

Bill nodded approvingly. 'Exactly. And, if you don't mind, I think we'll just go back the way we came without making too much fuss about the fact we were here.' He patted the envelope in his pocket. 'What I want to do is to show this to the chief, Sir Douglas Lynton, and take it from there.'

'I thought you said Scotland Yard couldn't do a thing unless you were called in?'

'There's such things as telephones, Miss Wingate,' said Bill with a smile. 'And if Sir Douglas has a word with the Chief Constable of Surrey Police, then I think all the pieces will fall into place.' He glanced up and down the road. 'Come on. The great thing now is to get away without anyone knowing we've been. I don't want to explain our presence here.'

As he spoke, the door of the chantry creaked open and a short elderly man came out. With a sinking of his heart, Jack recognised Henry Cadwallader.

'Come on,' he whispered. They backed off, hoping to slip away unobserved across the road to the field gate, but it was too late.

Henry Cadwallader stared at them for a moment, then stumped down the path towards them. Ignoring Bill and Betty completely, he made straight for Jack.

'So you came to see the chantry, young sir?'

Henry Cadwallader had the most direct approach of anyone he'd ever come across, thought Jack. Not for him the niceties of 'Hello', 'How d'you do?' or 'Nice to see you'. He spoke as if he'd last seen Jack a few minutes ago, rather than a couple of weeks previously.

'I'll show you round,' continued Cadwallader. 'It's a marvellous place.' His voice took on a reverent note. 'It was built by Mr Lythewell himself.'

'We'll get off,' murmured Bill.

'You will,' said Henry Cadwallader, leaning across the wall and seizing hold of Jack's arm firmly, 'enjoy it.'

'I'll meet you back at the car,' said Bill. He

spoke softly, but he needn't have bothered. If he'd bellowed the remark, it was doubtful Henry Cadwallader would've noticed. He was entirely taken up with Jack.

'Now then, young sir,' said Cadwallader, rubbing his hands together, 'let's get into the chantry. My word, have you got a treat in store!'

Five

Henry Cadwallader's complete absorption in the chantry was, Jack thought as he walked up the slope behind him, remarkable. He really did seem utterly oblivious to the departed Betty Wingate and Bill Rackham. Which was, of course, all to the good, but startling all the same.

Cadwallader stopped at the large, red, nail-studded doors. 'It isn't locked,' he said. 'I was coming back, so I left it open.'

'Is the chantry usually kept locked?' asked Jack.

'Oh yes. There's works of art and valuable artefacts inside that many a one would like to get their hands on.' He fumbled in the artist's satchel he wore and pulled out an ornate wrought iron key. 'Look at this! This key alone is a work of art.' It was certainly an imposing piece of metalwork. The key must've been at least eight inches long and weighed two to three pounds. 'There's plenty who would like to get their hands on this, I can tell you, but the chantry's always kept locked. This is my key,' he said with some pride.

'Who else has a key?' asked Jack.

Henry Cadwallader sucked his teeth. 'Mr Lythewell and Mr Askern have keys, of course. Not that they bother overmuch with the chantry,' he added disapprovingly. 'And there's a key in the office,' he added, obligingly answering what would've been Jack's next question, 'not that you ever see anyone from the office in here either, barring young Mr Askern. He drops in from time to time but he's not serious about the art. I don't want to speak out of turn, but I've often thought there's only me who values the chantry properly. If I've said to young Mr Askern once, I've said it a hundred times, that he should come and study how things should be done, but he just laughs. Youngsters,' he added in a rumbling undertone.

So anyone could get hold of the key. Okay...

'The first thing to look at,' said Cadwallader ponderously, 'are these nails in the door. These aren't your modern wire made rubbish. Modern nails split the timber, but these nails work with the wood. No *real* carpenter would use wire nails. Oh no.' He patted the head of a nail with pride. 'These are proper clouts, forged by the blacksmith for Mr Lythewell himself. That's craftsmanship. Look, you can see every clout is stamped with Mr Lythewell's initial. Now that's what I call taking pride in your work.'

There was, indeed, a capital L stamped onto the head of every nail, bearing testament to the departed Mr Lythewell's pride in the work. Or, thought Jack, his ego. However, fascinating as Henry Cadwallader obviously found the nails, Jack wanted to get inside the door.

He'd spotted the chantry as a major landmark from Signora Bianchi's garden. From what Cadwallader said it was seldom visited. A good place to leave a body? Maybe, especially if no one

100

knew a murder had been committed.

'Take your time, young sir,' grunted Cadwallader. 'Not that I blame you for being eager, mind.'

He pushed open the door. Completely involuntarily, Jack gave the reaction that Henry Cadwallader obviously expected: he gasped.

'I can see you appreciate it, young sir,' said Cadwallader with deep satisfaction.

The interior, which measured at least forty feet round, was a blaze of colour, dazzling in the light from the stained-glass windows. Flights of angels were painted around the walls, robed in white with sashes of reds, blues, yellows and greens. Their gold wings stretched up the walls and met round a circular window set in the middle of the ceiling thirty feet above their heads. The rest of the roof was painted in blue, picked out with stars. Oak panelling, painted crimson, ran round the walls to shoulder height, and above it the walls were a riot of intertwined leaves, fruits, flowers and vegetation

At the back of the chantry was a huge, highly carved and decorated oak altar, and above it, where Jack would've expected a crucifixion scene, was instead, an enormous mural, painted onto the circular plastered brickwork of the dome. It showed the gold and pearl gates of heaven wide open. God sat on a cloud above the gates and beneath him a white-robed, bearded figure welcomed another white-robed, bearded figure, watched by an audience of angels. Judging by the fact one of the figures was carrying keys, Jack correctly guessed he was St Peter.

'That's absolutely right,' said Cadwallader. 'I painted that picture, but it was Mr Lythewell's idea. I painted it under his direction. He thought an awful lot of that painting, did Mr Lythewell. It's an exact portrait of him. It shows him being taken up to heaven.'

'Gosh,' said Jack. He felt sand-bagged by the scene. He was fairly lost for words, but he tried hard. 'It's a remarkable piece of work.'

Fortunately, Henry Cadwallader didn't need much encouragement to take Jack's comment as unbounded enthusiasm. 'Exactly!' he agreed, his eyes shining. 'Now that's what church art should be like.'

Thank God, thought Jack, that for the most part it wasn't. 'Was the chantry ever consecrated?' he asked, falling back on neutral ground.

Cadwallader shook his head. 'No, it never was. Mr Lythewell, he had a falling out with the vicar about it. The vicar had very narrow views and said he thought it was all too Papist, would you believe.'

'Shocking,' murmured Jack. 'Papist, eh?' Privately his sympathies were entirely with the vicar. The late Mr Lythewell seemed to have as much modest self-effacement as a Borgia Pope. He tried hard and came up with a question. 'Is there any of Mr Lythewell's own artwork in here?'

'Oh, yes. He wanted to be interred here. He made his own tomb. He spent a lot of time on it, he did, but,' Cadwallader added with a curl of his lip, 'the family weren't allowed to carry out Mr Lythewell's wishes.'

'The family being...?'

'Mr Daniel Lythewell. No, Mr Lythewell had to be buried in the churchyard, like he might have been anyone, but this is the tomb he intended for himself.'

He led Jack across the chantry to where the light from the circular window in the ceiling shone directly on a stone coffin standing on a plinth in the middle of the floor, supported by four squat feet in the shape of lions' paws.

The stone coffin – or should that be sarcophagus, wondered Jack – was fairly plain, but the surrounding floor was covered with ornate tiles, decorated, as was the oak panelling, with intertwined leaves, fruits and flowers. The tile on the floor at the end of the sarcophagus showed a picture of the chantry, inlaid in silver metal and encircled with enough vegetation to make it look in imminent danger of being overgrown.

A life-size copper-coloured metal figure of a man knelt beside the coffin, his face covered by his arms, which were flung out over the coffin lid in an expression of grief. The coffin, its lid to one side, gaped open.

'Mr Lythewell made the tomb himself,' said Henry Cadwallader reverently. 'Wonderful work.'

The lid shielded part of the coffin. Jack felt his pulse quicken. Kneeling down beside the statue, he looked inside. Could this be the place the killer had put the body? It would be a bit obvious, but ... No. The coffin was empty.

'That was very respectful of you, young sir,' said Cadwallader approvingly. 'There's not many who'd think to kneel in prayer like that. I was glad to see you do it.'

'Just a gesture,' said Jack, rather embarrassed, when his attention was caught by the dust on the floor by the base of the plinth. There was plenty of ordinary grey dust, but this dust was a different colour, yellow and bright. He reached out and, picking up a handful, ran it through his fingers.

'What's that?' asked Henry Cadwallader.

'Sawdust,' said Jack, showing Cadwallader the dust in his hand.

Cadwallader sucked his teeth in disapproval. 'That woman isn't worth paying in washers.'

Jack looked a question.

'The cleaner, Mrs Whatever-it-is the woman's called, from the village. I told her there was some sawdust got in and she said she'd swept it all up.'

'It looks as if she swept most of it under Mr Lythewell's tomb,' said Jack, peering into the narrow gap under the plinth.

Henry Cadwallader was shocked. 'That's bordering on disrespectful, that is.'

'Yes, but where did it come from?' said Jack, rising to his feet.

'Sawdust?' Cadwallader looked puzzled. 'It comes from wood.'

'Yes, but *what* wood?'

'Any wood at all,' said Cadwallader, still puzzled. 'Even a very close-grained, dense wood produces sawdust.'

Jack sighed and gave up. He reached out and touched the metal statue. With the metallic

104

fingers grasping hold of the open stone lid of the coffin, it was difficult to see how the sarcophagus could ever have been intended to be used as a tomb. 'Is this statue Mr Lythewell's work as well?'

'No. At least, not Mr Josiah Lythewell, you understand. It was Mr Daniel who made that statue. He said if his father couldn't be buried where he wanted to be, at least his preferred last resting place should be treated with respect. That statue meant he'd always have at least one mourner. I thought it was very fitting.'

'I didn't know Mr Lythewell – Mr Daniel, that is – was a metalworker,' said Jack in surprise. It seemed hard, somehow, to imagine Mr Lythewell doing any sort of physical work.

'He hasn't done any for years,' said Cadwallader with a shrug. 'We used to do a lot of forging, electroplating and casting, but that's all gone now. We still have a forge but we haven't done any major work in metal for years. In fact, I think I'm right in saying that's Mr Daniel's last piece right there. Mr Lythewell, he was an expert in metal. He was a wonderful engraver and did beautiful inlaid work.' He stepped away from the empty tomb and pointed to a flagstone. 'You see? This lettering that's inlaid in the stone is Mr Lythewell's work.'

Jack obediently went to inspect the stone. As Henry Cadwallader said, a sentence in cursive script was inlaid into the stone in shiny metal.

Stop, my son, to pause and pray for treasure, read Jack. *Treasure*? It was probably metaphorical, but... 'What treasure is that?' asked Jack.

Henry Cadwallader gave a rusty laugh. 'Mr Lythewell's treasure. Mortal rich, he was, but no one knows what happened to it all. He left very little, as I've heard more than once. There's rumours that he buried a load of treasure before he died. I don't believe in it, myself. Young Mr Askern, he'd like to find it. He's been in here nosing round a few times lately. I thought he'd seen sense at last and come to see the art, but I reckon it's the treasure he's after.'

So Colin Askern had been looking round the chantry, had he? That, thought Jack uncomfortably, could be significant. He could have been looking for a hiding place...

'He's always on some money-making scheme or other,' continued Cadwallader. 'He's always wanting to bring in new ideas and new ways of working. He'd do better concentrating on the firm and how we've always done things. The firm did very well when Mr Lythewell was in charge.'

Jack looked across the chantry floor. Another engraved flagstone caught his eye. 'This talks about treasure, too,' he said, walking over to it. *'A far lesser treasure also behold.* What does that mean, I wonder?'

Henry Cadwallader looked blank. 'It's a sentiment,' he said. 'A funeral sentiment. Mr Lythewell wrote it.'

'Yes, but what does it mean?'

From Cadwallader's expression it was obvious he didn't expect a sentiment, however funereal, to mean anything.

Jack cast around for the next flagstone. It was

106

a few feet away. *'Be wise. Shun greed, let avarice be mute,'* he read. 'Well, it's good moral advice, I suppose.'

'Moral advice, you say?' said Henry Cadwallader in satisfaction. 'That's exactly what I'd expect of Mr Lythewell. He always had a word in season for those who were failing. See here,' he added, pointing to another flagstone. 'That's a warning, that is.'

'Art which is wrested from that evil root,' read Jack. 'I can't say I can exactly see what it's warning against, but it could mean the love of money.' Henry Cadwallader looked blank again. 'Money is supposed to be the root of all evil,' explained Jack. 'St Paul says as much.'

'Oh,' said Cadwallader, enlightened. 'Scripture. Well, that's fitting, isn't it?' He looked dubiously at Jack. He had obviously expected more enthusiasm and fewer questions. 'Anyway, you need to see the rest of the chantry.'

It took a good three quarters of an hour for Henry Cadwallader to show Jack the rest of the chantry. Fortunately, Cadwallader took Jack's keen – even minute – interest in any place that could possibly conceal a body as evidence of his overwhelming enthusiasm for the chantry, Mr Lythewell and all his works. Eventually, with a promise to return, Jack was able to make good his escape.

Bill was sitting on the bench under the oak tree outside the Brown Cow, smoking his pipe and reading the paper. With half a pint of bitter by his side he looked the picture of content. 'Miss

Wingate's gone back to Whimbrell House,' he said, shading his eyes from the sunshine. 'It's been very quiet. Your Spyker's received some admiring glances but nobody's paid me the slightest bit of notice. I saw Askern earlier on but I don't think he spotted me.'

Jack paused, his hand on the car door. 'Are you sure, Bill?'

'Fairly sure,' said Bill, climbing in. 'He certainly didn't say hello if he did see me, and there's no reason why he shouldn't.'

'Unless he is our man, of course.'

'If he is, he'd surely want to know what I was doing here. My real concern is that old fossil back at the chantry will tell everyone that Miss Wingate was there together with you and me.'

'Don't worry about that,' replied Jack, climbing into the driver's seat. 'I don't think he really registered you were there at all.' He started up the car. 'He's what you might call single minded, is our Mr Cadwallader, and, in my opinion, a bit cracked on the subject of the late Mr Lythewell.'

'He liked him, did he?'

'I'd say worshipped would be the precise verb,' said Jack with feeling. 'You may laugh, but it's a bit wearing after a time. Is there anywhere else you want to go, or do we head back to civilisation?'

'London for me, Jack. I want to have a word with Sir Douglas Lynton about what we've found. I don't mind telling you that those hairs trapped in the sofa and the silk caught on the wheelbarrow made quite an impression on me.'

'So you do think Signora Bianchi was murdered?' said Jack, letting in the clutch and pulling out onto the road.

'I think it's looking that way. Incidentally, I did see you put that photo of Askern's into your pocket, didn't I?'

'Absolutely you did,' said Jack. He took a hand off the wheel and, fishing the photo of Signora Bianchi out of his pocket, handed it to Bill. 'I can't help wondering if I've come across Signora Bianchi somewhere,' he said. 'She looks vaguely familiar.'

'Does she?' said Bill with interest. 'That might be useful.'

'Only if I can put my finger on where it was I saw her. I've been racking my brains, but I can't place her.'

Bill studied the photo for a few moments. 'She's certainly a good-looking woman.' He bit his lip and sighed. 'Askern's a fool to get involved with a woman like that. She looks like trouble to me.' He put the photograph down and drummed his fingers on his knee thoughtfully. 'I hope that's all there is to it – an affair, I mean. I could see you working out how Askern could be our man back at the cottage, and I must say I have to agree he's a possible.' He sighed once more. 'However, that's some way down the road.'

'Quite a long way, I'd say. Incidentally, Bill, you know Colin Askern is fairly keen on money?'

'He's not unique in that respect.'

'No, I daresay he isn't, but according to my pal Henry Cadwallader, there's a rumour old Mr

Lythewell left some buried treasure and Askern would love to get his hands on it.'

'Buried treasure?' repeated Bill sceptically. 'You're having me on.'

'No, I'm not. Apparently old Mr Lythewell was loaded. Absolutely bursting with money, so it was said, but when Mr Daniel Lythewell came to inherit the firm, it had all – or most of it anyway – mysteriously disappeared.'

'Money does that,' said Bill with a grin.

'So I thought, especially if you're given to building temples to an overwhelming ego with religious leanings.' Bill looked puzzled. 'That's what the chantry is, Bill. Nothing more or less. However, apparently the chantry money is all accounted for and there's still a massive hole where the dibs should be.'

'That's interesting. I can't see where it gets us, though.'

'No, me neither,' said Jack, giving the steering wheel a twiddle to avoid a straying hen. 'However, there's something about the thought of huge amounts of vanishing cash that always shouts, "Motive!" at me.'

'I can't see it's any sort of motive for bumping off Signora Whosit.'

'Not at the moment, no. We might come up with something, though.'

'We *might*,' said Bill guardedly. 'Did you spot anything interesting in the chantry? I know you thought it might be a good place to leave a body. And why is it called the chantry, anyway?'

'I asked Henry Cadwallader that. I don't suppose anyone ever went and chanted in it. No, it's called a chantry because it's a nice, medieval-sounding word that Mr Lythewell liked. The place was never consecrated because the local vicar had a bit more sense than Mr Lythewell bargained for. As far as spotting anything, the quick answer is I didn't. However, with Mr Cadwallader constantly at my side, I wasn't able to lift paving stones and tap walls.'

'No, I can see how you'd be hampered. It can't involve too much effort, though. Our chap didn't have unlimited time to dispose of the body.'

'No ... What do we think actually did happen that night?'

Bill clicked his tongue. 'I think the set-up is probably something along the lines of what you suggested back in Chandos Row. X, the murderer, waits until Signora Bianchi has said she's going to be away for an unspecified time, then gets her to come back to the cottage on some pretext or other. Then, knowing that her absence won't cause any sort of stir locally, he has days, if not weeks, to dispose of the body.'

'That's the local angle, certainly. However, where did Signora Bianchi stay when she went away? If it was a hotel, we might be stumped. She'd merely leave the hotel to return home and no one would be any the wiser, but if she was staying with friends, they'd notice she was missing.'

'They've kept pretty quiet about it if they have.'

'M'm, yes. Depending on who her friends were, they might not like the idea of contacting the police.'

'They were on the wrong side of the law, you mean?'

Jack shook his head. 'Not necessarily. As she was Italian, they could be Italian too, with limited English and a distrust of authority. Or, damnit, she could've just told them she was off home and therefore they wouldn't have any cause for alarm.'

'These are all paths we'll have to explore. I'm glad you picked up that photo. That'll make a search much easier.'

'A picture's worth a thousand words, as they say. There's one thing that I think is fairly certain. Our killer is a local man. The way the body was disposed of more or less proves that. I doubt anyone from outside the area would think of loading a body into a wheelbarrow and taking it across the fields.'

'I think you're right.' Bill scratched his chin. 'Jack, I know you had hopes for the chantry, but I'm not so sure. You can't get a car down Pollard Wynd to Signora Bianchi's cottage, but that field path is a fairly direct route to a proper road. What if the killer had a car waiting on the road by the field gate?'

'He could've done,' agreed Jack. 'He could easily have done. If that's the case, with any luck, someone will have seen it. I wonder if Lythewell and Askern employ a nightwatchman? He might've seen something.'

'Again, that's something we'll have to chase up. I'm trying to get the sequence of events clear.'

'Okay. The killer lures the Signora to the cottage, chloroforms her and then bumps her off. The chloroform tells us this is a planned murder, not an assignation that went tragically wrong, by the way. I don't believe anyone walks round with chloroform in their pocket just on the off-chance.'

'No, you're right there,' agreed Bill. 'So far, so good. Then poor Miss Wingate comes on the scene. She gets chloroformed in turn, while the killer does what?'

'He leaves the body in the pigsty. That could be because he was arranging an alibi.'

'Or moving his car into position.'

'Or, as you say, moving his car.' Jack drove for a couple of minutes in silence. 'It could be a lot simpler than that, of course. Say Miss Wingate is right and it was about half past nine when she was attacked. That's still fairly early in the evening. At this time of year it's still dusk. The killer might have been waiting until he thought it was safe to move.' He clicked his tongue in irritation. 'There's too many ifs, Bill. I'm not sure what our next step should be.'

'I know what mine is,' said Bill. 'I'm going to speak to Sir Douglas Lynton. What's more, I'll be very surprised if he doesn't want to have a word with you, as well.'

The next day, Jack received an invitation to call on Sir Douglas Lynton at Scotland Yard. When he was shown into Sir Douglas's office, he wasn't surprised to see Bill Rackham there.

'Come in, Haldean,' said Sir Douglas hospitably. 'I gather you've found an entirely new way for my chief inspectors to spend their days off. Help yourself to a cigarette, by the way. The box is on the table.'

Jack pulled up a chair and took a cigarette with a grin. 'I'm sorry, sir. I hope we didn't tread on any official toes.'

'Not exactly,' said Sir Douglas, 'although I had to be fairly diplomatic on the telephone this morning with Commander Pattishall, the Chief Constable of the Surrey force.'

'Very good of you, I'm sure, sir,' muttered Bill.

'Just a little oil to keep the wheels turning, you understand,' said Sir Douglas. 'It's difficult enough to get the local constabulary to refer matters to us at the best of times, without charging in and inventing murders for them.'

'Inventing, sir?' asked Jack.

Sir Douglas shrugged. 'The supposed crime is the murder of Signora Bianchi. Leaving aside the self-confessed report of trespass by Miss Elizabeth Wingate, which is hardly our concern, the Surrey police have no record of any crime. However, Pattishall's a sound man. I've met him a few times and, once I'd reassured him that there was no possible slur upon him or his men, he was prepared to listen. Like you – and I must say I share this view – he finds the evidence that you and Mr Rackham gathered yesterday disturbing. He could think of no good reason for anyone to transport expensive silk in a gardener's wheelbarrow. Added to the strands of hair you found caught up in the frame of the sofa and Miss Wingate's account of what she saw, it has, he agreed, an ugly suggestiveness about it.

Therefore, gentlemen, I am pleased to tell you that Commander Pattishall has agreed to call us in.' He raised an eyebrow in Jack's direction. 'Do I take it you want to continue to be involved in the case?'

'Absolutely, I do,' said Jack. 'I warned Archie Keyne, my editor, that I was going to be otherwise engaged for the next few days. This has the makings of a really meaty problem. Not only is there a disappearing body, there's disappearing treasure, too.'

Sir Douglas hid a smile. 'Disappearing treasure? Yes, Rackham told me about that. You'll probably find that the taxman's had it all.'

Jack grinned. 'That's very cynical, sir. It takes all the thrill out of discovery.'

'Cynical, eh?' said Sir Douglas with a laugh. 'No, Haldean, just realistic. If the taxman didn't take his cut beforehand, then he'll certainly have it afterwards. Now, I gather you think the murderer is a local man. I agree. Rackham told me of your concerns as to Miss Wingate's safety. Naturally, that's a concern I also share. Granted that our first priority is to ensure Miss Wingate's safety, there should be no doubt in anyone's mind that a full investigation is underway. I think the best way to achieve that is to go to Whimbrell Heath openly and make a proper search of Signora Bianchi's cottage.'

'Sir Douglas arranged a search warrant this morning, Jack,' put in Bill. 'You won't need to sweet talk the charwoman this time.'

'I didn't hear that remark,' said Sir Douglas with a smile. 'The other thing we can do is to find as much information as we can about Signora Bianchi. If she's an Italian national, as seems to be the case, she must have a passport, for instance. I want to know who she is, who saw her last and who her associates were. You know the drill.'

Bill nodded. 'I do, sir. Haldean picked up Colin Askern's photograph of her yesterday.'

'Have you got it, Haldean?' asked Sir Douglas.

Jack handed it over and Sir Douglas studied it for a few moments. 'She's a good-looking woman,' he commented. 'A very good-looking woman.'

'We can't use it without Colin Askern's permission,' said Jack. 'He took the photo, after all.'

'No, you're right, we can't,' said Sir Douglas. 'Never mind. If necessary, we can ask him. So, Rackham, I'd like you to return to Whimbrell Heath today. You could,' he suggested, 'start by asking questions about Signora Bianchi at the village post office. If Whimbrell Heath is like any other village, everyone will know within the hour exactly who you are and why you're there.'

'I'd say so, sir,' agreed Jack. 'The news'll go round like wildfire.'

Six

For the second day in a row, Jack parked the Spyker under the oak tree outside the Brown Cow. Whimbrell Heath Post Office and General Stores (*Mrs K. Sweetiman, Prop.*), their immediate destination, was in the middle of a parade of shops on the other side of the square.

The post office had the sharp, dusty smell of roast coffee and dried fruit. Open boxes of prunes, raisins, dried currants and apricots stood in front of the shelves of packets, tins, jars and bottles of sweets. Mrs Sweetiman herself stood with her back to a wooden counter weighed down with cheese, butter and ham, operating the bacon slicer.

'I'll be with you in a minute,' she said, turning her head as they joined the queue. She deftly wrapped the rashers of bacon into a neat parcel of greaseproof paper. 'Now then, Mrs Hawley,' she said to the woman in front of them, 'that's half a pound of bacon, a tin of tomatoes and a quarter of acid drops. That's sevenpence ha'penny, please. Did you hear about the burglary down Pollard Wynd?'

Jack and Bill exchanged glances.

'I did indeed,' said Mrs Hawley, delving into her purse. 'It's at that foreign woman's, isn't it?'

'It's Annie Hatton's fault,' said Mrs Sweetiman

117

knowledgeably. 'She told me she let two strange men into the house yesterday, which is a thing I'd never a-thought Annie Hatton would've done. I thought she'd have been more careful than that. She said they seemed like gents, but you can't tell nowadays, can you? They must've been eyeing the place up.'

'I wouldn't care to live down Pollard Wynd,' said Mrs Hawley. 'It's too cut off for me *and* there was that tale about a murder.'

'Excuse me,' said Bill. 'Has there been a burglary at Signora Bianchi's house?'

Mrs Sweetiman and Mrs Hawley looked at him. 'Yes, that's right,' said Mrs Sweetiman. 'She's away from home at the moment, so it must've been an easy job. I don't know what's been taken. What would you be wanting, sir?'

'We wanted Mrs Hatton's address. It concerns Signora Bianchi.' The two women looked at him quizzically. 'I'm from Scotland Yard.'

'Well, I never,' breathed Mrs Sweetiman, gaping at him.

'Mrs Hatton is the Signora's charwoman, isn't she?'

'Yes, that's right. Annie Hatton does for the foreign lady. If it's her you want, she's down Pollard Wynd at the moment, along with Bert Shaw. He's the police,' Mrs Sweetiman added helpfully.

'We'd better get along there right away,' said Jack, tipping his hat to the women. 'Thank you very much, ladies.'

They left the post office, a buzz of voices breaking out behind them.

'Do you realise we've been taken for burglars on the strength of our visit yesterday?' asked Jack. 'I'm glad we appear to be gentlemen, at any rate.'

'Yes, I did realise that. But we know we're not burglars, so who the dickens was the burglar? I don't know if Miss Wingate told anyone we'd been yesterday,' he said as they walked quickly down the street.

'After what we said to her? I thought she'd stay stum.'

'Then it's a pretty rum coincidence,' said Bill. 'Unless your old fossil, Cadwallader, told someone.'

'I thought we were safe there, but the charwoman could've gossiped about us,' said Jack. 'She could've easily mentioned that two strange men turned up with Miss Wingate.'

'Yes, she could,' agreed Bill reluctantly.

'And you were outside the pub,' pointed out Jack. 'You didn't think Colin Askern or anyone else spotted you, but...'

'Askern could've done, all the same,' finished Bill. 'Damn!'

The door of Signora Bianchi's cottage was standing open. Bill knocked and called as they went in to the hall, to be met by a wary 'Hello' from the kitchen.

Mrs Hatton and Constable Shaw were sitting at the kitchen table, with a cup of tea apiece.

Mrs Hatton looked at them apprehensively, then rose to her feet, clutched the table and pointed at them. Her voice rose to a squeak of fear. 'It's them! These are the men who broke in,

I tell you!'

'We're not burglars—' began Jack, but was interrupted by Mrs Hatton.

She looked wildly at Constable Shaw. 'Do something! Here they are, bold as brass! They're looking to see what else they can steal, I'll be bound.'

'We're not burglars,' repeated Jack patiently.

'Don't give me that! You were here yesterday! Don't try and deny it because I know better. I *seed* you, with my own eyes.' She turned to Constable Shaw again. 'These were the men I was telling you about. These are the ones who came yesterday. I told you, they knew all about the key under the plant plot and I didn't say nothing to them about it.'

PC Shaw stood up, stroked his moustache and eyed them dubiously. 'I have to ask you to state your business here,' he said ponderously. 'I may say that the circumstances seem very suspicious.'

'We're not burglars,' said Jack, this time with a great deal more emphasis.

Bill produced his official card. 'Relax, man. As Major Haldean says, we're not burglars. I'm from Scotland Yard.'

Constable Shaw looked at the card incredulously. 'And you've come all the way from London for a *burglary*? God strewth, you got here quick, didn't you? How did you know it had happened?'

'We haven't come about the burglary,' said Bill, with as much patience as he could muster. 'We've come about the disappearance of Signora

Bianchi.'

'Whatever for?'

Bill sighed. 'There was an eye-witness account of a murder.'

Constable Shaw stared at him. 'A murder? Here, you mean?' He gave a low, rumbling dismissive laugh. 'You've got the wrong end of the stick there. It was nonsense. That was just some young woman who'd had a bad dream, that's all.'

'We think there's a case to be investigated. As we are here, I want to know about this burglary. What happened?'

Constable Shaw looked at Mrs Hatton. 'You'd better tell them what's what. You reported it.'

Mrs Hatton bridled. *'Burglars!'* she sniffed in an undertone.

'Now, never you mind about that,' said Constable Shaw with heavy encouragement. 'It's all right,' he added, seeing Mrs Hatton still wasn't convinced. 'If these gentlemen are from Scotland Yard, they're not burglars, are they?'

'Well, you can see why I thought what I did,' said Mrs Hatton defensively. 'It seemed so strange, a burglary coming on top of your visit, and I was that upset, because Constable Shaw said as how I shouldn't have let you in yesterday, not knowing who you was, even if Miss Wingate was with you. I blamed myself, but I don't see how I could've known, even if you did know about the key.'

'You didn't do anything wrong, Mrs Hatton,' said Jack easily, taking a chair and sitting down. 'You're quite right, though. It is strange, to have

121

a burglary on top of everything else. Will you tell us what happened?'

His voice was gentle and his smile held nothing but anxious, sympathetic enquiry. A smothered laugh behind him made him guiltily aware that Bill knew only too well he was exerting the full force of what Bill half enviously, half mockingly, referred to as his Devastating Charm.

There was another smothered laugh as Mrs Hatton said, *'Oh!'* and, sitting down, patted her hair and smoothed her apron into place. 'What is it you want to know, sir?'

'Just what you saw and heard, Mrs Hatton,' said Jack, unleashing the smile once more. 'You're a very valuable witness.'

'Well, I don't know what there is to tell, really.' She gazed into his eyes. 'Not now I know you didn't do it, which,' she said earnestly, still gazing into his eyes, 'I'm sure you didn't. When I arrived this morning, I came in here to put the kettle on and then I went into the parlour and the window at the back was smashed in. I stood and screamed, so I did, then I went and got Constable Shaw here. I didn't want to stop here a minute. I thought the burglar might be upstairs. I couldn't wait to get out.'

'It must've been very frightening.'

'It was,' she said, looking at him gratefully. 'I was fearful.' She rolled her eyes and clasped her throat to indicate terror.

'That was really rotten for you.'

Mrs Hatton looked gratified. 'It was. *Awful.* Anyway, Constable Shaw came back with me, and we've gone through the house to see what's

122

missing. I mean, as I said to Constable Shaw, the place could've been ransacked. I took on ever so at the very thought of it!'

'And was it ransacked?'

'Well, no, it wasn't,' said Mrs Hatton, slightly put out. 'But it could've been.'

'There was one item you said was missing,' put in Constable Shaw ponderously. 'To wit, one cash box.'

'A cash box?' repeated Jack.

'Yes, sir,' said Mrs Hatton. 'You know the type. It was metal and black with a gold and red line round it, with a handle and a key. She didn't keep money in it, mind.'

'Do you know what Signora Bianchi did keep in it?'

'Papers,' said Mrs Hatton vaguely. 'Exactly what, I couldn't say. Oh, and I've just thought of something else that's gone. There was a picture of Mrs Bianchi, a photo what Mr Askern took. It was on the sideboard in the parlour. She was going to have it framed.'

Jack took it from his pocket. 'As a matter of fact, I picked it up yesterday,' he said, smiling at Mrs Hatton's reproachful look. 'I didn't intend to steal it, though. I just wanted an idea of what she looked like. Is it a good likeness?'

'It is, sir. It's just like her, that is. Why, looking at that, she could be sat here.'

'That's useful to know, Bill,' said Jack, with a glance at his friend. He turned back to Mrs Hatton. 'Will you show us where the window was smashed?'

'Of course I will.' She stood up and, leading

123

the way, took them into the parlour.

Bill dropped behind with Jack. 'You should bottle that manner of yours,' he murmured. 'You had her eating out of your hand.'

'Don't be vulgar,' said Jack softly. 'It worked, didn't it?'

He clicked his tongue in disappointment as he saw the parlour. The glass had been swept up and, apart from the smashed window itself, there was nothing to show that the room had been broken into.

'Constable Shaw said as how I could clean everything up,' said Mrs Hatton in response to a question from Bill.

'There's nothing to be gained from looking at broken glass, is there?' said the constable. 'It's clear enough that the malefactor smashed the window, put his hand in, caught hold of the catch and raised the window that way.'

'So he obviously didn't know about the key under the plant pot, then,' said Jack.

Mrs Hatton gave a defensive wriggle. 'As a matter of fact, I put the key under the mat yesterday.' She looked at Jack. 'I thought, what with you knowing all about it, others might too.'

'Let's see if there is any evidence left,' said Bill. He took a bottle of mercury powder from his bag, tipped some into an insufflator and puffed the powder onto the window frame.

'Here!' said Mrs Hatton indignantly. 'What are you doing, dirtying my woodwork?'

'I'm checking for fingerprints,' said Bill. 'Unfortunately, our man seems to have been wearing gloves.'

'If I was going to smash my way through a window, I'd want a pair of gloves, too,' said Jack.

'Yes, but it was worth checking, all the same.' Bill turned to Mrs Hatton. 'Where did the Signora keep the cash box?'

'In the drawer of her dressing table, in her bedroom.'

At their request, she took them upstairs, although, as she said, what they were going to tell by a-looking where it *had* been was more than she could say.

The dressing table, the conventional type of dark oak with an attached mirror, held a fine leather box.

'What's this?' asked Jack. 'It looks like a jewellery box.'

'It is.' Mrs Hatton looked at it with a puzzled frown. She opened it up. 'Look, the jewellery's still inside it. Now I come to think of it, it's funny that wasn't taken. Still, thank heaven for small mercies, that's what I say.'

Signora Bianchi's jewellery consisted of four necklaces of semi-precious stones, three brooches, three sets of earrings and five rings. She did have other jewellery. Some of it, according to Mrs Hatton, was lovely. The Signora had probably, thought Jack, taken her other jewellery away with her.

A thorough search of the cottage ensued but, despite all their efforts, they were no wiser as to who Signora Bianchi was, or who her friends or associates were, at the end of the search than at the beginning.

The only items that seemed personal were a few books with *Carlotta Bianchi* written on the fly leaf. There was some cash – four pounds in notes and a few coins – in the dressing table drawer but no letters, no documents and no passport. They must've been, agreed Jack and Bill as they walked away from the cottage, in the stolen cash box.

'And you can't tell me,' said Bill, 'that any thief who leaves jewellery, even cheap jewellery, and cash, is an everyday crook. According to Mrs Mop back there, the only thing taken was that cash box with the papers in. Somebody was looking for something very specific indeed.'

'Either that, Bill, or someone wanted to prevent us from finding it,' said Jack thoughtfully. 'I wonder which one it was?' He stopped at the cottage gate. 'What's our next port of call?'

'I think we'd better see Colin Askern next. In the light of what we both thought yesterday, that Askern could easily be our man, I wouldn't mind letting him know this is now an official investigation. And, granted we haven't found any other pictures of Signora Bianchi, I need to ask his permission to use his photo for the *Police Gazette*.'

They walked along the field path to Lythewell and Askern, coming out, as before, opposite the chantry. This time, thankfully, there was no Henry Cadwallader to impede them. They were guided to the workshops, a horseshoe of single-storey buildings enclosing a cobbled yard, by the sound of hammering. A blue-painted gate, large enough to admit wagons and lorries, stood open

126

and they walked into the yard.

An intelligent-looking, khaki-overalled man, a clipboard in his hand, was standing in the entrance to one of the buildings, totting up the numbers of a pile of barrels and long wooden boxes.

'Bill,' murmured Jack, indicating the pile. 'I know we were interested in the chantry, but you could easily fit a body in one of those barrels.'

Bill grinned. 'So you could, you old ghoul.'

The khaki-overalled man finished his calculations. 'All right, Harris,' he called to someone at the back of the shed. 'You can get them loaded onto the carts, now.' He turned as Bill and Jack approached. 'Can I help you, gents?' he asked. 'I'm the foreman. Were you looking for the offices?'

'We were actually looking for Mr Askern,' said Bill. 'Mr Colin Askern.'

The foreman pushed his cap back and scratched his head. 'I saw him go up to the house,' he said after a few minutes' thought. 'At least, that's where I think he was off to, but if it was about an order, though, you'd be better going to the office. They can get in touch with Mr Askern for you.'

'It isn't about an order,' said Bill. 'As a matter of fact, I'm a police officer and we're looking into a report of an incident that happened on Saturday night.'

'An incident? Here, you mean?'

'The incident actually happened in Pollard Wynd,' said Jack, 'but we wondered if anyone reported a car, say, waiting in the road near here on Saturday night.'

The foreman shook his head. 'I can't help you there, I'm afraid. There wasn't anything to do here on Saturday night, as far as I know. You'd better talk to old Stroud. He's the night-watchman. He might have seen something, I suppose. He doesn't start till six o'clock but he lives in Bryce Street, if you want a word. I'm not sure of the number, but it's next to the Guide Post pub.'

'Thanks,' said Bill. He took out his cigarette case and offered it companionably to the foreman. He nodded at the wooden boxes. 'What's in the crates, Mr...?'

'Jones, Andy Jones,' said the foreman, taking a cigarette. 'Thanks very much.' He took a light from Bill's match and leaned his elbow on the boxes. 'This is a consignment of church pews going up to...' He inclined his head to look at the label on the nearest box. 'Liverpool.'

'That's a fair old way,' said Jack.

The foreman grinned. 'That's nothing. We ship stuff from here all over the world. Australia, South Africa, New Zealand ... You'd be surprised. Mind you,' he added, 'those are usually single items, carved wood and statues and the like.'

'Can you take us through the routine?' asked Bill. 'What happens when an order comes in?'

Mr Jones nodded affably, nothing loath to take a few minutes off. 'I organised the way we do things. Someone places an order, maybe from the catalogue or perhaps after having corresponded with the office, for a custom-made piece, then the exact details of what's to be made up are sent down to the yard. This is wood and

128

stone I'm talking about, you understand. Mr Askern sees to anything that you might call fine art, pictures and suchlike, but all the craftwork is produced here.'

'It's all despatched from here, though, isn't it?' asked Jack. 'To the customer, I mean?'

Mr Jones nodded. 'Yes, it's all checked by me.'

'So say I'd ordered a wooden pew. What would happen?'

Mr Jones pointed across the yard. 'First it would be made in the wood shed, then it would be carved and varnished. Once it's finished, one of the bosses, Mr Askern, say, will take a look if it's a single item, or, if it's part of a larger consignment, I'll check it over to see it's up to our standards. Then it'll be marked as passed and taken to the packaging shed where it's crated up and labelled. All our crates are custom made for each item, of course. As each piece is made, there's a label attached.' He smiled. 'We don't want anything going to the wrong address, as you can imagine.'

'No, I can see you wouldn't,' said Jack, looking at the hefty crates.

'After it's crated up, the final despatch labels are fixed on, and it's brought here, to the despatch shed. Then it's loaded onto the wagons and taken to the railway station.'

He tapped his clipboard. 'I've got copies of all the labels of the goods we're working on here. Then, when they're despatched, they're filed away with a note of the carrier. If it's only a small package, such as a statue or a wood carving, that's the end of it, but for larger items, such as these pews, for instance, we send a team of workmen to the church or chapel in question and make sure everything's assembled and in place to the customer's satisfaction.'

'That seems a very thorough system,' said Jack.

'It's not bad,' agreed Mr Jones thoughtfully. 'I wish I could organise the way we do a few other things. This is a great business, you know, but...' He broke off, shrugging. 'It's not my place to offer suggestions. Anyway, I've worked here for nearly ten years and we've never had a consignment go astray yet.'

'That's an impressive record,' said Bill, finishing his cigarette. He glanced at Jack who nodded in agreement. 'Can you direct us to Mr Askern's house?'

'Go out of the yard,' said Mr Jones, pointing, 'turn left, and walk along the road for a little while and you'll see a big house. Heath House, it's called. It's less than ten minutes' walk. You can't miss it. Don't,' added the man helpfully, 'take the turn to the right or you'll come to Whimbrell House. That's Mr Lythewell's. It's easy to get the two mixed up, but Heath House is smaller.'

'Thanks,' said Bill easily. 'Much obliged.'

Jack was thoughtful as they walked away. 'It's difficult to see,' he said eventually, 'how a body could be slipped into a crate without Mr Jones noticing.'

'I knew you were trying to work that out,' said Bill with a laugh. 'It's tempting, isn't it? There's lots of crates and boxes and it'd seem easy to get rid of it that way, but I just can't see it, Jack, not with every crate made to order for the individual item. They do know what they're crating up. No. If there's a solution to where this body has disappeared to, I think we're going to find it a lot closer to home.'

A butler opened the door of Heath House to them. 'Mr Colin Askern, gentlemen? I will enquire if he is at home.'

'I'm aware of the social conventions,' said Bill, 'but if he is at home, we need to see him. I'm from Scotland Yard and this is official business.'

The butler, startled out of his deferential imperturbability, allowed his eyebrows to rise. 'Indeed, sir?' He coughed. 'I do believe Mr Askern is partaking of morning coffee in the garden. If you follow me, sir, I will take you to him.'

They went through the house and came out onto a delightful, sun-filled terrace where, under the shade of a tree, a stout lady, dressed in pastel violet, together with Colin Askern and Betty Wingate were sitting at a table with a tray of coffee. Askern had his back to them, but Betty started and gazed at them apprehensively.

The butler coughed politely. He was about to announce them when Colin Askern turned round and got to his feet in surprise. 'That's all right, Kingsdown,' he said, dismissing the butler. 'I know these men. Rackham, Haldean, what on earth are you doing here?'

'Colin,' chided the stout lady. 'That's not the way to greet guests.' She adjusted her lorgnette and gazed at them. 'Won't you introduce us?'

Colin took a deep breath. 'This is Chief Inspector Rackham and Major Haldean. I knew Rackham in the war. This,' he said rapidly, completing the introductions, 'is my stepmother, Mrs Askern, and you know Betty, of course.'

'I remember you mentioning both Mr Rackham and Major Haldean, Colin,' said Mrs Askern. 'Pleased to meet you...' She stopped, obviously taking on board Colin's unease and Betty's awkward silence. 'Excuse me, did you say *Chief Inspector*?'

'That's correct, Ma'am,' said Bill. 'And I'm sorry to say, we're here on official business.'

Betty's startled squeak was amplified by Mrs Askern. 'Official business?' she repeated waveringly.

Colin turned on Betty Wingate accusingly. 'Betty! You didn't ask Rackham to come here, did you?'

She nodded dumbly.

'Well, of all the...' said Colin in disgust. 'For heaven's sake, Betty, we've been through this *endlessly.*' He looked at Bill apologetically. 'You'd better sit down. All I can say is that I'm sorry you've been dragged down here on a wild goose chase. You too, Haldean. This,' he explained to Mrs Askern, 'is about Betty's nightmare,' adding, seeing she was still flummoxed, 'when Betty thought she saw a murder.'

'Good heavens! But that was just a dream, surely?'

'Unfortunately,' said Bill heavily, taking a seat, 'we have good reason to think it wasn't.'

The silence was absolute.

132

'Miss Wingate,' said Bill, 'made a full statement to us of what she saw and, as a result of that statement, we are proceeding with an investigation.'

'They believe me, Colin,' said Betty in a small voice. 'They don't think I'm making it all up.' She stuck her chin out defiantly. 'I told you so.'

'I think the less you say, the better,' said Colin icily. 'It's a great pity you didn't talk to me before running to the police.'

Betty's eyes glinted dangerously. 'I did talk to you. And you told me I was dreaming.'

'Precisely.'

'Excuse me, Askern,' said Bill, 'but why are you so sure nothing occurred?'

'Because it's all complete and utter nonsense, that's why! I was there, at the cottage. I even went and got the police because Betty was so sure she'd seen God knows what. There was nothing there!'

'Bodies can be moved,' said Jack. 'In this case, we're fairly certain it was.'

Mrs Askern gripped the table. 'Colin,' she said, in a voice brittle with control, 'go and get your father.' She looked at Bill and Jack and shuddered. 'And perhaps these ... these *gentlemen* had better wait inside the house.'

'Shall I take them into the morning room?' asked Betty.

Mrs Askern shuddered again. 'Just as you please.'

'You'd better come with us, Miss Wingate,' said Jack quickly. Out of sheer humanity he didn't want Betty to be left alone with either of the Askerns at that moment.

'I'll talk to you later, Betty,' said Colin Askern grimly as he pushed his chair back from the table.

'And that,' said Jack, as the three of them trooped into the morning room and Betty clicked the door shut behind them, 'is what being sent off with a flea in your ear feels like. Whoa, easy there!'

Betty Wingate had broken into sobs.

Jack hesitated for a moment, then put a comforting arm around her shoulders. 'Hold on. I've got a handkerchief somewhere. Go on, dry your eyes with that. I'm not surprised you were upset. It's rotten when no one believes you, isn't it?'

Between sobs, Betty agreed that was exactly it.

'We believe you, though.'

'But Colin was so angry!' She gulped for breath. 'Why have you come back? Now, I mean?'

'Because,' said Bill, 'I've got official permission to do so. That was pretty hard evidence we uncovered yesterday, Miss Wingate, and it needs acting upon.'

'There ... There wasn't very much. I was thinking about it all yesterday and there wasn't much.'

'We can't expect to find dripping daggers and bloodstained footprints every time we turn up, Miss Wingate,' said Jack encouragingly.

There was an attempt at a giggle between the sobs.

'It would be very satisfying if it was so, but

134

sometimes evidence is just little bits and pieces that look like nothing much. Why, Bill here once solved a murder because of a pin. And there was a burglary at Signora Bianchi's last night. That's evidence of something not quite as mother makes going on.'

Betty dried her eyes. 'Burglary? What burglary?'

Jack and Bill explained.

'But that *proves* I'm not making it up,' said Betty, indignation mixing with relief. 'They have to believe me now!'

'Whether they do or not, it certainly needs explaining. Now, why don't you go and have a wash and tidy up before all the Askerns pile in on us? There must be a bathroom somewhere and I'm sure you've got some face powder or whatever in your handbag. Keep the handkerchief,' he added hastily as Betty attempted to give it back. 'Go on. You'll feel much better afterwards.'

'When did I solve a murder because of a pin?' asked Bill with interest once Betty had left the room.

'It was Sir Ernest Childerton, if you recall, and it wasn't so much the pin, it was the note attached to it that gave the game away, but I thought she needed cheering up,' said Jack wandering aimlessly round the room. He paused beside the bookcase. 'I feel really sorry for that poor girl. I'm glad she came to you, Bill. I want to see her proved right.'

'Don't take your eye off the ball, Jack. What we're actually here to do is to solve a murder, not cheer up young ladies, however pleasant they may be.'

'She is nice, isn't she?' said Jack, taking a book from the shelf and idly thumbing through it. 'Very nice indeed. Hello! There's a brief biography of Mr Askern senior in here.'

'Really? What's the book?'

'It's a history of the firm. Privately printed, of course. I say, Bill, listen to this! It says that Mr John Cedric Askern studied art in Milan before joining the firm. That was when the original Lythewell was in charge.'

'Milan?' asked Bill sharply. 'And Signora Bianchi's an Italian.'

'Yes, I thought you'd be interested. It could be a coincidence, of course.'

'Or it could be a link. What else is in that book?'

'Nothing much about Mr Askern that I can see. There's that perfectly hideous painting from the chantry as a frontispiece. The firm was established in 1866 ... Great success ... Daniel Vincent Lythewell, after studying in New York, took control of the firm following his father's death in 1898. Snapshot of Daniel Lythewell on the deck of the *SS Concordia*, also snapshot of John Askern with Whistler.'

'Whistler? Oh, the artist, you mean. The chap who painted his mother.'

'That's the one.'

The door opened and Jack absently pocketed the book.

Daphne Askern, together with John and Colin Askern, came into the room, followed, rather to Jack's surprise, by Daniel Lythewell.

'Where's Betty?' asked Colin.

'She'll be joining us in a minute,' said Bill. 'Mr Lythewell, what are you doing here?'

'I was with Mr Askern when Colin telephoned, Chief Inspector, and I must admit to my share of curiosity. Do I understand that you think there is some truth in this extraordinary tale of young Betty's?'

'Of course there isn't any truth,' said Colin vigorously. 'It's just a storm in a teacup. Furthermore—'

Mr Lythewell held up his hand and Colin subsided into angry silence. 'If there is any truth in the story, Mr Rackham, may I ask what you want with us?'

Daniel Lythewell, thought Jack, was definitely wary. That was understandable. Colin Askern was angry and defensive, Mrs Askern looked apprehensive, but John Askern ... John Askern looked frightened.

Bill smiled. 'In the first instance, Mr Lythewell, nothing very much. We conducted a search of Signora Bianchi's cottage and found a photograph of her which, I believe, is your work, Askern.'

Jack produced the photograph.

'Yes, that's mine,' agreed Colin reluctantly.

'As Signora Bianchi is currently missing, if I can put it like that, I want your permission to use it in the official police investigation.'

Colin hesitated. 'No.' He shook his head. 'No. I have the greatest regard for Signora Bianchi and I don't want to see her image posted up for everyone to see. She wouldn't like it. And,' he added, holding out his hand, 'as it's mine, I'll have it back.'

'I'm sorry, Askern, this is the only picture of the Signora we have. I'll need to hold on to it for the time being, even if we can't reproduce it. I'll let you have a receipt for it, of course.'

'But nothing's happened to her!' broke out John Askern. There were tiny beads of sweat on his forehead. 'She's gone away for a few days, that's all.'

'As you say, sir,' said Bill smoothly. 'Tell me, sir, were you personally acquainted with Signora Bianchi?'

John Askern licked his lips before replying, 'No.' Beside him, Daphne Askern moved uneasily. 'That is, I met her once or twice, but I wouldn't call that an acquaintance.'

'I see.' Bill looked at him thoughtfully and decided to try a shot at random. 'I don't suppose you knew her when you studied in Italy, by any chance?'

There was no mistaking his reaction this time. Askern's face was ghastly and he swayed on his feet. 'No! No, I swear I didn't! You've got this all wrong, I tell you.'

Colin Askern reached out a hand to support his father. 'Get me a chair for him, will you?'

'Italy?' repeated Daphne Askern in a stunned whisper.

Mr Lythewell helped Colin escort Mr Askern to a chair.

Bill waited until he was sitting down. 'Mr Askern, where were you on the evening of Saturday the twenty-eighth of April? Last Saturday?'

138

Mr Lythewell cleared his throat. 'Is that the evening my niece says she saw this ... er ... occurrence?'

'It is, sir.'

'I was here!' broke out Askern desperately. 'Daphne, tell them I was here.'

Daphne Askern looked bewildered. 'Of course you were here, John. We had dinner and then you said you had some work to finish off, so you went into the study. I know you were here. I came to ask you about something or other, but you'd gone for a stroll on the terrace with your cigar. I looked around for you, then you came in through the French windows and told me that's what you'd been doing.'

Bill couldn't help exchanging a satisfied glance with Jack.

'Askern,' said Mr Lythewell quickly. He'd seen the glance. 'Don't answer any questions. You're obviously in no fit state to defend yourself.'

'But there's nothing to defend myself *from*,' blustered Askern, some of his self-assurance returning. 'I tell you, I hardly knew the woman. Why on earth should I take it into my head to run off and strangle her, eh?'

'Did we say Signora Bianchi had been strangled, sir?'

Once again the colour drained from John Askern's face.

'Betty told you,' said Colin sharply. 'Betty told me, at any rate, and I told you. Speaking of which, where the devil is she?'

As if on cue, the door opened once more and

139

Betty came in. She was holding something wrapped up in a towel in her hands.

Colin gazed at the towel, then at her. 'Betty...' he began. There was real anxiety in his voice.

'I'm sorry, Colin. I don't know what's going on, but I'm tired of lies and I'm tired of having you not believe me.'

'Betty, please!'

'I was in the bathroom. I heard you and your father whispering on the landing. You were talking about *"It"* and you said *"It"* was in your wardrobe, so I went to have a look. I found this.'

She unwrapped the towel. Inside was a black metal cash box with a red and gold line round it.

They all gazed at the box. Colin swore. John Askern gave a frightened whimper.

'It's Signora Bianchi's,' said Betty. 'It's got her name on the bottom of the box. You're the burglar, aren't you, Colin? You broke into Signora Bianchi's cottage. You stole this last night.'

Colin Askern said nothing.

Bill Rackham walked across the room and took the box from Betty's hands. 'Let's see what's inside it, shall we? Askern, have you got the key?'

'Don't give it to him, Colin!' said John Askern urgently.

Colin Askern shrugged. He looked utterly defeated. 'What's the point? It'll be opened anyway.' He reached in his pocket and, pulling out a key on a piece of string, passed it over to Bill.

'Thank you,' said Bill, putting the box on the table and turning the key. 'What have we got here? A passport for one Carlotta Bianchi and

140

various papers ... And look at this. A marriage certificate for Carlotta Santarelli and John Cedric Askern.'

There was a strangled gasp from John Askern.

'I take it,' said Bill quietly, 'that Carlotta Bianchi and Carlotta Santarelli are the same woman?'

John Askern hid his head in his hands but Colin Askern nodded reluctantly. 'Yes, they are.'

'Marriage!' yelped Daphne Askern. *'Married?'* Her voice rose to a scream. 'You were *married* to that woman!'

Once again, Bill exchanged looks with Jack. 'A concealed marriage seems like a pretty good motive for murder to me, especially in the light of everything else that's gone on.'

'It wasn't like that,' began John Askern helplessly. 'Daphne, *please*!'

'Married,' Daphne Askern repeated. 'Oh, dear Lord, married!'

Bill cleared his throat with an official-sounding cough. 'Mr Askern – John Cedric Askern – I arrest you on suspicion of having murdered Signora Carlotta Bianchi, formerly Carlotta Santarelli. I would be obliged if you would accompany me to the nearest police station where you will be questioned. You do not have to say anything, but anything you do say will be noted down and may be used as evidence at your trial.'

'Let me tell you what really happened—' began Askern.

Lythewell cut across him. 'No, Askern! Don't say a thing. You're not guilty of anything. I know that and when we get a lawyer we can prove it.'

Once again the door opened. Kingsdown, the butler, stepped into the room. He attempted to get Mrs Askern's attention, but she had collapsed into a chair, brokenly muttering, *'Married!'*

The butler coughed and then coughed again. Colin Askern, distracted nearly to fury, swung round on him. 'What the hell is it?'

Deeply affronted, the butler blinked and drew himself up to his full height.

'Signora Bianchi, sir.'

'Who?' yelled Bill.

Everyone froze in their place.

A woman, a beautiful woman, clearly the original of Colin Askern's photograph, came into the room. She was naturally poised but warily on the defensive. As she gazed round at the stilled group, she drew back in puzzled surprise. 'What is the matter? Is something wrong?'

No one answered.

She shook her head impatiently, then turned to Colin. 'Colin, *tesoro mio,* what is going on?'

'Mother,' he said weakly, 'where have you been?'

Seven

'Mother?' echoed Betty. 'Colin, d'you mean to tell me Signora Bianchi is your *mother*?'

'I didn't mean to tell you any such thing,' he said gruffly. He buried his face in his hands for a moment. 'Look, this is just all too complicated to explain.'

'I think you'd better try,' said Bill grimly. 'Signora Bianchi, where on earth have you been?'

She looked at him coolly. 'And who are you, to demand where I have been?'

'Don't get on your high horse, Mother,' said Colin. 'Not now. This is Chief Inspector Rackham of Scotland Yard. Would you believe he's just arrested Dad for your murder?'

She stared at him, open mouthed, then threw back her head and laughed. 'My murder! But I am not dead.'

'I can see that, Madam,' said Bill, whose patience was obviously being stretched very thinly indeed. 'However, in view of the circumstances, it was a natural conclusion to reach.'

Signora Bianchi gave an expressive shrug, pulled up a chair and, with complete self-possession, unpinned her hat, peeled off her gloves and sat down. She seemed very much at home.

Daphne Askern gave an outraged shudder. *'Impudence,'* she muttered.

143

Signora Bianchi looked at her appraisingly. 'You disapprove, yes? You are John's wife, yes? You disapprove?'

'I most certainly do! What are you doing here? Why did you come to Whimbrell Heath?'

For the first time since Signora Bianchi had entered the room, John Askern spoke. His voice was little more than a croak. 'They know we were married. You'd better tell them everything, Carlotta. I can't think straight.'

'Everything?'

He nodded and she shrugged once more. 'Very well. John and I were married in Italy. Hastily.'

John Askern winced and Daphne Askern raised her eyebrows in horror. 'Well, really!'

Carlotta Bianchi gave a frank, open smile and Jack suddenly realised she was enjoying herself very much. Wherever Signora Bianchi was, she was the centre of attention and that's exactly how she liked it.

'John was very respectable, a man of appearances, a man to whom the opinion of others mattered – oh, so much. Me,' she added, with another expressive shrug, 'I am not so, but I was young, and the good and holy nuns who brought me up, they said I should be married, so I was. However, John, he says it is wrong for me to entertain myself with parties and balls and I should think no more about dresses and affairs, but stay in our tiny house with no visitors and no society, just content with baby. Me' – she crossed herself rapidly – 'I am not the Blessed Madonna.'

'No,' growled John Askern, recovering some

144

of his self-assurance. 'You're right there. You led me up the garden path, all right, but I married you fair and square, then you ran away with Marco Bianchi and left me holding the baby.' He looked up at Colin. 'You. So what could I do? I came back to England.'

'You told me Colin's mother had died,' said Daphne Askern.

'She was as good as dead to me,' said John Askern. 'Yes, I said she was dead. As far as I was concerned, she was in the past.' He looked at Daphne pleadingly. 'What could I say? It was all so long ago. It was fine. It's been fine for years until *she* showed up again.'

'Yes,' said Jack. 'Why did you show up again, Signora Bianchi?'

'I have my reasons,' said Signora Bianchi proudly. 'I wanted to see Colin. I knew he must be big and strong and I wanted to see my son.'

'I'll tell you why you showed up again,' said John Askern. 'Your precious Marco had died, you wanted to embark on another affair, but this time you wanted some money. You came here, shamelessly told Colin the truth, got him on your side...'

'Not entirely, Dad,' put in Colin.

'Not entirely?' repeated John Askern scornfully. 'The woman bewitched you. You said I should give her everything she wanted. Well, let me tell you, my boy, I haven't *got* the money.'

'But you're well-off.'

'It's my money,' said Daphne Askern coldly. 'Protected by trusts. Even if I'd known the truth of this disgraceful business – which I most certainly did not – I would never countenance handing money over to this woman.' She glared at Signora Bianchi, then averted her eyes.

Jack looked at Bill. 'Does that sound suspiciously like blackmail to you?'

Bill nodded. 'It's beginning to.'

Signora Bianchi's eyes narrowed. 'Blackmail? No, I tell you. Signora Askern, what would you have done if I announce myself openly to you? Told you that your 'usband is not your 'usband but mine? That your marriage was never a marriage? That you are not married in the eyes of the law or of the holy church? That is important to you, yes?'

'I ... I...'

'You would have paid. You would have been grateful to me for going away and you would have paid,' she said with satisfaction. 'That is not blackmail.'

'Well...' began Bill.

She ignored him and turned on John Askern. 'I told you that is what I should have done, but you would not hear of it. I wanted to be – what is it you say? Open and above the board. Besides, it is not for me I want the money. It is for Luigi Mantonelli, my – my companion, shall I call him? He is a gifted man, he makes the moving pictures, the films, yes? Before the war, in Italy, he made moving pictures. Italian films, they were good, yes, good, I tell you, and Luigi made them. But now?' She shrugged. 'Everyone is in Hollywood, in America. He wants to go to Hollywood, to make the perfect picture, and Colin will come with us and be a star.'

146

'I'm not sure about that,' put in Colin, his colour rising.

'But yes! You have the good looks, you have the talent and, with Luigi behind you, it will be a wonderful film, believe me. But in Italy, since the war, we are poor, so I tell him, I tell Luigi, I will get the money, and my son, he will be a star. That is business, yes? That is not blackmail.'

Bill drew his breath in. 'Whatever it is, it certainly isn't murder.' He looked at Colin Askern with scarcely concealed anger. 'If you knew your mother was alive, why the devil didn't you tell us?'

'I *did*,' bit back Colin. 'God help me, Rackham, I've been saying nothing else! When Betty first came to me with that cock-and-bull story, I was scared witless. I honestly thought she had seen something in the cottage, but there was *nothing there*. I knew my mother was going away for a few days. I knew everything was all right. How could it be anything else? Was I supposed to believe that my father – because if anyone *had* murdered my mother it would have to be my father – had somehow managed to lure her back to the cottage, without letting me know a thing about it, and then concealed her body so cleverly that it couldn't be found?'

'Nevertheless,' persisted Bill, 'why didn't you just tell us the truth about who the Signora was?'

'How the devil could I? It wasn't my secret. My father's been like a cat on hot bricks about this.' He glanced at Daphne Askern. 'He was worried stupid you'd find out the truth. Then, yesterday, I heard in the post office that Betty and two strange men had been in my mother's house. I knew something was up and knew I had to act. I didn't know where my mother had got to but I knew she'd gone to see – er – her friend. I didn't have his address but thought I might find it on a letter or something.'

'So you broke in,' said Bill flatly.

'Yes, so I broke in! The key had been moved from where it's usually kept, so I broke in. I found the address but I found a lot of other papers, too, in that cash box. I knew once you got sight of that marriage certificate, the cat really would be amongst the pigeons, so I took the lot. It seemed the safest thing to do. I fired off a telegram this morning, pleading with my mother to come back and stop this nonsense, and here she is. Now, if Betty can stop insisting she saw horrors when she obviously didn't, and you, Rackham, and you, Haldean, can leave us in peace, we'll do our best to sort everything out.'

Bill took a long breath. 'Very well, Askern.' He pocketed his notebook with a sigh. 'There really doesn't seem to be any reason why we should stay.'

Daphne Askern, who'd been gazing at Signora Bianchi with a sort of fascinated horror, levered her attention away for a moment to glance at the butler. 'Kingsdown, show these – er – *gentlemen* out, please.'

'Very good, Ma'am.'

They left the room in a state of very artificial silence, but they could hear the cacophony of furious voices breaking out behind them once more before they got to the front door.

'Case,' murmured Jack, as they trudged down the drive of Heath House, 'dismissed.'

Bill made an impatient noise. 'Come on, Jack. I need a drink.'

Over a pint of bitter in the saloon bar of the Brown Cow, Bill, despite having thoroughly vented his frustration, was still going strong. 'What did Askern call it? A wild-goose chase? Well, he was right there and no mistake. I've never felt such a fool in all my born days.'

'So you said,' agreed Jack mildly.

'And what Sir Douglas is going to say, I don't know.'

'So you remarked before.'

'And he, poor beggar, has to explain it to the chief of the Surrey force.'

'You mentioned that, too.'

'I can tell you this much. The next young woman who turns up at the Yard yelling she's seen a murder, better have a damn sight more proof than our Miss Wingate, no matter how personable she is. Women!'

'That,' said Jack, running his finger round the top of his tankard, 'is rather unfair, Bill.'

'Unfair? *Unfair?* You have no idea how unfair I'd like to be at the moment.'

'What I'm saying,' Jack explained patiently, 'is that the case – our case – remains exactly the same.'

Bill stared at him incredulously. 'Excuse me? You were at Heath House just now, weren't you? You do remember when the murder victim – the victim I'd just arrested John Askern for murdering – came waltzing through the door, large as life? Because, believe you me, that's something *I'm* not going to forget in a hurry.' He drank his beer broodingly. 'When I think of all the trouble we've been to over that ruddy woman and it turns out she was doing nothing more than having a ruddy few high jinks with her ruddy boyfriend somewhere! I couldn't credit it when she turned out to be Askern's mother. His *mother*, for God's sake! She doesn't look like *anyone*'s mother! She's far too glamorous by half.'

'Mothers come in all shapes and sizes, I suppose,' said Jack. 'I'm surprised no one guessed about Signora Bianchi and Colin Askern, though. They do have quite a marked likeness. I nearly got it when I looked at that photo.'

'I'll never forget it,' rumbled Bill. 'Never.'

'No, of course you won't forget it, old bean,' said Jack in a placatory way. 'Incidentally, what were you going to do with Mr Askern, once you had arrested him?'

'Keep a damn good eye on him to see he stayed put, yell for Constable Shaw or whatever his name is, then haul him off to the police station.'

'So really, it's just as well Signora Bianchi came in when she did.'

Bill finished his beer. 'I suppose it is,' he admitted grudgingly. 'Come on, Jack. The sooner we leave, the better. Motion pictures, indeed! I'd like to give them motion pictures! I've got to face Sir Douglas, and what he's going to say I can only guess. I wish I could use motion pictures to break the news to him.'

'Hold on a minute,' said Jack, pulling him back

into his seat. 'If you'll just stop snorting with righteous disapproval for a moment and look at the facts, what have we got?'

'A mare's nest, I'd say.'

'No, we haven't. We've got the wrong victim – that's obvious – but we've still got the facts. Miss Wingate saw a strangled woman. Yes?'

'So she says.'

'Miss Wingate suffered from chloroform blisters around her mouth. Yes?'

'Again, so she says.'

'And, when we investigated, we found hair trapped in that very odd angle of the sofa arm. There were threads of brown silk on the wheelbarrow, tracks where the wheelbarrow had been pushed along the field path and threads of brown silk on the barbed wire fence. That's what we were investigating, Bill. Naturally we assumed the victim was Signora Bianchi—'

'Because that's what Miss Wingate said.'

'Because, as you rightly say, that's what Miss Wingate said. To be fair to Miss Wingate, she told us she only caught a glimpse of the victim and that was by the flare of a match. She was expecting to see Signora Bianchi, so that's who she assumed she had seen. There was so clearly something rum about Signora Bianchi, she seemed an ideal candidate to be the victim, but I always kept in mind that the victim could be someone else.'

Bill's eyebrows crawled upwards. 'As a matter of fact,' he admitted grudgingly, as he lit a cigarette, 'you did say as much. At least, you floated the possibility that Signora Bianchi could be the murderer. You don't think that's it, do you?'

Jack shook his head. 'It's possible, but she's a slightly built woman. I think she'd find it hard to push the wheelbarrow all the way through the fields. I'm not saying she couldn't do it if she was desperate, but I think she'd come up with another plan to dispose of the body when she was thinking things through beforehand.'

Bill laughed, the first sign of amusement he'd shown for a good hour. 'You're sure it was that well-planned?'

'I'm convinced of it. For one thing, the murderer used chloroform, which needs to be bought in advance. It wasn't an impulsive murder.'

Bill sat back down on the settle. 'I don't know what it is about you,' he complained. 'A few minutes ago I was ready to storm out of Whimbrell Heath and go crawling apologetically to Sir Douglas. And now...'

'And now?' prompted Jack.

'And now...' Bill tapped his cigarette on the ashtray. 'Now, dammit Jack, I think you're right.' He pushed his cigarette case over. 'Help yourself, by the way. There is something to be investigated. But if the victim isn't Signora Bianchi, which it clearly isn't, and if the murderer isn't Signora Bianchi herself, who the dickens is it? It all happened in her house, after all.'

'Okay,' said Jack, taking a cigarette and striking a match. 'I'm not sure we can make any guesses about the victim yet, but let's think about the murderer. It's clearly someone who knows enough about Signora Bianchi to know she was

152

going to be away, so that's someone who knows her and, I'd say, knows Whimbrell Heath.'

Bill nodded. 'Yes, all right, I can see that. It can't just be happenstance. There was too much to hand to make life easy for the murderer for it to be coincidental. The empty cottage, the wheelbarrow – those things are necessary to make this work.'

'And, of course, the wheelbarrow, complete with cargo, pitched up on the road outside Lythewell and Askern where there might or might not have been a car waiting.'

Bill stubbed his cigarette out in the ashtray. 'All right. Let's have some lunch, then go and have a word with the nightwatchman. I want to know if he saw anything. I suppose I'd better tell Mr Lythewell what I'm doing. He strikes me as the sort who could make life very awkward indeed if he thought I was exceeding my authority. Incidentally, you don't think either Lythewell or Askern could be our man, do you?'

Jack shrugged. 'They *could* be. At the moment it could be anybody, including,' he added with a grin, 'Henry Cadwallader. If anyone said anything untoward about old Mr Lythewell, I'm sure he'd find that an adequate motive for murder.'

'He had quite an effect on you, didn't he?' said Bill with a laugh.

'You have no idea,' said Jack earnestly. 'I wonder if this pub does steak and kidney pie?'

After lunch (which, to Jack's satisfaction, was steak and kidney pie), they walked back along the road to Lythewell and Askern.

153

It would be overstating the case to say Mr Lythewell was pleased to see them.

'I assumed, gentlemen, that after this morning's fiasco, you would have decided to let this matter drop,' he said, glaring at them over the desk in his office.

The office, thought Jack, was designed to impress. Mr Lythewell's portrait hung above the mantelpiece. The desk was large, oak, and inlaid with green leather. The files on the shelves round the room were solidly bound and gave the office the look of a gentleman's library.

'I agree,' continued Mr Lythewell, 'that Mr Askern's problems were not of your making, but there is no doubt that your intrusion into the affair made a difficult situation very much worse. I naturally assumed, once your suspicions had been proved groundless, you would return to London.'

'We can't do that, sir,' said Jack with his most charming smile. 'You see, although Signora Bianchi is still very much with us, it really does look as if *someone* came to grief that night. We certainly found evidence pointing that way.'

Mr Lythewell's eyebrows beetled upwards. 'Evidence? What evidence could there possibly be?'

Bill cleared his throat. 'That, sir, I'm not at liberty to disclose, but I would take it as a favour if you would let us interview your nightwatchman.'

'Eh? You want to interview one of my men? But why?'

'Again, sir, I'm not at liberty to explain.'

154

Mr Lythewell sighed in a much-put-upon manner. 'Oh, very well. I can't recall the fellow's name but you'd better ask Jones, the foreman, in the yard. Tell him I sent you. Oh, and Mr Rackham! Your time may be paid for out of the public purse, but my men's time is paid for by me. Please ensure you waste as little of it as possible.'

Bill preserved a poker face until they were out in the corridor and safely out of earshot. 'The pompous old devil,' he said with feeling.

'Yes, he was a bit ratty, wasn't he? Still, I don't suppose that's anything to be amazed by. I doubt his partner will be pulling his weight in the office for a while.'

They ran the nightwatchman, Gilbert Stroud, to earth in the public bar of the Guide Post Inn, where he was enjoying a leisurely lunch of pork pie, pickles and a half of mild.

His routine was a simple one. He went round the yard with his lantern every couple of hours during the night. 'There's plenty of tools worth pinching. I have to keep an eye on things. A car? No, I can't recollect seeing no car, or hearing one either, unless it was Mr Askern's going past.'

'How d'you know it was Mr Askern's?' asked Bill.

'It went up the road to Heath House, that's how. Who else could it be? Late, that was. He didn't stop, though. Last Saturday night, you say? No, we don't get many cars parked up along the road. The other end of the village, yes, with all the new houses and what have you, but we don't get much traffic near the works. There

155

wasn't none the other Saturday. None at all, that I can recollect.'

'It needn't have been a car,' said Jack. 'Did you see a lorry, perhaps?'

Mr Stroud shook his head. 'No, no lorry either.' Further questions elicited the fact that Lythewell and Askern had no motor transport of any kind. Anything that needed moving inside the yard was done by cart and muscle power, and anything that was bound for despatch out of the yard was loaded up and taken by horse and cart to the railway station. And no, there weren't any horse and carts stood round on Saturday night, either. Jack regretfully dismissed the mental image of a murderer making a very slow getaway by horse and cart.

He took out his tobacco pouch and offered it to Stroud. 'Did you see anything at all odd or out of the way near the works or the chantry last Saturday night?'

'Odd, now,' said Mr Stroud. He filled his pipe and tamped the tobacco down with his thumb. 'Thank'e sir.' He blew his cheeks out in an effort at recollection. 'No, I can't say as I did.'

The landlady, a sharp-faced woman, looked up from where she was washing glasses. She had, Jack had noticed, been washing the glasses at a slower and slower rate, obviously interested in their conversation. 'Excuse me, sirs, but are you Annie Hatton's gents from London?'

Jack smiled. 'That's us. I'm glad to say Signora Bianchi turned up safe and sound.'

'Oh, I know *that,* sir,' said the landlady dismissively. 'That's all round the village, that is, and her no better than she should be, I'm sure. Foreigners,' she added with a sniff. 'No, it was with you mentioning the chantry. I'm sorry, I'm sure, but I couldn't help overhearing.' She leaned forward across the mahogany-stained bar. 'There are rumours that it's haunted.'

'Garn,' said Mr Stroud in disgust. 'Some folks are frightened of their own shadows.'

'Who says it's haunted?' asked Jack.

'Kids,' opined Mr Stroud. 'Kids and,' he added with a sideways look at the landlady, 'women who should know better.'

'I've seen some strange things in my time, Gilbert Stroud,' said the landlady. 'Things that can't be explained.' She gestured across the bar to a table where a burly man was sitting, newspaper propped in front of him, a grey-muzzled lurcher curled up under the table beneath him, chomping his way stolidly through a ham sandwich. 'Sam Catton wouldn't agree with you. Sam! Have you got a minute?'

Man and dog made their way heavily to the bar. Jack leaned down to let the dog sniff his hand. The dog inhaled warily before letting Jack scratch the top of his head, then licked his hand and flopped to the floor.

'Can I get you a drink?' asked Jack hospitably.

'I don't mind if I do,' said Mr Catton, evidently approving of his dog's acceptance of Jack.

'These are gentlemen from London,' said the landlady. 'Annie Hatton knows them. They're asking about anything odd up at the chantry.'

'There's plenty that's odd there,' said Sam. 'I'll have a Worthington White Shield, if it's all the

157

same to you, gents.' The landlady took a bottle off the shelf and started to pour the White Shield carefully into a glass. 'There's lights,' continued Sam. 'Lights at all hours.'

'That's that mad old artist geezer,' said Mr Stroud. 'Cadwallader. He's always up there.'

Sam weighed up Jack and Bill thoughtfully, as if calculating the chances of being believed. 'There's more'n Cadwallader, if you ask me,' said Sam eventually. He picked up the White Shield and held it up to the light.

'You've got to be careful with the sediment,' said Jack conversationally.

'You have,' said Sam, pleased at this evidence of fellow feeling. 'There's plenty who don't understand a White Shield. That's well poured,' said Sam, nodding to the landlady in approval.

'That's only what you'd expect in this house,' said the landlady, accepting the praise as her due. 'These gents were asking if anyone had seen a car or a lorry near the chantry on Saturday night.'

Sam Catton took a sip of his White Shield. 'I don't know about no car, but I was near the chantry on Saturday night. It would be about quarter past one, I reckon. I heard the church clock strike a bit before.'

The landlady leaned forward and lowered her voice portentously. 'The thing about the chantry is that it's not a *normal* place.'

'I couldn't agree more,' said Jack fervently.

'How come no one hardly ever goes in?' demanded the landlady. 'It's not a proper church, that's why. There's a tomb there. And treasure,

158

so I've heard. They do say,' she added, lowering her voice, 'as how the old man comes looking for his treasure.' Mr Stroud made another dismissive noise which she ignored. 'It's because he weren't buried properly where he wanted to be. Sam heard *noises*, didn't you?'

'On Saturday night?' asked Bill sharply.

Mr Stroud laughed. 'Oh yes? What was it? A ghost going "Whoo" and clanking its chains?'

'Of course not, you daft old beggar,' said Sam. 'No.' He hunched his shoulders and breathed stentoriously. 'No, this was *knocking*. You can laugh, Gilbert Stroud, but I know what I heard. As I say, that was gone one in the morning.'

'And what was you doing up at the chantry at gone one in the morning?'

Jack let his eyes flicker to the cut of Sam's coat, with its large pockets and the dog flopped at his feet. Both the dog and the coat were suggestive. 'Rabbits?' he said softly.

Sam hesitated, then slowly grinned. 'Perhaps.'

'You told me it sounded like someone was trying to get out,' put in the landlady. 'Gave me shivers, that did.'

Mr Stroud in his role as sceptic, laughed once more. 'That's a good 'un. How come you didn't go and let 'em out then?'

'Not ruddy likely,' said Sam. He reached down and ruffled the dog's head. 'It isn't natural. Even old Bessie here wouldn't face *that*. Dogs know more than we think.'

Mr Stroud didn't say anything but his face registered complete disbelief.

'Why don't you take a walk round one night

with your Shep?' asked Sam. 'I'll be surprised if she wants to go anywhere near the chantry. Maybe you'll trust her even if you don't believe me.'

Mr Stroud's face fell. 'Poor old Shep,' he said. 'Didn't you hear, Sam? I lost her last week. She must've eaten some rat poison or some such, because she took ill and died. Had that dog for years, I did.'

The haunting or non-haunting of the chantry was forgotten in a wave of sympathy for the departed Shep.

'Rat poison,' said Bill thoughtfully as they walked away. 'That could be nothing more than a coincidence or...'

'Or it could be very useful for someone not to have a dog around to put the nightwatchman on the alert,' said Jack.

'Exactly,' agreed Bill. 'Come on, Jack. I want to get back to London. After being handed a lead like that about the chantry, I want a search warrant and Sir Douglas Lynton's blessing. *Something* was going on there on Saturday night and I'm going to find out what it was without any chance that pompous stuffed shirt Lythewell will step in to raise any objections.'

'Right you are,' agreed Jack.

They reached the Spyker, still safely parked by the bench under the shade of the oak tree.

'Let's see what we know,' said Jack as he slipped the clutch and drove up the hill out of Whimbrell Heath. 'First things first. Someone – someone from this village – committed a murder on Saturday night.'

Bill took a deep breath. 'Murder it is. Even though we haven't any irrefutable evidence of that.'

'You're planning to take the chantry apart on a hunch?'

'All right,' conceded Bill. 'We've got more than a hunch. Murder it is,' he repeated. 'I doubt I'd get a warrant for anything less than suspected murder in the circumstances. I wish we had a line on the victim, though.'

'Let's see where we get, yes? Righty-ho. Someone – someone local – knew Signora Bianchi was going to be away and someone thought they would be undisturbed.'

'How did the murderer get their victim into the cottage?'

Jack shrugged. 'That's something I can't answer at the moment, but presumably, unless the victim was local and came on foot, they arrived by car or train.'

'Where would the car be parked?' asked Bill. 'We know a car can't get down Pollard Wynd.'

'There's the other road, Greymare Lane, that runs along the bottom of the village. Pollard Wynd leads off it. Miss Wingate didn't see a car, but it could be parked out of sight somewhere along there. In fact,' said Jack, 'why don't we go and have a look now?'

Greymare Lane was much as Betty Wingate had described. It was a long dirt-track with deep ditches on either side, with trees overhanging the lane. Jack drove slowly along the lane until the turning for Pollard Wynd and the brick bulk of Signora Bianchi's cottage came into sight. After

161

Pollard Wynd the road curved in a long bend.

Jack stopped the car and they both got out.

'There have been cars along here,' said Bill. 'I can see tyre tracks.' He looked back along the lane. 'I can't see the cottage from here.'

Jack looked up at the arching beeches. 'It'd be very gloomy at night under these trees. A car could be left here quite easily, out of sight of both the cottage and Pollard Wynd. What d'you think? The victim could've arrived by car. If it was parked along here, Miss Wingate wouldn't have seen it.'

'That's true,' agreed Bill as they got back into the Spyker. Jack reversed the car in the entrance to Pollard Wynd and headed back down Greymare Lane.

'The victim could have come to Whimbrell Heath by train and been picked up at the station,' said Bill. 'I suppose we can make enquiries. The porter or ticket collector might remember a stranger.'

Jack pulled a face. 'They *might*. The trouble is that this is Surrey, not the wilds of the countryside. I imagine the railway station is fairly busy, especially with the new building going on.'

'I wish we had a line on the victim,' said Bill once more. 'We know the victim's a woman, but that's about all we do know.'

Jack went to speak, then hesitated. 'Leave that to one side for a moment, eh?'

'Okay,' said Bill after a pause. 'I can see you've got an idea, but all in good time. Now, because the victim was a woman and because we know from Miss Wingate the woman was strangled, I'm going to presume the murderer was a man. Strangulation takes some strength.'

'Not if a scarf or something similar is used,' objected Jack, driving out of the shadows of Greymare Lane and back onto the main road. 'However, for the time being, I agree. We can take as read it was a planned crime because of the chloroform and what-have-you, but what we've found out today makes it seem even more planned.'

'Poisoning the watchman's dog?' asked Bill with a lift of his eyebrows.

'Exactly.'

'And that brings us to where the body was taken. The chantry.' Rather to Bill's surprise, Jack didn't reply. 'Do you think the body's hidden in there?' demanded Bill bluntly.

Jack made an impatient gesture. 'I don't know what else *to* think. Anyone in Lythewell and Askern can get hold of the key, but I'm blowed if I know where they hid the body once they got it in there. I had a fairly good look round.'

'Behind something? Underneath something? Inside something?' suggested Bill. 'That knocking Sam Catton heard at one in the morning means there was something going on in there. Whatever it is, we'll find it if it's there to be found. I just wish I could get some sort of angle on who the victim was.'

'Yes...' said Jack, again with the hesitation in his voice. 'Bill, I'm going to make an assumption. I'm going to assume the murderer is connected with Lythewell and Askern.'

'Fair enough,' said Bill in mild surprise. 'I

can't say that's too far-fetched, especially now we know about the chantry.'

'A murder,' said Jack, 'is one way to solve a problem. A person is inconvenient and therefore they are removed. Right?'

'All right,' agreed Bill. 'I don't know where you're going and it all sounds a bit cold blooded, but yes, you're right.'

'Now we thought, quite reasonably, that Signora Bianchi was the problem. And, indeed, she certainly was and is a problem, but not *the* problem.' He grinned. 'She proved that, very conclusively.'

'Don't remind me,' muttered Bill. 'I'll never forget her waltzing in like that. Never.'

'However,' said Jack, disregarding his friend's grumbles, 'I think we may have witnessed the birth of another problem for someone connected with Lythewell and Askern.'

Bill looked at him blankly.

'The exhibition?' prompted Jack. 'There was a woman there who behaved very oddly indeed, if you recall.'

'The flag-seller, you mean?'

Jack nodded. 'The flag-seller. What's more, because it was at the exhibition, all the Lythewell and Askern lot were present.'

Bill laughed. 'And because of that, you think our victim might be Mrs Whatever-she-was-called? The flag-seller?'

'Mrs Joan McAllister. Yes, I think she might be. I ran into her after the exhibition, if you remember, and I thought she definitely had something up her sleeve.'

164

Bill shrugged. 'Just as you like. At least we've got her name. She was taken to the Charing Cross hospital, wasn't she? I presume she gave her address to the hospital, so we can check up on her. But Jack, she struck me as more or less off her rocker. Didn't she tell you she fainted away because of the contrast between the idle rich – us, in other words – and the waifs and strays she was collecting for? It sounds downright cuckoo to me.'

'That is, or would be, as loopy as a corkscrew,' agreed Jack. 'But I didn't believe her. She certainly had a shock that day – that was real enough – but I didn't believe her account of what had shocked her. It'd be interesting to see if we can find her, don't you think?'

'If you want to go looking for nutty flag-sellers, be my guest,' said Bill tolerantly. 'I want a warrant for the chantry.'

Eight

'Mrs McAllister?' said Miss Sharpe. 'I don't know, I'm sure.' She was about as unlike her name as it was possible to be – a sagging, faded woman who looked, Jack thought, as if she could do with some fresh air and some good food.

She certainly wouldn't find any fresh air in 46, Purbeck Terrace. The house was redolent with the odour of stale cooked cabbage, which seemed to kick the idea of good food into touch, too.

It was the following morning. A telephone call from Scotland Yard to the Charing Cross hospital had established Mrs Joan McAllister's address as 46, Purbeck Terrace, Paddington, and Jack, with Bill Rackham's rather amused blessing, had taken himself off to investigate.

46, Purbeck Terrace was a boarding house. At one time it had evidently been a prosperous Victorian residence, but age, grime and changes in fashion had taken their toll. The down-at-heel nature of the house took him by surprise. Not that he'd thought Mrs McAllister was particularly affluent, but she was a flag-seller, after all, and collecting for charity was, in his experience, an occupation limited to the middle classes.

The landlady, Mrs Kiddle, after bearing up under her disappointment that Jack did not require a room, informed him that Mrs McAllister had left them. Was it a fortnight ago? No, wait, she told a lie. It was more like three weeks since. No, she didn't know Mrs McAllister's present address, but if he'd like to speak to Miss Sharpe – if Mrs McAllister had been friendly with anyone, it was Miss Sharpe – she might know where she'd got to.

Mrs Kiddle showed him into a room she referred to as the Residents' Lounge. It didn't invite lounging. It had a worn carpet on which the pattern was still just about discernable, and the sofa and armchairs had seen better days. Lots of better days. Three stuffed birds under a glass dome and a dusty aspidistra in a streakily polished brass pot on a stand added to the general funereal joy.

After a few minutes, a woman, patting an untidy bird's nest of grey hair into position, came in. To say she fitted her surroundings was unkind but true.

'Miss Sharpe?' asked Jack, standing up. 'I wondered if you'd be able to help me.'

'I don't know, I'm sure,' said Miss Sharpe, in a voice about as faded as the carpet, perching on the edge of one of the shabby chairs. 'Mrs Kiddle said you were looking for Mrs McAllister. She's your aunt, I believe.'

Jack had adopted this innocent deception to explain his interest in Mrs McAllister. 'Yes, that's right. My Aunt Joan. I haven't seen her for a long time.'

'Are you from America?' asked Miss Sharpe.

'I beg your pardon?' said Jack, pausing as he

sat down. This was unexpected, to say the least.

'I wondered if you were from America. I thought you might be.' She put her head to one side. 'You look foreign, and I know they've got a lot of foreigners in America. And gangsters and millionaires and so on,' she added, regarding Jack with vague hopefulness.

'No, I'm not from America,' said Jack, taken aback. 'Or a gangster or a millionaire, come to that. I'm not even foreign.'

'No?' said Miss Sharpe. Jack felt he had let Miss Sharpe down in some obscure way. 'Mrs McAllister had lived in America. I thought you might be American.'

So that's what Mrs McAllister's accent had been! Not pure American, but an English accent with American inflections.

'I suppose,' she said, looking at him dubiously, 'that you could call Americans foreigners, but they're not *foreign* foreigners, if you see what I mean? I know they express themselves oddly on occasion, but at least they do speak English.'

Having thus admitted kinship with one hundred and ten million people, Miss Sharpe moved on. 'I know Mrs McAllister's been back a few years now and I wondered if that's why you hadn't seen her for a while.'

Once again, Jack felt he'd let Miss Sharpe down. 'Because I've been in America, you mean? Sorry, that's not the reason.'

'She used to talk about America,' she said sadly, and heaved a wistful sigh. 'How good it was over there, how big the shops were and how there were lifts in all of them, so you didn't have to bother with stairs, which must be *such* a boon to those who are getting on in years. Even those of us who aren't exactly old find stairs such a sad trial. I sometimes,' she added with an air of resigned martyrdom, 'get positively breathless when faced with a flight of stairs, with such shooting pains in my legs, you wouldn't believe. Mrs McAllister was *most* sympathetic.'

'That was very nice of her,' said Jack.

'I feel it in my knees, most of all, but it goes all the way up to my hips,' she said with a sort of weary persistence. 'Mrs McAllister said that in America I wouldn't notice I had legs. Not notice! I'm always aware of my legs. And my knees. I used to talk to Mrs McAllister about my legs all the time.'

She looked at him hopefully, obviously willing to continue the discussion, but Jack had no intention of getting sidelined by Miss Sharpe's legs. Miss Sharpe, he felt, could quite happily allow her legs to dominate any conversation. Instead he hazarded a guess. He'd better show some sort of knowledge of Aunt Joan.

'She loved New York, didn't she?'

'Oh, *yes*,' said Miss Sharpe, thankfully dropping the legs *motif*. 'She talked a lot about New York. She lived in a lovely house, near a big park.' She frowned. 'Now, where was it?'

'Central Park?' asked Jack, guessing wildly.

Miss Sharpe's face cleared. 'That's it! I couldn't remember for the moment.'

Jack decided to try another guess. From his two meetings with Mrs McAllister, to say nothing of the shabbiness of Purbeck Terrace, it seemed unlikely she would own or rent 'a lovely house' near Central Park. There was, he thought, only one way she could live there. 'She enjoyed her time in service, didn't she?'

Miss Sharpe looked worried. 'In service?' She leaned forward confidentially. 'Well, yes, she did, but she didn't like people to know she'd been in service. *I* didn't mind, but there are some who would. People are so prejudiced, aren't they? She wouldn't have liked it to have got about. She never was in service here, you understand, only in America, and that's not the same, is it? It's different in America, I daresay. Of course, when she got married – her husband would be your Uncle Michael, wouldn't he? – she had to give it up. Not that she minded, as he did quite well for himself, didn't he?'

'So I believe.' Jack decided to draw another bow at a venture. 'Was he in grocery?'

From Miss Sharpe's expression it was clear that Uncle Michael wasn't a grocer.

'Or was that my Uncle Arnold?' he mused out loud. 'Or my Uncle Stephen?'

'He was a barber, I believe.'

Now that was something he wouldn't have guessed.

'Of course! Hair today, gone tomorrow, as you might say,' said Jack with a disarming smile.

Miss Sharpe tittered. 'That's exactly what your Aunt Joan used to say! She did use to make me laugh.' She looked upon him kindly. 'I can see you've got her sense of humour.'

Blimey, had he? Remembering Mrs McAllister, it wasn't the best compliment he'd ever received, but it was something. 'As a matter of fact, I never met Uncle Michael,' he said, truthfully enough.

'No? She was very happy with him. He restored her faith in men, she used to say, after having been so dreadfully let down.'

Jack looked a question.

'I don't know any *details*, of course,' said Miss Sharpe, lowering her voice, 'but your poor Aunt Joan had supped sorrow with a spoon, as she used to say. With a spoon,' she repeated impressively. She sighed deeply. 'Some men, Mr Haldean, see a woman's trusting heart as a mere plaything, but your Uncle Michael was her knight in shining armour and an excellent barber as well.'

'I'm very glad to hear it,' said Jack. There didn't seem to be much else he could say. 'I was hoping to mend a few bridges,' he added. 'We were never a close family. My father had a huge quarrel with Aunt Joan after my grandparents died, all about who should own a sideboard, I think. It seemed very trivial, I must say, but you know how families can be.'

'Oh, I *do* know,' said Miss Sharpe earnestly. 'Why, my own mother could never abide to hear her own sister, Doris, mentioned after she'd married. She gave herself airs, my mother said. Just fancy, Mr Haldean, I never knew Mrs McAllister had any living relatives at all. She certainly never mentioned you.'

This wasn't, perhaps, surprising.

'I'm sure she'd like to see you, though. These quarrels in families are so silly, aren't they?'

171

'They certainly are,' agreed Jack heartily. 'Tell me, Miss Sharpe, what happens if any letters arrive for my Aunt Joan? Is there an address to send them on to?'

Miss Sharpe shook her head. 'She hasn't had any letters. It's just as well, because she didn't leave a forwarding address. I wish she had, because I've got her collecting box upstairs and I'd like to give it back to her.'

'Her collecting box?'

'Yes, and her tray.'

Enlightenment dawned. 'Oh, for the Waifs and Strays Society, you mean?'

'That's right. I don't know what to do with it, I'm sure.' Miss Sharpe, it seemed, was only sure of negatives. 'I thought she'd come back for it, as she was a very dedicated worker for the cause.'

'That does her great credit,' said Jack, seeing some comment was called for.

'Oh yes, she was. She went out such a lot.' Miss Sharpe heaved a sigh. 'Tireless, she was. She left the box in her room, so I took care of it, but really, I'd like to see she has it safely.' She regarded him with perplexed anxiety. 'It's a worry to me, having to look after it. Mrs Kiddle didn't know what to do with it. Another lady – a Miss Richardson, a very nice lady indeed – has Mrs McAllister's room now and she didn't want it in the room as it takes up so much space, but we couldn't just throw it away or use the tray for kindling. No, indeed. I mean, it's *official*, isn't it?'

'Perhaps,' said Jack, a suspicion forming in his

172

mind, 'you'd let me have it, Miss Sharpe. I'll see she gets it back when I finally get in touch with her.'

'Would you? I'd be so grateful.' She stood up. 'I'll go and get it for you.'

A few minutes later he was in possession of a wooden tray containing a few flags and the tin collecting box that he'd last seen outside the art exhibition.

'I only wish I could wrap it up for you,' said Miss Sharpe. 'It seems such a bulky thing to carry around.'

'Don't worry,' said Jack cheerfully. 'I haven't got to carry it far.'

He carried the tray and the tin as far as Scotland Yard.

'Hello,' said Bill, as Jack came into his office. 'I'm still waiting to get the go ahead on that warrant for the chantry.' He looked at the tray suspiciously. 'Have you taken to good works? I hope you're not going to ask me to brass up.'

'Not money, old thing,' said Jack, pulling out a chair and sitting at the desk, 'but I'd like some information about this.' He tapped the tray. 'This is Mrs McAllister's and so's the tin.'

He told Bill about his encounter with Miss Sharpe. 'And, Bill, although I don't want to sound snobbish, I thought the general ambiance of 46, Purbeck Terrace, made it an unlikely place to find a flag-seller.'

Bill nodded. 'I know what you mean. Flag-sellers are usually fairly upper class, aren't they?'

173

'Middling to upper, yes. Which doesn't describe our Mrs McAllister. Add to which I thought she was a right old fraud when I met her outside Lowther's Arcade, and I wondered if there might be something not quite as mother makes about this particular tray and tin.'

'It *looks* authentic enough,' said Bill, pulling the tray towards him.

'I agree. So if the tray and tin are authentic but Mrs M. struck me as a phoney, that means what?' asked Jack, lighting a cigarette.

'That means...' Bill broke off and stared at his friend. 'Blimey, Jack, are you telling me you think it was pinched?' Jack nodded. 'Hell's bells! You made me cough up a fortune to that ruddy woman. I put two ten bob notes – two, mark you! – into that tin.'

Jack laughed. 'D'you know, I didn't think of that.'

'A pound,' muttered Bill. 'A whole quid, just thrown away on your say-so because you made me feel guilty.'

'Get over it,' said Jack easily. 'I put a shilling in.'

'Yes, and I put in a damn sight more. This needs checking right away.' He reached out his hand to the telephone. After a conversation with the operator, he was put through to the Waifs and Strays Society. Pencil in hand, he jotted down notes as he talked.

'Well,' said Bill, putting the phone down, 'I bet you're right. They've got no record of a Mrs Joan McAllister as a collector, but a tray and tin has been stolen. All the other trays are accounted for, by the way, so this has to be the stolen tray. One of their collectors, a Miss Marjoriebanks-Smythe, reported the theft last year.'

'How did it happen?'

'Miss Marjoriebanks-Smythe was caught short, poor woman, in King's Cross Station, and needed to use the facilities. Obviously, she couldn't take the tray into the cubicle with her, so asked the attendant to keep an eye on it for her. However, the attendant was distracted by a mother with two small children, and when Miss Marjoriebanks-Smythe came to collect her tray and tin, they were gone. There was a fair old crowd in and out of the lavatories, so the attendant couldn't say who was the likely thief. It was reported as stolen at the time, but that was that. Incidentally, the Society didn't have a flag day on the Saturday we got collared by the wretched woman – McAllister, I mean – so that proves it, not that we needed any proof.'

'So she was a fraud,' said Jack. 'I thought so.'

'I wish you'd thought so before I paid up,' grumbled Bill. 'There's one thing, though. Now I know she obtained money under false pretences, I can circulate a description of her. We could find her like that.'

'Not if Mrs McAllister was the body in Signora Bianchi's cottage.'

'No...' Bill drummed a tattoo with his pencil on the desk, then looked at his friend hesitantly. 'Doesn't it seem awfully far-fetched to you, Jack? I mean, it was only yesterday we thought the dead woman was Signora Bianchi, and we know how that turned out. I'm a bit leery about

175

giving a name to the victim until we know a damn sight more.'

'The only reason we thought the victim was Signora Bianchi was because the body was in her cottage,' said Jack impatiently.

'And because Miss Wingate told us so. She seemed very certain about it.'

'That's because, not unnaturally, she'd been expecting to see Signora Bianchi in her own house.'

'Yes, well, that's the point, isn't it? It's one thing having Signora Bianchi murdered in her own cottage...'

'Amidst all the comforts of home,' murmured Jack.

'...but it's quite another having a complete stranger bumped off there,' continued Bill, ignoring him. 'Why pick on the cottage? Doesn't it seem odd to you?'

Jack shook his head. 'Not really. It was common knowledge that Signora Bianchi was away. It's isolated yet accessible, and he – the murderer – should have been uninterrupted.'

'It's still a bit of a coincidence, don't you think? That it could be Mrs McAllister, I mean.'

'Is it?' Jack put his hands behind his head and leaned back in his chair. 'Look at what we've got. Mrs McAllister, who we now know to be a right old fraud, is collecting money...'

'Don't I know it?' muttered Bill.

'...who, by coincidence,' continued Jack, 'if you like, is drawn to a well-dressed and, as far as she was concerned, well-heeled crowd outside Gospel Commons. Now she might be a fraud but

176

she wasn't faking her faint. Something rattled her badly and I think it's someone she saw.'

Bill pulled a face. 'Perhaps.'

'I'll tell you something else, too, Doubting Thomas,' said Jack, leaning forward. 'When I ran into Mrs McAllister that day outside Lowther's Arcade, I congratulated her on her recovery and said something along the lines that I hoped she was taking things easy. She reacted as if I'd said something funny, and said she certainly intended to take things very easy indeed in the near future.' He looked at his friend expectantly. 'Put those things together and what have you got? I think she recognised someone at the exhibition.'

Bill wriggled impatiently. 'I know what you want me to say. You want me to slap my forehead and say *blackmail*!'

'Well? Why don't you say blackmail?' demanded Jack. 'You can slap your forehead into the bargain, if you like. I bring you a victim and a motive, all neatly packaged up, and all you do is sit there and look as if you're sucking lemons. What on earth's the matter with you?'

'The matter is that I've had to explain what happened yesterday to Sir Douglas and I'm not desperately keen to go bowling in and tell him that I'm fearfully sorry, sir, wrong victim an' all that, but here's another that'll do just as well. I agree there's a connection with Lythewell and Askern. The carry-on at one o'clock on Saturday morning in the chantry proves that, unless our poacher pal, Sam Whatisname, in the pub yesterday was having us on. I also agree that all the

Lythewell and Askern crowd were present when this wretched woman started frothing at the mouth and drumming her heels on the pavement.'

'When she fainted, at any rate. Don't get carried away.'

Bill held his hands up. 'Okay, when she fainted. But if I even whisper the suggestion to the Chief that the victim is this Mrs McAllister and *she* turns out to be alive and well, then my name will be mud and no mistake.'

'Sometimes,' said Jack, 'I feel downright unappreciated.' He took a cigarette from the box on Bill's desk and lit it. 'If you didn't like that suggestion, you're going to love my next one.'

'What's that?' asked Bill suspiciously.

'Well, it struck me that as Mrs McAllister lived in New York and Mr Daniel Lythewell lived in New York, Mr Daniel Lythewell might be the man we're looking for.' His smile widened at Bill's expression. 'I can see you're not struck by that idea.'

'Oh, my good God! *Jack!* Will you stop leaping to conclusions? Since when was living in New York a criminal offence?'

'It isn't, of course.'

'And how d'you know Lythewell lived in New York anyway?'

'It said so, in that printed history of the firm I picked up yesterday. He came back home in 1898.'

'1898?' Bill repeated in bewilderment. '1898? What the devil has anything that happened in 1898 got to do with what happened a fortnight ago? For Pete's sake, Jack, that's twenty-odd years ago. I'll tell you something else, too. If you think I'm going to mention that idea to Sir Douglas, you've got another think coming.'

Jack held his hands up. 'All right, all right, you've made your point. There's one thing you could do, though, without agitating the Chief. Miss Sharpe obviously thought Mrs McAllister was living on the money left to her by her husband, but, as we know, she was supplementing it by other means.'

'Thieving, not to wrap it up in fancy language.'

'As you say, thieving. Has she got a record?' He nodded at the tin. 'I know there'll be other prints on it, but, with any luck, Mrs McAllister might have left a fingerprint or two on it.'

'She might,' agreed Bill. 'That's something I can find out, at any rate. I can't see we'll get anything from the tray, as the wood's too rough, but the tin should be okay.'

He stood the tin on a piece of white paper and, taking an insufflator from the drawer, puffed a fine film of grey powder over the surface. A satisfying array of fingerprints was revealed. 'Are your prints on here, Jack?' he asked.

'No. I was careful to pick up the tin by the string.'

'All right, I'll get this down to Records,' he said, pushing his chair back. 'You never know your luck.'

He was back within ten minutes. 'They'll let me know as soon as possible,' he said. 'I presume you're not interested in nailing Mrs McAllister for petty fraud. What do you hope to show if it turns out she does have a record?'

'I'm not sure at the moment,' admitted Jack frankly. 'It's too much to hope she'll have left her fingerprints at Signora Bianchi's cottage, as we know it's been cleaned, but we might get an idea of her associates and so on. She moved out of Purbeck Terrace about three weeks ago, according to the landlady. Where did she go? And,' he added, 'what was she living on? I know you scouted my idea of blackmail, but you must admit the dates tie up. If she does have a record and she's seen any of her old associates, it could give us a way of tracking her down.'

Bill drew a couple of doodles on the corner of his blotting pad. 'Okay.' He clicked his tongue in irritation. 'I wish I could hurry up the warrant for the chantry.'

'Are you having trouble?'

'The Surrey force are being a bit sticky. I know it's our investigation, but we like to keep everyone as happy as we can. I gather that Commander Pattishall, the Chief Constable of the Surrey force, is reluctant to make any waves with a firm as well respected as Lythewell and Askern on the say-so of a self-confessed poacher, especially after yesterday's fiasco. With any luck we'll get there, but Sir Douglas is having to be diplomatic. That's another reason I don't want to start sounding off about your precious Mrs McAllister to him.'

He looked up as a knock sounded on the door. 'Come in!'

A sergeant poked his head into the room. 'I'm sorry to disturb you, sir, but there's a lady asking for you. A Miss Elizabeth Wingate.'

Bill sighed heavily. 'Very well. Ask her to come up, will you?' He turned to Jack. 'I wonder what she wants?' He broke off, looking at his friend suspiciously. 'What the devil's the matter with you? You look very pleased with yourself all of a sudden.'

'Nothing much,' said Jack, adjusting his tie and pulling his jacket straight. 'I just wondered if there'd been any further developments, that's all. And I was looking forward to seeing Miss Wingate again.'

Escorted by the sergeant, Betty came into the room. She looked both surprised and pleased to see Jack. 'I'm glad you're here, Mr Haldean,' she said, as he pulled out a chair for her.

'And we're glad too, aren't we, Bill?'

'It's nice that someone's pleased to see me,' she said with a weary smile. 'It's been pretty beastly at home. I slipped away without making any fuss. Everyone blames me for what's happened.'

'And what has happened?' asked Jack.

'The most appalling row. After you left yesterday, Mrs Askern worked out that if Mr Askern was still married to Signora Bianchi – and he is, because they were never divorced – then Mr Askern's been living with her under false pretences all these years, dragging, as she said, her good name through the mud. He told her not to be ridiculous and she...' She shrugged. 'Well, you can imagine.'

'I imagine she went pop,' said Jack.

'More or less. Anyway, it ended with Mrs Askern saying that she never *was* married to Mr Askern, she never *will* be married to Mr Askern and, as it's her money he's been living on all these years, she feels utterly betrayed and he could take himself off just as soon as he liked and never darken the door again. So, to cut a very long story short, Mr Askern's moved into his club. Uncle Daniel said, "What about the firm?" and Mr Askern said, "Damn the firm," and Colin told them both not to worry as Mr Askern could travel to work from London very easily, and as far as that was concerned, it shouldn't make any difference.'

'Gosh,' said Jack, blinking. 'That's a very practical way of looking at things.'

'Colin is practical,' said Betty. 'It's one of the things I like about him. Anyway, then Signora Bianchi put her oar in, and told Mrs Askern she ought to be grateful for any husband and that she had no chance whatsoever of getting another man at her age, so she'd be better off counting her blessings and forgiving and forgetting.'

'Gosh,' said Jack once more. 'I don't suppose Mrs Askern liked that idea, did she?'

'Mrs Askern,' said Betty, 'really let things rip. Apparently Mr Askern's taken some money from the bank recently and can't account for it, and Mrs Askern accused Signora Bianchi of having it. Signora Bianchi denied any such thing and so did Mr Askern, but she – Mrs Askern, I mean – refused to believe either of them. She called Signora Bianchi a few things I'd rather not repeat, but she was very angry.'

'Unexplained money, eh?' said Jack, looking at

Bill quickly. 'Have you any idea how much?'

'I don't know for certain. About a hundred pounds, I think.'

'Are you sure about that, Miss Wingate?' Bill asked sharply. 'That Signora Bianchi denied receiving any money, I mean?'

'She denied Mr Askern had given her that much but I don't know if I believed her. Apparently he'd paid the rent for the cottage. When Mrs Askern found that out, she was furious. She worked out that the big attraction about the cottage was that it was an easy walk across the fields to Heath House, and accused Signora Bianchi of having assignations with Mr Askern. Anyway, Colin pitched in and told Mrs Askern not to talk to his mother in that way, Signora Bianchi said lots in Italian, and then everyone turned on me for producing the cash box.'

Her lip wobbled and she lit a cigarette with shaky hands.

'You poor kid,' muttered Jack.

She gave him a grateful, if watery smile. 'Thanks.'

'Where's Mr Askern now?' asked Bill. 'At his club?'

'Yes. It's the Reynolds in St James. Uncle Daniel and Colin have both come up to see him today. I came on a different train and they don't know I'm here. Both Uncle Daniel and Colin more or less forbade me to come and see you. They think my latest idea's crazy, but I don't see why I should have to do exactly what they say.'

'No, no, of course not,' said Jack. 'Excuse me, what is your latest idea?'

'I mean, I know I'm living with Uncle Daniel and Aunt Maud,' she said, ignoring the question, 'but, after all, Uncle Daniel isn't my father or anything and, as for Colin, we're not engaged, and even if we were I'd still have come. Colin thinks the fact his mother's alive *proves* I was making it all up, but it doesn't prove anything of the sort, does it?'

Bill cleared his throat. 'Have you anything to tell us, Miss Wingate? Anything new, I mean?'

She nodded vigorously. 'Oh, yes. That's why I've come. Only...' She broke off and pulled nervously on her cigarette. 'I want the truth. I want everyone to know I was telling the truth about what I saw that night, and most of all I want everything back to how it was between Colin and myself. That'll only happen once we find out who was murdered in the cottage that night.'

'That's very true,' said Bill with commendable patience. 'And your idea is?'

'I thought of it this morning.' She swallowed. 'I'm not going to say I'm certain, because I'm not, and you'll probably think I'm as crazy as Uncle Daniel and Colin do, but when I woke up this morning, I'd been dreaming of that night in the cottage and ... and...' She braced herself and looked him straight in the eye. 'I wondered if the woman I'd seen could be the woman who fainted on the steps of the exhibition.'

184

Nine

There was a long pause, then Jack threw back his head and laughed.

Betty flushed angrily. 'If all you're going to do is laugh at me, I might as well have listened to Colin and not come.' She picked up her bag and made to stand up.

'No, please stay,' said Jack, gently pushing her back into her chair. 'You don't realise, but we've just been talking about that very possibility. The coincidence, if that's what you want to call it, struck me as funny, that's all.'

'*You've* been talking about it,' corrected Bill. 'Not me. Miss Wingate, whatever gave you the idea?'

'I've been thinking about it, obviously,' she said. 'If it wasn't Signora Bianchi who was murdered, then who was it? I wondered if it was someone who lived in Whimbrell Heath, but, if it was, they'd be missed and their absence talked about. I know I only saw her for a brief second, but there was something vaguely familiar about her. I couldn't swear to her face, but I think it was her posture, the way she was slumped on the sofa. That made me wonder if she was someone I'd met, and if so, where? It came to me this morning. It was the woman at the exhibition. I remembered how she looked, sprawled out on

185

the steps, and I couldn't help thinking it was the same woman.'

Bill leaned back in his chair. 'How do you account for her being in the cottage that night?'

She looked at him helplessly. 'I can't.'

'Fair enough,' said Bill, nodding. 'Well, Miss Wingate, thank you very much for coming to see us. I very much appreciate the effort you've made. I'll certainly think about what you've said.'

'So you don't think I'm crazy?'

'Certainly not,' said Jack. 'Do you have to rush back, Miss Wingate, or will you let me buy you lunch?'

She stopped, obviously surprised, then smiled at him. 'That's awfully nice of you, but I really should get back.' She hesitated. 'It really is nice of you, Mr Haldean. Perhaps another time?'

'I hope so,' said Jack. He got up and opened the door. 'I'll look forward to it.'

He waited until she was safely down the stairs and out of earshot before returning to the desk. 'Well? What d'you think?'

Bill looked at him with a knowing smile. 'I think you're in danger of falling for her, that's what I think.'

He had the pleasure of seeing Jack lost for words. 'How on earth d'you work that out?' said Jack eventually. 'I feel sorry for her. It sounds as if she's having a rotten time at home. She's a nice enough girl, I grant you, but that's all.'

'She's a nice enough girl who's just swanned in, Mr I-feel-sorry-for-her Chivalry, fingered Mrs McAllister as the victim *and* told us that

John Askern has taken unexplained amounts of money from his bank account and has now decamped to his club. But instead of wanting to race round to see John Askern, your first thought was to take her out to lunch. Apart from anything else, we're waiting for the results from Records. Where's your detective instinct?'

'Damn my detective instinct,' said Jack crossly. 'I can figure things out and still retain the rudiments of manners, I suppose?' He would have said more, but the telephone rang.

'Records,' Bill breathed to Jack as he picked it up. There was the crackle of a voice on the other end. 'Well,' he said, hanging up the phone. 'You were right about the McAllister woman having a record. She's never been convicted, but she's also known to us as Mrs Joan Morton, Mrs Joan Manning and Mrs Joan Middleton, all of whom are wanted in connection with thefts from the various households where she was employed either as a cook or a housekeeper. She first came to our attention fifteen years ago. The latest incident was eighteen months ago, when a Mrs Joan Middleton disappeared from a Dr and Mrs Pratchett's house in Canterbury, Kent, with about a hundred and fifty quid's worth of jewellery and forty pounds in cash.'

'Does she have any associates?'

'Apparently not, more's the pity. Anyway, I've got a few more names to fire at John Askern. If he's ever employed a cook or a housekeeper whose initials are J.M., I'll be interested, to say the least.' He got up and handed Jack his hat and stick. 'Come on, let's go.'

'Where to?'

'To see Askern, of course. We've every reason to believe the murderer is associated with Lythewell and Askern. You worked out the victim could be Joan McAllister. Miss Wingate thinks the same. You worked out that if the victim is Joan McAllister, then the motive is blackmail. Miss Wingate's just told us that John Askern, who couldn't be more associated with Lythewell and Askern, has unexplained amounts of money missing from his account. I can't help feeling the very least we should do is ask him about it, don't you? And by the time we've done that and had lunch, with any luck the warrant for the chantry should've arrived and we can really start getting somewhere.'

'Okey-doke,' agreed Jack mildly, taking his hat and his stick. 'I feel as if I'm in the presence of a suddenly awakened human dynamo. Lead on, old thing. I'm right behind you.'

Colin Askern was with his father in his room at the Reynolds, a brooding, unfriendly presence. However, if it hadn't been for Colin, Jack doubted they would have got any sense at all out of John Askern. He looked as if he'd aged years since yesterday and he moved like an old man. He didn't, Jack thought, really register who they were.

'Questions?' said Mr Askern vaguely. 'Yes, I suppose I can answer some questions.' He looked at them hopefully. 'Have you come from my wife? From Daphne?'

'No, Dad,' said Colin Askern firmly. 'This is

188

Chief Inspector Rackham and Mr Haldean.'

John Askern passed a hand over his face. 'I'd hoped Daphne would've sent a message. Daphne's always been so sensible. Such a nice, sensible woman. I don't know why she was so upset about Carlotta.'

'You can't blame her for being shirty, Dad,' said Colin, appeasingly.

Shirty, thought Jack, was a magnificent understatement.

'It must've been a nasty shock for her,' continued Colin, looking at Jack and Bill. 'My stepmother is a sensible woman, though. I'm hoping she'll forget about it and we can all let things settle down.'

Bill cleared his throat. 'Mr Askern, did you give Signora Bianchi any money?'

'Money?' Askern looked evasive. 'What money?'

'I believe an unexplained amount of money has gone from your bank account.'

'How d'you know that?' broke in Colin angrily. 'You can't go rummaging in my father's accounts. He hasn't committed any crime.'

'Bigamy's a crime,' Bill reminded him. 'Quite a serious one.'

'That was years ago! For heaven's sake, Rackham, you know the circumstances.'

'Nevertheless, I'd like to have this missing money explained. Mr Askern?'

John Askern passed a hand over his forehead. 'Money? Missing, you say? I ... I must've lost it.'

'How, sir?'

There was a pause. 'You gave it to me, didn't you, Dad?' stated Colin firmly. 'Don't you remember?'

'No, I...'

'You gave it to me, all the same,' repeated Colin. 'It was a hundred pounds, wasn't it?'

'Askern,' said Bill warningly, 'can I remind you this is police business?'

'What does it *matter*?' said Colin Askern impatiently. 'What does a few pounds here or there matter?'

Bill sighed and tried again. 'Mr Askern, can I ask you about Mrs Joan McAllister?'

If he was hoping for a reaction, he didn't get one. Bill repeated the question but Mr Askern remained blank.

'Who the devil's Mrs McAllister?' asked Colin. 'What's she got to do with anything?'

'We'd like to question her in connection with thefts from the houses where she's been employed. She's also known to us as Joan Morton, Joan Manning and Joan Middleton. I don't suppose you've ever employed a cook or a housekeeper called Joan whose surname began with an M, have you? She seems to stick to her initials.'

'No, I can't say that we have,' said Colin, seeing his father wasn't going to respond. 'We've never had any trouble with dishonest servants, either. My stepmother's always been pretty fortunate in that way. She's a generous woman and the servants have all been with us for ages.' He looked at Bill curiously. 'I must say I didn't expect to be questioned about cooks or housekeepers. It's funny, though. The name rings a faint bell.'

'Mrs Joan McAllister, to call her that,' said Bill, choosing his words carefully, 'is the woman who collapsed outside the art exhibition.'

Mr Askern was so sunk in apathy it was doubtful if he had heard, but Colin smacked his fist into his palm angrily.

'Betty's been to see you! Damn it, I told her not to! She's caused quite enough trouble as it is without coming up with another cock-and-bull story. There wasn't a body in my mother's cottage. There just can't have been. The whole thing's incredible and, as for it being that flagseller, the idea's utterly ridiculous.'

Bill ignored him, turned to Mr Askern and tried again. 'Mr Askern, do you know anything about a Mrs Joan McAllister? The woman who collapsed outside the exhibition?'

Mr Askern took a deep breath. 'No.'

'It has been,' said Bill, persevering, 'suggested she was blackmailing you.'

There was a disbelieving snort from Colin, but Bill waved him quiet.

'Blackmail?' John Askern's voice wavered. 'No. No, she couldn't have been. I – I don't know her.' His voice grew distant. 'Carlotta wanted money.'

He gazed unseeingly at his son. 'Carlotta loved you. You mustn't think she didn't care, but she found life very dull. She wanted money. I knew she wanted money and excitement. I couldn't give her either. That's why she went away with Bianchi. I thought ... I thought once I had some money, something to offer her, she'd come back,

191

but she'd gone too far by then.' He looked at them helplessly. 'I did it for Carlotta. Perhaps I shouldn't have done it. She never did know what I'd done. I tried to tell her but she never knew. Then there was nothing for it but to carry on. It didn't make any difference, not really. Carlotta didn't come back.' He buried his head in his hands. 'I shouldn't have done it.'

Jack and Bill glanced at each other, puzzled.

'Excuse me, Mr Askern,' said Jack gently. 'What shouldn't you have done?'

Colin moved uneasily. 'I don't think you should answer that, Dad.'

'So much money,' said Mr Askern. 'Gone.' He laughed. 'Where? Did he hide it? Did he ever have it?' He shook his head sadly. 'It drove him mad.' He lowered his voice. 'He thought they were after him, you know. That's why he hid it.'

'Who hid what, Mr Askern?' demanded Bill.

'Dad!' warned Colin. 'Be quiet.' He looked pleadingly at Jack and Bill. 'You can see he's not fit to answer any questions.'

'Do you know what he's talking about?' asked Bill quietly.

Tiny beads of sweat stood out on Colin Askern's forehead. 'No, I don't. I've never heard of any hidden money.'

Money? Hidden money? And Colin Askern was obviously not telling the truth....

With a flash of insight, Jack remembered what Henry Cadwallader had said to him in the chantry about old Mr Lythewell.

There's rumours that he buried a load of treasure before he died ... Young Mr Askern, he'd like to find it. He's been in here nosing round a few times lately.

'Mr Lythewell's treasure,' said Jack slowly. He looked at Colin Askern. 'That's what your father's talking about. This is all about the past, isn't it? Mr Lythewell's treasure.' Colin's reaction told him he'd guessed correctly. 'You searched in the chantry for it.'

'All right, what if I did?' said Colin. 'It's our chantry, after all. I didn't find anything,' he added grumpily. 'Nor has anyone else, and if you want to know where any money vanished to, all you have to do is look at that damned museum old Lythewell built. That bloody chantry must've cost a fortune.'

'Does your father know anything about old Mr Lythewell's missing treasure?' It seemed easier to ask Colin than the silent, distressed man beside him.

Colin sighed impatiently. 'No, he doesn't. I've asked him. There's rumours about hidden treasure but it's all nonsense. It's those stupid mottoes or whatever they are, engraved into the flagstones. They talk about treasure, but it's not *real* treasure, the proper sort that you can spend. Old Lythewell was a religious maniac. He was talking about eternal life and his immortal soul, not pounds, shillings and pence.'

'Treasure in heaven, you mean?' said Jack.

Mr Askern suddenly gave a high-pitched laugh that was horribly unsettling to hear. *'Treasure!'* he exclaimed, and laughed once more.

'For Pete's sake,' muttered Colin.

Bill shifted in his chair. 'I hardly like to con-

193

tinue, Jack,' he muttered. 'Not with Mr Askern in this state.'

'I think,' said Colin, 'that you'd better leave.'

'That was unpleasant,' said Bill with feeling, as they walked down the stairs to the lobby of the Reynolds. 'It strikes me that poor old Mr Askern is a fair way to losing his marbles.'

Jack nodded. 'I can't help thinking Colin Askern feels the same.'

'Colin Askern,' said Bill tartly, 'is becoming a real pain in the neck. I hope Mrs Askern is as sensible as they say. The sooner that Italian baggage takes herself off, the better for everyone. I don't think Mr Askern does know anything about Mrs McAllister, though, do you?'

'Not under that name, certainly,' said Jack absently. He suddenly stopped and clicked his fingers together. 'Got it!' He turned to Bill, his face alight. 'I think I've pinned down that memory!'

He stepped to the kerb and, raising his stick, hailed an approaching taxi. 'Fleet Street,' he said to the driver as they got into the cab. '*On The Town* magazine.'

'What memory?' demanded Bill as Jack hustled him into the taxi. 'What's all this about?'

'It's the reason why the name Lythewell seemed familiar. It was a phrase Colin Askern used. He called the chantry a damned museum. You know I write an occasional series for *On The Town* about historic crimes? Well, years ago there was something called the Great Museum Scandal, or something like that, and I'm sure there was a Lythewell connected with it.'

'Daniel Lythewell?' asked Bill hopefully.

'I don't know. It's ages since I wrote the article but they'll have it on file in the office.'

A quarter of an hour later, they were in the dusty light of a small, book-lined room over-looking Fleet Street. 'I think it should be in the winter issues of about three years ago,' said Jack, pulling a bound volume off the shelf. 'Check 1922, will you, Bill? I'll take 1923.'

'Right you are,' said Bill. He blinked as the leather-bound volume, which looked as if it should contain a Bible or, at the very least, law reports, opened on the prismatic colours of the cover of *On The Town*. 'I'm looking for a historic crime to do with a museum, right?'

Silence followed, broken only by the rustle of pages.

Jack grunted in disappointment and pulled another volume off the shelf. 'It must be earlier than I thought...'

More silence.

Bill took a volume for 1921 from the shelf and, flicking through the magazines it held, read through the contents patiently. 'Is this it, Jack?' he asked, slewing the book round. '"The Great Museum Scandal that cost a man's life! Number five in our series of enthralling real-life mysteries from the past. By Jack Haldean."'

'That's the one,' said Jack in satisfaction. He walked round the desk to Bill. 'Of course! It's a Victorian crime so it's in the Christmas number. I don't know why Victorians, crime and Christmas go together, but they do. I'll read it out.

'"On the ninth of November, 1868, Dr Jacob Anstruther, B.A., M.A., D.Phil (Cantab.), the highly respected curator of the Jannard Street Museum of Oriental and Eastern Antiquities, announced to his astonished audience consisting of distinguished and learned academics, interested onlookers and gentlemen of the Press, that the technique of electroplating, far from having been invented by the Italian chemist Luigi Brugnatelli in 1805, had, in fact, been in use thousands of years earlier by the Qui Dynasty of Ancient China." Gosh.'

'When does Lythewell come into the story?'

'Later. Perpend, will you, and don't be so impatient. "Electroplating, as our more scientifically-minded readers will know, is a method of coating one metal with a thin layer of another metal by the application of electricity."'

'Does it have to be metal, Jack?' asked Bill. 'I'm not particularly scientifically minded, so I may be wrong, but I thought you could electroplate just about anything. There's a shoe shop on Oxford Street which has got a pair of metal shoes in the window as an advertising gimmick.'

'I know the shop you mean,' said Jack. 'They're advertising Nevascuff shoes, aren't they? "Nevascuff! Really Tuff! As strong as steel with all the comfort of leather." I think you have to brush the leather shoes or what-have-you with a sort of metal paint first, but yes, you're right. Anyway, back to poor old Dr Anstruther and his amazing discovery. "Dr Anstruther showed his astonished audience a golden statue,"' he continued, '"dating from the reign of King Zhao..."'

He broke off. 'Blimey, did I really write this? I can't even pronounce it.' He blinked and tried again. '"Of King Zhaoxiang" – I think that's how you say it – "who reigned from 306 to 255 B.C., celebrating the battle of somewhere called Yique. The statue, he explained, was actually base metal with a fine layer of gold electroplated on to its surface. This, explained Dr Anstruther, was, perhaps, the major discovery of his life. To use electroplating, the Ancient Chinese must have had electricity in the form of Voltaic Piles" – they sound painful – "and, granted the exquisite workmanship of the statue displayed, were highly skilled in its use."'

Jack quickly ran his finger down the rest of the magazine page. 'It's all coming back to me now. The gist of it, not to bore you stupid and to get to the bit with Lythewell in it, was that Dr Anstruther, very unwisely, had crowed too soon. Other museum curators started to examine the valuables in their possession. The more worldly-wise amongst them were worried stiff. It's one thing to have priceless gold and silver articles, it's quite another to find they're made by the same process as cheap jewellery.'

'I imagine it is,' said Bill with a grin.

'Anyway, to cut my fairly long story short – I got paid by the word in those days – it turned out that, far from being the invention of the Ancient Chinese, electroplating seemed to have been invented independently by the Ancient Persians, the Ancient Greeks, the Mughal Empire and the Ancient Assyrians, to say nothing of the Ancient Egyptians.'

'That seems remarkable,' said Bill, his grin widening. 'I suppose all the dodgy items were knocked off in a workshop in Birmingham and flogged to the museums in question?'

'Actually, no,' said Jack. 'That was the puzzling thing. A great many of the items had been in the possession of some of the museums for years. Nearly all of the artefacts had impeccable credentials and, in the case of some of the more recent acquisitions, the curators had been on the archaeological digs when the articles had been uncovered. That was particularly worrying. Archaeological digs, for the most part, aren't desperately keen on precious metals, as the dig organiser has to pay the workmen the value of the piece in hard cash to prevent the article being stolen and melted down. It ups the cost of the dig tremendously, as you can imagine.'

'But there is some jiggery-pokery going on, isn't there?' asked Bill. 'I mean, all this about Ancient Whoevers discovering electroplating all at the same time is nonsense. It just has to be.'

'Exactly. It turned out that Scotland Yard, when it was reported to them, thought the same. What had happened was that a forgery gang had broken into the various museums, taken wax copies of the articles – as they were precious they were all fairly small – made forgeries and then substituted the forged item for the real thing. The real things were sold to collectors, and, in some cases, to other museums. By and large, the purchases were shown to have been made in good faith, but it's simply not known how many forgeries were made. The beauty of these particular thefts, you see, was that nobody knew a theft had taken place.'

Bill whistled. 'I see. And I don't suppose that any museum curator is desperate to tell the public that the pride of his collection is actually a fake.'

'No. There was a great deal of highly embarrassed covering-up and, in many cases, a flat refusal to investigate.'

'They must have been damn good forgeries. Did Scotland Yard get to the bottom of who'd done it?'

Jack nodded. 'Yes, they did, and that's where, as far as we're concerned, it gets interesting. Frederick Bannister, a highly skilled thief, and Cornelius Croft, an expert model-maker, both of whom had previous convictions, were caught, tried and sentenced to twenty years' hard labour. Poor old Dr Jacob Anstruther, who had been absolutely convinced that he was on to the discovery of a lifetime, shot himself, but the man popularly supposed to be the brains behind the scheme, the electroplater himself, was never convicted. However, suspicion fell on someone whose name we know, a highly respected church artist.'

'Lythewell,' said Bill softly.

'He's the man. Josiah Lythewell, Daniel Lythewell's father. There's no mention of this, by the way, in that printed history I picked up.'

'No, I don't suppose there is. It's not something to boast about.'

'No, I'd say not. The firm was simply Lythewells, then, of course, not Lythewell and Askern, as it later became. Lythewell did stand trial, but he was defended by Sir Havelock Collison Soames, a noted orator. There was a lot of attention given to the fact that Lythewell was a skilled electroplater, but, as Sir Havelock said, expertise in one's chosen profession is not usually taken as a sign of guilt. In his address to the jury, he roared – he was a great roarer – "Does this mean, gentlemen, that a great surgeon is to be suspected of murder because he knows how to use a scalpel? Or a butcher, a tailor or a cabinet-maker because they, too, are skilled in the use of sharp implements? Nonsense, I say! Let a man have the tools of his trade without let, hindrance or fear!" Anyway, the jury, who, co-incidentally I'm sure, had amongst its members a butcher, a tailor and a cabinet-maker, loved it, and Lythewell got off.'

'Was he guilty, Jack?'

Jack shrugged. 'It's hard to tell. The police never suspected anyone else of being involved, that's for sure. It's interesting, though, isn't it? If Lythewell really was the brains behind the scheme, he was certainly in a position to have lots and lots of lovely loot. Or, to put it another way, treasure.'

'Yes,' said Bill, 'he was. What about his con-federates? The model-maker and the thief? If they kept quiet, they'd want their share once they got out.'

'They both died inside. That, by the way, wasn't unexpected, as they were both men in their fifties, but it could account for Lythewell hiding his treasure.' He looked at the magazine article again. 'Here we are. Their trial was in 1869, so they'd be due for release in 1889, by which time Lythewell had built the chantry and, presumably, stowed away the swag.' He looked at Bill with bright eyes. 'Interesting, eh?'

'Very,' said Bill. 'If I mention this to the Chief, I think any difficulties about the warrant should fade away pretty fast. A breath of an old scandal should do the trick nicely. Thanks, Jack. Let's get back to the Yard.'

'I understand,' said Daniel Lythewell, leading the way up the path to the chantry, the key in his hand, 'that you've got hold of the old story about my unfortunate father.'

Bill, warrant safely in his possession, had arrived at the chantry together with a detective sergeant and two constables. Jack had driven down and met Bill and his men at the station and they had arrived together at Lythewell and Askern.

'Commander Pattishall,' continued Mr Lythewell, 'mentioned as much to me on the telephone.'

'It's a matter of public record, sir,' said Bill smoothly.

'Yes,' agreed Lythewell unenthusiastically. 'As long as you remember that it's also a matter of public record that my father was discharged without a stain upon his character.'

'It must have been hard for him, to have been caught up in an affair like that, sir,' said Jack.

'Oh, I believe it was, Major Haldean,' said Daniel Lythewell, unbending slightly at this show of sympathy. 'I was only a child at the time, but, as I understand it, my mother took it very hard. Indeed, she found life here completely impossible after the trial. My grandparents had established themselves in New York some years previously and my mother decided to go and live with them, until the fuss had died down. She took me with her, of course.'

'Did she ever return home?'

Daniel Lythewell shook his head. 'No, she didn't. She was never very strong-minded, and the anxiety affected her greatly. I have very few memories of my mother, but, as I understand it, it became obvious that she, poor woman, was completely incapable of making any rational decisions either for herself or her family.' He cleared his throat in a meaningful way. 'It was thought better that she should live away from the world. It was many years, of course, before I understood the truth of the matter and, by that time, she had been dead for some time.'

He heaved a sigh. 'A thoughtless accusation, Major, can have many unpleasant and unlooked for consequences. Take this story of my niece's, for example. I have no doubt that, but for her interference, this whole unhappy business between Askern and his wife could've been discreetly cleared up without any real harm having been done. As it is...' He sighed once more and shrugged his shoulders expressively. 'Suffice it to say that young Askern is very concerned about his father, as, indeed, speaking as John Askern's old friend and business partner, so am I.'

He unlocked the chantry door and stood back.

'Well, there you are, gentlemen. I must say I'm at a loss to even guess what you hope to find?'

There was a question there which Bill decided to ignore. 'There probably is nothing to find, sir,' he said cheerfully, 'but if your property has been used for anything untoward, I'm sure you want us to get to the bottom of the matter.'

'Very well,' agreed Lythewell reluctantly. 'Please be careful with the fabric of the building and its contents. It might not be to everyone's taste, but, as you say, it is my property and I would be very unhappy if it was damaged in any way.'

'There's no danger of that, sir,' said Bill evenly. 'We'll be very careful.'

With a final disapproving look, Lythewell left them. Bill relaxed as they heard his departing footsteps down the path.

'Now we can get on with things.' He rubbed his hands together, looked round the chantry and shook his head. 'What a mausoleum!' He stared at the painting of Josiah Lythewell being received into heaven and shuddered. 'I see what you mean about old Lythewell, Jack. He must've been as mad as a hatter.' He raised his voice. 'As I said, men, there was a report of a light and the sound of knocking was heard from here at about half-one last Saturday night.'

'Knocking, is it?' repeated Constable Morgan in his Welsh lilt, looking round the chantry. 'I'm not surprised. Is this place meant to be haunted?'

'Don't run away with any fanciful ideas, Morgan. We're looking for evidence of a crime, not a ghost.'

203

The other men laughed.

'It wouldn't be the first time that someone's allowed the idea of ghosts to cover up some very real wrongdoings,' said Jack. Constable Morgan looked pleased at his support. 'We think there's a body in here. Let's see if we can find it.'

After a very dusty hour or so, Bill was ready to throw in the towel. They had covered the entire chantry to shoulder height, exploring, measuring, testing every place, probable or improbable, that could conceal a body.

The empty tomb merited special attention. Jack's half-formed idea that the stone sarcophagus could be moved or perhaps rotated, revealing a cavity beneath, was tested, but the open tomb, with the metal statue of the grieving man, remained obstinately in place.

Armed, as the police were, with powerful torches, it was easy, if depressing, to see that the fine film of dust that covered most of the surfaces and floor hadn't been disturbed for some time.

Bill straightened his aching back and slumped onto an elaborately carved pew. 'I'm just about ready to call it a day,' he announced.

Jack looked up from where he was copying the last of the inscriptions on the flagstones into his notebook.

'It's depressing, isn't it?' he remarked, joining Bill on the pew. 'At first sight, this place looks as if it should be bulging with secret passages and hidden chambers, but if they're secret, they're very secret indeed.'

'And yet I'd swear that chap, Sam Catton,

wasn't making things up.' Bill broodingly took his cigarette case from his pocket, then, with a glance at his surroundings, thrust it back. 'I don't suppose we'd better smoke in here. It's too much like a church for comfort. Dammit, Catton heard knocking! That surely means something was moved, but what, for heaven's sake? There's nothing to move.'

'Unfortunately, I agree. I did wonder if the inscriptions on the flagstones might contain directions to a hidden chamber, but if they do, I can't see it.' Jack passed his notebook to Bill. 'See what you make of it.'

'"The church is your true and worthy treasure",' read Bill. 'It seems like pious advice, to me. "Stop, my son, to pause and pray for treasure. A far lesser treasure also behold."' He frowned. 'He's got treasure on the brain, if you ask me, not secret passages. "Worldly goods will always fade and wither." That's the sort of sentiment you'd expect to read in a church, I suppose. "Art which is wrested from that evil root". Is that the root-of-all-evil root?'

'I thought so,' agreed Jack. 'That's an interesting line, isn't it? If he was the crook behind the museum forgeries and used the money to build this place, it'd fit, certainly.'

'It would, but I can't see it helps us. "That doorway, greater than man can measure." He can't mean a real doorway, can he?'

'I don't think so. Not if it's really greater than man can measure. Look, the next inscription is: "The doorway's here to eternal life".'

Bill sighed. 'A fat lot of good that is, then.' He

gestured to the painting of Josiah Lythewell before the gates of heaven. 'That's probably the door he's got in mind. What's the next inscription? "Open – look! – to all curious eyes." I say! I don't suppose that's the secret hiding place we've been looking for, is it?'

'The flagstone seemed solid, but come and see for yourself.' Jack took him to the flagstone set off to one side. 'It had the same amount of dust on it as everything else. If it does move, I can't shift it.'

Bill carefully examined the joints around the stone, then trod heavily on each corner. Nothing happened. 'I bet he's talking about the doorway to eternal life again,' he said regretfully. 'That's meant to be open to everyone, isn't it?'

'That's sound theology, but if he really is talking about the doorway to eternal life, I'm surprised he says it's "Open to all curious eyes". I'd have expected him to say pious or reverent, not curious, but you're probably right.'

'Blimey, Jack, I'll be amazed if these mottoes mean anything at all. I think he was nuts. After all,' he added, lowering his voice, 'that's more or less what Mr Askern said, isn't it? What's the next inscription?'

'It's by the tomb. "It is yours, O my son, but for your soul".'

'But for your soul *what*?' Bill asked blankly.

'I dunno,' said Jack. 'But for your soul's sake be careful, perhaps? It sounds as if the son – Daniel Lythewell, I presume – might have to trade in his soul in some kind of bargain.' Bill looked puzzled. 'Like Faust,' Jack added helpfully. 'A bargain with the Devil, that sort of thing.'

Bill shook his head. 'Perhaps.' He read the next inscription in Jack's notebook. '"Be wise. Shun greed, let avarice be mute". That sounds like all-round good advice. What's next? "But true metal wrought, cast, forged, small in size".'

'That's over by the tomb, as well.' Jack grinned. 'It's interesting that true metal is wrought, cast or forged, not electroplated. I imagine electroplating could've been a sensitive subject.'

'I'd say so.' Bill read the next entry and tapped his finger on the book. 'Look, all these things he writes about doors that open, they do mean eternal life. "Is opened for you after earthly strife." That's life after death, isn't it? He's got an odd way of expressing himself though, hasn't he? What's next? "Not copper, silver, precious stones or gold." I think we're back to treasure again.'

'Or the absence of treasure, perhaps, if it's not copper, silver, precious stones or gold. There's not much left, unless it's banknotes, I suppose.'

'I don't think you're taking this as seriously as you might be,' said Bill. 'Of course it's not banknotes, you idiot. It's eternal life again, isn't it? Here's a religious sentiment for you: "In penitence here's shown the greater whole."'

'Yes, but what does it mean, Bill?'

'Absolutely nothing, in my considered opinion,' said Bill, closing the notebook with a snap and giving it back. He looked up, startled, as the door to the chantry swung back and a figure, arm outstretched and finger pointing dramatically, was outlined in the sunshine from the doorway.

'Stop!' boomed a voice. 'In the name of God, stop!'

'Oh, by crikey,' muttered Bill. 'Here's another one who's very odd indeed.'

'Henry Cadwallader,' said Jack with a sinking feeling.

And it was.

Ten

Henry Cadwallader strode up the chantry towards them, coat flying behind him. 'Desecration!' he shouted. 'Wanton desecration! Sacrilege!'

Bill stepped up to him. 'Mr Cadwallader, calm down!'

Henry Cadwallader's eyes were wild. 'Calm down! Calm down when Mr Lythewell's life work – Mr *Lythewell*'s work! – is being torn apart!'

'That's nonsense, sir,' said Bill firmly. 'See for yourself.'

'We haven't torn anything apart, Mr Cadwallader,' said Jack. 'Honestly. We've treated everything with the utmost respect.' Cadwallader, chest heaving, cast darting glances round the chantry. 'You can see for yourself,' continued Jack. 'Nothing's been harmed in any way.'

Henry Cadwallader put a trembling hand to his face. 'No. No, I can see that.' He dropped his hand and glared at Jack. 'When I heard what was happening, I was sure of the worst.' He blinked at him. Jack could see recognition dawning. 'It's you! I didn't know it was you. They told me the police were in here.'

'As you can see, Mr Cadwallader, the police are here,' said Jack. 'Leave this to me, Bill,' he murmured. Putting a hand on Cadwallader's trembling arm, he led the old man to one of the pews. 'We're having a look to see if anyone's been in here, using the chantry for some purpose they shouldn't.'

Cadwallader drew back in fastidious disgust. 'Are you talking about a common assignation? No one would dare.'

'Of course they wouldn't.' Jack couldn't agree more fervently. The chantry was the last place he'd expect to find anyone engaged in a romantic encounter. It was far too forbidding. 'No, but we believe someone was here the Saturday before last.'

'They mustn't!' Henry Cadwallader jumped to his feet. 'They might damage the chantry!'

'Exactly,' said Jack soothingly, taking his arm and drawing him back to his seat. 'Look, Mr Cadwallader, you probably know this place better than any man on earth. Have you noticed anything out of place or any recent damage?'

Henry Cadwallader reluctantly shook his head. 'No.' He took a deep breath. 'You're right, young sir. I'd know if there was any damage.' The lines on his face softened. 'I love this building. I know every inch of it, every stone that Mr Lythewell placed here.'

He swallowed noisily and, taking a large, paint-stained cotton handkerchief from his pocket, wiped his eyes. 'It's all I've got left of him. No one looked up to Mr Lythewell as I did.' He pointed to the painting of Josiah Lythewell and St Peter. 'I painted that. Mr Lythewell let me paint him from life. I've still got all my sketches.

They're my greatest treasures.'

'Why did Mr Lythewell mean so much to you?' asked Jack. 'He obviously did.'

Mr Cadwallader blew his nose. 'You'd never understand,' he said distantly. 'You're an educated man. I was never educated, not at any fancy school. Art, yes, but not what you'd call an education. Things were different then. Lads now, they get free schooling and everything done for them. It wasn't like that then. When I first met Mr Lythewell I could just about read and write. I was sharp-like, but not educated, but Mr Lythewell, he took me in. I was only a youngster and he took me in.'

'I might understand,' said Jack. 'I know you were very poor.'

Cadwallader's eyes were distant. 'I was alone in the world. I lived on what I could pick up, sweeping the street and running errands and the like. Then – pray you'll never be tempted – I fell into bad ways with bad company.' He shook his head and lowered his voice. 'I've testified to this at chapel, many a time. If you can believe it, I was a pickpocket, far gone in sin.'

Jack wondered if he should comment, but Henry Cadwallader didn't seem to need any encouragement. His voice took on a well-worn quality. It was obvious he'd told this story many times.

'One day – and my hand must've been guided that day – I stole a bag from none other than Mr Lythewell. But see how good can come from evil! A passer-by gave the hue and cry. I emptied the bag and threw it away but I was pursued.

211

Pursued and cornered! Then Mr Lythewell arrived. "Do you give this lad in charge?" said the policeman, but Mr Lythewell, instead of having me thrown into prison, where I would have received my just deserts, refused. "No," he said. "I have my bag back. No harm has been done." He knew the bag was empty and the stolen goods were in my pocket and so did the policeman. They argued, but Mr Lythewell wouldn't be budged. Mr Lythewell took me under his wing, and, when he realised I had the talent, had me trained in art.' He paused in reverent silence. 'He was a truly great man.'

'He must've been,' agreed Jack. 'That's an inspiring story.' And it should've been an inspiring story, but he was curious. Why hadn't Lythewell wanted to press charges? It could have been simple altruism, but... 'What was in the bag? The one you took from Mr Lythewell?'

This was clearly an unexpected question. Henry Cadwallader blinked and seemed to realise that he was speaking to Jack and not addressing a congregation. 'What does it matter what was in the bag?' He ran a distracted hand across his forehead. 'I can hardly remember. It was a small metal statue of some sort, a heathen thing. It had no value. It was only lead or some such, but Mr Lythewell, with his goodness, he turned it into gold.'

Yes, thought Jack. That's precisely what did happen to the statue, at a guess. And if Lythewell had pressed charges, he'd have been asked to account for the fact the lead statue was in his bag and his part in the Great Museum Scandal would've been exposed. The game would've been up. No wonder Josiah Lythewell took such pains to get the young urchin on his side.

'I'm not surprised you venerate his memory, Mr Cadwallader. You know the chantry – Mr Lythewell's life's work – inside out. Is there a secret chamber or hidden room somewhere? Perhaps even a hidden cupboard or hiding place? We wondered, you see, if someone was trying to hide something in here and perhaps the sound of knocking was the sound of a door being forced.'

Henry Cadwallader looked at Jack with sudden sly craftiness. 'You're looking for Mr Lythewell's treasure, aren't you?'

'No, we're not. However, if we do find it, we'll restore it to its rightful owner, Mr Lythewell's son, Mr Daniel Lythewell.' Jack didn't miss the expression of mulish obstinacy. 'Mr Lythewell wanted his son to benefit. I've just read all the inscriptions he had engraved into the flagstones. "Stop, my son, to pause and pray for treasure",' he prompted. 'That's inlaid in stone in letters of silver.'

Cadwallader ran a hand over his whiskery chin. 'I suppose so,' he grudgingly agreed. 'Not that Mr Daniel has ever shown the proper veneration for his father's memory.'

'Oh, I don't know,' said Jack, trying a little provocation. 'After all,' he said, gesturing to the empty tomb, 'he had that statue of the mourner made, didn't he?'

'It's not up to Mr Lythewell's standards,' said Cadwallader. 'It's a great shame Mr Lythewell didn't make it. Now that would've been worth

213

looking at. He was a wonder when it came to electroplating.'

I bet he was, thought Jack.

'I've never seen his like,' continued Cadwallader. 'Mr Daniel, he tried his hand, but couldn't produce real quality.'

'But it did show proper feeling, didn't it, though?'

Cadwallader reluctantly nodded. 'If you say so. There were changes, though,' he added darkly. 'Right from the beginning there were changes. Mr Daniel, he shut down the metal workshop and sold everything off. Then there's all this rubbish about a new sort of art. What do we want a new sort of art for? The old sort was good enough.'

Jack had no intention of being sidelined into a discussion of art. 'So do you know of any hiding place?'

'I might,' said Cadwallader unexpectedly. 'That is, I know there is one.'

Jack tried to keep the excitement out of his voice. 'Really?'

'I don't know where it is, though.'

Jack's spirits drooped. 'Are you sure?'

'Certain. Mr Lythewell, he was worried. You're quite right, young sir. He wanted to hide his treasure away from thieves and the ungodly. He told me that his true treasure was in the church.'

'Oh.' That didn't sound very promising, and yet Lythewell had been the brains of the Museum Scandal gang. He'd had money, all right. 'Did he mean actual wealth? Money, I

214

mean?'

Cadwallader nodded matter of factly. 'Yes, he did, but he took his secret to the grave with him. Where it is, is something not I, or any other man, will ever discover.'

Which was wretchedly inconvenient of him, thought Jack. No wonder John Askern thought old Lythewell had gone off his head. 'Thank you, Mr Cadwallader,' he said, getting to his feet. He took his card case from his pocket and gave Cadwallader one of his visiting cards. 'That's my address. If you do remember anything about this hiding place, or come to know where the hiding place is or might be, please let me know. I'll see Mr Lythewell's memory is respected.'

Cadwallader examined the card carefully before putting it away. 'Respect,' he echoed. 'That's what's needed. Respect.' He raised his head and gazed round the chantry. 'I'll do a painting,' he said softly. 'Not just a great painting, but a painting on a great scale. I'll paint the chantry. People talk about Panini's *Interior of St Peter's*, but that will be nothing to what I'll paint.' His eyes gleamed with enthusiasm. 'It'll be shown at the Royal Academy and, when it is, people will flock here. Then everyone will know about Mr Lythewell and his genius. I'll show them! I'll show them the man he was. Respect!'

He turned to Jack and gripped his hand. 'Thank you, young sir! You've given me the spark of inspiration I needed. I'll start work right away on the preliminary sketches. This painting will be a fitting tribute, the culmination of a life's work.' He rifled through his satchel. 'Where's my sketch pad? I must get my sketch pad. Work! I have to work! Work!'

He hurried off, leaving a slightly bemused Jack staring after him.

'What on earth did you say to him?' asked Bill, coming over to the pew. 'I thought he was either going to attack us, burst into tears or have a nervous breakdown, then he jumped up like a jack-rabbit and scarpered off yelling, *Work*!'

'He's decided he's going to do a monster painting of the chantry, exhibit it at the Royal Academy and, after everyone's fainted in awe at the sight, they'll run excursion trains and charabancs to Whimbrell Heath to see the chantry in real life.'

'I beg your pardon? I heard what you said but I don't think I understood it.'

Jack gave him the gist of his conversation with Cadwallader.

'So Lythewell really was a forger, eh? And Cadwallader reckons there's a real treasure hidden in the church but hasn't a clue what or where it is?' Bill sighed. 'I can't see that gets us much further forward.' He looked round in mounting irritation. 'I'm going to call it a day. Treasure, to my mind, especially when you think of the sort of treasure Lythewell could've had, means something small and precious, like a diamond, say. That could be hidden in a very small space, but to hide a body takes a fair old bit of room. It could be here, but if it is, I don't know where to look. Come on. Let's return the key to Mr Lythewell and get back to town.'

* * *

For the next fortnight, nothing much happened.

A note was added to the record of the long-closed Great Museum Scandal case, and Mrs Joan McAllister's details, plus a list of aliases, were published in the *Police Gazette* as wanted for obtaining money under false pretences.

There was a brief stir of excitement when a Mr Andrew Alistair McKenzie, a senior clerk employed by the London, Midland and Scottish Railway in the left luggage department of Euston Station, followed his nose and his instinct for something out of place, and opened a trunk which had been despatched from Manchester London Road to be left until called for. The unappealing contents turned out to be an unclothed woman in an advanced state of decay.

Is this, Jack asked Bill hopefully, *our* body? No, it isn't, Bill replied, quashing Jack's hopes and theories at a stroke. The trunk had been despatched back to Manchester where the Mancunian Police had welcomed it enthusiastically as the main plank in their case against a Mr Nathan Ormskirk, a builder from Ardwick. Mr Ormskirk, a notoriously heavy and ill-tempered drinker, had a long history of disagreements with his wife, who had mysteriously vanished. It wasn't, Bill asserted, much to Jack's disappointment, anything to do with their non-murder in Surrey.

Jack, following his own train of thought, visited the British Museum Newspaper Library and, much to his private distaste, Bill Rackham was forced to interview John Askern once more.

'It's a case of bigamy, Jack,' he said to his

217

friend that evening in Jack's rooms in Chandos Row. 'And bigamy, no matter how broad-minded we've all become since the war, is a crime.'

'I don't know much about bigamy,' said Jack, adding a splash of soda water to the two glasses of whisky he'd poured and handing one to his friend. 'Here you are, Bill. Bung-ho.'

'Cheers,' said Bill gloomily, raising his glass.

Jack, glass in hand, sprawled comfortably on the sofa. 'I've only ever used bigamy in passing, so to speak, when I've been writing a story. I've never used it as a proper motive, only to set things up, so that, say, a chap will go about marrying illicitly and often in order to bump off the newly-wedded for her insurance money.'

'Bigamy's a crime, all right.'

'A real crime?' asked Jack dubiously. 'I can imagine, if you've managed to acquire more wives than are usually thought desirable, it's not something you'd want talked about, but are we talking about a ticking-off from a magistrate or chokey?'

'It's chokey. Jail, prison, incarceration, detention at His Majesty's pleasure or however else you want to phrase it. Under the Offences Against The Person Act of 1861, it's penal servitude for not less than five years. I read up on it before I tackled Mr Askern.'

'Five years?' Jack whistled. 'As much as that? That's pretty serious. Isn't there any way of wriggling out of it?'

Bill swirled his whisky round in his glass. 'Yes, but I'm not sure if it applies. If the bigamist in question acted in good faith, then there isn't any offence. By "good faith" the law means that the first husband or wife made themselves scarce for seven years before the second marriage and – this is the rub – the abandoned husband or wife didn't know their spouse was alive during that period.'

'How are you meant to prove what the abandoned did or didn't know?'

Bill shrugged. 'By investigation. Letters, diary entries, newspaper clippings or dated photographs that have been preserved, for instance. I'll tell you something. Mrs Daphne Askern-as-was is blistering. She's more than happy for us to dig away in John Askern's papers to see what we can turn up. She's suffering from a massive sense of injustice and, I must say, I have a lot of sympathy for her. Before she married Askern she was a widow and, by all accounts, was left very well-off by her first husband. She's been, particularly where John Askern's concerned, very generous with her money.'

'I can see why she'd feel hard done by.'

'Absolutely. Our Mr Askern was feeling the pinch a bit before she came along – admittedly, this is what Mrs Askern says – but not only does she feel as if she's been made to look like a gullible fool, Signora Bianchi added some pretty deadly insults to her feeling of injury. D'you know Daphne Askern thought John Askern and Signora Bianchi were having an affair? She was prepared to overlook that, as long as it came to an end, but she has no intention of letting this be swept under the carpet.'

'I imagine it's out of her hands anyway.'

'Legally speaking, yes it is. This seven-year rule is a beggar, though. If Mrs Askern has a change of heart and decides to hunt through Askern's papers and destroy anything that's incriminating, I doubt we'll ever be able to prove a charge of bigamy.'

'You'd better not let Colin Askern know that. I can imagine him destroying his father's papers without turning a hair in order to get him out of trouble.'

'So can I. He's a very determined character altogether. And, Jack, the law is the law. Colin Askern is perfectly capable of finding out how things stand for his father without us telling him.'

'Mmm, yes.' Jack pulled the tobacco jar across the table and, reaming out his pipe into the ashtray, stuffed in fresh tobacco. 'Forgetting about what can or can't be proved for the moment, you've seen Mr Askern. Do you think he knew the Bianchi was still alive? For seven years before he married Mrs Daphne, I mean? And when was the date of the marriage?'

'It was the fourteenth of May, 1921, which takes us back to the fourteenth of May 1914. As far as what I believe is concerned, well...' Bill pulled a face. 'It's difficult to get him to make any sort of statement, he's so rambling and disconnected. I honestly do wonder about his mental state. He's drinking heavily as well, which doesn't help matters.'

Jack raised an eyebrow. 'So it's not a case of *in vino veritas*?'

'It's a case of *in vino* making him talk a load of

220

old rubbish, as it often does. Half the time I couldn't make out if he was talking about now or when Carlotta Bianchi left him, years ago. She clearly wanted money – a lot of money – then, just as much as she does now. John Askern kept maundering on about old Lythewell's treasure.'

Jack put a match to his pipe. 'He talked about old Lythewell's treasure that day we saw him at his club. That's before we knew old man Lythewell had been part of the Great Museum Scandal and was in a position to have enough dosh for it to be described as treasure. I've thought about what he said. *They were after him. It drove him mad.* It didn't seem to make much sense at the time, but surely he has to be talking about old Lythewell and his fear that the little gang of forgers would come after him once they'd got out of prison.'

He pulled his notebook out of his pocket. 'I copied down the inscriptions from the chantry flagstones, as you know. There's frequent references to *My son* in those inscriptions. I think Lythewell wanted his son, Daniel, to have the treasure and so hid it from the gang to keep it safe.'

Bill looked at him quizzically. 'Which is all very interesting, Jack, but hardly helps with trying to decide if there's enough proof to proceed against Mr Askern for bigamy.'

'No, but I was wondering if there was another crime hidden in Mr Askern's ramblings. Do you remember what he said? *I did it for Carlotta. She never knew what I'd done*, and so on?'

'I can't say I do, but he's certainly said words

221

to that effect since. Goodness knows what he's talking about.'

'Can't you guess?' asked Jack quietly.

Bill put his hands wide. 'Search me. I tell you, the man's got a bottle of whisky beside him and he seems half-seas over most of the time. I haven't a clue what he's going on about.'

Jack sat upright and put his pipe and glass on the table with a sharp click. 'Okay, let me tell you what I've got in mind.' He leaned forward and ticked the points off on his fingers. 'Point one. Old Lythewell, as we now know, had money. How much money is anyone's guess but let's say it was a lot. It sounds as if it was a lot. Point two. In order to keep the money out of the hands of his former gang, he hid it. Point three. He hid it, so it's believed, in the chantry.'

'So what?'

'Where, Bill, it could be discovered and stolen, yes?'

'I suppose so, if anyone knew where it was,' said Bill with a shrug. 'We didn't get a sniff of it and you can't say we didn't look. You can't tell me Mr Askern discovered and stole it. I told you, he's never been well off and, what's more, before he married Daphne Banks, as she was then, in 1921, he was even less well off.'

'Agreed.'

'Besides that, if John Askern did find the treasure, old Lythewell would kick up a dickens of a fuss about it. He wouldn't just calmly sit back and let his young assistant, as John Askern was then, walk off with the loot.'

'Exactly,' said Jack with a grin. 'Unless – and

this is point four – what happened?'

Bill looked at him blankly. 'Unless old Mr Lythewell was dead.'

'Exactly,' repeated Jack. 'And, to quote Mr Askern once more, *I did it for Carlotta. She never knew what I'd done.* Doesn't that sound like a guilty conscience to you?'

Bill gaped at him. 'Hold on. A guilty conscience? Are you telling me you suspect John Askern of *murder*?'

Jack nodded. 'Of murdering old Mr Lythewell, yes.'

Bill shook his head and gave a dismissive laugh. 'Come off it, Jack. You haven't got a shred of proof. Old Mr Lythewell could've died of anything. Heart disease or TB or pneumonia or something.'

'That's what I thought,' said Jack. 'So I paid a visit to the Newspaper Library and looked up Josiah Lythewell's obituary. He made it into *The Times*, you know. He died as a result of a fall down the stairs.'

Bill hesitated, then picked up his glass. 'That's interesting,' he said slowly. 'Where was John Askern when old Lythewell died? I don't suppose that was in *The Times* was it?'

'No, but there was a very full account in the local paper, *The Whimbrell Heath and Broomwater Intelligencer.* Josiah Lythewell's body was discovered by none other than our old pal, Henry Cadwallader, but John Askern was in the house all right. It said as much in the local paper.'

'That's very interesting, but it doesn't prove anything.'

'No, but it could explain things. Look at it this way. I think John Askern was driven nearly demented by Carlotta Bianchi. She would come back to him, so he thought, if he had money. That's a pretty powerful motive. What's more, it makes sense of John Askern's ramblings, doesn't it? He's knows he's guilty, but he doesn't really think he's guilty of bigamy. What he knows he's guilty of is murder; a totally pointless murder, carried out in desperation to allow him to get his hands on Lythewell's treasure. He believed in that treasure. Virtually no one else did. Two dead crooks did and Henry Cadwallader does, but who'd listen to Henry Cadwallader? Daniel Lythewell can return from New York, inherit his father's estate, and John Askern can hang on to the loot without anyone being any the wiser.'

'So why isn't John Askern rich?' demanded Bill.

'It's obvious, isn't it?' said Jack, picking up his pipe once more. 'He didn't find the treasure, any more than we did.' He looked at his friend's expression and smiled. 'C'mon, Bill. Stop being so cautious. I can't prove anything but it does make sense.'

Bill took a deep breath and sat back in his chair. 'You're right,' he said eventually. 'It does make sense. I've just been going over in my mind what John Askern's actually said to me and yes, it makes sense.' He relapsed into thought once more. 'I'm not sure what to do, and that's a fact. I can hardly charge John Askern with a crime no one suspected and, granted how long ago it was, can't even prove happened. In fact,'

224

he added, with a cynical smile, 'this bigamy business is a relief. At least we know that *has* happened, unlike Signora Bianchi's murder and your idea about Josiah Lythewell's untimely end. What do you want me to do about it?'

'Keep it in mind,' said Jack, relighting his pipe. 'I know there isn't any proof and, I agree, after all this time I doubt if there ever will be any, but as long as you've got it in mind, it might help you to piece together what John Askern's talking about. You could just try asking him,' he added brightly.

'Not unless I want to be accused of bullying a suspect,' said Bill. 'There are rules.' He sipped his whisky broodingly. 'I'll tell you something that unsettles me, though,' he added after a time. 'A man who's committed a murder and got away with it, a man who has, to all intents and purposes, gone on to lead a successful life – I'd say that man was dangerous. You think Joan McAllister was murdered in Signora Bianchi's cottage, don't you?'

'I think it's possible,' said Jack.

Bill grinned. 'Now who's being cautious?'

'All right, I think it's more than possible. I think it's likely.'

'And John Askern knew Signora Bianchi was away and therefore her cottage would be untenanted.'

Bill finished his whisky, got up from his chair and, going over to the sideboard, poured himself another drink. 'I've been after him for bigamy,' he said. 'You think he could've bumped off Josiah Lythewell. However, we *know* – really *know* – that something untoward happened in Signora Bianchi's cottage that night and both of us think it's murder. John Askern was there when Joan McAllister fainted outside the exhibition. You think that's because she recognised someone. I wonder if it was John Askern. He's clearly guilty of something. He's told me that, if he's told me nothing else. I'm beginning to wonder if there's a much more recent murder than that of Josiah Lythewell's on his conscience and I've been asking him the wrong questions.'

Jack looked at Bill. His friend was suddenly grimly determined. 'So what are you going to do, Bill?'

'In the first instance, have a word with Sir Douglas. And then, perhaps, start asking the right questions.'

Three days later Colin Askern called into Scotland Yard to see Bill Rackham. 'I want this police persecution of my father to stop,' he said without preamble. 'For heaven's sake, it's driving him mad.'

Colin Askern's handsome face was so strained, he obviously wasn't the only member of the Askern family feeling the pressure.

'I'd hardly call it persecution,' said Bill. 'When I've called in to ask him a few questions, you've been present, his solicitor was there on one occasion, and yesterday Mr Lythewell turned up.'

'But damnit, Rackham, what are you looking for? You know as well as I do there was nothing in that stupid story of Betty's. My mother's alive, for heaven's sake.'

'There is the question of bigamy,' said Bill, ignoring Colin Askern's snort of disbelief.

'But that's nonsense! I asked the solicitor and he explained how the law stood. When he married my stepmother, Dad thought my mother was dead.'

'Did he? After all, your mother knew exactly where your father was living. She obviously knew he wasn't dead.'

'That doesn't prove my father knew she was alive. Askern's not a common name and my father hasn't been in hiding. I didn't know my mother was alive until she turned up in Whimbrell Heath.'

'Are you sure?'

'Certain.' Colin Askern met his gaze squarely, then his mouth quivered and he buried his face in his hands. 'Just leave us alone, will you? Ever since Betty came to you with that fanciful tale, you've been determined to prove there's been a murder. When it became obvious my mother wasn't the victim, you've been trying to prove some unknown woman was murdered instead. For some extraordinary reason of her own, Betty believes it's that woman who keeled over outside the art exhibition. We've all tried to reason with her, but she just won't have it. Can't you see what this is doing to my father? It's as if you think *he* might be a murderer.'

Bill said nothing.

'This is ridiculous!' Colin broke out. 'If my father was going to murder anyone, he'd have murdered my mother, not a complete stranger. You know he didn't murder my mother, but at least you can see there'd be a reason for it. But this? This is complete and utter nonsense from beginning to end. I've told Betty so, but I don't know what's got into her recently.'

Bill traced an abstract pattern on the desk with his forefinger. 'Can you think of any reason why Miss Wingate should make up such a story?'

'God knows,' said Colin, with another snort of impatience. 'I'm not a psychologist but I'm beginning to think she needs one. I used to think Betty was a nice, straightforward girl. I used to feel sorry for her, for Pete's sake! I don't feel sorry for her any longer. She's either subject to nightmares or she's looking for attention.' He gave a little shiver. 'To be honest, it scares me a little, she's so determined. She ... well, she can't have had such an easy time of it with Mrs Lythewell. I don't know. Maybe she really does just want attention.'

Bill thought of Betty Wingate. She must be having a hard time at home. 'We did find evidence that there'd been a crime.'

Colin Askern made a dismissive noise. 'So Betty says, but I'd like to know exactly what evidence there was. I don't see how there can be any.' Bill was aware that Askern was watching him very closely. 'There isn't any real evidence, is there?' said Askern acutely. 'None that Betty couldn't have put there herself.'

Although Bill could've sworn his expression had given nothing away, Askern smacked his fist down on the desk in triumph. 'I knew it!' He pushed his chair back and, standing up, rubbed his tired eyes with his hand. 'Look, when I said

228

I felt sorry for Betty, I meant it. She's had a rotten run of luck and it can't be easy, living at her Aunt Maud's beck and call. It wouldn't be surprising if it did drive her mental. Maybe she really does need a psychologist. I could understand that, but what I can't understand is why my father's being hounded. I want it to stop.'

Bill put his head to one side. 'I don't think you're in a position to tell me what to do.'

Askern drew a deep breath. 'Maybe not. But I'll tell you this. Betty didn't understand the true facts about the relationship between my mother and myself. I hardly like to say as much, but she thought there was an affair of sorts going on.'

'Almost everyone did think that, as far as I can make out,' said Bill dryly.

Askern had the grace to look abashed. 'All right, but I'd told Betty there was nothing to worry about. If the silly girl had only taken me at my word, she'd have saved herself a lot of heartache.' He rubbed the side of his nose in embarrassment. 'Don't you understand? Betty was jealous. Despite everything I'd said, she was jealous of my mother.'

'And?'

'Jealous women are capable of just about *anything*. As I said, God knows what's going on in Betty's mind, but she could've seen exactly what she wanted to see and have trumped up some so-called evidence to prove it when no one believed her. It's possible, you know.'

Was it possible? Just about. Perhaps.

Askern saw the question in Bill's eyes and pressed home the advantage. 'My father's not a

229

strong man. If you're going to formally charge him with bigamy, then charge him. At least he'll have something concrete to fight. But this cloud of suspicion has to be lifted, otherwise there's every chance you'll send him over the edge.'

'Are you going to charge Mr Askern with bigamy?' asked Jack, when Bill reported the conversation to him. 'It sounds suspiciously like a challenge or a diversion to me.'

'I don't see how we can, unless we've got some hard evidence.' Bill paused. 'How d'you mean? A challenge or a diversion?'

'To take your eye off the real crime, dumbbell.'

'If there is a real crime,' Bill said gloomily. 'Askern was quite right, you know. There wasn't anything we turned up in Signora Bianchi's cottage that Miss Wingate couldn't have placed there herself.'

Jack laughed dismissively. 'Come off it, Bill. That didn't occur to you before you spoke to Askern.'

'As a matter of fact, it did. When Miss Wingate first told me her story, I did wonder how much of it was real and how much imagined.'

'You've changed your mind since then, though.'

Bill sighed. 'I *had*. If only we could find the body, Jack. That would make all the difference. You can't argue with a body. At the moment, we can't do a damn thing. It's all suspicion and hearsay and ifs, mights and buts. I'm tired of the whole wretched business.'

230

'Cheer up,' said Jack encouragingly. 'You never know what tomorrow might bring.'

The next day, Miss Betty Wingate, letter in hand, walked into the small lobby of Dorian House, the block of flats that straddled the corner of Ransome Gardens and Buchanan Street. The hum of traffic from Tottenham Court Road faded as the door closed behind her. There was a porter's desk and chair in the lobby, but the chair was empty. On the desk was a bell with a notice beside it: *Please ring for attention.*

Betty reached out her hand, then hesitated, looking at the letter once more. The instructions in the letter were perfectly clear and she wanted a few moments to compose herself.

Flat 22. Three o'clock. Knock and enter.

She didn't really need anyone to show her the way to the second floor, did she? And she was grateful for these last few moments to gather her thoughts, to think exactly what she was going to say, without interruption.

Flat 22. Three o'clock. Knock and enter.

Miss Betty Wingate mounted the stairs.

Eleven

It was twenty past six when Jack's telephone rang.

'Jack?' It was Bill Rackham. 'I'm at 22, Dorian House. It's a block of flats on the corner of Ransome Gardens and Buchanan Street. Do you know it?'

'Buchanan Street? Near Tottenham Court Road?'

'That's the one. Can you get over here? Now, I mean? It's important.'

Jack mentally rearranged his evening. Bill's voice sounded urgent. 'Yes, of course. What's happened?'

'I'd rather not say over the phone. Just get here as fast as you can.'

What the dickens was all this about? There was a police constable on duty in the lobby of Dorian House who politely directed him upstairs, but who equally politely refused to give him any details.

It has to be murder or a death at least, Jack thought, as he took the stairs two at a time. Nothing else would warrant the constable's bland, official secrecy, and surely – *surely* – it had to do with what he had privately labelled the Chantry Case. But where did Dorian House fit into that?

232

Dorian House was a good, solid Victorian building divided into good, solid apartments which, judging from the lobby, stairs and hallways, were kept up to a high standard. The rents probably ran to six or seven pounds a week. They were the sort of flats where he'd expect the occupants to have a maid or a man-servant. To the best of his knowledge, no one had ever mentioned Dorian House before.

The door of number 22 stood ajar and Jack could hear voices coming from the flat. He pushed open the door and went along the hallway to the sitting-room.

Bill was standing to one side of the room, beside a chintz-covered armchair. With him was a man Jack recognised, the police surgeon Dr Roude. Beside him, packing away his camera, was a police photographer, three uniformed constables and two plain-clothes officers, who, from their briefcases, Jack thought were probably the fingerprint men.

'Jack!' said Bill as he came in, stepping away from the armchair.

In the chair, sitting with his head thrown back, a man was slumped. Round his throat, wrapped very tightly, was what looked like a woman's blue silk scarf with a knotted fringe. His posture seemed that of sleep, but the utter rigid stillness of his hands on the arms of the chair told its own story.

Jack stopped short. 'It's *John Askern*,' he said incredulously. He gazed at Bill in bewilderment. 'John Askern? But damnit, that's impossible.'

'Impossible or not, here he is.'

233

'But Bill, we'd had him pegged as a likely murderer, not a victim.' He glanced at Dr Roude. 'It is murder, isn't it? I mean, it looks pretty unlikely, but there's no chance he could have committed suicide, is there? I could've believed that.'

Dr Roude shook his head. 'None whatsoever, I'd say, Haldean. Inspector Rackham asked me the same question.'

'It has to be murder,' said Bill. 'You can see for yourself, Jack, that a man simply couldn't commit suicide in that position.'

'Could he have been moved after he died? Could he have been put in the chair?'

'That occurred to me,' said Bill, 'but the doctor says that, medically speaking, there's no indication the body's been moved. I examined the area around the chair pretty closely, as you can imagine, but there's no scuff marks on the carpet or anything else to suggest that he was carried or dragged here.'

Jack's mind was racing. It seemed impossible that John Askern could've been murdered, and yet here he was. *You can't argue with a body.* Bill had said that only yesterday. 'How long has he been dead?'

'I saw him at twenty to five,' said Dr Roude. 'I'd estimate that by that time he'd been dead for about two and a half to four hours or so. That's the absolute outside. Certainly not earlier, but I can't be more accurate than that. There's too many variable factors to take into account.'

'Would three o'clock be a possible time?' asked Bill.

Dr Roude pulled a face. 'I'd veer to an earlier time, perhaps, but three is certainly possible, yes.'

'And it's murder,' said Bill. 'Murder by strangulation.' He reached out and touched the blue silk scarf with his forefinger. 'He was strangled with this, despite the fact he looks so peaceful.'

Dr Roude cleared his throat. 'To be technical, what I believe actually occurred was attempted strangulation, causing compression of the vagus nerve, which runs alongside the jugular vein. That led to over-stimulation of the heart, so the cause of death was actually heart failure, which explains the lack of usual signs of asphyxia.' He snapped his briefcase shut. 'Which, I may say, is a relief for all of us, as an asphyxiated victim is not a pleasant sight. We'll probably find he had a weak heart, but that's something which I only can ascertain in the P.M.' He looked at Bill. 'If you don't need me for anything else, I've finished here.'

'No, that's fine, Doctor,' said Bill. He looked up as a knock sounded on the door and a constable came in.

'The mortuary men are outside, sir.'

'Good.' He looked at the fingerprint men. 'Can the body be taken away now?'

'Yes, sir, we've finished,' said one of the men. 'You can touch anything you like now.' He nodded towards the photographer. 'We've got it all on record.'

'Good,' said Bill. He turned to the uniformed constables. 'Ask the mortuary chaps to come and remove the body, then return to making enquiries

235

at the other flats, will you? Let me know right away if anything new turns up.'

The mortuary men came in, loaded the mortal remains of John Askern onto a stretcher, covered the body with a green canvas cover and took it away.

Once everyone had gone, the flat seemed very quiet.

Bill lit a cigarette and, sinking into an armchair, tossed his cigarette case over to Jack. 'Help yourself. This is a turn up for the books, isn't it? All our theories kicked into touch.'

'That poor beggar Askern,' said Jack, taking a cigarette and striking a match. 'I know I suggested he was the villain of the piece, but it was horrible to see him like that.' He shook his head impatiently, as if to rid himself of the image.

'Incidentally, it's kind of you to say *our* theories,' he added glumly, after a pause. 'It's me who was so damn certain John Askern was our man. I wouldn't say I had it all worked out, but I was getting there. Mrs McAllister seemed to fit so well as the victim in Signora Bianchi's cottage. I'd guessed that she'd been a servant, perhaps in old Mr Lythewell's household, perhaps elsewhere in Whimbrell Heath, but certainly somewhere she knew John Askern in a context associated with art.'

Bill looked at him acutely. 'I see. That explains why she said what she did outside the exhibition. That's not a bad explanation, Jack.'

'I thought it was credible. It'd do as a working hypothesis, at any rate. However...'

'Carry on,' said Bill. 'You've not spelt your

ideas out for me like this before.'

'No? That's because ideas are all they are – or were, I should say. There's damn all I can prove. It was no secret that John Askern had been married, but I guessed Joan McAllister may have found out Colin's mother was alive. And you know I thought John Askern had seen off old Mr Lythewell to have a crack at Lythewell's treasure?'

Bill nodded. 'D'you still think that?'

Jack shrugged. 'I think it's feasible. I thought Joan McAllister had guessed either that Colin's mother was alive or the truth about Lythewell's death, two facts that Askern would want kept quiet. John Askern bought her off and Joan McAllister went to America. Then, years later, she sees him outside the exhibition and – bingo! She recognises him and starts to cash in. Askern, already worried to death by the reappearance of Signora Bianchi, found Joan McAllister popping up again just about the last straw. So, knowing that Signora Bianchi's cottage is unoccupied, he asks her to meet him there and bumps her off, disposing of her body God knows where. And that, Bill,' he said, flicking the ash off his cigarette, 'was more or less it. The fact that poor old Askern was murdered himself does make me think I was on the wrong lines.'

'Unfortunately,' said Bill, 'you are. Which is a pity, because it sounds very plausible. You aren't in possession of all the facts, though.'

Jack looked up with a cynical smile. 'That sounds as if you're awarding me a pat on the back, an A for effort and a gold star. Go on. What facts am I lacking?'

'Well, you haven't asked me who this flat belongs to, for instance.'

'I was going to. We're obviously firmly in upper middle-class territory. It didn't belong to John Askern, did it?'

'Not as far as we can tell. Not unless he was the man who really paid the rent, if you see what I mean. The porter tells me the flat belongs to a Colonel and Mrs Pearson, but they're in Egypt for six months. The Colonel and his wife approached a lettings agency to let the flat while they were away.' Bill couldn't help but pause. 'You're going to love this, Jack. The flat was taken three weeks ago by none other than Mrs Joan McAllister.'

If Bill had been hoping for a reaction, he certainly got one. Jack gaped at him. *'Who?'*

'Mrs Joan McAllister,' repeated Bill.

'Bloody hell, Bill, that's impossible! Joan McAllister *couldn't* have rented the flat. We'd worked out she was dead, for heaven's sake!'

'You worked out she was dead,' Bill reminded him. 'You and Miss Wingate.'

'So where's Joan McAllister now?'

'I only wish I knew. I've looked in the bedroom and it seems to me as if she's made a complete get-away. The wardrobe's empty and there's no suitcase. It looks as if she's scarpered. I've had a good look round and there aren't any personal bits and pieces that might give us a clue. I've got men calling at the other flats in the building to see if anyone's seen her recently, but, so far, we've drawn a blank.'

'*Joan McAllister?*' repeated Jack, dumbfounded. 'But...' He smoked his cigarette down to the stump and crushed it out in the ashtray. He got up and, going to the fireplace, braced his arms against the mantelpiece, sinking his head between his shoulders.

It was a little while before he turned to face Bill. 'I've been wrong,' he said flatly. 'I've been wrong from beginning to end.'

'You might not be wrong about the association between Joan McAllister and John Askern,' said Bill. 'There had to be something between them, otherwise he wouldn't have been murdered here, in her flat.'

'I was wrong about Joan McAllister being murdered in Signora Bianchi's cottage, though, wasn't I? Hell's bells, Bill, I couldn't have been more wrong! You're sure – absolutely sure – that Joan McAllister rents this flat?'

'I've got a description of her from the porter and from the neighbours, and I'm bound to say, their description ties in with my memory of her.'

Jack lit another cigarette. 'Did she have a maid or any other servant?'

Bill shook his head. 'No, I asked that. Mrs McAllister told one of the neighbours, a Mrs Conway-Lloyd, that her maid had left to go back home to Ireland to be married a few weeks ago and she was trying to find a nice girl to take her place.'

'Well, that's a complete fairy tale for a start. A few weeks ago Mrs Joan McAllister was living at that grim boarding house in Purbeck Terrace, swiping pennies and tuppences from the Waifs

239

and Strays Society.' Jack paused, trying to adjust his thoughts. 'I can hardly believe it. You say this neighbour – what's she called?'

'Mrs Conway-Lloyd.'

'This Mrs Conway-Lloyd actually *spoke* to Joan McAllister?'

'Absolutely, she did. It sounds as if she was quite pally with her. As I said, I've got the men checking who saw her last, but a good few people have seen her and spoken to her in the last three weeks. Mrs Conway-Lloyd, for instance, thought she seemed a very nice sort of woman with a great interest in charities.'

'Well, that's certainly true. The charity part, at least.' Jack shook his head. 'I need hardly tell you, Bill, this is a complete facer. I was practically certain Mrs McAllister was the missing victim from Signora Bianchi's cottage. Dammit, you believed it, too.'

'I thought she might be, but that's as far as I was prepared to go. It was you and Miss Wingate who were so sure about it. And, while we're on the subject of Miss Wingate, guess who discovered the body?'

Jack gazed at him. 'Go on,' he said in a dried-up voice.

'It sounds as if you've guessed.'

'It was Betty Wingate, wasn't it?'

Bill nodded. 'Got it in one.'

'Oh, my God.' Jack was quiet for some time. 'What on earth was she doing here? Tell me what happened.'

'She received a letter, supposedly from John Askern, asking her to meet him here at three

240

o'clock this afternoon. It contained a warning of danger.'

'Did it, by George?'

'He said that she was in danger and, for the sake of her own safety and his, he asked her not to tell anyone about the letter. He went on to say that he was very sorry to hear that she and Colin had had a disagreement but, if she was in possession of certain facts, she might see his son's actions in a different light. He also said he was now able to give her the truth of what lay behind her unpleasant experience that night in Signora Bianchi's cottage.'

Jack nodded. 'That's a fairly powerful invitation. I notice you say the letter was supposedly from John Askern. Was it?'

Bill shrugged. 'I don't know. She had the letter with her but I haven't had time to examine it properly.'

'What happened then? I take it Miss Wingate kept the appointment?'

'She did. She says she followed the instructions literally to the letter, which were to come here at three, knock and enter. She showed up at three, walked in and found John Askern much as we saw him. Or, at least, that's what she says.'

Jack frowned. 'Do you doubt her word, Bill?'

Bill clicked his tongue. 'Come on, Jack, you know as well as I do that we can't blindly accept what any witness says as being the unvarnished truth. And,' he added, obviously picking his words carefully, 'you must admit that she does seem to have a habit of being in the wrong place at the wrong time.'

Jack said nothing.

'I don't like it any more than you do,' said Bill uncomfortably, 'but you have to see that her story is open to question. For all I know, she could've written the letter herself, to provide an excuse for being here.'

'But *why*, Bill? You're saying, not to wrap it up, that you suspect Miss Wingate of murdering John Askern, but why? What on earth does she have to gain?'

'To say I suspect Miss Wingate is putting it far too strongly, but I have to question what she says. As to what she has to gain, what does anyone have to gain?'

'Well, if this flat does belong to Joan McAllister, Mrs McAllister might have decided that Askern knew a damn sight too much about her and decided to put him out of the way. There was a warning of danger in that letter, after all. What happened after Miss Wingate discovered John Askern?'

'She got out of the flat and found the porter who, after seeing for himself what had happened, ran into the street and called the nearest policeman. He telephoned the Yard. I got over here as fast as I could. Miss Wingate was very upset, so I arranged for her to be taken back to the Yard and left in the care of a couple of women police officers.'

'Does Colin Askern know what's happened?'

'I've asked for him to be informed. John Askern was his father, after all. Naturally I didn't want him here, so I suggested he should come into the Yard. Do you want to take a look round before we go? As I said, I've already been through the place, but you might see something I've missed.'

'All right, but it sounds as if Mrs McAllister made a clean escape.'

A thorough and frustrating search turned up nothing of any importance. Indeed, the total lack of any personal possessions whatsoever made Jack pause. 'I know she's only been living here for three weeks, but she's obviously gone to some pains to clear the place out completely. This wasn't a hurried escape, Bill. She's taken her time over this.'

A knock came at the door and a police constable came in. 'We've completed our round of the flats, sir. The last person to see Mrs McAllister was the porter. He saw her this morning, round about midday.'

'Was she carrying a suitcase?'

'No, sir. According to the porter, she was coming in, not going out. He didn't actually speak to her, apart from to say good morning. He didn't take any especial notice of her, but he says it was Mrs McAllister all right.'

'I see. Well, I think we've done all we can for the time being. I'll lock up and leave instructions with the porter.' He looked at Jack. 'Do you want to come back to the Yard with me, Jack? We'll probably find Colin Askern there.'

As they expected, Colin Askern was with Betty Wingate at Scotland Yard. Slightly more unexpectedly, he was accompanied by Daphne Askern, and Maud and Daniel Lythewell.

243

'I'm surprised to see you here, Mrs Askern,' said Bill.

'I had to come,' she said, dabbing her eyes. She'd obviously been crying. She swallowed a sob and dabbed her eyes again. 'I know what I said and what I did, but I was bitterly hurt, Inspector. I felt betrayed and so horribly let down, but now the worst has happened, I can't believe I was so harsh and unfeeling towards poor John. He tried to tell me that terrible woman meant nothing to him, but I wouldn't listen, and now she's *murdered* him.'

'Terrible woman?' asked Bill.

'S-S-S-Signora Bianchi,' said Daphne Askern in a flood of renewed sobs.

'There, there, Daphne, don't take on so,' said Maud Lythewell, slipping an arm round her shoulders. 'I'm quite sure the Inspector will be able to track her down, and then,' she added, her face growing stern, 'she'll pay the full price for her crimes.'

'It won't bring back poor dear John,' wailed Daphne Askern. 'He's gone and I was so horrible to him!'

'Signora Bianchi?' repeated Bill. 'Excuse me, Mrs Askern, whatever makes you think that it was Signora Bianchi who was responsible for your husband's death?'

Colin wriggled impatiently. 'Of course she wasn't responsible! The idea's ridiculous!'

Bill waved him quiet.

Mrs Askern lowered her handkerchief. 'Mr Lythewell said so,' she said uncertainly. 'It has to be her. She's been behind all poor John's troubles from beginning to end.'

'Mr Lythewell?' asked Bill enquiringly.

Daniel Lythewell put his hands wide. 'Who else could it be, Inspector? Signora Bianchi attempted to blackmail poor John – be quiet, Askern! – and, when she'd come to the end of that little game, I'm afraid this was the next step.'

'My mother,' said Colin, who was obviously holding himself in check with some effort, 'is *not* a murderer.'

'She can twist you round her little finger, Colin,' said Betty. She was still pale and shocked, but her voice was composed. 'She always could. You'd do anything for her.'

'She's my *mother,* for Pete's sake!' He rubbed his face with his hands. 'Look, I know she has her faults–' there was a concerted sniff from all the women in the room – 'but she isn't a violent person. She simply wouldn't do that sort of thing. She just wouldn't.'

Bill nodded. 'I have to say, Askern, that I agree with you.' Colin Askern looked at him gratefully. 'Not,' continued Bill, 'from any knowledge of your mother's character. As far as that goes, I haven't really got any. Our chief suspect in the affair has to be the woman who rented 22, Dorian House, where your father was found, and I'm bound to say the description of her doesn't sound remotely like your mother.'

'I don't understand,' wailed Daphne Askern. 'What was John doing in some woman's flat? Who was she?' She gulped. 'He wasn't having an affair with this woman, was he? I don't think

I could stand it!'

'Now, now, Daphne,' said Daniel Lythewell with heavy-handed sympathy. 'Perhaps there are some questions that are better not answered just at the moment.'

Daphne Askern's face crumpled and she gathered herself for another outbreak of sobs.

'I think you can rest assured there's no question of Mr Askern having an affair with the woman who rented the flat,' said Bill hastily. Daphne subsided, her chest heaving.

Colin looked at him, puzzled. 'But who was she, Rackham? Oh, my God, this is like a nightmare!' His voice broke. 'First of all poor Dad goes to pieces and then *this* happens. Who was this woman? The one who rented the flat, I mean?'

'Her name,' said Bill, 'is Mrs Joan McAllister.'

There was a complete and puzzled silence.

'Who?' asked Colin eventually.

Betty gave a little gasp. 'Mrs McAllister? She's the woman who collapsed at the art exhibition. But...' She glanced at Jack and stopped, biting her lip.

'I know,' said Jack, speaking for the first time. 'I thought she was dead. I was obviously wrong.'

Betty shook her head in bewilderment. 'I don't understand. I just don't understand any of it. What was Mr Askern going to tell me? And why did he ask me to meet him at this Mrs McAllister's flat?'

'I don't know what John was thinking of,' said Daphne Askern tremulously. 'Why should he write to you, Miss Wingate? If he had written to anyone, it should've been me. I was his *wife*.'

'If my father wrote the letter at all,' said Colin darkly.

'That's easy enough to prove,' said Bill. He glanced at Daphne Askern. 'You would recognise your husband's writing, wouldn't you?' he asked. She nodded. 'Can I see the letter, Miss Wingate? I didn't have time to look at it properly when you showed it to me before.'

'Of course,' said Betty, picking up her handbag. 'I've got it here.' She rummaged in her bag and Jack saw her face change. 'Where is it? I know I had it!'

'Honestly, Betty, come on,' said Colin Askern brusquely. 'It's important.'

'I know it's important, Colin,' she snapped. 'I had it in my bag.'

Betty Wingate's handbag, an openwork bag with a bamboo handle and a cheerful jazz design, was tipped up on the desk. There was a purse, a lipstick, a powder compact, an enamelled cigarette case with a sunburst design, a lighter and a bunch of keys, but no letter.

'I couldn't have lost it,' she said despairingly. 'I don't know where it's got to.'

'Could someone have taken it?' asked Jack. 'Have you had your bag with you all the time?'

'I don't know,' she said helplessly. 'I suppose someone could have taken it, but why?'

'Where is it?' demanded Daphne Askern, her voice rising. 'I want to see John's letter! What have you done with it?'

'It really is *most* careless of you, Betty,' said Maud Lythewell. 'I would've thought you'd

247

have taken the greatest care of it after what happened. You must've known how important it was.'

'But I *did* know,' protested Betty. 'I had it safely in my bag, I know I did.'

'If it ever existed at all,' Colin Askern said grimly. She stared at him speechlessly. 'After all,' he continued, 'why you? Why did Dad write to you – if he did? Why is it you who supposedly discovered first my mother's body and now my father's? I don't know what's going on, Betty, but I don't like it.'

Betty swallowed and went pale.

'The letter certainly did exist,' interposed Jack quickly. 'Miss Wingate showed it to Inspector Rackham at Dorian House.'

She glanced at him gratefully. 'See, Colin? I'm not making this up.'

Colin snorted in disbelief. 'You could've written it yourself, for all I know.' He ignored her shocked denial. 'I thought you wanted attention, Betty. I thought that was all it was. I was sympathetic up to a point, but enough's enough. I don't believe and never did believe there was a murder in my mother's cottage, and you hated me saying so. So what's going on?' His voice cracked. 'My father's dead and I want to know why.'

'Jack,' said Bill quietly, nodding his head towards the door, 'can I have a word?'

As they went into the corridor, they could hear a furious argument breaking out behind them.

'I don't believe it,' said Bill, his face grim. 'What else can go wrong with this ruddy case? I

248

saw her put that letter back in her bag myself. I suppose Askern could be right, that Miss Wingate wrote it herself.'

'Either that or she's lost it,' said Jack quickly. He held up his hand to ward off Bill's protest. 'I know that doesn't seem likely. Or it could've been stolen.' He jerked his thumb at the door. 'If it has been stolen, it has to have been taken by one of the bright crew in there. You could make everyone turn their pockets out, I suppose.'

Bill winced. 'I could, but where that's going to get me, I don't know. These people aren't under arrest. I can't demand a thorough search without really upsetting the apple cart, and anything else is useless. Besides that, if it has been taken, there's been ample opportunity for any of them to have disposed of it. We're stuck.'

'Unfortunately, I think you're right.' Jack glanced round as the noise from the room intensified. 'Blimey, that's a dickens of a row they're having. We'd better go back in before there's another murder.'

'What do we do now?'

'Well, I know what I'm going to do,' said Jack. 'I'm going to ask Miss Wingate out to dinner.'

Bill's eyebrows shot up. 'Why?'

'Why? For one thing, I think she needs a break and for another ... Well, I'd quite like to get to know Miss Wingate better.'

'Really?' Bill sucked his cheeks in dubiously. 'She does seem to have an unfortunate habit of coming across bodies. Watch your step, Jack.'

Twelve

The Cafe de Bologna, with its resident dance band, potted palms, linen tablecloths and gold-rimmed chairs, was bright and cheerful. Unlike Betty Wingate, Jack thought sympathetically, looking across the table at her strained face and troubled eyes.

Damn Colin Askern! He shouldn't have let Betty go to that flat alone. *I wish I'd been there*, thought Jack. It was such a strong wish it brought him up sharp.

Bill had accused him of falling for Betty Wingate. He was honest enough to ask himself the question squarely. Was he? He felt sorry for her, intrigued by her, and enjoyed being with her. Her hair caught the light as it waved. He wanted to make her smile and see her eyes light up, as they'd lit up that first day, when he met her at the exhibition. But then, his memory warned, she'd smiled for Colin Askern.

'I wish,' she said, as she picked up her glass of wine, 'you'd been there this afternoon.'

It was such an echo of his thoughts that his heart gave a leap. 'Me in particular?' he asked, 'or would you rather Askern had been there?'

'Colin?' she said, shocked. 'Of course not. I'd hate him to have discovered his father. It was horrible. Colin would've gone to pieces.' She shuddered. 'It was rotten enough finding Mr Askern without having to cope with poor Colin as well.'

Poor Colin. Ah well...

'He can't face unpleasant things. That's why he keeps denying what I've seen. It would be so much easier if I really had dreamt it all.' She gave a wan, tired smile. 'Poor Colin. He likes everything to be just so, and if it isn't, he just can't cope.'

'Can you cope?'

'Me?' She was surprised at the question. 'Well, of course I can. I have to, don't I?'

'I think you're wonderful,' said Jack, with a surge of admiration. Dammit, she shouldn't *have* to cope.

Someone had tried to incriminate her, to make her discover John Askern's body. Someone had stolen that letter from her bag. Someone wanted to harm Betty.

Harm Betty... His stomach lurched. No! No one was going to harm Betty. That wasn't going to happen. The thought was like a sudden, raging flame, so fierce it hurt. *What about Colin Askern? She was in love with Colin Askern, wasn't she?*

He forced himself to smile, forced his voice to show nothing but friendly concern. 'C'mon, funny face,' he said gently. 'Cheer up.'

'Why did you ask me to dinner?' she asked, rearranging the napkin on her knee.

'I thought you needed some time away from everyone,' he said, forcing the smile once more. 'Besides that, I enjoy your company.'

She looked down, flushing. 'I wish I could believe it was as simple as that,' she said in a small voice. 'You want to know what happened, don't you?'

'Yes, of course I do, but not now.'

'Colin thinks he knows what happened,' she said sadly. 'I used to have such fun with him.'

Hell. Did she?

'He used to tease me for being so solemn, but I don't think I could've stood living with Aunt Maud if it hadn't been for Colin.' Her voice wobbled dangerously. 'I'm sorry,' she said with a sniff and an attempt at a smile. 'I don't want to cry or make a scene or anything embarrassing like that.'

This time Jack did reach out for her hand. 'Miss Wingate – Betty – you've had a horrible experience. It's only natural you should feel upset.'

She gave him a watery smile. 'Thanks,' she said eventually.

Her hand trembled in his. She could look after herself, but he suddenly realised he wanted, wanted more than anything, to shield her from harm. 'Look, this probably isn't the time to mention it, but I think you're nothing short of wonderful.'

She drew back in startled wariness, her eyes narrowed.

Jack fiddled unnecessarily with his cutlery, avoiding her gaze. 'If, by any chance, you decide to return Askern to the store, you could give me a chance, you know?'

Her wariness increased. 'Why are you asking?'

He glanced up in surprise. 'Because I think you're the tops. What other reason could there be?'

'Do you know the reason why I left my last job?' She looked at him appraisingly. 'And the one before that, for that matter? Men.'

'I don't quite follow...' began Jack.

'There's plenty of men,' continued Betty, 'who think a single girl is fair game. That's why I liked Colin so much. He wasn't after anything, unlike most men. Married men,' she added bitterly, 'are the worst of all.'

Jack flinched and she drew back, so startled she nearly knocked over her wine glass. 'I'm sorry,' she apologised, 'but you looked so fierce that it was a bit of a shock.'

Jack took a deep breath and got a grip on his temper. That fire inside had flared at her words. He wanted to shout, *I'm not like that!*, but he couldn't shout, not here in the Cafe de Bologna, so instead he settled for making her smile.

He put his hands to his heart in a deliberately florid gesture. 'I'm not married. You see before you a totally blameless bachelor with a completely clean record. Snow white, in fact. I'm guaranteed one hundred per cent wholesome, free from all contamination and any inspection is welcomed.'

Much to his relief, she giggled. 'Idiot! Are you serious?'

'Completely and utterly so,' he declared. 'My intentions are pure.'

Her eyes sparkled. 'I'm glad to hear it. What are your intentions?'

For a fraction of a heartbeat the question caught him off guard. Until that moment he'd intended nothing more than to see she had a fair deal, to enjoy her company, to get to know her better, to simply spend time with her, but that *wasn't* what he wanted.

He wanted her. He wanted to come home to her. It was simple, straightforward, life changing and shattering.

He picked up the bread roll and crumbled it between his fingers. 'My intentions? Just the usual, I suppose.' *He wanted to come home to her.* 'Two hearts that beat as one, as you might say.' He heard her intake of breath and looked up with a smile. 'I'm sorry if it seems a bit soon to mention it, but, what with one thing and another, I've never been married. I wouldn't mind,' he added, his smile widening at her expression, 'giving it a try. How about you?'

Betty stared at him. 'Marry you, you mean?'

Jack nodded. 'That's the general idea, yes.' Betty glanced around quickly and he knew she was on the verge of picking up her things and leaving. 'Mind you, that's about chapter two or three of how I see the future,' he added, leaning back in his chair. 'We go out to dinner a few times or perhaps take a picnic to the park. We go dancing, you're overwhelmed by the fact I don't tread on your feet, and there we are. A perfect union.'

Betty subsided. 'But we hardly know each other,' she said weakly. 'You can't possibly expect me to marry you.'

'Why not? I told you my intentions were pure.

Come on, Betty – you don't mind me calling you Betty, do you? Miss Wingate seems absurdly formal when I'm offering you my hand and heart, don't you think? What with one thing and another, granted I am offering the aforesaid hand and heart, it only seemed polite to mention it. I didn't want to escape your attention.'

Betty gazed at him, shaking her head in disbelief. 'I don't think you could ever escape my attention.'

'I'll take that as a positive sign. In case it makes a difference, I can also do a wide range of farmyard imitations. Oh, and I can recite the whole of "The Green Eye of the Little Yellow God".'

'I don't believe you,' said Betty with a giggle.

'Don't you?' Jack cleared his throat. *There's a one-eyed yellow idol to the north of Khatmandu. There's a little marble cross below the town. There a broken-hearted woman tends the grave of Mad Carew. And the yellow god forever gazes down.* I can do the second and subsequent verses upon request. The second verse introduces what you may call the love interest, in the person of the Colonel's daughter. Mad Carew came to a sticky end as a result of pinching the green eye of the little yellow god for the Colonel's daughter, but she loved him madly, all the same. You could follow her example.'

'You can't possibly be serious,' said Betty, laughing.

'Well, if you don't fancy poetry, what about dinner from time to time?'

'And what about Colin?'

255

'Forget about Colin,' he said, rather more crossly than he intended.

'I can't! I care for him – care for him a lot.'

Jack swallowed. 'Just for the time being?' he pleaded. 'Tell me about yourself instead.'

Three quarters of an hour later they had covered Betty's early life and interests. She answered his questions shyly at first, unused to talking about herself. 'You write, don't you?' she asked. 'I love reading. Colin loves your stories, but mysteries aren't much fun in real life. It's all so horribly puzzling and real.'

And that, of course, brought them back full circle to the events of the day, focusing on the missing letter.

'Did you have your bag with you all the time?' asked Jack, as he led her round the dance floor. He raised his voice to carry above the noise fuelled by the clarinets, drums, saxophones and trombone of Art Burrell and his Seven Brooklyn Buddies.

'I thought I did,' she said, 'but I wasn't keeping an especial guard on it. Who would want to steal Mr Askern's letter? Mrs Askern might want to see it, but she wouldn't steal it, surely. Why should she? Why should anyone?'

'Because if Mr Askern didn't write it, someone else did, and if we could tie up the handwriting, it'd give us a dickens of a clue, wouldn't you say?'

'But that's stupid, too,' said Betty, wrinkling her nose. 'I could've easily handed it over to Inspector Rackham at the flat. It's only a matter of complete chance he didn't take it there and then.

I wish he had done,' she added moodily. 'If he had done, Colin wouldn't be able to make such idiotic suggestions. He says ... I can't believe he really thinks this, but he says that I'm doing it to attract attention. Anyone would think I *wanted* to discover dead bodies all the time and I most certainly don't.'

'That seems a very reasonable aspiration,' said Jack, executing a daring glide past four couples who were blocking the way. 'I can see it's not something you'd want to make a hobby of.'

She giggled and it was lovely to hear her laugh. 'Jack,' she said shyly. 'Inspector Rackham said you were good at finding out the truth about things. I wish you could find out the truth about all this.'

'I will,' he said firmly. Come hell or high water, he was going to get to the bottom of this business. She needed him. She needed him to find out what was going on, and he only wished he had more of a clue.

What Betty said was absolutely right. It was merely a matter of chance that Bill hadn't taken the letter from her when she'd shown it to him at the flat. So therefore it was either a very good imitation of John Askern's handwriting or John Askern really had written the letter. But both of those solutions seemed to raise as many problems as they solved. He shook his head impatiently. There must be an answer but he couldn't think of it.

'The other thing I don't understand is, who is Mrs McAllister?' asked Betty. 'I thought she was dead but she can't be, can she? I suppose,' she added, her brow wrinkling doubtfully, 'that Mrs McAllister – the one who had the flat, I mean – could really be someone else, someone pretending to be Mrs McAllister, but then who is she?'

'She'd have to know Mr Askern,' said Jack.

Betty bit her lip. 'Do you mean Mrs Askern? She's the only one who really fits the bill. I can't think of anyone else. Not that we know.'

'Perhaps,' said Jack.

The dance came to an end. Everyone applauded, the band tipped out the moisture from their instruments and struck up with 'Sweet Georgia Brown'.

Betty shook her head impatiently. 'None of it makes any sense! Can we forget about it all for a while?' She tapped her foot to the music. 'I like this one,' she said. 'Can we dance again?'

Mrs Askern? thought Jack as he led Betty round the floor in a foxtrot. As Betty said, like everything else in this affair, it didn't make much sense.

The lyrics of 'Sweet Georgia Brown' struck him with unusual force. He just hoped the significance wasn't ironic.

They all sigh and want to die, for Sweet Georgia Brown! I'll tell you just why, you know I don't lie... sang Art Burrell.

Art Burrell had a deep, powerful voice. Art Burrell...

'Art!' muttered Jack, missing his step.

'I beg your pardon?'

'Art! She said art!'

And a piece of the puzzle clicked into place.

* * *

258

'So let me get this straight,' said Bill Rackham doubtfully the next day. 'Miss Wingate thinks our mysterious Mrs McAllister who rented 22, Dorian House, may be none other than Mrs Daphne Askern herself?' He broke off and stared at Jack. 'You seem very pleased with yourself this morning, by the way. Have you got something up your sleeve?'

'Me?' said Jack, wiping the grin from his face. 'My sleeves are completely empty, old thing. I had a very pleasant evening with Betty Wingate, that's all. She still has the shocking bad taste to prefer Colin Askern to yours truly, but at least I was able to let her know I was in the frame.'

Bill stared at him. 'Are you serious?'

'Why does everyone ask me if I'm serious?' complained Jack. 'Yes, dammit, of course I'm serious. Why shouldn't I be?'

'She's a suspect in a murder investigation,' Bill reminded him.

'That's a mere detail. She won't be a suspect once I've cracked the case.'

'I admire your confidence,' said Bill dryly. 'So your girlfriend—'

'Colin Askern's girlfriend, you mean.'

'So the girlfriend thinks that the mysterious Mrs McAllister of Dorian House could be Mrs Daphne Askern?' He drummed a tattoo on his desk with his pencil. 'I'll say this for the idea. Mrs Askern was very bitter about how she'd been treated.' He cocked an eyebrow at Jack. 'Did you think Mrs Askern's grief yesterday was a bit excessive?'

'I'm not sure,' said Jack frankly. 'It could've

been put on easily enough, but I must say she struck me as someone who was deeply shocked. As far as her being Mrs McAllister goes, she *could* be, if all we're going off is Mrs McAllister's description – that's an above average height, stout, middle-aged, jowly-faced woman. I did wonder briefly if Mrs flat McAllister, if I can call her that, could be Signora Bianchi, but I don't think that's on the cards.'

'Not unless she's gained about five stone in weight and developed a double chin, no. Apart from her, though, Mrs blasted McAllister could easily be a whole raft of middle-aged women,' said Bill moodily. 'That had occurred to me. What d'you think?'

Jack shrugged. 'Mrs Askern certainly had a motive to kill her husband. As you say, John Askern hadn't treated her well, not by any stretch of the imagination.'

'But what about this blasted vanishing letter? If – and it's a big if – the Mrs McAllister who rented the flat is none other than Mrs Askern, then why should she pinch the letter? If she'd told me it was her husband's handwriting, I'd have believed her without question.'

'You may not question it in the first instance, but you very well might later on. There's one thing for sure. Having the letter vanish hasn't half made everything a lot more obscure.'

'As if I didn't know that!'

'And therefore more difficult to pin onto one particular person,' continued Jack patiently.

'I suppose so,' Bill grudgingly admitted. 'Anyway, to put these and other speculative ideas to one side for the moment, what we do know is that Mrs Joan McAllister, petty fraudster and thief – I still haven't forgotten that pound I put in her collecting tin – lived at 46, Purbeck Terrace until seven weeks ago or thereabouts. We saw her at the exhibition, she was admitted to Charing Cross hospital, but she was discharged on the same day.'

'She certainly seemed in good health when I ran into her on the Strand, later that same week. She must've left Purbeck Terrace shortly after I saw her.'

'Very shortly afterwards, but where she went to then, we just don't know. That's one of the things I want to find out. Then, some three weeks ago, she pops up at Dorian House. It's possible, not to put it more strongly than that, that the Mrs McAllister who lived at Purbeck Terrace and the Mrs McAllister who rented Dorian House are not the same woman, but for the moment I've got to assume they are and work on that basis.' He boxed his papers together in a gesture of finality. 'Now, what's this other idea you've got?'

'It's a question of names,' said Jack. 'You remember, don't you, that Mrs McAllister – the Mrs exhibition McAllister – yelled, *Art!* before she keeled over. Now, at the Cafe de Bologna last night, the dance band was Art Burrell and his Seven Brooklyn Buddies.'

'It's nice of you to keep me up to date with your social calendar,' muttered Bill. 'Do let me know if you've any more excursions planned, won't you? I love to hear all about you and your little outings.'

'Keep up, old prune,' said Jack pityingly. 'Don't you get it? Art Burrell, yes?' Bill looked blank. 'You see? *Art.* Art isn't just art, it's a name as well.'

'I'll take your word for it. Art? That's a rum sort of name.'

'It's the American abbreviation for Arthur. It's not an abbreviation anyone English would normally use, but Mrs McAllister had lived in America. She might very well address an Arthur as Art.'

Bill looked frankly puzzled. 'I suppose she *might*, if there was anyone called Arthur in the case, but there isn't. Besides that, I thought you'd worked out that the wretched woman yelled *Art!* because she associated John Askern with art. Now, I did like that idea.'

'Don't you like my art is Arthur idea?'

Bill hesitated. 'It's interesting, Jack, but I can't see how it'll help me pin down how John Askern came to be murdered by a woman you were convinced was dead in a flat off the Tottenham Court Road yesterday.'

'Put like that, it's awfully deflating,' complained Jack.

'Well, pick up your ball and go and play somewhere else,' said Bill. 'I've got some work to do. What I could really do with is a photograph of Mrs McAllister, but there isn't one. There isn't even a passport photograph of her, for all the fact she lived in the States.'

'No. She wouldn't have needed a passport before the war, and afterwards she could've travelled on her husband's passport, if he had one.'

'Exactly. It all adds up to no photo.' Bill sighed heavily. 'What are you up to for the rest of the day?'

'I thought I'd have another look at those mottoes I copied down from the chantry. You know, the ones inscribed on the flagstones. Are you at home this evening? I'll ankle round to your rooms if you are and let you know what, if anything, I've come up with.'

'I should be in, unless anything crops up in the meantime. What are you hoping to find?'

Jack shrugged. 'Some sort of meaning in the mottoes, I suppose.' He grinned. 'That sounds a bit twee, but you know what I mean. I might have to go down to Whimbrell Heath again. It could be that the mottoes only make sense when you see them in context.'

Bill blinked. 'Just as you like. Er ... I'm sorry to repeat myself, but I can't see how that'll help me work out how John Askern came to be murdered by a woman you were convinced was dead in a flat off the Tottenham Court Road yesterday.'

'It might,' said Jack, with dignity.

'As you say,' said Bill. 'I can't see the point, but don't let me stop you.'

Jack creaked open the door of the chantry and stopped. He'd parked the Spyker under the tree by the pub in the village and walked along to Lythewell and Askern. Rather than call in at the offices to get the key, he decided to see if the chantry door was unlocked. It was. He expected to see Henry Cadwallader but, to his surprise, it wasn't Henry Cadwallader inside the chantry but Daphne Askern.

She was sitting on one of the pews, gazing at the flights of painted angels.

She gave a little start as he came in. 'Mr Haldean? It is Mr Haldean, isn't it?' She tried to smile. 'Are you looking for someone?'

'Not really,' said Jack. 'It was more the chantry itself I wanted to see.' She looked at him, puzzled. 'I wanted an insight,' he explained. 'An insight into old Mr Lythewell's character.'

She shuddered. 'This place is a monument to old Mr Lythewell. Colin hates the chantry, but I was thinking of John.'

'What did Mr Askern think of it?' asked Jack. 'Do you mind if I sit down?'

She moved along the pew. 'No, please do.' She heaved a sigh. 'John admired the workmanship, but the whole thing struck him as too...' She frowned and hunted for the right word. 'Ornate? Would that be fair to say?'

'Very fair,' agreed Jack. 'When Mr Askern was a young man he worked for Mr Lythewell, didn't he? Did he get on well with him?'

She looked at him sharply, then her gaze dropped. 'Old Mr Lythewell was long before my time,' she said quietly. 'Funnily enough, I've been trying to understand what sort of man he was, too. I've been in here a lot, recently. I've been thinking about old Mr Lythewell a great deal.' She smiled once more, an odd, tight smile. 'You asked me if John got on well with him.' She hesitated, picking her words carefully. 'I think it's fair to say he didn't.'

Her eyes met his. It was as dramatic, as sudden, and as illuminating as a flash of lightning. *She knew!*

Jack felt a shiver of expectation and waited.

Daphne Askern was quiet for a moment, then sighed. 'Yes, I've been in here a great deal. I've been trying to understand.' She waved her hand to indicate the building. 'Mr Lythewell had all these religious feelings, I know, but when you look around, it's not about religion or holy things, it's all about him.' She shuddered. 'It's a bit frightening, I think. Instead of Mr Lythewell looking up to God, God is looking up to Mr Lythewell, and that's wrong.'

'That's the definition of the old sin of pride,' said Jack softly, moved by her insight. *Closer. Getting closer...*

Daphne Askern nodded. 'Pride is a sin. It poisons things. John...' Her voice broke. 'John could be proud.'

Again, she was quiet.

Now for it.

'Mrs Askern,' said Jack, very gently. 'Don't take this the wrong way, but I know more than you think.'

She looked at him in startled apprehension. 'Go on,' she said, her voice scarcely more than a whisper.

'I think,' said Jack, looking directly at her and keeping his voice level, 'that you've been doing a lot of hunting around in old papers recently.'

He sensed rather than saw her body stiffen. She

265

was very much on her guard and if he said the wrong thing he'd lose her. He didn't want to lead her, but to make her feel it was safe to speak.

'You wanted to find out if your husband had known that Carlotta Bianchi was alive when he married you.'

'He knew,' she said with sudden vehemence. 'He knew all right, but John never would face up to things. He always buried his head in the sand and hoped they'd go away. Still...' Her voice wavered again. 'Signora Bianchi's magic, her glamour, whatever you call it – that had worn off when he married me. That's what makes it so bitterly ironic.' She stopped abruptly.

'I know,' said Jack, still keeping his voice level, 'that you know why that was so ironic. After she'd left him, abandoned him for another man, leaving him to look after their baby son, your husband desperately wanted Carlotta Bianchi to return to him. He was employed by Josiah Lythewell, an old man driven by pride, a man who had hidden away great wealth, a man who, by any objective standard, could only be thought of as insane.'

Her eyes were fixed on him and he could feel her tension, waiting for his next words.

'It must,' said Jack, allowing nothing but sympathy in his voice, 'in many ways, have seemed like a mercy.'

She leapt to her feet. 'It wasn't! That's kind. Much too kind! I *knew* John, knew him through and through. He wanted Lythewell's treasure – wanted it desperately – so he could entice her back to him. He loathed facing unpleasant facts

266

and, when he was forced to face them, when he couldn't avoid facing them any longer, he would get suddenly, irrationally angry. He was always so amenable, so easy-going, that it was a dreadful shock to see him in a rage. Then, afterwards, when he'd calmed down, he would never admit that he'd lost his temper. Mr Lythewell might've been all those things you said – old, mad, eaten up with rotten pride, anything you like – but he was *alive* and John killed him.'

She stood trembling, twisting her hands together. 'He pushed old Mr Lythewell down the stairs. It was a complete impulse and he never regretted it. It was as if someone else had done it. All he ever regretted was that he never did find the treasure and he still couldn't get Carlotta Bianchi back. Once I found out what he'd done, I knew there could be no going back, not ever. It's only...' She stopped, breathing quickly, then gathered herself together. 'I'm sorry John's dead,' she said wonderingly. 'I don't know what he was doing in that woman's flat yesterday or how or why he died, but for a long time I was happy with him. Who would want to kill John?'

'You haven't any idea?' asked Jack.

She shook her head. 'No. I thought, when I got the news, that he might've killed himself, but it seems he couldn't have done.'

'No, he couldn't,' agreed Jack.

She shook her head. 'It doesn't make any sense.'

That seemed to be the constant refrain. 'Mrs Askern,' asked Jack, after a pause. 'How d'you know about your husband and Mr Lythewell?'

She pushed the hair out of her eyes and gathered her thoughts. 'There was a series of letters, letters to that woman, Carlotta Bianchi. He told her quite openly what he'd done.' Her face twisted. 'He said that it proved how much he cared. He must've been mad.' She shrugged. 'In the end, it didn't matter. The letters were returned with *Not known at this address* on them, so I don't suppose she ever knew. She did write to him, two years before we were married, to ask for money and for news of Colin. He kept that letter and he must've replied to it, because there's a brief note from her thanking him.'

'Have you still got those letters?'

'Yes. I was going to give the letters from that woman to my solicitor, as it proved my case. He knew she was alive when we married. The other letters – well, I thought I might burn them. I wouldn't like Colin to see them.'

Jack looked up as the chantry door opened. He groaned inwardly. Henry Cadwallader, complete with sketch book, paint box and easel came in.

Cadwallader frowned as he saw them, then brightened as he recognised Jack. 'I wondered who was in here. I'm glad to see it's you, young sir. It's a pleasure to meet someone who appreciates the chantry as it deserves. You'll be glad to hear I've been working hard. My painting will be a masterpiece, sir, an absolute masterpiece, and a fitting tribute to Mr Lythewell. Let me show you the work I've done.'

'I think I'd better go,' said Mrs Askern.

'Now,' said Cadwallader, with an air of maddening leisure and completely ignoring Mrs Askern, 'I know you're a man of method, young sir, so I'm going to take you back to my original idea. You remember how you were a witness to my inspiration?' He opened the sketch pad, laid it out on the adjoining pew, then put a firm hand on Jack's shoulder. 'You'll be interested in this.'

Mrs Askern stood up, walked out of the pew at the other end and went quickly to the door.

'Mrs Askern!' called Jack. 'Wait a moment!' He shook off Cadwallader's restraining hand. The man looked thunderstruck but he could blinking well get over it. 'I'm sorry, Mr Cadwallader, but I have to go.'

'But...'

'I'll be back soon.'

Jack ducked under Cadwallader's arm and caught up with Mrs Askern on the chantry path. 'Mrs Askern, would you let me have those letters?'

'Let you have them? Why? Why do you want them?'

'I'll hand them over to Scotland Yard. Those letters are so important, Scotland Yard really is the best place to look after them.'

'Scotland Yard?' She looked worried. 'I don't know. John's dead and gone but Colin's still alive and he cared deeply for his father.'

'I can promise you this, Mrs Askern,' said Jack earnestly. 'Unless it's absolutely vital – and I do mean vital – the contents of those letters will never be publicly revealed. As it is, they could be the missing link in a chain of evidence. They could even, perhaps, help save an innocent man from being hanged.'

She winced and drew back. 'I don't see how.'

'Don't you? I'd guessed that old Mr Lythewell didn't die of natural causes. A murder case is never closed. What if the police, at some stage, suspect someone else? With those letters his innocence can be proved, but without them it's all guesswork.'

She thought for a few moments. 'All right. Heaven knows, I don't want them in the house.'

Jack smiled in relief. 'Thank you. I'll come and get them now if that's all right?'

Half an hour later, with the precious letters safely in his pocket, Jack returned to the chantry.

'So you've decided to come back,' said Cadwallader grumpily. 'I'd have thought that art was more important than running off after females. You need to be careful of females,' he added. 'I'm glad to say that Mr Lythewell had no truck with females, not even his wife after she upped and left for America. If everyone followed his example, the world would be a better place.'

If, thought Jack, underpopulated. The idea that he was 'running after' Daphne Askern would usually strike him as funny, but he was suddenly annoyed with this ridiculous man and his ridiculous obsession. 'That *lady*,' he said, emphasising the word, 'is Mrs Askern. Didn't you hear the news? She lost her husband yesterday.'

Mr Cadwallader's eyes widened and he stepped back in horror. 'Lost him? Mr Askern's dead, you mean?' Jack nodded. 'But that's shocking news. I didn't always hold with his views, but he was a real artist. He understood art. What's the firm going to do?' He reached for the

270

nearest pew and sat down, trembling. 'Who's going to carry on? Young Mr Lythewell isn't an artist. This is dreadful, just dreadful! I can't believe Mr Askern's been taken so sudden.'

He sat for a good few minutes, staring sightlessly in front of him. 'The ways of the Almighty are hard to fathom,' he said eventually. 'It isn't given to us to understand the workings of Providence, but this is a sad day for the firm. Do you know what young Mr Lythewell intends to do? Has he got anyone to replace Mr Askern?'

'For heaven's sake, Mr Askern only died yesterday. It's a bit soon to look for a replacement, don't you think?'

'At one time I'd have taken the burden upon my shoulders, but those days are past, I'm afraid,' said Cadwallader, oblivious to what Jack had said. 'Besides, I've got my own work to think of. I must complete my work. It's a tribute to Mr Lythewell. A monumental tribute that will show the world what sort of man he was.'

Or perhaps not, commented Jack to himself.

Mr Cadwallader sat in silence for a few more minutes, then rose shakily to his feet. 'I must carry on. I know you want to see the work I've been doing.'

As a matter of fact, Jack didn't want anything of the kind, but Henry Cadwallader's complete certainty was hard to argue with. There was a sort of hypnotic inevitability in the way Cadwallader took Jack's enthusiastic interest for granted.

'To do the chantry justice,' said Cadwallader, deep within his sketch book, 'needs a real grasp

271

of perspective to get the whole picture, but the detail is vital. Now, as I told you before, I was honoured to have Mr Lythewell himself sit for the work depicting him being received on the steps of Glory...'

He made it sound like a civic function, with God standing in for the Lord Mayor, thought Jack, his sense of humour fully restored.

'...and, of course, I have the original sketches.' He opened his portfolio and took out an old sketch book. 'Now, you just look at these. They show the modelling of the head.'

Jack nodded. The sketches were, as a matter of fact, very good. Henry Cadwallader might approach a conversation with the unstoppable force of a lava flow, but there was no doubt he could draw.

'Looking at these sketches, I have to admit I've been in error,' said Cadwallader gravely.

'Error?' repeated Jack. That was unexpected.

'Error,' echoed Cadwallader. 'For many a year, I've dismissed Mr Daniel Lythewell's skills. I cannot bring myself to feel overly guilty, because Mr Lythewell abandoned his proper calling early on, but, you mark my words, he could have been as great a metal worker as his father.'

Jack blinked. This was really unexpected. 'Er ... How d'you know?'

Cadwallader gazed at him. 'Isn't it obvious?'

'Not to me, no.'

'Look at his metalwork, man. On the tomb,' he added with ponderous impatience. 'The detail of the head.'

Jack got up from the pew and went to crouch beside the statue of the grieving man. With the man's face hidden by his crooked arm as he sprawled across the lid of the open tomb, there was really only part of his forehead and his ear to admire. It looked perfectly fine, but Jack could not see why, after having looked at it for years, Cadwallader should suddenly consider it a masterpiece.

'It's such a graceful tribute,' said Cadwallader reverently. 'When I saw what Mr Daniel had done, when I really understood it, I was awestruck. You might consider me slow, young sir, but after all these years, the chantry can still surprise me with the depth and the quality of its art.'

'I'm sorry,' said Jack, 'I just don't get what I'm supposed to be looking at.'

'This,' said Cadwallader in astonishment at Jack's slowness. He tapped the statue. 'This isn't just any figure. This is a depiction of Mr Lythewell *himself*. I've never understood it before. I wish Mr Daniel had told me what was in his mind, because I could've helped him in his work.' He thumbed through his sketch book. 'You'll see from these drawings that he got the proportions of the body wrong, which is a crying shame.'

'Yes,' agreed Jack, looking from the sketch book to the statue. 'Mr Lythewell wasn't so tall and he's a good deal portlier than the statue.'

'Yes, well it's a tribute, not a replica.' Cadwallader allowed himself a slow smile. 'That's the privilege of the artist, sir, to make a few graceful improvements on nature, but the modelling of the head is perfect. Compare it with my drawings and you'll see.'

Jack took the sketch book Cadwallader was holding. 'Yes, it is,' he agreed. 'It really is remarkable.'

He stood in silence before the empty tomb. An idea, a tentative idea, was beginning to grow. Besides that, he really needed to distract Cadwallader for a little while, to get some time by the tomb unobserved. Mr Cadwallader might have his virtues but the man was positively adhesive.

'Mr Cadwallader,' said Jack eventually, 'can I ask a favour? I'd very much like to have a drawing of Mr Lythewell.'

Cadwallader clutched his sketch book to his chest defensively, as if Jack was about to wrench it from him. 'These drawings are precious to me, young sir!'

Jack smiled. 'Of course they are, but would it be too much to ask you to copy one for me? Could you do it now? I'd be very grateful.'

Mr Cadwallader relaxed. 'A drawing of Mr Lythewell? It'd be a pleasure.' He looked at Jack with warm approval. 'It's gratifying to come across someone with a true appreciation of who Mr Lythewell was and what he did.'

And that, thought Jack cynically, was a good deal more accurate than Mr Cadwallader could ever guess.

'Which picture would you like?' asked Cadwallader, holding out the sketch book. 'I'll draw it for you right away.'

Jack thumbed through the book and selected a drawing – a profile of Josiah Lythewell – and waited until Cadwallader had set to work.

Then, as if he had nothing in particular on his mind, he set off for a stroll round the chantry. Glancing round, he saw Cadwallader, pencils and charcoal on the pew beside him, his head bent over his sketch, completely engrossed in his drawing.

Jack strolled back to the tomb and, with his back to Cadwallader, knelt down by the flagstone that held the silver inlaid picture of the chantry. Taking an envelope and a metal file from his pocket he scraped a few shavings from the silver inlay, coughing to cover the sound of the file.

He glanced round. Cadwallader, wrapped up in his work, was completely oblivious. Although it really didn't seem necessary, Jack coughed once more, taking a few more shavings.

The metal came up brilliantly silver. Jack carefully put the shavings into the envelope and safely into his pocket.

Job done.

Thirteen

At half past eight that evening, Jack was enjoying a well-earned whisky and soda in Bill's sitting room. Bill had two rooms on the upper floor of an inconvenient but beautifully proportioned Georgian building in Melbourne Road off Russell Square. The sash windows stood open, gilding the well-worn carpet and comfortable chairs with the last of the evening sun.

John Askern's letters had been duly handed over and were safely in Bill's possession, to be delivered into the safekeeping of Scotland Yard tomorrow.

'Those letters are stunning,' said Bill, topping up Jack's glass. 'Askern must've been mad to have written them.'

Jack swirled the whisky round in his glass. 'If you're defining mad as the courts do when someone's topped themselves, that the balance of his mind was disturbed, I think you're probably right.'

He reached for a cigarette from the box Bill had companionably placed on the table by his elbow. 'John Askern was in the grip of an obsession, and that's an unbalanced mind, all right.' He half-smiled. 'Mrs Askern called the situation ironic. What really is ironic is that if those letters had reached Signora Bianchi, I bet poor old

Askern would've spent the rest of his life being blackmailed, instead of the Bianchi suckering up for money in fits and starts.'

'I bet you're right.' Bill raised his glass. 'You were right about John Askern seeing off old Lythewell. Well done. It didn't,' he added, after a liquid pause, 'do him any good though. I mean, he didn't find this treasure of old Lythewell's, did he?'

'No, he didn't. I think things would've worked out very differently if he had. Which is, of course, where those metal shavings I acquir-ed—'

'Pinched.'

'Acquired,' corrected Jack, 'come into it. I dropped them into Johnson and Cooke, the analytical chemist on the Strand. They stay open till all hours. I hope you don't mind, but I gave them your telephone number as I knew I'd be coming here.'

'As long as they don't ring at four in the morning.'

'Don't worry. They might stay open late but they aren't nocturnal.'

'What are you hoping the metal will be, Jack?'

'I think – this is only a guess, mind – but I think the metal might be platinum.'

Bill swallowed a mouthful of whisky the wrong way. *'Platinum!'* he exclaimed, once he had finished choking. 'But I remember looking at that picture of the chantry. You do mean the one inlaid into the flagstone, don't you?' Jack, his eyes bright, nodded in agreement. 'But by crikey, Jack, there's a whole plate of metal in that flagstone! It must be worth an absolute fortune.'

'Exactly. That's treasure in anyone's book, isn't it?'

'You didn't give all of the metal shavings to Johnson and Cooke, did you?' asked Bill anxiously. 'If it is platinum, I want the Yard to be able to analyse a sample too.'

'Relax,' said Jack. 'Johnson and Cooke only needed a small amount. Besides that, the inlaid stone in the chantry isn't going anywhere.'

'It will, if any of the Whimbrell Heath lot get the slightest hint of what you've been up to,' said Bill in an agitated way. 'Colin Askern would have it crowbarred out before you could say knife. You're sure no one guessed why you were there?'

'Strewth, Bill, calm down! Poor Mrs Askern was far too caught up in her own affairs to ask me any questions, and Henry Cadwallader is convinced that I'm as enthralled by Josiah Lythewell as he is.'

'But how come no one's ever realised what the plate's made of?' Bill shook his head. 'I can't believe it! A fortune – a whole ruddy fortune – literally underfoot. How did you get onto it?'

'I looked at what we've been referring to as the mottoes,' said Jack, taking his notebook from his pocket. He gave a self-conscious grin. 'Now, I thought I was blinking clever about this. If you want to say so, you're at perfect liberty to do so. I won't disagree.'

'You're absolutely brilliant. Is that enough praise? Now tell me how you came to guess the truth about the treasure, damn you.'

'Okay. I'll need a few sheets of paper though, to show you properly. Have you got some letter paper?'

Bill rummaged in his desk and produced a pad of Basildon Bond. 'Will this do?'

'That's perfect,' said Jack, putting the pad on the sofa beside him. 'Now, let's pretend this room is the chantry.'

Bill shuddered. 'God forbid. I thought the place was a nightmare. Go on.'

Jack picked up an armful of cushions and laid them on the carpet in a line. 'I want you to imagine these cushions are the empty tomb with the picture of the chantry at the bottom.' He quickly drew a picture of the chantry on one of the sheets of notepaper and placed it at the bottom of the line of cushions. 'You see?'

'Tomb, picture. Fine. What next?'

Jack picked up the pad of paper. 'The flag-stones in the chantry with the mottoes on them were laid out like this.'

Tearing off sheets of paper, he moved round the cushions. 'Now, tell me what you see, Bill.'

Jack had laid out the rectangles of paper on the carpet. They formed two sideways-on V shapes. The point of both V's pointed to the picture of the chantry at the base of the tomb.

Bill looked at the sheets of paper on the floor. 'It's obvious,' he said slowly. 'It's like two arrowheads pointing to the chantry flagstone.' He glanced at Jack, his frown deepening. 'I went over the chantry with a fine-tooth comb. How come I didn't see where the inlaid slabs were pointing?'

'The shape is much easier to see here than it is in the actual chantry,' said Jack. 'They're a lot further apart there. However, you agree, don't you, that the inlaid slabs act as pointers?'

'Of course,' said Bill. 'Laid out like that you can't miss it.'

'Good. Now for what was written on the inlaid flagstones. We'll start with the arm of the left-hand V furthest away from the tomb and work up and round. Here goes.'

He picked up a piece of the letter paper from the carpet and, with his notebook beside him, wrote: *The church is your true and worthy treasure*, then replaced it. He worked his way up the V until the papers read, in order: *The church is your true and worthy treasure. Stop, my son, to pause and pray for treasure. A far lesser treasure also behold.*

At the point of the V he wrote: *Worldly goods will always fade and wither*, then continued down the other side with: *Art which is wrested from that evil root. That doorway, greater than man can measure*, and finished with: *The doorway's here to eternal life!* Moving to the other side, and once more starting from the left-hand side of the V, he wrote: *Open – look! – to all curious eyes*, continuing with: *It is yours, O my son, but for your soul. Be wise. Shun greed, let avarice be mute.* At the point of this V he wrote: *But true metal wrought, cast, forged, small in size*, then carried on down the other side with: *Is opened for you after earthly strife. Not copper, silver, precious stones or gold* and finished with: *In penitence here's shown the greater whole.*

Bill pointed to the paper with: *Not copper, silver, precious stones or gold* written on it. 'I see why you guessed the treasure was platinum, Jack. Once you've taken out copper, silver, precious stones and gold, there's not a great deal left.'

'Got it in one. My thoughts exactly,' agreed Jack. He cocked his head to one side. 'Can you see anything else significant about what we've got here, Bill?'

Bill gazed at the sheets of paper. 'I'm sorry, I'm stumped,' he said after some thought.

'How many sheets of paper – that's inlaid flag-stones in reality, of course – are there?'

Bill puffed his cheeks out. 'There's seven sheets or flagstones in each V. Three down each side and one at the point of the V.'

Jack nodded. 'And that gives us fourteen inlaid flagstones altogether.' He stepped back from the pieces of paper and lit a cigarette. He glanced across to his friend and raised his eyebrows. 'I don't suppose the fact there's fourteen means anything to you, does it?'

'I'm sorry, it doesn't,' said Bill after some cogitation.

'How about,' said Jack, 'if you stop thinking of these lines as mottoes, as Henry Cadwallader describes them, and think of them as poetry?'

'Poetry?' repeated Bill in surprise. 'What, as in *"Drake is in his hammock and a thousand miles away. Captain art thou sleeping there below?"* type of thing, you mean?'

'I was thinking about a form of poetry a step or two up from "Drake's Drum",' said Jack with a

281

grin. 'Not that I've got anything against "Drake's Drum", you understand. But think of Shake-speare, Bill.'

'Er ... *Hamlet, Romeo and Juliet, Macbeth*, you mean?'

'Not plays but poetry,' said Jack. 'What form of poetry do you associate with Shakespeare?'

'Blimey, I'm blowed if I know.' Bill shrugged. 'The sonnet, I suppose.' He stopped. 'Hang on a minute! I *do* know! I remember learning this in school. A sonnet's got fourteen lines, hasn't it?' He looked at the sheets of paper laid out on the carpet and snapped his fingers together. 'Jack! There's fourteen flagstones!'

'Give that man a cigar,' said Jack with a broad grin. He indicated the sheets of paper. 'These aren't random jottings from the loony bin as we first thought, but the fourteen lines of a sonnet.'

'You're not telling me Shakespeare wrote this,' said Bill in frank disbelief. 'He wrote things like, *"Shall I compare thee to a summer's day?"*.'

'Well, only if you feel you must,' murmured Jack. 'It's a little fulsome, but I'm touched.'

'Idiot! What I mean is, is that Shakespeare's good. This is a bit – well, not so good.'

'That's because old Josiah Lythewell wrote it, and Bill, my old pal, I bet Lythewell thought his sonnet was every bit as good as anything the Bard ever produced. Modest self-effacement doesn't seem to have been one of old Lythewell's chief characteristics.'

'Not judging from the chantry, no.'

'The thing is that a sonnet, the classic Shake-spearian sonnet, I mean, follows a very set pattern. There's fourteen lines, each line containing ten syllables. There's a pattern of an unstressed syllable, followed by a stressed syllable, which is repeated five times. The last two lines are a rhyming couplet which is usually a reversal of what the sonnet's been saying and, at the same time, an affirmation of the theme of the poem.'

'I beg your pardon?' asked Bill, blinking. 'Can you say that again, but slowly?'

'Well, take a classic, that sonnet that starts, *"My mistress' eyes are nothing like the sun"*.'

'Hang on, that's one I know.'

'Can you remember it?'

'Not to quote great chunks from, no.'

'I can manage a couple of lines from memory, I think. *"My mistress' eyes are nothing like the sun. Coral is far more red than her lips' red,"* and so on. *"I grant I never saw a goddess go; My mistress, when she walks, treads on the ground"*. Shakespeare gives us all these extravagant comparisons and says his girlfriend's nothing like that, then he flips it over in the last two lines by saying, *"And yet, by heaven, I think my love as rare, As any she belied with false compare"*. You see? The sincerity of the last two lines reverses and yet affirms what he's been saying.'

Bill nodded. 'I do see that, of course. But how did that help you with working out what old Lythewell was on about, Jack?'

'Well, once I'd noticed there were fourteen lines and had the idea it was a sonnet, I had a set pattern to follow. Lythewell wanted to hide what he was up to, so it was obvious that he'd mixed the lines up, so they appeared disjointed. To put

283

the sonnet back together again – which sounds as if Humpty Dumpty, to quote more poetry, had a hand in it, all I had to do was follow the rules. I didn't do all this off the top of my head, of course. I lugged out my old guide to Eng. Lit.' He reached for his notebook again and found the page he wanted. 'And my old guide to Eng. Lit. tells me that the rhyme scheme in a Shakespearean sonnet is *a-b-a-b, c-d-c-d, e-f-e-f, g-g*, where the two a's rhyme, the two b's rhyme, and so on.'

'I'll take your word for it,' said Bill.

'And that rhyme scheme,' said Jack with a grin, 'helped me rearrange Lythewell's sub-Shakespearian sonnet into its proper order.'

He picked up the sheets of paper from the floor and, referring to his notebook and numbering the sheets as he went, laid them out on the floor once more. Once he had finished, he stood back. 'There you are. One sonnet as written by Josiah Lythewell, to be used for reflections on life and the afterlife, with directions to the discovery of treasure thrown in as a bonus. Not bad, eh?'

Stop, my son, to pause and pray for treasure
The doorway's here to eternal life
That doorway, greater than man can measure
Is opened for you after earthly strife
A far lesser treasure also behold,
Open – look! – to all curious eyes
Not copper, silver, precious stones or gold
But true metal wrought, cast, forged, small in size
In penitence here's shown the greater whole

Art which is wrested from that evil root
It is yours, O my son, but for your soul
Be wise. Shun greed, let avarice be mute.
Worldly goods will always fade and wither
The church is your true and worthy treasure

Bill stood up and raised his glass in salute. 'That is brilliant, Jack,' he said sincerely.

Jack flushed. 'Come off it, Bill.'

'No, really. Everyone but everyone, including me, has looked at those flagstones and thought they were nothing more than random lines meaning God knows what, if anything, but you've teased the meaning out of them.' He read through the sonnet once more. 'Take me through it,' he said. 'I think I've got the gist of the thing, but poetry isn't my strongest point.'

'Okey-doke,' said Jack obligingly. 'I think there's no doubt that it's addressed to Daniel Lythewell. *"Stop, my son, to pause and pray for treasure"*, is a real instruction. The doorway, as you guessed before, is the doorway to eternal life or heaven, where old Lythewell clearly thought he was bound for, with no quibbling from the choirs of angels at the back.'

'And the *"far lesser treasure"* is the platinum?' asked Bill with a grin.

'Yep, that's how I see it. He tells us it's not copper, silver or gold, but *"true metal"*. Then, I think, he registers his claim to enter the heavenly kingdom, as shown in its full splendour in that appalling painting by Henry Cadwallader, by saying that the *"true metal"* was placed there because he's penitent.'

'He wasn't penitent enough to own up to what he'd done, though, was he?'

'Steady on, Bill,' said Jack with a smile. 'There's no point overdoing this penitence lark. But you see how he describes his picture of the chantry inlaid into the flagstone? At least, I'm fairly sure that's what he's describing, at any rate. *"The greater whole"* is the chantry depicted by *"art which is wrested from that evil root"*. The evil root just has to be the love of money, which is the root of all evil, as even Henry Cadwallader saw, turned into art by none other than J. Lythewell, Esquire, and passed on to Daniel Lythewell. *"It is yours, O my son"*. Now there's a piece of straightforward parental advice. For the sake of Daniel's soul, he tells him not to be avaricious or greedy but to be wise.'

'So Daniel Lythewell can have the treasure as long as he doesn't get too excited about it?'

'More or less. I think, to be fair, he's telling Daniel not to let the treasure take over his life, which is good advice, even if it is old Lythewell giving it. That's backed up by the penultimate line, *"Worldly goods will always fade and wither"*, which sounds wonderfully Victorian, if true enough for all that, but I'm sure the last line is a pun or a play on words, at least, where the two sorts of treasure, eternal life and worldly wealth, come together. *"The church is your true and worthy treasure"* makes a lot of sense if the church is a platinum slab.'

'A platinum slab,' repeated Bill in a dazed sort of way. 'Good grief. My father had plenty of good advice to pass on, but he was a bit short in the platinum slab department.'

'It'd be worth listening to all sorts of good advice, even from a sanctimonious old beggar like Lythewell, to get your hands on that, wouldn't it?'

'I'll say...' Bill hesitated, stroking his chin. 'The thing is, Jack, was it old Lythewell's to pass on? I mean, we know that his wealth – this wealth – came from his career as a forger.'

'He was found innocent at his trial,' Jack reminded him. 'In the eyes of the law, he was an innocent man.'

'We know damn well he was no such thing, though.' Bill indicated the sheets of paper. 'How come, if old Lythewell was so keen for his son to have the treasure, he hid its location so well? I can see that he'd want to conceal it, to keep it out of the hands of his fellow crooks, but you'd have thought, wouldn't you, that he might have dropped a hint to his son that there was a fortune in platinum lying on the floor of the chantry.'

'That's something I just don't know,' admitted Jack. 'I think that this treasure was something Daniel Lythewell was supposed to inherit.'

'Well, of course it was. You've just explained all that.'

'What I mean is, it's something that old Lythewell was perfectly happy for his son to have once he, Josiah, was dead and gone. He obviously didn't leave instructions in his will, otherwise Daniel Lythewell would surely have followed them and we wouldn't be having this discussion.'

'That's true enough.'

287

'Or,' said Jack, 'old Pop Lythewell was so far off his crumpet that he expected Daniel to be able to read the sonnet and follow the instructions, but that seems a bit unlikely, I agree.' He shrugged. 'You might find, once you tell Mr Lythewell that there's a fortune in the chantry floor, that old Lythewell did leave instructions that simply weren't understood.'

'M'yes,' agreed Bill in a dissatisfied way.

'Or he might have planned to tell him at a later date, of course. After all, old Lythewell didn't expect to die. Don't forget John Askern took matters into his own hands by bumping him off.'

'Which is,' said Bill, rubbing his hands together, 'something I've now got concrete evidence to prove. Those letters Mrs Askern gave you really are dynamite. I'm thoroughly looking forward to seeing Sir Douglas tomorrow.'

'When are you going to tell Mr Lythewell?'

'I just don't know,' Bill admitted frankly. 'That's a decision for Sir Douglas to make. We've still got a murder investigation on our hands.' He waved a hand at the papers on the floor. 'All this has been fascinating and I honestly can't congratulate you enough, Jack, but d'you think it has any bearing on Askern's murder?'

Jack lit another cigarette. 'It's difficult to see how it can have. On the other hand, it's so much money that I really do find it intrusive.'

'The root of all evil, eh?'

'More or less,' agreed Jack. He was about to say more but was interrupted by the shrill ring of the telephone.

With a muttered excuse, Bill picked up the receiver. 'It's the chemists, Johnson and Cooke,' he whispered to Jack, clamping his hand over the phone. 'They've got the results of the analysis of the metal shavings. Yes,' he said loudly into the receiver, 'I can pass a message on to Major Haldean.'

Jack saw Bill's expression alter during the brief conversation. 'Are you sure? No doubt at all. None whatsoever ... I see. Thank you.'

Bill replaced the receiver on its hook and stared sightlessly in front of him for a few moments.

'Bill?' prompted Jack. 'Bill? What is it?'

Bill turned to face him. 'I'm sorry, old man,' he said sympathetically. 'I was sure you were right. I still am sure you got the meaning of that wretched poem worked out correctly, but...'

'But *what?*' demanded Jack.

Bill shook his head. 'Somehow or other, you've got it wrong.' He smiled wryly. 'I'm sorry to tell you this but the metal's not platinum but aluminium. And, I'm afraid, it's absolutely worthless.'

Fourteen

The two men said nothing for a few moments. Outside, the sound of the traffic in Russell Square seemed to get louder as the silence continued, then Jack shook his head with a weary laugh. 'Game, set and match to old Pop Lythewell,' he said, going to the sideboard. 'You don't mind if I have another, do you?' he asked, his hand on the whisky decanter.

'Go ahead, Jack. You deserve it, you poor beggar.' Bill walked to the sideboard and put a friendly hand on his shoulder. 'You can give me a top-up, too. But why the devil would old Lythewell go to all that trouble to direct his son to a worthless piece of junk? You're right about the flagstones and the sonnet. You just have to be right.' He shook his head wonderingly. 'I don't suppose that picture of the chantry – the inlaid picture – lifts out, does it? And the real treasure is hidden underneath?'

'What, like a coal-hole cover, you mean?' Jack clicked his tongue. 'We could look, I suppose, but I don't honestly think it does. I was looking for a concealed hiding place, you see. That was my first thought. I was pretty pleased with myself when I worked out that the chantry picture itself was the treasure. Only it's not, of course.' He sighed deeply. 'Ah well, at least you don't have to worry about what you tell Mr Lythewell. We can hardly roll up and say, "Excuse me, we've found this wonderful hidden treasure of your father's that everyone's talked about for years. By the way, it's worth about fourpence to a scrap-metal merchant."'

'He wouldn't be very impressed, I agree,' said Bill. He twisted his head round to read the last line of the sonnet from the paper on the carpet. '"The church is your true and worthy treasure". Maybe he's talking about eternal life, after all. Maybe he meant that the church, the chantry itself, I mean, is the treasure?'

'In that case, why direct us so precisely to the engraved slab? And where does the "true metal" come into the picture? The chantry's made of brick, not metal.'

'That's a thought,' said Bill. 'Actually...' He frowned. 'Jack, there's a metal statue on top of the tomb, isn't there? Could that be made of something precious?'

'Not by old Lythewell, it wasn't. That was Daniel Lythewell's handiwork. I've heard Henry Cadwallader wax lyrical on the topic.'

'Henry Cadwallader,' murmured Bill. 'Jack, I know he's about a hundred and ninety and as mad as a hatter, but he was young once. He seems to spend his life in the chantry and he's an artist. Could he have cottoned on to what the slab was, levered it up, and made a replica to go in its place?'

'What, interfere with his beloved Mr Lythewell's handiwork and go against his wishes, you mean? I don't honestly think he would, Bill. He's as nutty as a fruit cake and fairly tapped on the subject of the late J. Lythewell, but I think he's honest enough.' He shook his head. 'No. I'll have a look to see if the chantry picture is the entrance to a hiding place, but I don't think it is.' He drank his whisky and grinned ruefully. 'At least it's not my treasure I was hunting. That really would be annoying.'

The next morning, Jack finished his bacon and eggs whilst reading the account in the *Daily Messenger* by his old pal, Ernest Stanhope, of the arrest of one Nathan Ormskirk, a builder from Ardwick, Manchester, for murdering his wife. He cast his mind back. Mrs Ormskirk had been the body in the trunk found at Euston Station, hadn't she? Apparently not. Mr Ormskirk, it was alleged, as Stanhope was careful to phrase it, had incorporated Mrs Ormskirk into the foundations of a new public convenience in Deansgate.

That, thought Jack, was interesting. He took his breakfast coffee over to the desk by the window and pinned up on the wall, where the sunlight caught it, the drawing of Josiah Lythewell Mr Cadwallader had copied for him yesterday. Then he picked out from the bookshelf the printed history of Lythewell and Askern he had taken from John Askern's house.

He was just about to open the book when the telephone rang.

'Jack?' It was Bill. His voice was urgent. 'I've got news. There's been another murder. Henry Cadwallader's been found dead in the chantry.'

It was as if time stood still. The sunlight still

shone on Cadwallader's drawing of Josiah Lythewell, the drawing he had copied with such pride. It was only yesterday...

'Jack? Are you there?' demanded Bill.

Jack shook himself. 'Henry Cadwallader's been murdered, you say?'

'Yes. Mrs Askern found him.'

At least it wasn't Betty Wingate this time, thought Jack with a surge of relief.

'I don't know anything more than that,' continued Bill. 'Can you get away? Now, I mean?'

'Yes, of course. Do you want me to drive you down?'

'Thanks, Jack. It'll probably be quicker than the train. Can you pick me up at the Yard?'

'I'll be there as fast as I can.'

On the drive down, Bill brought Jack up to date with what he knew, which wasn't, as he admitted, very much.

Daphne Askern had gone into the chantry early that morning. The time, as nearly as she could judge, must've been about quarter to nine. 'And what,' said Bill, 'she was doing in there, I don't know.'

'I met her in there yesterday,' said Jack. 'That's when she told me about the letters. She said she'd visited the chantry a lot recently. She'd been thinking about John Askern and old Lythewell.'

'I see – or I think I do, anyway. Incidentally, Jack, Sir Douglas sends his congratulations to you on getting hold of those letters. It doesn't explain Askern's murder, but it fills in some very valuable background detail. Anyway, Mrs Askern went into the chantry and there was Cad-wallader, as stiff as a board.'

'He was murdered, was he? He hadn't just keeled over?'

Bill shook his head. 'By the sound of things, there was blood everywhere. He'd had a wallop to the back of his head. And that's more or less all I know. The local police are meeting me at the chantry, together with the Whimbrell Heath doctor and a photographer. I just hope they've had enough sense to leave everything well alone until I get there.'

They were greeted at the door of the chantry by none other than the Chief Constable himself, Commander Pattishall, a grey-haired, broad-shouldered, ex-naval officer, whose beard and moustache gave him the look of King George the Fifth. He was accompanied by a Dr Oxenhall and a twitchy young man called Clough, the town photographer.

'I've arranged for the body to be removed by the local undertakers in about an hour or so,' said Commander Pattishall. 'Dr Oxenhall's agreed to perform the post-mortem.'

Bill nodded. 'What about Mrs Askern? Where is she now?'

'Mrs Askern's being looked after by Mrs Lythewell at Whimbrell House. I've already had a word with her, of course, poor lady. I'm afraid it's going to be some time before you can question her.' He cocked an eyebrow at the doctor. 'I had to insist, but you weren't overly keen on me having a word, eh, Oxenhall?'

Dr Oxenhall shook his head. 'Mrs Askern was

very distressed. Coming on top of Mr Askern's death, this has been a severe shock to her. I thought it best to give her a sleeping draught.'

'She didn't have very much to tell us, in any case,' put in Commander Pattishall, seeing Bill's politely unexpressed but obvious annoyance. 'She came into the chantry shortly before nine this morning, saw Henry Cadwallader's body, screamed and ran for help to the nearest place she could think of, which is Whimbrell House. Mr and Mrs Lythewell were at breakfast. Mrs Lythewell took care of Mrs Askern and Mr Lythewell telephoned Colin Askern. Together the two men came into the chantry and saw Cadwallader's body. They locked the chantry and telephoned the police from Whimbrell House. In view of the gravity of the situation, the local man got in touch with me right away. I called Sir Douglas Lynton and here we are.'

'Do you know if Mr Lythewell or Colin Askern touched anything?' asked Bill.

'Nothing more than they could help, apparently. Naturally enough, they ascertained whether poor Cadwallader really was dead, but there wasn't much doubt about it, I'm afraid, as you'll see for yourself. I've had a look inside, of course, but I left things exactly as they were.'

'Was the chantry open?' asked Jack. 'When Mrs Askern arrived, I mean?'

'I asked her that,' said the Commander. 'She unlocked it with her own key. Anyway,' he added, smoothing his moustache, 'I did a little detective work on my own account. Cadwallader had a house in Pincer Lane off Bridge Street, the

295

main street in the village. He lived alone, but a local woman, a Mrs Treadmire, came in and did for him, as the expression is. I've spoken to her. She went in twice a day. Once in the morning, to get his breakfast and to clean and wash up and prepare lunch, and again in the early evening to prepare his evening meal, which she'd leave in the oven for him. Cadwallader had a fairly set routine. He was always up at seven, breakfast at eight, and then would either work in his studio, which is at the back of the house, or come here, to the chantry. He'd have his evening meal at six o'clock or so. He'd recently taken to coming back here in the evenings. He wasn't a communicative man, but Mrs Treadmire says he was excited about a painting he was working on.'

'That's right,' agreed Jack. 'He spoke to me about it when I last saw him. It was a painting of the chantry. Did he come here last night?'

'Apparently so, yes. He'd eaten his evening meal but she thinks he must've gone out after that and not returned. He invariably had a night-cap of whisky and hot water before he went to bed, but he didn't last night.'

'So it looks as if Cadwallader was killed after six o'clock yesterday evening,' said Bill. 'You'll be able to tell us more about that, Doctor.'

'I haven't seen him yet,' said Dr Oxenhall. 'I've been too taken up with Mrs Askern and the other ladies. This business has bowled everyone over. Mrs Lythewell is terribly upset, of course, and so's Lythewell's niece, Miss Wingate.'

Commander Pattishall cleared his throat in what Jack could only think of as a marked manner. 'I understand that it was Miss Wingate who actually discovered John Askern's body in London?'

'That's right, sir,' agreed Bill.

The Commander's brow furrowed into a series of straight lines. 'And it was Miss Wingate who reported the supposed murder of Signora Bianchi, wasn't it?'

'Yes, sir. That incident is still under investigation.'

The Commander's eyebrows shot up. 'Really? Considering Signora Bianchi is alive and kicking, I wouldn't have thought there was much to investigate.' He stroked his moustache into place. 'Still, no doubt you know your own business best.' He paused with his hand on the chantry door. 'It's interesting how that young woman, Miss Wingate, seems to crop up, isn't it?'

His meaning was unmistakable, but Jack, with great restraint, refrained from saying anything.

'Shall we go in?' asked the Commander, and opened the chantry door. 'It all looks pretty normal at first, if you can call this place normal. I've passed it by hundreds of times, but I've never been inside before. Quite extraordinary place. Lythewell and Askern have always been a most well-respected firm, as indeed are the two senior partners themselves. Mr Askern will be a sad loss as he was a very well-thought-of man, but I really do think that old Mr Lythewell must've been a little eccentric, to say the least. I never knew him, of course, as he was long before my time.'

He led the way into the main body of the

297

chantry where, sprawled across the empty tomb, lay the body of Henry Cadwallader. His arms were flung wide and the back of his head was matted and dark with blood.

Bill turned to the photographer. 'I'll tell you what I need photos of later, Mr Clough. Just keep clear until I say otherwise, yes?'

The photographer, who'd taken one look at Cadwallader's body, gulped ominously and retreated hastily to a pew at the back.

The doctor drew his breath in sharply and, clearly nerving himself, took his thermometer out and feeling under Cadwallader's jacket slipped it under his arm. 'The body's completely rigid,' he remarked. 'That ties in with the idea he was killed after six o'clock last night.'

Jack knelt down beside Cadwallader. By his outstretched hand was a pencil, where it had evidently dropped when he was struck down. A sketch book, open at a half-finished drawing of the tomb, lay beside it. Half hidden by Cadwallader's body was the old sketch book containing his original drawings of Josiah Lythewell.

'I don't think he anticipated the attack, Bill,' he said quietly. 'It looks as if he was working on his sketch when the blow was struck.'

'Could the murderer have crept up unnoticed, d'you think?' asked Bill.

'I don't think so,' said Jack. 'Cadwallader was a bit deaf, but he was used to having this place to himself. I think he'd have noticed someone come in, if he didn't notice anything else. I think it's more probable that he knew the person who attacked him and was taken completely off his guard.'

Dr Oxenhall shuddered. 'Dreadful, quite dreadful,' he muttered. He removed the thermometer and held it up to the light, his lips moving as he calculated the times. 'I'd say he's been dead for ten to twelve hours at least.' He stood back from the body and shook his head. 'I had taken it for granted that this must be a random attack, perhaps by a passing tramp or vagrant, but that doesn't seem to be possible, does it?'

Bill shook his head. 'The fact that Mrs Askern had to unlock the door to get in this morning rules that out, sir. A tramp wouldn't lock up after himself.'

'That's right,' agreed Jack. 'Besides that, poor old Cadwallader would hardly continue placidly drawing while a tramp came poking round the building.' He rummaged in Cadwallader's satchel and drew out a large key. 'That's Cadwallader's key to the chantry, so the murderer must've used their own key to lock up behind them.'

'That should narrow things down,' said Bill in satisfaction.

'Maybe,' agreed Jack. 'However, Cadwallader told me that not only did the Lythewells and the Askerns have keys, there was another openly on display in the offices. Hello,' he added suddenly. 'What's this? There's something gleaming under here.'

Wrapping his handkerchief round his hand he reached under the plinth of the tomb and, holding it delicately by the edge, brought out a heavy brass vase.

The vase was roughly cylindrical with a bulbous bottom and waisted to form the shape of an elongated tulip. It was about eight inches high with a wide, round, heavy base. The base was matted with blood and white hair. Its weight and shape made it an excellent weapon.

The doctor drew his breath in. 'That's the murder weapon,' he asserted confidently.

'Look at the hair caught up on the base. Besides that...' He gingerly lifted the matted hair round the wound on Cadwallader's head and nodded. 'If I had a magnifying glass you could see this more clearly.'

Bill opened his briefcase, took out a magnifying glass and handed it to the doctor.

'Thank you, Inspector. Look at the shape of the wound. Yes, I'd say there's no doubt about that whatsoever.'

He handed the glass back to Bill. 'Look at this, Jack,' said Bill, glancing from the wound to the base of the brass vase and back again. 'You can see for yourself how the edge of the wound corresponds with the base of the vase.'

Jack took the glass. 'That's very clear, isn't it? The wound's deeper in the middle but the edges are shallow, just as you'd expect if poor old Cadwallader was sloshed with a circular object.' He measured the wound between his thumb and index finger, then measured the base of the vase. 'Yep, that certainly ties up.'

'You'll take the precise measurements in the post-mortem, won't you, Doctor?' said Bill, returning the magnifying glass to his bag. 'I don't want there to be any doubt about it in court.'

He took out his insufflator and mercury

powder and, carefully placing the vase on a pew, puffed the powder over the vase. An array of fingerprints sprang into view. 'Excellent,' he breathed, then raised his voice. 'Mr Clough! Come and photograph this, will you?'

Mr Clough reluctantly came forward and, under Bill's direction, set to work photographing the vase and the body.

After Clough had finished with the vase, Bill went to pack it carefully away in his bag, but Jack stopped him.

'Wait a mo, Bill.' He felt inside the vase. 'It's still a bit damp inside. I think it's recently held water and flowers.' He glanced round the chantry. 'I don't think the vase belongs in here. The shape's very modern in comparison with the rest of the ornaments. It's certainly not a Victorian vase, but it could have been brought here at a later date, I suppose. Vases like this usually come in pairs. Can you see the other one, Bill? I'd expect to find some discarded flowers, too.'

They stood up and, with the help of the doctor and Commander Pattishall, started to look for the other vase.

'There aren't any cut flowers in the chantry at all,' said Bill after a search. 'I can't see any vase that looks like the one you found. I think you're right, Jack. I think it's been brought in from elsewhere.'

'Which makes me think this was a premeditated crime, Bill,' Jack said quietly. 'No one carries one brass vase round with them just for the fun of the thing. By the way, it seems like old news now, but I had a dekko at the chantry

301

picture while we were looking for the flowers. If that flagstone or inlay can be moved, I'm a Dutchman.'

'So no hiding place for hidden treasure?'

'Not there, at any rate.'

He turned as a top-hatted, frock-coated man, who was, judging from his clothes, the local undertaker, creaked open the chantry door and came in, reverently doffing his hat. 'Can we remove the remains now, sir?' he asked Commander Pattishall.

The Commander looked to Bill, who nodded. 'I don't see why not. I think we've got everything we need from here.'

The undertaker called his men in, who produced a stretcher and with difficulty started to manhandle the rigid body away from the tomb and on to the canvas. This, thought Jack, was not nice to watch. There was a grimly comic element to the way even Cadwallader's corpse, rigid in death, resisted being taken from his beloved chantry, he supposed, but Jack didn't feel remotely amused. He looked away, oddly moved that this gifted – for he had been very gifted – fussy, infuriating but rather pathetic personality of Henry Cadwallader should end with so little dignity.

'By George, look at this!' called Commander Pattishall sharply.

He stooped down and picked up a gleaming blue and green little square case from the floor, where it had been hidden by Cadwallader's body.

They all crowded round. It was an enamelled

cigarette case with a sunburst design on it. 'It's a dainty thing, isn't it?' said the Commander, evidently very pleased with himself. 'I can't see Cadwallader owning a case like that.'

Bill reached out and carefully took the cigarette case, holding it by the edges. 'This is a woman's cigarette case.' His eyes were bright. 'It was under the body, Jack. It could be the murderer's. It's very distinctive.' He snapped his fingers together. 'I've seen it before! I wonder if there's a name engraved in it?'

'There is,' said Jack, his mouth suddenly dry. 'It's engraved inside the lid. I've seen that case before as well. It belongs to Miss Wingate.'

Commander Pattishall's eyebrows shot up. 'Does it, by Jove!' He stroked his moustache vigorously into place. 'I told you that young woman's name kept cropping up. I think we'd better have a word with Miss Wingate.'

Jack was unusually quiet as they walked to Whimbrell House. Dr Oxenhall had accompanied the undertaker's men to his surgery, where he was going to perform the post-mortem, and Mr Clough departed to his studio to develop the photographs.

Bill allowed Commander Pattishall to get ahead of them. 'Jack,' he said quietly, 'you must see I've got no choice but to question Miss Wingate. She has to account for the fact her cigarette case was found under Cadwallader's body. What's more, coming on top of the fact she was the one who discovered John Askern, I have to say it's not looking good.'

303

'It's looking,' said Jack, picking his words with care, 'bloody awful. I know you know that Betty Wingate's cigarette case isn't proof positive that Miss Wingate was there, but I can see how it looks, all right. What's more, that brass vase was certainly the murder weapon. If the fingerprints on the vase match Betty Wingate's, what then?'

'Then I haven't got any choice, Jack. I'll have to take her into custody.'

'But *why,* Bill? Why should she bump off old Cadwallader? Come to that, why should anybody bump him off?'

'Why should anyone have killed anyone in this case?' replied Bill with some asperity. 'From our first mysteriously vanishing body in Signora Bianchi's cottage to John Askern in Mrs McAllister's flat to that poor beggar Cadwallader, I can't see the reason for any of it. I'll grant you Miss Wingate doesn't seem to benefit, but no one seems to benefit.'

'Mrs Askern certainly had a motive to kill her husband.'

'Yes, she did,' said Bill fairly. 'And if it turns out that John Askern, in addition to his other failings, was running that flat as a love nest where he'd installed Mrs McAllister, a very compelling motive. The trouble is, we both saw Mrs McAllister *and* spoke to her. She's hardly anyone's idea of a siren, is she?'

'No, I have to say that's true.' Jack shook his head unhappily. 'There has to be a reason for the murders, though.'

'I can't say I like it much more than you, but the trouble is, the reason may be something we

304

wouldn't recognise as a real reason at all. For all I know, Colin Askern might have put his finger on it right at the start, when he talked about Miss Wingate wanting attention.'

'Psychology?' asked Jack, raising his eyebrows with the faint ghost of a smile.

'Yes, psychology, damn you. Look, I know you don't want to hear this, but she could easily be suffering from wounded pride. She's a poor relation, Jack. She could feel constantly overlooked, with no future to look forward to and a festering sense of inadequacy.'

'Good grief, Bill, this is positively creepy.'

'I know. And it doesn't make sense to you or to me or to anyone else that's normal and well-balanced. But if all murderers were normal and well-balanced, my job would be a great deal easier. Lots of murders have been committed for reasons that are utterly trivial.'

'Yes,' said Jack unhappily. 'I know.'

A maid showed them into the drawing room of Whimbrell House and informed them that Mrs Lythewell would be down shortly.

The drawing room clearly showed the hand of Mrs Lythewell, being fashionably decorated in brilliant lemon, green and black. Stylised yellow and green tulips embroidered the cushions on the angular black sofa and chairs and entwined themselves across the rug in front of the gleaming chromium fireplace.

'It's not exactly to my taste,' said Commander Pattishall, looking round the room disparagingly, 'but it's bright enough. Ladies have to have their fancies, eh?'

Jack pointed to the brass vase full of fresh freesias in the middle of the mantelpiece. 'Does that look familiar?'

'Great heavens!' exclaimed the Commander, reaching out to pick it up. 'Why, it's the same as the other vase we found!'

Jack caught hold of his hand. 'Excuse me, Commander, but it would be as well if no one touched it. Bill, can you test it for prints?'

The Commander snorted, causing the ends of his moustache to lift. 'But dash it, man, whatever for?'

'Just for the sake of completeness, Commander,' said Bill.

Mrs Lythewell entered the room to find her three guests grouped round the mantelpiece, gazing intently at her vase. 'Good morning, gentlemen...' She stood back in surprise. 'Is there something I can help you with?'

'We'd like to see if there're any fingerprints on this vase,' explained Jack cheerfully. 'Is there a newspaper or something we can use to stand it on?'

Mrs Lythewell's eyebrows shot up. 'That seems rather peculiar.' She shrugged. 'Just as you like.'

She produced a newspaper from the rack by the fireplace and Jack spread it on the table near the window. Then, holding the vase by the lip, Bill carried it over to the table.

'Freesias have such a beautiful smell, don't they,' remarked Jack conversationally, 'and these are really lovely.'

'Oh, yes. I *love* fresh flowers – so sweetly

pretty – but the gardeners are always so tiresome about letting you cut them when they're at their best. They want them to make a show in the garden but Betty brought the freesias in yesterday. She can always get her own way with the men.'

Taking out his insufflator and mercury powder, Bill puffed it over the highly polished brass surface of the vase.

'This is *very* dramatic,' drawled Maud Lythewell, stepping forward and running her long pearl necklace between her fingers. 'What happens now?'

'Nothing,' snapped Commander Pattishall in disapproval, peering at the vase. 'You can see for yourselves there's nothing there.'

'No, there isn't,' agreed Jack, an odd note of repressed excitement in his voice. Bill glanced at him in surprise. 'There isn't a single fingerprint on that vase. Mrs Lythewell, can we take this vase, please? Inspector Rackham will give you a receipt for it.'

Maud Lythewell shrugged. 'I suppose, if you really feel you must. You can put the freesias in the other vase.' She looked at the mantelpiece and her brow furrowed. 'Where's the other vase? There were two here yesterday.'

'Are you sure, Mrs Lythewell?' asked Bill.

'Of course I'm sure,' she snapped. 'I bought those vases as a pair from Heals when I had the room redecorated last year. They act as a *motif* for the whole room.'

'Exactly,' said Jack, again with that note of suppressed excitement. 'There were two of them.'

'If you really are going to take my vase, I'll have to get another one for the flowers. I wonder what Betty's done with the other one? She must've moved it.' Maud Lythewell frowned. 'How very tiresome.'

She went to the mantelpiece and rang the bell. 'Mabel,' she said to the maid when she appeared, 'ask Miss Betty to join us, will you? And can you,' she added, waving a languid hand at the brass vase, 'find a suitable vase for these freesias?'

'Major Haldean,' said Commander Pattishall, with some irritation, 'can you explain *why* you want to deprive this good lady of her property?'

With a glance at Maud Lythewell, Jack hesitated. 'Do you ever read Sherlock Holmes, Commander?'

'Eh? What the dickens has Sherlock Holmes got to do with it, man?'

'The famous incident of the dog in the night time,' said Jack.

Commander Pattishall reached the limits of his patience. 'Would you mind explaining yourself, sir?'

Bill, who'd looked equally puzzled, smiled slowly. 'Got it,' he said quietly. 'Never mind the reasons just at the moment, sir,' he said, with a significant glance at Maud Lythewell. 'Suffice it to say that we'll take good care of this vase and it may be very valuable evidence.'

The Commander snorted in disapproval and was clearly about to demand a fuller explanation, when the door opened and Betty Wingate came in. She looked drawn and anxious.

'You want to see me, Aunt Maud?' she began, and stopped as she saw the men in the room. 'Jack! Inspector Rackham! I didn't know you were here.'

She looked at them with worried anxiety. 'I suppose you've come about poor Mr Cadwallader. Mrs Askern's asleep upstairs. She was dreadfully upset.' She stopped and looked quizzically at the brass vase on the sheet of newspaper. 'Whatever are you doing with that vase? And why's it got grey powder all over it?'

'We've been testing it for fingerprints,' explained Jack. 'We didn't find any.'

'Oh! I see – or I don't really, but I suppose you know what you're doing.'

'Betty,' cut in Maud Lythewell sharply. 'One of the vases is missing. What do you know about it?'

Betty drew back. 'Nothing.' She pushed her hair back from her forehead in a puzzled way. 'Missing, you say? I don't know where it can be. There were certainly two there yesterday. I filled both of them with fresh flowers yesterday afternoon.'

'Were you in this room last night?' asked Jack, including Mrs Lythewell in the question with a look. 'Did you notice if there were one or two vases on the mantelpiece then?'

Both women looked at each other. 'We were certainly in here,' said Maud Lythewell. 'I listened to the wireless and read for a while, but I didn't notice the vases particularly. Betty? How about you?'

Betty shook her head. 'I'm afraid I didn't give the vases a thought.' She frowned in an effort of remembrance. 'No, I'm sorry,' she said eventually. 'I can't help you.'

'Perhaps you can help us with another matter,' said Bill. Avoiding Jack's eyes, he opened his briefcase and took out the enamelled cigarette case.

'That's mine!' exclaimed Betty, reaching out her hand.

Bill drew back. 'When did you last have it, Miss Wingate?'

'Yesterday afternoon, I think. It was after lunch. I was in the garden and wanted a cigarette, but I couldn't find my case. Colin was here and gave me one of his, but he always smokes Player's Weights and I find them too strong.'

'What time was that?'

'Round about two o'clock, I suppose. I looked for my cigarette case all day after that, off and on, but couldn't find it. Look, what is all this? Can I have my case back?'

'Not just yet, I'm afraid,' said Bill. 'Miss Wingate, would you mind if I took your fingerprints?'

Commander Pattishall grunted in approval. 'That's more like it!'

'My fingerprints?' repeated Betty in alarm. Instinctively she put her hands behind her back. 'Why? What for?'

'Yes, Inspector,' drawled Maud Lythewell. 'What for?'

'We wish to eliminate Miss Wingate from a certain line of enquiry,' said Bill stiffly.

The Commander snorted once more. 'Eliminate, yes. Very good.'

Jack, who'd been standing back, nodded at her
encouragingly. 'It'll be all right, you know. You
needn't worry.'

Betty bit her lip nervously. 'All right,' she said
apprehensively. 'I suppose so. What do I have to
do?'

Bill produced a card, ink pad and cloth from
his briefcase and put them on the table. 'Just put
your fingers on the pad like so – and now on the
card – and there we are.' He handed the cloth to
Betty to wipe her hands.

'Well?' barked Commander Pattishall, unable
to restrain himself. 'Are the prints a match,
man?'

'A match?' questioned Betty anxiously. 'A
match for what?'

'I can't tell yet, Commander,' said Bill firmly.
'I need to have the photographs from the chantry
developed before I can compare them properly.'

Commander Pattishall sighed dangerously. 'I
don't hold with this shilly-shallying. Miss Wingate, do you confirm this cigarette case belongs
to you?'

'Certainly I do,' said Betty, scrubbing her
hands. 'My name's engraved in the lid.'

The Commander squared his shoulders. 'Then,
unpleasant as it is, it is my duty to inform you
that, because of the circumstances in which that
cigarette case was found, you are under arrest on
suspicion of murdering the late Henry Cadwallader. You are under no obligation to say anything but anything you do say—'

The rest of his sentence was lost in Maud Lythewell's screams.

Betty, paper-white, stared at him unseeingly. She swayed as if she might faint.

'It's all right,' hissed Jack, catching her round the waist. 'It's going to be all right. Trust me.'

Fifteen

The next day saw Bill back at Scotland Yard where, with Jack's help, he was going through the case for the benefit of Sir Douglas Lynton.

On Sir Douglas's desk were the two brass vases and a collection of photographs. Sir Douglas looked from the enlarged photographs of Betty Wingate's fingerprints to the photographs of the fingerprints found on the brass vase. 'They're a match,' he said. 'That's very clear.'

'It is, sir,' said Bill. 'There's no doubt about it. Miss Wingate's prints match those on the vase found in the chantry. To sum up the rest of the evidence from yesterday, Dr Oxenhall's examination of the stomach contents in the post-mortem showed that Cadwallader died about an hour to two hours after eating his evening meal. That, along with the temperature and rigidity of the body, gives us a time of death of between seven to eight o'clock in the evening or thereabouts. Although Miss Wingate was seen at intervals during that time, she doesn't have a real alibi. In addition, her cigarette case – her very distinctive cigarette case – was found under Cadwallader's body. On the face of it, it's an open and shut case.'

Sir Douglas leaned back in his chair with an

encouraging expression. 'I know Miss Wingate's in custody. Commander Pattishall has informed me. However, I gather you don't think it's quite as simple as that.'

'It could be, sir,' said Bill seriously. 'Right from the start, the start being Miss Wingate reporting the supposed murder of Signora Bianchi, Mr Colin Askern, who knows Miss Wingate well, has said that Miss Wingate is prompted by a desire to be in the limelight. And,' he added with a shrug, 'I have to say, there's a lot to be said in favour of that theory. Miss Wingate discovered John Askern's body. She *says* Askern wrote to her, asking her to meet him at Dorian House at three that afternoon, but the letter has been lost. She could've easily written that letter herself. If the motive is simply a desire to be in the spotlight, then it all adds up.'

'Motives,' said Sir Douglas, 'can be tricky to understand.'

'I know, sir,' agreed Bill. 'However,' he said, with a glance at Jack, 'what isn't hard to understand is Major Haldean's observation about the murder weapon that killed Cadwallader.'

'I found the vase under the empty tomb near Cadwallader's body,' said Jack, in response to Sir Douglas's enquiring look. 'As you can see, it's a modern design, quite out of place in the chantry. It looked to me as if it was one of a pair of vases.'

'Which it is, of course,' muttered Sir Douglas.

'Yes, but we couldn't find the other vase in the chantry. That made me think it was a premeditated crime. No one happens to have one vase from a pair with them by chance. The blood and hair, the size and shape of the wound, plus the fingerprints, make it seem obvious that not only is the chantry vase, if I can call it that, the murder weapon, but it was wielded by Betty Wingate. However, when we were shown into the drawing room of Whimbrell House, we found the other vase from the pair. Now,' said Jack, leaning forward. 'That vase had no prints on it at all.'

'And?' questioned Sir Douglas.

'It should've done, sir. Miss Wingate had put flowers in those vases the previous day. She handled both vases. Mrs Lythewell said as much and Miss Wingate didn't dispute it. I didn't particularly want to spell this out in front of Miss Wingate or Mrs Lythewell, but it struck me as the perfect example of Sherlock Holmes' famous dog in the night time.'

Sir Douglas smiled. 'Is that what Commander Pattishall meant when he said to me on the telephone...' he consulted his notes and cleared his throat '...*That Haldean feller seems to think he's Sherlock Holmes, eh?*'

'That's it,' said Jack with a grin. 'Inspector Rackham twigged it right away, I'm glad to say. The dog in the night time didn't bark when it should've done and there were no prints on the vase when there should've been. Somebody *must* have taken not one vase but two to the chantry. They used one to kill Cadwallader and wiped it clean. That vase was returned to the drawing-room mantelpiece of Whimbrell House. They then took the other vase, being careful not to disturb those prints of Miss Wingate's, daubed

315

Cadwallader's blood and hair on the base and left it under the tomb for us to find.'

'It's an interesting theory,' began Sir Douglas, when he was interrupted by a meaningful cough from Bill. 'Yes, Rackham?'

'It's more than a theory, sir. After hearing what Major Haldean had to say, I examined the Whimbrell House vase carefully. It looks clean, right enough, but there's traces of blood beneath the screw-head fitting the base to the vase proper. I'd testify that, despite appearances, the clean vase is the murder weapon.'

Sir Douglas reached out his hand for the clean vase and hesitated. 'I can pick it up?'

'Yes, sir. It's been thoroughly examined and the evidence documented.'

Sir Douglas weighed the vase in his hand. 'It's a nice weapon,' he said thoughtfully. 'Very heavy for its size and it fits nicely into the hand. It's the sort of weapon it might occur to a woman to use.' He replaced the vase on the desk. 'I suppose, in view of what you've told me, we'd better recommend that Miss Wingate is released.'

Jack shook his head vigorously. 'I'd rather you didn't, sir. Somebody took some pains to incriminate Miss Wingate. I'd far rather they thought their plan had succeeded. For her own safety, I'd much prefer her to remain in custody. Besides that, if we're going to nail the real murderer – a murderer who I firmly believe has killed at least three people – we need to lull them into a false sense of security.'

Sir Douglas digested this with a long face. 'That's all very well, Major Haldean, and I do

316

appreciate your point...' He stopped abruptly. 'What d'you mean, *at least* three people? We only know of two for certain. The third, the murder in the cottage, is very problematic, but that's the end of it, surely?'

'It's just an idea I've got,' Jack replied disarmingly. 'At the moment that's all it is and it may very well come to nothing.'

'An idea, eh?' Sir Douglas chewed his moustache. 'The trouble is, Major, we can't keep Miss Wingate locked up indefinitely while we try to get to the bottom of this business, ideas or no ideas. This all started with the supposed murder of Signora Bianchi in her cottage. That proved to be an absolute mare's nest, but since then we've had John Askern's murder and now Henry Cadwallader. None of it seems to make any sense. These ideas of yours. D'you think they might help?'

'They might, sir. I'll tell you one thing I'd like to know. Who is Mrs McAllister?'

Sir Douglas gave a short laugh. 'If you can answer that, you're doing well. The wretched woman seems as elusive as gas.'

Jack laced his fingers together and, stretching out his long legs, put his hands behind his head and leaned back. 'Miss Wingate thought that the dead woman she saw in Signora Bianchi's cottage could've been Mrs McAllister.' Ignoring Sir Douglas's dismissive snort, he carried on. 'I must say that chimed in with certain ideas of my own.'

'But that woman – if she existed at all – can't be Mrs McAllister, man! Mrs McAllister rented

317

the flat in Dorian House. She's made herself scarce now, but she lived there openly for three weeks. She was seen frequently and spoken to by the neighbours and the porter during that time. There's no doubt she was there.'

'There's no doubt a Mrs McAllister lived in Dorian House, but was she *our* Mrs McAllister, if I can phrase it like that? The same woman that Inspector Rackham and I saw at the art exhibition at Lyon House?'

'Well, if she wasn't the same woman, who was she?'

'I'm afraid I don't know,' Jack admitted. 'However, there was a woman's body found in Euston Station in a trunk that had been despatched from Manchester. She was thought to be a Mrs Ormskirk, but I understand from the report in the *Daily Messenger* that's not so.' He hesitated. 'I wondered if that woman was actually Mrs McAllister.'

'What?' Sir Douglas shook his head. 'But she can't be, man!'

'Can't she, sir? On the one hand we have a woman who Betty Wingate reported as murdered in Signora Bianchi's cottage and, on the other, an unclaimed and unidentified body. Are they one and the same?'

Sir Douglas shifted uncomfortably in his chair. 'That sounds like a very neat solution. A little too neat, perhaps?'

'That's what Bill thought,' said Jack, turning to his friend with a grin. 'He said I was chasing moonbeams when I floated the idea past him.'

'That's right, Jack,' agreed Bill. 'I couldn't see

318

how a body that had disappeared in Surrey ended up in a trunk despatched from Manchester. They're at different ends of the country, to which you replied that it was Manchester, not Timbuktu, and could I get the report from the Manchester police?'

'And did you get the report from the Manchester police, Chief Inspector?' asked Sir Douglas.

'I did, sir,' said Bill. He took a thin official file from his briefcase and put it on the desk. 'As you can see, there's not much in it. It's mainly a collection of negatives, as the Manchester police were really concerned with proving if the woman was or wasn't Mrs Ormskirk. The body was badly decomposed, so there's no facial features and no chance of fingerprints. Of course, we know hardly anything about the body Miss Wingate says she saw in Signora Bianchi's cottage. However, we did find some hair on the sofa in the cottage and threads of a brown silk scarf on the wheelbarrow in the pigsty in the cottage garden. And that, sir, made me think Major Haldean might be right after all. The hair on the trunk corpse – I had a sample of the hair examined under a microscope – is similar to the few hairs we found in the cottage, and snagged up on the lock inside the trunk were a few silk threads which, although badly contaminated by the body, had been brown.'

Sir Douglas stared at him. 'Good Lord!'

'My thoughts exactly, sir. We can't *prove* they're the same, as the contamination is very extensive, but you'll agree it's a remarkable coincidence.'

'It most certainly is.' Sir Douglas reached out his hand for the police report and, pulling it towards him, read through it.

Jack lit a cigarette and waited.

'Well, that is interesting,' said Sir Douglas at last. He looked up and tapped the file thoughtfully. 'As Inspector Rackham said, this isn't proof, but it's a remarkable coincidence.'

He reached for a cigarette and read the report through once more. 'This has to be followed up,' he said eventually. 'We simply can't ignore it. But if this body really is Mrs McAllister's – the Mrs McAllister you saw at the exhibition – then how did she come to be in Signora Bianchi's cottage? Who killed her? And how did her body turn up in a trunk despatched from Manchester?'

He stubbed his cigarette out in the ashtray. 'And who, for heaven's sake, is the woman who lived for three weeks as Mrs McAllister in Dorian House? Because I need hardly tell either of you gentlemen that *if* Miss Wingate is an innocent woman, then the Mrs McAllister from Dorian House is our prime suspect for the murder of John Askern.'

'That's exactly right, sir,' agreed Bill. 'I'd like to add something to that. Miss Wingate says she was invited to Dorian House by a letter purporting to come from John Askern. That letter disappeared. If Miss Wingate is innocent, then someone stole it. The only people who were in a position to steal the letter were the people with her that day. One of them has to be the fake Mrs McAllister.'

Sir Douglas's eyebrows rose. 'But that narrows

320

it down to Mrs Lythewell and Mrs Askern. Of the two, Mrs Askern has by far the most compelling motive.' He glanced at Jack. 'Don't you agree, Major?'

'Absolutely,' said Jack. 'If that letter was stolen, it was stolen by someone in the same room as Betty Wingate. However, I wouldn't exclude either of the men. They could be in cahoots with Mrs McAllister quite easily.'

'I could get them all in for questioning,' said Bill. 'That should give us some answers.'

'Yes, you could,' agreed Jack. 'The trouble is, that would tell the real crook that you don't believe that Betty Wingate's guilty. It'll put them on their guard, which is exactly what we're trying to avoid.'

'But what *can* we do?' asked Bill in exasperation.

'Give me a day,' said Jack. 'Two days at the most.' With his head to one side, he scratched his chin thoughtfully. 'You asked me if I had any ideas.' His voice was hesitant. 'The answer's yes, but my ideas might come to nothing. If it proves to be a washout, I'll have to try again, but one thing that struck me was the series of drawings that Cadwallader did of the chantry.'

'There's nothing special about them,' said Bill. 'I had a look at the drawings he'd worked on. He didn't sketch a likely murderer if that's what you're thinking.'

Jack shook his head. 'No, that wasn't what I was thinking of.'

'Well, what's special about his drawings? They are just details of the chantry. There's nothing there you can't see with your own eyes. What are you getting at, Jack?'

'Just at the moment it's all a bit vague,' Jack admitted, 'but I'm convinced the roots of this business go back a long way. I want to start by looking up the records of the Nordic Atlantic shipping company.'

'The *who*?' repeated Bill blankly.

'The Nordic Atlantic. They've got an office on Cockspur Street. They operated the *SS Concordia,* the ship Daniel Lythewell came to England on in 1898. I want to see who else was onboard that ship with him. And then, I think, I might be able to tell you a bit more about our mysterious Mrs McAllister.'

That afternoon Jack met Bill outside 46, Purbeck Terrace, Paddington. 'I got your message,' said Bill. 'Why did you want me to meet you here?'

'I've got a little experiment in mind,' said Jack. 'Mrs McAllister lived here for a while. She was friendly with a Miss Sharpe, who knew her as well as anyone.' He tapped the briefcase he was carrying. 'I've brought my sketch pad and pencils, and I'm hoping that, my artistic talents permitting, by the end of the afternoon I'll be able to get a working likeness of Mrs McAllister.'

'That'd be useful. How did you get on at the shipping office, by the way? Was Mrs McAllister one of the passengers on board the *Concordia?* I presume that's who you were looking for.'

'Not exactly,' said Jack. He grinned. 'Just bear with me for a while, will you? I've already made one massive gaffe in this case, by being so ruddy confident the slab in the chantry was made of platinum. I don't know if I can stand another blow to the ego like that so soon. Mind you, I've had an idea about that, too.' He walked up the steps and rang the bell. 'I'll let you know exactly what's what as soon as I'm sure of it myself.'

The landlady, Mrs Kiddle, ushered them into the Resident's Lounge, where, after a little while, Miss Sharpe joined them.

Her face brightened as she saw Jack. 'It's Mr Haldean, isn't it? Did you find your Aunt Joan?'

'I'm afraid not,' said Jack with a funereal face.

Miss Sharpe clasped her hands together. 'How sad! Families are so precious, aren't they? I said to Miss Richardson – such a nice lady who's taken your aunt's old room – that it was so tragic to think of an entire family torn asunder over a sideboard.'

'A ... I beg your pardon?' asked Bill, blinking.

'The sideboard!' said Jack hastily, a wayward memory coming to his aid. What on earth had he told the woman? 'The sideboard my ... my uncle quarrelled with my Aunt Joan about.'

'You said it was your father who quarrelled,' corrected Miss Sharpe, frowning at him.

'Did I? The sideboard went to my uncle, of course. Miss Sharpe, d'you think you could help us?' he went on quickly, before her inconveniently retentive memory could trip him up any further. 'This is my brother, William,' he added, indicating Bill with a wave of his hand.

Bill looked perplexed but accepting of the relationship.

'William and I thought it would be much easier

to find Aunt Joan if we had a picture of her.'

'There aren't any photographs,' began Miss Sharpe worriedly, but Jack interrupted her.

'No, I realise that, so I thought I'd try the next best thing.' He opened his briefcase and took out his sketch pad. 'Now, I've drawn as good a likeness as I can of my mother, as she was supposed to favour Aunt Joan, but, as you can see, I haven't added any hair or eyebrows or any little personal touches. I was hoping, with your help, I could make the picture a lot more life-like.'

Miss Sharpe gave a murmur of surprise and, putting on her spectacles, which were on a chain round her neck, looked at the picture. She drew back in unspoken dissent. 'That's not very like her.'

Bill saw the picture and drew his breath in with a hiss. 'Good God! She's not what you'd call glamorous, is she? It's a funny thing, though,' he added with a frown, 'I'm sure I've seen her somewhere before, but with no hair, it's difficult...'

'William,' said Jack solemnly, 'of course you have seen her before. This is our late mother you're talking about. Show a bit more respect, please, both to the memory of our dear departed mother and to my art.'

'Art, indeed,' muttered Bill.

Miss Sharpe screwed up her face and tried hard. 'I suppose it *could* be Mrs McAllister, but I really don't know.'

'Let's try,' said Jack cheerfully. 'Now, did Aunt Joan wear glasses?'

Details of glasses, hair, earrings and dress were

added at Miss Sharpe's direction. 'She's very like our mother,' said Jack with a sentimental sigh when the picture was complete. 'Isn't she, William?'

Bill blinked at the picture. 'That's not how I remember my – our – mother, I must say.'

'Is this a good likeness of Aunt Joan, Miss Sharpe?' asked Jack. He gazed at her with wide, hopeful eyes. 'Please say yes.'

Miss Sharpe studied the picture carefully. She clasped her hands together once more in an expression of sorrow. 'Poor boys,' she said woefully. 'Such a *sweet* idea and yet ... I'm sorry, Mr Haldean. I'm sorry to crush your hopes when you've gone to so much trouble, but I'm afraid this lady is nothing like your Aunt Joan.'

'Well,' said Bill, once they were free of Purbeck Terrace and Miss Sharpe. Miss Sharpe had been insistent they should drown their sorrows in afternoon tea with caraway seed cake, and it was only by adroit footwork and a plea of a prior engagement they had made good their escape. 'That's one idea come to nothing.' He clapped Jack on the shoulder with a grin. 'Never mind. I'm sorry Miss Sharpe didn't recognise your – sorry, *our* – mother. How's the ego bearing up?'

'Very well,' said Jack with undisguised satisfaction. 'I gave Miss Sharpe every encouragement to identify Aunt Joan but I'd have been devastated if she had. That little experiment, Bill, old bean, was to demonstrate who Mrs McAllister *isn't*.'

'What's the point of that?' said Bill in exasperated disbelief. 'Now, if you could find out a way of demonstrating who Mrs McAllister *is*...'

'That's part two of the experiment,' said Jack. 'I propose to carry out the next segment at Dorian House. Who's the neighbour you mentioned? The one you said who'd spoken to Mrs McAllister the most?'

'Do you mean Mrs Conway-Lloyd?' asked Bill, after a few moments' thought.

'That's the one. Now, we can't be looking for Aunt Joan, of course, and she knows you, so I think you'd better be yourself.'

'That's a relief,' grunted Bill. 'I've got quite enough relatives to be going on with without adding you to their number, brother.'

Mrs Conway-Lloyd was at home and willing to co-operate. She remembered Bill perfectly well and Jack, introduced as 'an artist', produced his sketch pad in which he'd drawn a duplicate of the picture Miss Sharpe would've recognised as his mother.

'I've managed to put together a basic outline of Mrs McAllister's face from descriptions of people who met her,' explained Jack to a fascinated Mrs Conway-Lloyd. 'The main facial features are there, but the details of hair and eyebrows and even such seeming trivialities as jewellery and what sort of neckline she preferred on her dresses I've left blank to be filled in with your help. Those are the details that really make a difference to identification.'

Mrs Conway-Lloyd nodded in vigorous agreement. 'Yes, indeed, Mr Haldean,' she said, without stopping to reflect those were precisely the details any witness would've mentioned.

'Now,' said Jack, picking up his pencil, 'did Mrs McAllister wear spectacles?'

The same litany of questions Miss Sharpe had answered earlier in the afternoon followed, with Mrs Conway-Lloyd's enthusiastic help.

'Don't forget the lipstick, Mr Haldean. Mrs McAllister was always so careful about her make-up. She was very up-to-date. No, not that shade,' as Jack reached for his vermilion coloured pencil. 'A little darker, I think. Yes, that's right. Quite a pale powder and rouge, of course, and her eyes rimmed with kohl – with mascara, too. Colour makes such a difference, doesn't it?'

Eventually the picture was completed. Mrs Conway-Lloyd surveyed it in satisfaction. 'You've really captured her likeness remarkably well, Mr Haldean. That's exactly her.'

Bill took the sketch pad and gazed at it. 'Excuse me, Mrs Conway-Lloyd, but are you sure?'

'Absolutely, my good man,' asserted Mrs Conway-Lloyd. 'No doubt about it whatsoever.'

Bill did have his doubts, though. Before they left Dorian House, he showed the portrait to two more neighbours and the porter. They all identified the woman in the picture as Mrs McAllister.

Once they got outside, Bill looked at a justifiably smug Jack in bewilderment. 'I just don't understand, Jack. Why this elaborate charade? I'll grant that's a picture of Mrs McAllister. I don't understand it, but I believe it. All those witnesses can't be wrong, but how, in the name of goodness, did the real Mrs McAllister end up in a trunk despatched from Manchester? What's it all about?'

'I told you the roots of this case went back a long way,' said Jack, suddenly serious. 'Old Mr Lythewell, John Askern, Signora Bianchi and that poor trusting beggar, Daniel Lythewell – I feel especially sorry for him – they all played their part, but as to how Mrs McAllister ended up in a trunk? Well, if you'll be in Whimbrell Heath tonight, I hope I can show you.'

Sixteen

The nightwatchman's lantern flickered round the yard of Lythewell and Askern. Overhead an owl hooted and, far in the distance, came the faint noise of a car changing gear.

Gilbert Stroud rattled the door of the despatch shed, then came a sound Jack had feared. A dog – a young, excited dog, by the sound of its bark – gave a high-pitched yip and scrabbled its paws against the door.

The door rattled once more as Stroud tried it again.

'C'mere, boy,' Stroud said in deep disapproval. 'Down, I say! It's locked. There's nothing there.'

The puppy whined in disappointment as Stroud stumped away, the sound of his footsteps ringing on the cobbles.

On the other side of the door, Jack flicked on his torch, shielding the light with his hand. He'd been waiting for Stroud. When he and Bill had talked to the nightwatchman a few weeks ago in the bar of the Guide Post, he said he made his rounds every couple of hours. It was just on midnight now so they should have until two in the morning. The dog was a ruddy nuisance though, with far better instincts than his master gave him credit for.

He opened the metal filing cabinet that stood

against the wall and grinned as he saw the foreman's clipboard and a pile of address and despatch labels. He shut the drawer and turned to the stack of waiting crates.

Working as quietly as he could, he manhandled a crate about five and a half feet long by two feet deep off the stack in the middle of the shed. It was heavy but manageable. That was good. It probably contained wood of some sort, which was a relief. He didn't want to try shifting a stone pillar, say, single anded.

Despite his care, it fell with a thump, end up, on the floor. Jack paused and listened.

Silence.

There was a sack trolley leant against the wall. Jack heaved the crate onto the trolley and, taking the weight on the handles, pushed it to the doors. Even though the crate was heavy, the trolley was surprisingly easy to control.

He took the picklocks, which Bill had provided, and, unlocking the doors, looked out onto the silent, moonlit yard.

This was the danger point. Leaving the crate and trolley, he slipped across the yard and unlocked the heavy gates but didn't pull them back. In the distance, the puppy yipped again and he heard the faint sound of Gilbert Stroud's voice.

He had to risk it. Keeping to the shadows, he got back to the despatch shed and, checking the coast was clear, pushed the sack trolley across the yard and out of the gates.

He pulled the gates to after himself and, again using the picklocks, locked them. The only sound was the rustle of the wind through the trees. About a hundred and fifty yards away was the black bulk of the chantry.

With its heavy load, the trolley was more difficult to pull over the uneven, gritty ground, and it was a relief when he reached the smoother ground of the chantry path. With some effort, he heaved the trolley up the slope and to the door of the chantry.

The door was closed but unlocked. He pushed the door open and, bringing the trolley into the chantry, closed the door behind him.

'Bill?' he called softly. 'Bill?'

There was the click of a torch and a light shone out. Bill got up from a pew.

'Everything all right?' he asked quietly.

'Fine,' said Jack, catching his breath. 'The watchman's got another dog, which is a nuisance. Fortunately it's only a puppy and Stroud ignored it, thank God.'

Bill struck a match and lit the oil lamp he'd brought with him. 'That's better. We can see what we're doing now.' He looked at the crate on the trolley. 'Are you going to tackle this part of the process by yourself?'

'I'd better. After all, the point of this demonstration is to show how it could be done alone, so I don't want to cheat.'

Jack wheeled the crate into the middle of the chantry and, taking it from the trolley, laid it on the floor.

'You remember what Mr Jones, the foreman, told us about the way the crates were despatched? I haven't got a real corpse to play with, as recreations should only go so far, but you'll agree that it was perfectly feasible to bring a body here from Signora Bianchi's cottage in the gardener's wheelbarrow?'

'Yes, of course I do.'

'Okey-doke. The body was then left in the wheelbarrow inside the chantry while our bright spark went and got a crate, yes?' Bill looked dubious. 'It's possible,' said Jack impatiently. 'As I've just gone and got a crate, you've got to agree it's possible.'

'It's certainly possible, yes.'

'What happens now is that I open up the crate.'

He selected a claw-headed hammer from the metal toolbox they'd brought earlier and set to work. 'A crowbar would get the lid off faster,' he remarked, 'but I don't want to damage the crate. Obviously, dog or no dog, the watchman would notice if I started hammering in the despatch shed at the dead of night. It more or less has to be done up here, as there isn't really anywhere else to work in private.'

It took Jack a little time to work round all the nails, but, once done, he levered off the lid to reveal a mass of sawdust.

'When I first looked round here with Cad-wallader, I found sawdust on the chantry floor,' he said. 'I was puzzled at the time as to where it came from.'

He delved into the crate and, grunting with the weight, pulled out a highly polished pew bench. He laid it on the floor and slapped his hands together to get rid of the sawdust.

'Now, as I said, we haven't got a body, but we want something to go in the crate.' He looked

332

round, and pointed to two brass candlesticks that stood about three foot high. 'They should do for starters, and we can fill up with other bits and pieces so the weight is about right.'

'I'm not very happy about taking the candlesticks,' said Bill. 'Or anything else, for that matter.'

'We're not stealing them,' Jack reassured him. 'They'll be recovered. I just don't want there to be any doubt that this will work.' He hefted a candlestick across to the crate.

'So what happens now?' asked Bill.

'Well, as a matter of fact, it's all quite simple,' said Jack, casting round the chantry in search of more items. 'I'm going to put the candlesticks and various bits and pieces into the crate and hammer it shut again. You remember Sam Catton, that chap in the Guide Post pub who believed in ghosts? He said he heard knocking from the chantry on the night of the murder. That, I imagine, was the sound of the crate being boxed up. Then, when it's all ship-shape and Bristol fashion, I'll take the crate on the sack trolley down to the despatch shed and put it back with the other boxes.'

'What about the address label?'

'It's easy enough to write an address label. There's a stack of blank labels in the despatch shed. All I have to do is write on any name I fancy – say, my old friend, the Reverend Father Peter Crabb, for instance – and address it to Manchester London Road Station, to be left until called for. I'll put the pew bench back in the packaging shed, where it'll be repacked and despatched to its proper home. Then I tootle up to Manchester, and, as Father Peter, collect the crate, take it to a convenient house or shed that I've previously rented and pack the body into a trunk. These crates would make good kindling and would be easy to chop up and burn, together with any clothes I saw fit to remove from the victim. I then have the trunk collected and taken to the station, where it can be sent to London to be left until called for.'

Bill shook his head. 'It's all so easy and straightforward when you explain it.'

'Yes, it is,' said Jack, 'but only if you can plan it beforehand and know the routine of the firm inside out...' His voice died away. 'Bill! There's someone coming. Hide!'

The door swung open with an ominous creak and a beam of light swept across the chantry. Jack tried to hide but the beam of light caught him squarely. He flung an arm over his face to protect his eyes from the dazzling glare.

'Mr Haldean!' called an astonished voice from behind the light. It was Daniel Lythewell. Lythewell shone the light from the torch downwards and walked towards Jack. He was, Jack noticed with a stab of alarm, holding an automatic pistol in his hand.

Lythewell's face changed as he saw the open crate on the floor. 'What on earth are you doing?' He snapped off the torch. The two men looked at each other in the soft glow of the oil lamp.

Jack said nothing.

Lythewell looked at the candlestick beside the

crate. 'I suspected robbery when I saw the light. I came armed.' His voice was thin with anger. 'I never suspected you of theft.'

'This isn't theft, Mr Lythewell,' said Jack quietly. 'This is a reconstruction of how a murderer disposed of a body.' His hand moved to his pocket.

'Keep your hands where I can see them,' snarled Lythewell, gesturing with the gun.

'I'm just reaching for a cigarette,' said Jack mildly. 'You don't mind if I smoke in here, I suppose?'

Lythewell's eyes narrowed. 'Feel free.' His eyes flicked to the crate. 'You obviously don't mind desecrating a sacred edifice.'

Jack lit a cigarette. 'I would, as a matter of fact. But this isn't a sacred edifice, is it? It's a monument to a monstrous ego, the ego of a man who, by forgery and fraud, amassed a fortune and who wanted to pass a substantial part of that fortune on to his son. You knew about that fortune, didn't you? It was a pretty open secret, after all. I think Josiah Lythewell probably wrote to Daniel Lythewell and told him how to read the secret of the chantry, how to discover the fortune hidden in here. But you didn't know the secret, did you?'

Daniel Lythewell froze. 'I beg your pardon? I am Daniel Lythewell.'

Jack shook his head. 'No, you're not. You were Daniel Lythewell's valet. Your name is Arthur Croft.'

There was a hiss of indrawn breath followed by a spluttering protest.

Jack raised his hand for silence. 'You were employed by Daniel Lythewell in New York. One of your fellow servants was the woman known to us as Joan McAllister. You had an affair with her, didn't you? And many years later, she recognised you and called you *Art*. You travelled with Daniel Lythewell to England on the *SS Concordia*. Your name, occupation and employer are listed in the shipping records.'

'This is absolute nonsense!'

'Is it? When you arrived in England, you realised – realised very quickly – that John Askern had a guilty secret. He'd murdered Josiah Lythewell. Perhaps Daniel Lythewell realised it, too.'

Croft drew his breath in sharply. 'It's not true,' he said unsteadily.

'Yes, it is. John Askern confessed what he'd done in letters to his wife.'

'The bloody fool!'

'You could say that. He was lucky. His wife returned the letters unread. Mrs Daphne Askern's got them. However, it's an interesting fact that young John Askern, with no money and no influence, was suddenly made a full partner in the firm. I believe you kept silent about his guilty secret, just as he kept silent about yours.'

'Silence? Guilty secrets?' Arthur Croft laughed. 'I've never heard such rubbish. Why should I need his silence?'

'Because you murdered Daniel Lythewell.'

The automatic pistol came up. 'I think you'd better prove that statement before you say another word. There wasn't any fortune. You know damn well there wasn't any fortune. There was

336

no motive to kill Daniel Lythewell and all this rigmarole is a complete fairy tale.'

'You want proof?' Jack stepped forward and was stopped by a gesture from the gun. He put his hands wide. 'I was going to show you something interesting, Mr Croft.'

'My name's Lythewell, damnit! Go on. Show me *something interesting.*'

Jack knelt down beside the inlaid chantry slab and, reaching out, tapped the metal. 'This is aluminium.'

'So what?'

'Aluminium was once more precious than gold or silver. Old Josiah Lythewell *could* have made this slab of platinum but chose, instead, to use the more valuable aluminium. Then, in 1886, an American called Charles Hall and a French bloke called Héroult extracted aluminium from bauxite. The price of aluminium dropped through the floor. I think the knowledge that his fortune, his wonderful treasure, was worthless, added to Lythewell's madness. So you see, Mr Croft, it was all for nothing.'

Arthur Croft licked very dry lips. 'The bloody fool,' he said again, his voice a croak.

'Unfortunate, certainly.'

Jack picked up the hammer he had used to take the nails from the crate.

'Put that hammer down!' Croft said sharply.

'Relax,' said Jack with a smile, still kneeling on the floor. 'I've got something else to show you.'

He swung the hammer and brought it down with a thunderous smash on the leg of the

337

grieving man. A white leg bone showed through in the gleam from the oil lamp.

'That's Daniel Lythewell!' yelled Jack.

He hurled himself to one side as Croft fired. He lay on the floor, hands scrabbling backwards as Croft, laughing, advanced. His eyes were wide and staring. He looked completely mad. 'You can't hide forever, Haldean. You're right. That is Daniel Lythewell and I put him there. How much do you know, I wonder? Does my name mean anything to you?'

'Croft,' said Jack, desperate to keep him talking. 'One of the men Lythewell used in his museum forgeries was called Croft.'

'Well done,' purred Croft. 'Cornelius Croft was my father. He taught Josiah Lythewell everything he knew about electroplating. Josiah Lythewell used him, cheated him, and left him to rot in Dartmoor. My father died, a broken man, and the money that should have been mine was stolen by Lythewell for his precious son. That's why I took employment with Josiah Lythewell's son. I wanted to get to Josiah Lythewell. My only regret is that he was killed before I could do the job. When I heard that Josiah Lythewell had escaped me, his son was doomed.'

'What about John Askern? He was supposed to be your friend.'

A flicker of regret crossed Croft's face. 'I was truly sorry to have to kill poor John. He remembered, you see? He remembered who we were and what we'd done before we became respectable. It was our shared secret, the thing we had in common. I felt lost without John, but he had to

338

go. He was getting dangerous. He knew too much, just as you know too much.'

He raised the pistol to fire, then his eyes rolled backwards in his head and he fell in a crumpled heap to the floor.

'Blimey, Bill,' said Jack with a shaky laugh as he got to his feet. 'Did you have to leave it so late? He's not dead, is he?'

Bill put down the candlestick he had walloped Croft with and rolled the unconscious man over. 'No, he's still breathing,' he said. 'I realised, once you were cornered, that you wanted to draw a confession out of him and, quite honestly, Jack, I wanted to hear it.' He looked at the statue of the grieving man with the white leg bone clearly visible and shuddered. 'Daniel Lythewell's body's in there? That's disgusting.'

'Yes it is, the poor beggar,' said Jack. 'The tomb wasn't so empty after all.'

'I don't believe it,' said Betty Wingate blankly. 'I just don't see how Uncle Daniel can be guilty.'

She had been released from prison that morning and was now with Jack and Bill in the sun-filled private room of the Brown Cow, where they had invited her and a bewildered Colin Askern to join them for breakfast.

'He's guilty sure enough, Miss Wingate,' said Bill. 'He confessed what he'd done last night in the chantry before he tried to kill Haldean.'

Betty shuddered and looked at Jack. 'You're all right now though, aren't you?'

'I'm fine,' said Jack, uncovering a dish of bacon and eggs and filling his plate. 'My word,

I'm hungry. Come and have something to eat, Askern.'

Colin Askern reluctantly came and stood by the table. 'I don't understand!' he broke out, ignoring the dishes before him. 'When I went to bed last night it all seemed so hopeless, and now...' He shrugged. 'You tell me Mr Lythewell's guilty of everything, but I just don't understand.'

'I think you'd better explain things, Jack,' said Bill. 'Both Askern and Miss Wingate need to know what really happened.'

'Before I do that,' said Jack, glancing at Colin Askern, 'I think an apology is due to Miss Wingate.'

Colin Askern started guiltily. 'Eh?' He looked at Betty and rubbed his hand across his face. 'Yes, I suppose you're right. Betty, I'm sorry. I was a fool to think you could be mixed up on the wrong side of this business, but I was so worried, first of all by my mother and then poor Dad, that I couldn't think straight.'

'You could've trusted me, Colin,' said Betty.

'I did!' he said desperately. 'I did really, but after poor Dad died, I didn't know what to think. When your fingerprints were found on that vase, it seemed like a nightmare. None of it made any sense. I believe you now,' he said, with the ghost of a smile on his handsome face. 'I always did, deep down, you know.' He reached out his hand to her. 'I'll never doubt you again.'

Betty hesitated.

Jack couldn't help feeling a sudden surge of hope at her hesitation. It was one thing for Betty to accept Askern's apology, but surely things couldn't just go back to how they were before. Could they?

Betty reached out and took Colin's hand. 'You promise?' she asked. 'You'll never doubt me?'

'Absolutely not,' he said earnestly. 'We can start again.' He squeezed her hand. 'You'd better tell us what happened, Haldean,' he said cheerfully. 'I can't make head or tail of it.'

Jack avoided his eyes. This was Betty's choice, he told himself. It was up to Betty to decide, but ... He'd believed her. Askern hadn't. Yes, Askern had his reasons, but he, Jack, had believed her. That should count for something.

'You've told us how old Lythewell made a mint from electroplating forgeries of antiques he'd stolen from museums,' went on Colin, pulling the dish of sausages towards him. 'That's clear enough. I also understand about the aluminium plate in the chantry. I know that his famous treasure is worthless, worse luck, but what about the rest of it? Where did it all start?'

Jack swallowed hard. For the sake of his own self-respect he was damned if he was going to let Askern – or Betty, for that matter – have the slightest hint of how he felt.

'It started years ago, when Daniel Lythewell came back from America together with his valet, Arthur Croft,' he said, his voice as even as he could make it. 'You remember the dance band at the Cafe de Bologna, Betty? The singer was called Art Burrell. It was then I realised that art wasn't necessarily art, but could be a name as well. I was convinced that Mrs McAllister had

341

recognised someone at the exhibition and, what's more, that their name was Art or Arthur. The name, together with Mrs McAllister's past, suggested an American connection. Daniel Lythewell, I knew, had sailed from New York on the *Concordia*, and when I checked the records and found Lythewell's valet was one Arthur Croft, I knew I'd struck gold. *Art* explained what Mrs McAllister said, but the surname Croft gave me the connection with the loot stolen as part of the Great Museum Scandal. I knew I was on the right track.'

He swallowed hard. It was no use. If he carried on speaking, somehow or other he'd give himself away. 'Bill, why don't you tell the story? I want to finish my breakfast,' he said, rather too heartily. 'You know what happened.'

'All right,' said Bill, with a sideways glance at his friend. 'I don't mind if I do. The thing is, Askern, Croft wanted revenge on the Lythewells. He knew Josiah Lythewell had amassed a fortune.' He paused awkwardly. 'Before I tell you this, Askern, can I say that we've got absolute proof of what I'm about to say? The thing is, Croft also discovered – I'm not sure how – that your father killed old Mr Lythewell.'

Colin drew a long breath. 'I wondered if you knew about that.'

Jack, Bill and Betty gaped at him.

'Dad never intended to kill old Lythewell,' said Colin quickly. 'It just sort of happened. It was an accident. He should've owned up, I suppose, but it was much better for everyone to let sleeping dogs lie. I told you he wasn't good at covering things up. It wouldn't take much for Mr Lythe-well – Croft, I mean – to get the truth out of Dad.'

'Well, I'll be damned,' muttered Bill. There was a long pause.

Colin, avoiding Bill's gaze, concentrated on his breakfast.

'Anyway, Arthur Croft saw his chance,' Bill continued eventually. 'Your father must've covered up for him, Askern, because no one ever suspected that the real Daniel Lythewell was dead and Croft had taken his place. Granted what happened to Croft's father, electroplating Daniel Lythewell's body had a horrible symmetry to it. And then, of course, the awful truth must've dawned, that old Mr Lythewell's treasure was well and truly hidden and the murder hadn't gained him a fortune but only a business.'

'It was a very lucrative business in those days,' said Colin. 'He did very well out of it.'

Bill nodded. 'Anyway, as we know, things continued until he had the misfortune to run into Mrs Joan McAllister at the exhibition. Jack put this part of the story together. A Miss Sharpe, who knew Mrs McAllister, told Jack that Mrs McAllister had been involved with a man who'd let her down badly before her marriage.'

'She'd been a servant in New York,' said Jack. He was relieved to hear his voice sounded normal in his own ears. 'Putting two and two together with what else we knew, that man had to be her fellow-servant, Arthur Croft.'

'I feel sorry for her, of course,' said Betty, 'especially when I think what happened to her,

343

but, even so, she doesn't sound a very nice person.'

'No, she doesn't,' agreed Jack. 'I'm not sure who contacted who, but she was certainly looking forward to a spot of blackmail. She virtually told me so that day I met her on the Strand. It wouldn't take her long to find out that the man she knew as Arthur Croft was calling himself Daniel Lythewell. Arthur Croft, of course, was anxious to keep her quiet. I think he initially paid up – she moved out of Purbeck Terrace pretty quickly – and, perhaps lulled into a sense of false security, she must've agreed to come down to Whimbrell Heath.'

Betty swallowed. 'This is my night in the cottage, isn't it?'

'That's right,' Jack agreed. He looked at Colin. 'He knew about your mother, of course, and knew she was away. Her cottage was the perfect place to stage a murder. I think he met Mrs McAllister at the station and drove her to the cottage. God knows what tale he told her to get her into the cottage, but he chloroformed her and strangled her. And then, just as everything was going according to plan, Betty, you walked in on him.'

'I've never been so frightened in my life,' she said. 'But Jack, why didn't he kill me?'

'Don't you see, Betty?' said Jack. 'He couldn't. He knew what he was going to do with Mrs McAllister's body. He'd planned it all in fine detail, even down to poisoning the watchman's dog. But two bodies? That's a very different kettle of fish.'

'He was fairly safe with Mrs McAllister,' put in Bill. 'It was no one's business to find out what had happened to her. You, on the other hand, Miss Wingate, would be missed. Anyway, when you said what had happened, no one believed you, did they?'

Colin Askern looked very sheepish. 'It all seemed so incredible,' he said. 'When you would not let the matter drop, I got really worried.'

'That's why I went to Scotland Yard,' said Betty tartly. 'I was desperate for *someone* to believe me. I didn't realise who Signora Bianchi was, of course.'

'It went really wrong for Dad when my mother turned up,' said Colin. He put down his knife and fork and looked at Jack squarely. 'Don't get me wrong. I can't excuse what my father did, but he really cared for my stepmother. He fell to pieces when she cut up rough, poor beggar. He wasn't really rational the last few days of his life. I realise now that you'd started to put two and two together about what had happened to old Mr Lythewell. I suppose that's why that devil killed him, isn't it?'

'That's right,' agreed Jack. 'If your father had been arrested or even properly questioned about Josiah Lythewell's death, then the whole truth would've probably come out. Arthur Croft couldn't risk it.'

'Why did he pretend to be Mrs McAllister?' asked Betty. 'I still can't get over the idea that Uncle Daniel dressed up as a woman. He must-'ve been a very convincing woman,' she said wonderingly. 'No one seemed to suspect him.'

345

'Just think of the female impersonators on the music halls,' said Bill. 'They can be very convincing. With the right dress, make-up and hair, Arthur Croft obviously did a very good job. And, of course, to have Mrs McAllister apparently rent a flat in Dorian House after he'd murdered her did make it seem as if she wasn't dead. I suppose you had mentioned to him that you thought the woman in the cottage could be Mrs McAllister, hadn't you?'

'I did, as a matter of fact,' said Betty slowly.

'That put you in danger,' said Jack. 'He didn't want any connection between Mrs McAllister and the body in the cottage, so he arranged for you to discover John Askern. He hoped we'd think of you as a liar and a murderer. That was certainly his intention when he killed Henry Cadwallader.'

'That was just cold-blooded,' said Colin in disgust. 'But why kill Cadwallader? I can't believe he knew a thing.'

'Can't you?' asked Jack. 'Cadwallader was doing a series of drawings of the chantry. He showed me the statue of the grieving man. He pointed out that the grieving man's ear was identical to that of Josiah Lythewell's. The shape of an ear is very distinctive and often identical in fathers and sons. That's a fairly well-known fact. Cadwallader was convinced that the statue was nothing more than a tribute, as he put it, by Daniel Lythewell to his father, but, looking at the shape of that ear and comparing it to the drawing I had of Josiah Lythewell, I was convinced, on top of everything else we knew, that there was a far more straightforward and sinister explanation. Cadwallader would've told anyone who'd listen about the similarity between the statue and Josiah Lythewell. Arthur Croft couldn't risk it. All it needed was one tap with a hammer and the truth would be revealed. And, of course, it was.'

Betty pushed her plate away in disgust. 'I can't bear to think of it. It's horrible!' She looked at Jack. 'When I was arrested, I knew I was innocent, but, once again, no one seemed to believe me.' Her blue eyes met his. 'You said, *"Trust me"*,' she said wonderingly. 'I did.'

There was something in her look that suddenly made hope surge once more, then Colin Askern broke the moment.

'Betty, you're Daniel Lythewell's niece, aren't you? The real Daniel Lythewell, I mean.' He looked at Betty with a new respect in his eyes.

'Of course I am,' she said puzzled. 'I'll have to see that he's properly buried, poor man. We can't leave him in the chantry in that hideous statue.'

'He died without marrying though, didn't he? I mean, your Aunt Maud isn't really your aunt, even by marriage. Your uncle – your real uncle – died without having children. Josiah Lythewell doesn't have any other living descendants, apart from you. Don't you see, Betty? You're Lythewell's heir. The firm belongs to us. You and me. We're partners.'

'Colin,' she said, shocked. 'You can't possibly think of things like that now!'

'Why not?' he asked with a shrug. 'It's how things are. We might as well be practical.'

'But...' Betty stopped, lost for words. 'I don't

347

want anything to do with the firm, Colin, and I know you don't. You only worked there because it's what your father wanted.' Her eyes were suddenly bright with excitement. 'Why don't you go to Hollywood with your mother? It's what you've always wanted.'

'Go to Hollywood?' Colin grasped both her hands in his. 'Betty, come with me. Let's do it!'

Arthur Croft was tried and convicted. Daphne Askern stayed on at Heath House, but Maud Lythewell left Whimbrell Heath. Colin Askern, meeting Jack after the trial, was alive with enthusiasm for his new plans. Things, it appeared, were working out wonderfully.

'This friend of my mother's, Luigi Mantonelli, really is everything she said. He made some classic Italian films before the war. He's got some connections in Hollywood. All he needs is money.'

'Where's he going to raise the funds?' asked Jack without much interest. 'Has he got a backer?'

'That isn't a problem. Betty's found the money. Betty's been wonderful,' said Colin fervently. 'She said we should forget art and work on repairs and restoration. Betty suggested we put the foreman, Jones, in charge, and he's taken to it like a duck to water. For the first time in five years or so, it looks as if the firm's going to make a profit. What's really turned the scale, though, is getting some capital. Betty suggested we sell off the surplus land for building and it's been snapped up. I tell you, Haldean, things are going from

348

strength to strength. Mantonelli and my mother are in Los Angeles already and he's promised me that once I've learned the ropes, I can do what I really want, and that's direct as well as act in my own films. Now the trial's out of the way, Betty and I are sailing for New York. I've got the tickets.'

'So Betty's going with you?' asked Jack, his mouth suddenly dry.

'Oh, yes. We'll get married once we're out West. It's a wonderful chance for both of us. Betty's really looking forward to Hollywood. We're leaving on the *Olympic* next Tuesday.'

Tuesday. The days spread out, each one a grey desert, each night bringing the sailing of the *Olympic* that much closer, then Tuesday arrived.

Hollywood. The land of dreams. Why shouldn't Betty go to Hollywood? Askern was going to succeed. He had no doubts about that. Askern would be a star.

He looked at the clock. The *Olympic* should be clear of Southampton Water by now, feeling the first rush of the ocean current beneath her keel.

Life went on. There were friends, work, places to go, things to see ... but the colour was drained out of his world. It was all dreary, dull routine, with one damn thing after another. Nothing was any *fun* any more.

The phone rang.

'Jack?' said Betty. 'Jack, is that you?'

A wild hope gripped him. 'Betty! Aren't you on board the ship?'

'I couldn't leave, Jack.' He could hear the hesitation in her voice. She sounded nervous.

'There's a lot to keep me here. Colin doesn't need me. He's got his future. You believed me and...' She hesitated once more and he could hear the smile in her voice. 'Ages ago you invited me out to lunch. Is the invitation still open?'

Unable to speak, Jack gazed at the telephone, then silently punched the air in delight.

'Jack? Are you there?'

'Lunch,' he said with a broad grin. 'That sounds fun.'